THE INVERTED PYRAMID

BY BERTRAND W. SINCLAIR

Raw Gold (1908)

The Land of the Frozen Suns (1909)

North of Fifty-Three (1914)

Big Timber (1916)

Burned Bridges (1919)

Poor Man's Rock (1920)

The Hidden Places (1922)

The Inverted Pyramid (1924)

Wild West (1926)

Pirates of the Plain (1928)

Gunpowder Lightning (1930)

Down the Dark Alley (1935)

Both Sides of the Law (1951)

Room for the Rolling M (1954)

THE INVERTED PYRAMID

BERTRAND W. SINCLAIR

RONSDALE PRESS

THE INVERTED PYRAMID
Copyright © 1924
LITTLE, BROWN, AND COMPANY.
First published 1924; 2nd edition, Ronsdale Press, 2011

RONSDALE PRESS
3350 West 21st Avenue, Vancouver, B.C.
Canada V6S 1G7
www.ronsdalepress.com

Typesetting: Julie Cochrane, in Granjon 11.5 pt on 15
Cover Design: David Drummond
Paper: Ancient Forest Friendly "Silva" (FSC) — 100% post-consumer waste, totally chlorine-free

Ronsdale Press wishes to thank the following for their support of its publishing program: the Canada Council for the Arts, the Government of Canada through the Canada Book Fund, the British Columbia Arts Council, and the Province of British Columbia through the British Columbia Book Publishing Tax Credit program.

This publication is also made possible with support from the City of Vancouver's 125th Anniversary Grants Program, the Office of Vancouver's Poet Laureate Brad Cran, and the participation of the Government of Canada.

Library and Archives Canada Cataloguing in Publication

Sinclair, Bertrand W., 1881–1972
The inverted pyramid / Bertrand W. Sinclair.

Originally publ.: Toronto : F.D. Goodchild, 1924.
Issued also in electronic format.
ISBN 978-1-55380-128-3

I. Title.

PS8487.I565I68 2011 C813'.52 C2011-903008-X

At Ronsdale Press we are committed to protecting the environment. To this end we are working with Canopy (formerly Markets Initiative) and printers to phase out our use of paper produced from ancient forests. This book is one step towards that goal.

Printed in Canada by Marquis Printing, Quebec

"From the duality of man's nature
and the competition of individuals
the life-history of the earth must in
the last instance be a history of a
really very relentless warfare.
Neither his fellows, nor his gods,
nor his passions will leave
a man alone."

—JOSEPH CONRAD

CHAPTER I

ITEM: ONE BOY AGED eighteen, name Roderick Norquay; one girl aged fifteen, named Mary Thorn; one gaudy cedar dugout canoe got up in the Siwash style of high-curving bow and stern, both ends grotesquely carved and brilliantly coloured in flaming red, blinding yellow, piercing blue; one stretch of tiderace running swiftly between an island shore and a forbidding rock-strewn point.

The tides of Fundy and the maelstroms of the Scandinavian coast have been variously hymned since Jules Verne vulgarized holy science and proved himself an unwitting prophet with Captain Nemo's submersible. But there are tides and maelstroms on the Pacific seaboard as worthy as these others, which have as yet no place in literature save through the dull medium of admiralty charts and blue-bound North Pacific pilot books. These sheets and tomes are thumbed and conned by men nowise concerned with that colour, form, and substance which imparts magic to the written word. They seek therein only knowledge of reef and shoal, of anchorages, currents, depths, for the safe passage of their sea-borne keels.

Rod Norquay, sitting on the shore of Little Dent, waiting for the flood tide to wax strong and the race of it through the choked pass to grow swifter, found himself wondering why no poet had sung the song of this swirling water; why no novelist had lovingly portrayed this land as a backdrop for his comic and tragic puppets? Why was there no *Iliad* of the pioneers, no Human Comedy of men and manners peculiar to the North Coast? If McAndrews sighed for a Burns to sing the song of steam, so young Norquay found himself wishing that someone with the gift of living words could catch and transfix the beauty and majesty, the invisible yet pulsing spirit of his native land. That it deserved a Homer and a Burns he did not doubt. Rod had been reading Homer with his tutor that morning. Perhaps the thought in his mind now was only the reflex of a question put then.

"Why should a fellow have to learn all about these frowsy old Greeks?" he had demanded, as much in mild mischief, to scandalize his tutor, as for any reason. Yet he was suddenly earnest when he followed up this by saying, "It would be much more interesting to read poetry about our own people. How they sailed this coast in small ships, how they fought Indians and settled the country and founded families, and all that sort of thing."

He could not quite comprehend when Mr. Spence shook his grey head and gravely stated in a precise, tutorial voice:

"There is, my dear Rod, no epic literature dealing with the pioneer. That is merely in the nature of things. It takes leisure and culture to embody a tradition in language that will live. American civilization has been too occupied with grasping material power, with cutting trees and digging mines, making machinery and so on. This country has tradition, but little culture. It is too young and lusty, too new and crude — raw, one might say."

Rod Norquay had muttered "rats!" under his breath. He did not accept as gospel *all* that his elderly tutor vouchsafed. Young? Four generations of men had been born in the house where they sat. Its stone walls had been fabricated by English masons who rounded the Horn before the day of steam. Rod believed the Anglo-Saxon took his culture with him insofar as he possessed culture — wherever he went. It was not something indigenous to the soil in which he planted his roots.

At any rate that was a passing thought and Rod put it by as youth so easily puts abstractions aside. His eyes rested critically on the flooding tide, the line of current that poured with accelerating speed through its narrow gate. Northward, up Cardero Channel, the level was beginning to rise. Southward, where the four-mile boomerang curve of the Euclataw Passage opened into the Gulf the tide was falling fast. Vancouver Island, spreading its sinuous length like a barrier against the Pacific, crowded the sea into the shape of an enormous hourglass. Queen Charlotte Sound formed one bulb, the Gulf of Georgia the other. An hourglass three hundred miles from north to south. The Euclataw Passage was the neck, and the rapids between Little Dent and Valdez was a constriction of this neck to a span six hundred feet across, through which at the full strength of the tidal flow the sea ran with hurrying feet and a loud, complaining voice, as a mountain river hastens roaring over its stony bed.

Rod turned to the girl.

"It's running pretty good," he remarked. "Let's go, Mary."

She smiled assent. They got off the mossy rock. The green-bodied dugout with its futuristic bow and stern rubbed against a shelf convenient for embarking. The girl sat amidships, Rod in the stern, squatting on their knees, paddles in hand. Forty feet out from shore the water dropped with a murmur over a sunken ledge. It stood like a low, green wall, curling over with a white-edged crest. In two hours that murmur would rise to a thunderous roar, the low green wall would be a man's height with hissing whirlpools below. Already the suction was strong. The indraught took the canoe backward the instant they let go the shore hold. They bent to the paddles, plying short, swift strokes, won clear to the slack water well above the rapids and pointed for the Valdez side.

Here the current, thirty fathoms deep, free of all obstruction, shot through the Euclataws in a clear, straight line, pitching down in a slant perceptible to the eye, a strip of smooth jade-green bordered to right and left by eddies, whirlpools, white-tipped waves where conflicting currents met and slashed up foam. The song of running water crooned gently between wooded banks — that song which would presently fill the air with deep-toned antiphony to the whisper of the winds.

"Now," Rod commanded. "Stow your paddle till I shout."

It was like a path between precipices, that strip of smooth, swift-flowing water, after the first dizzy swoop at the overfall. A boat length on either hand spun whirlpools. A sudden sheer of their craft meant almost sure destruction. The guiding thrust of Rod's paddle held the dugout true. Their breath came quickly. Their eyes glowed. Their lips parted in a set smile, as if an alteration of feature might destroy their equilibrium.

"Right," young Norquay said curtly.

The girl's paddle dipped with a sure, vigorous thrust. In the stern Rod held his blade at an angle, like a rudder, and the dugout shaved a whirling hollow in the vortex of which a drift log stood upended, spinning like a top, going slowly down end-on in the suction.

"Steady."

She held her paddle poised again. The canoe came back to midway of the green path. The Valdez shore flew by, stubs of trees, tall cedars with lancelike crests and drooping boughs. A gull swooped over them, crying. The swiftness made a cool breeze in their faces, flung the girl's hair in a loose brown cloud about her head.

The high, carved bow dipped into broken water, among cross-surges. They rode over "boils" — deflecting currents that shot up from the depths and broke into strange watery mounds with a sinister muttering. They shipped a little spray, rolled uncertainly in this agitation. Then they were through, floating in a great eddy that swept them back toward Little Dent. They had shot the rapids.

Mary looked over her shoulder. They smiled at each other in perfect understanding, and young Norquay thought:

"I'd like to take old Spence through. *He* wouldn't grin. Poor old duffer, he gets all his fun second-hand — out of books."

Aloud he said, "We'd better get under the Dent shore before the eddy carries us back among the swirls."

"Among the Devil's Dishpans, you mean," she laughed, keeping stroke with him. "That's what daddy calls them."

"Good name," he grunted. "They're devil's something when they get to spinning good. Paddle, Brownie. We're losing ground."

They got in under the weedy shore of Little Dent and worked up to the overfall. They got ashore. Rod took a light line from the bow and hauled. Mary held the canoe off with a slender pole. Thus they worked their craft up over the jump-off and reached the northern side of the small island where the flood tide parted and where its sweep was slow. Then they re-embarked and stood clear, paddling in a wide detour until they drove into the straight current again and were swept down like a gaudy arrow.

Close on their heels as they made the second voyage came a white power cruiser, all agleam in the afternoon sun, her housework varnished oak, bright flashes reflected off polished brass and copper. She plowed down the green spillway, her bow wave spreading like an ostrich plume. When Rod and Mary skilfully picked smooths in the broken water and swung aside into the comparative calm of the great eddy the white cruiser followed and hauled up close to them.

Out her pilot-house window a capped, red face grinned genially. On her low afterdeck half a dozen people sat in wicker chairs, the women in cool summer stuff, the men in flannels and coloured sweaters. A girl about Mary Thorn's age, a fair-haired, blue-eyed creature like a bisque doll, stood with one arm around the slender signal mast. A little below her a tall young man with the reddish-brown hair and fine clear skin and greyish-blue eyes of the boy in the canoe leaned over the pipe rail.

"Hello, everybody," Rod greeted casually.

His brother disregarded this.

"Better climb aboard and tow that thing," he suggested. "How did you manage to get caught in the rapids?"

"We didn't get caught," Rod answered mildly.

"Then what the deuce are you doing in them?" Phil demanded.

"Oh, just running 'em for fun," Rod drawled.

"For fun!" One of the matrons on the afterdeck contrived a horrified inflection.

Phil Norquay's brow wrinkled a trifle. He looked inquiringly down at his brother. That youth gazed up at him with bland innocence.

"You'll be getting in among those big swirls if you don't watch out," Rod said to him. "Never mind about us."

Phil glanced up and ahead, called an order to the man leaning out the pilot house.

"You'd better —"

But his sentence to Rod was cut off, for that imperturbable youth drove the dugout well clear of the power boat with a thrust of his paddle, and Mary Thorn's blade dipped in unison. They pointed straight for shore.

The launch swung in a short circle, gathered way, passed up the channel. Rod steered the canoe over to Little Dent, caught a drooping bough and held it against the streaming tide.

Mary looked after the white cruiser, turning now into Mermaid Bay.

"What a pretty girl that was by the mast. Who is she?"

"Oh, Isabel Wall. Sister to a girl Phil's got half a crush on," Rod answered carelessly. "I don't think she's so pretty. Too dolly-dolly. Shall we run 'em once more?"

"She looked pretty to me. She was so beautifully dressed," Mary said thoughtfully.

"Oh, clothes," Rod answered disdainfully. "That's all the bunch around our place does these days; doll up and look pretty. Come on, let's shoot the shoots again."

"No. It's running too fast now. The boils are beginning to break in the straight current," Mary said. "I want to go home."

"All right."

Rod let go the branch. They paddled against the eddy, crossed the small stretch of broken water where a lesser flood poured in from behind Little Dent, and slid down on the tide along the Valdez shore to a point a mile inside the rapids. Facing north, looking across the channel into Mermaid Bay, a planked float gave them landing. Back from the beach an unpainted house of split cedar lifted in a square of cleared land in the edge of virgin forest.

Mary sprang lightly to the float.

"What's the rush?" Rod asked, breaking a long silence. "What's wrong anyway? What made you turn clam all at once?"

"Me?" she turned a pair of clear hazel eyes on him with every indication of surprise. "Nothing. I have to pick some blackberries for Mamma before supper."

Rod sawed the paddle blade up and down in the green water streaming under the float.

"Shall I come and help?"

"No," she said decisively. Then mockingly, "Thanks very much for your offer of assistance, just the same, Mr. Norquay."

Rod smiled at her.

"All right," he acquiesced. "I'll go home, if you're going to be haughty. Listen. If I can get away from that bunch tomorrow, I'll bring my tackle and we'll hike up to the lake and get some trout. Eh?"

"Maybe. If Mamma'll let me."

"She will, if I ask her," he observed. "Bye, Mary."

"Bye, Rod."

He tied the gaudy dugout — which in its barbaric colour scheme of Rod's own devising was alternately a joke and a provocation to his brothers — to the Hawk's Nest landing, after the lapse of an hour, which hour he spent coasting under the western shore of Big Dent, alone in the canoe, watching the herring flash in silver shoals among the kelp, the scuttle of crabs over the shingle, the deep purple and brick-red of starfish against flat rocks, in gazing up at a blue dome arched over the hurrying tide and the encircling mountains. Vast peaks, from the green-mantled cones nearby, to distant pinnacles lifting far above timber line and capped with everlasting white.

Rod did not consciously apply his intellect to considering his environment. He felt it. It satisfied him, filled him with an indefinable sense of well-being. His people for a hundred years had filled their eyes with that and found it good. Against this background they had lived and loved and died. No matter. Rod, floating lazily in his canoe, was not looking backward, introspectively considering if he were the sum of five generations, each of which had contributed its quota to subduing a wild land to its use and need, to its ambition as well as to its necessity, and becoming one at last with that portion of the earth the first Roderick Norquay had made his own and handed to his sons.

No, eighteen mercifully wears invisible blinkers, and Rod was no exception. Life sat lightly on him. No emotional spur had as yet been forged to rowel him with the barbed thrust of ambition, desire, hot struggle, frustrated hopes and keen dissatisfactions, glows of possession and achievement, dead ashes of loss, all the curious patterns a man must weave with uncertain fingers in the tapestry of his life. So far as Rod was concerned on this bright August day, these things were not.

He walked up from the float toward a stone house with a warm red roof of tiles sitting amid a reach of emerald grass and clumps of exotic shrubbery against a background of magnificent native trees, his hands in his trousers pockets, bare-headed, whistling.

CHAPTER II

THE PATH ROD WALKED approached the house by a circuitous route. It turned aside here and there like a leisurely pedestrian to skirt red-trunked arbutus with oily-green leaves and clusters of unripe berries, to curve around the base of massive firs that rose like dun pillars in a blue-vaulted forum, to pass great fibrous-barked cedars with drooping boughs wherein unseen squirrels chattered. Everywhere grass clothed the ground, a carpet with green velvet pile, close shorn. Stones great and small had been gathered in artless piles so long ago that their granite nakedness was hidden under thick moss, disguised with ivy, or bright with flowering plants, brilliant dabs of colour against vivid greens and sombre browns. This walk brought him at last to one end of a great stone house with wide, cool porches, deep window recesses, a roof of tiles that glowed in the sun like a cardinal's hat.

There were people sitting about on the porch, a dozen or more. Rod greeted them without halting until he reached the corner. Then he looked back over his shoulder. Through the trees on the parked slope he got a flash of the racing tide. The voice of the rapids waxed strong. Across the channel Oliver Thorn's weather-beaten house was a drab spot on the forest's edge. Over the low shoulders of Valdez the distant backbone of Vancouver Island cut the skyline into jagged tracery. That three-hundred-mile wall which stopped the marching surges from tropical seas loomed in a bluish haze out of which rose high, conical peaks, far and white and faintly shining.

He skirted the house. If he had destination or purpose Rod was not conscious of either as a definite urge. He was simply strolling. But as he turned the corner he came upon a girl leaning on a parasol and staring at some letters cut in a massive cornerstone where the thick foundation rose out of the earth.

"Oh, Rod," she said. "Do answer about a million questions for me, please."

"Have you got a list?" he asked.

"A list? Oh, no," she chuckled. "I'm still on an even keel."

"Nautically all right," Rod smiled.

He didn't know Laska Wall very well. He hadn't seen much of her. She had only been at Hawk's Nest three days. Prior to that he had heard more or less about the Walls. They were people who had lately begun to cut quite a figure in Vancouver society. His brothers knew them. Both Phil and Grove had pretty well monopolized Laska since her arrival here. But what Rod had seen of her he liked. She was a quiet girl, with a slow smile that wonderfully transformed a piquant, delicately tinted face. Rod looked at her now admiringly. He wondered if Isabel, the pretty, bisque-doll creature upon whose dainty clothes Mary Thorn had remarked, would be like that when she was twenty-one. He supposed so, since they were sisters, but he could scarcely believe it. He detested Isabel. She giggled incessantly, flaunted herself before him with an irritating archness, annoyed him with her glib French, with numerous manifestations of what Rod contemptuously termed (to himself) "kindergarten stuff." He was a man — in his own estimation. It was a trial, which he bore as a gentleman, to be expected to act as Isabel's cavalier, merely because they were the juveniles of this house party. Isabel was juvenile enough, Rod admitted. He exempted himself from the charge of extreme youth. But it was provoking to have everyone else blandly proceed on that assumption.

Perhaps that was why he warmed to this fair-haired young woman who addressed him as an intellectual equal who could impart knowledge.

"What does that signify, Rod?" she asked, pointing to a group of letters and figures graven deep in the stone.

"Oh, that's the cornerstone of the first course of masonry above ground, of the first wing of the old house, built by the first Norquay," Rod told her with a trace of pride that he covered by assumed casualness. "Those are his initials. R.S.N. for Roderick Sylvester Norquay. And the year."

"1809," the girl murmured. "A hundred years exactly. You know I have always thought of this country as a semi-wilderness — the last American frontier. How many generations, Rod?"

"We're the fifth from his time." He indicated the chiselled stone. "Grove and Phil and myself and Dorothy. I don't know if you've met Dorothy. She's married to a chap named Hale. Lives in Victoria."

"A century since that stone was laid by a man's hands," Laska continued musingly. "Five generations. No, certainly I did not imagine one would find any such well-established ancestral heritage on this wild coast."

"What's a century?" Rod commented. "Greece and Egypt had philosophers and poets and noble ruins when our ancestors were wearing skins and killing their meat with clumsy spears."

The girl paid no heed to this.

"I knew this place was old the moment I stepped ashore," she continued. "I knew it must have a history. Who was this first enterprising Norquay, Rod? Where did he come from and how did he pitch on this spot so long ago as the place for his baronial hall? I wonder if you realize what a — an air of distinction this place has? As if it were so well established that all the crudities had been ironed out — an atmosphere like — well, of permanency and power."

"Well, it's home, and that's a good deal," Rod answered, a little doubtful of too eager response. "I don't know about the power, but it's permanent enough."

"You can hardly imagine other people dispossessing you and making it *their* home, eh?" Laska asked mischievously.

"No chance," Rod grinned at the suggestion. "I should say not."

"Tell me about the first Norquay," she wheedled. "I am sure it's vivid history. What was he — great — great —"

"Great-great-grandfather," Rod supplied. "Have you seen the family boneyard?

She shook her head.

"I have seen most of the interior of the house. I have sat on the porch and drank tea and stared at these wonderful mountains that stick up everywhere, I have walked about on this lovely turf, in these grounds that are like an English park — and marvelled how it had been made so beautiful. But I haven't seen the family boneyard. Is that literal?"

The boy nodded.

"There have been quite a few of us born here at one time and another," he said in his pleasant low-toned voice, "and buried here finally. Come and I'll show you, Miss Wall."

"My name's Laska," she smiled at him.

"All right then, Laska," he agreed. "Odd name. I like the sound."

"R.S.N. Eighteen hundred and nine. *Hoc saxum posuit.* I've forgotten all my Latin, Rod."

"*He placed this stone*," Rod translated. "Come on. I'll show you where the old chap's buried and tell you something about him."

Big Dent passes on map and chart for an island, by a geographical laxity. But it is an island only for brief moments at an extremely high tide. Otherwise it is a peninsular out-thrust, that helps to choke the Euclataw Passage.

Big Dent was a mile wide and twice as long. From side to side and from end to end it stood clothed in its ancient garment, the forest. Everywhere lifted enormous firs in whose plumy crests had sighed the winds that blew the first Norquay's trading vessel down Cardero Channel, cedars that were lusty when Columbus crossed the Western Ocean. For profit there had never been axe laid to tree on that twelve hundred acres. On its northern extremity Big Dent remained the natural forest of the region, a hushed jungle of devil's club, salal brush, ferns that grew man-high, salmonberry, branchy dogwood, vine maple.

Out of this lesser growth the great trees rose in their majesty, silent, immobile, brooding. The sun blazed on their lofty heads. About their boles were silence and shade, a coolness at midday heat, the commingled smells of moist, fecund earth and rotting wood.

But all across the southern portion, the greater half of Big Dent, the thickets had been cut away, the patriarchal trees freed of the litter about their solidly planted feet, the sun let in, grass sowed, so that the eye could reach far down wooded corridors and get glimpses of sparkling sea; so that a Norquay or his guests could walk abroad in those friendly places and observe — if they were minded to observe — how man had imposed order and beauty upon the wasteful processes of nature by sweeping away all the detritus of the arboreal struggle to survive.

Leaving the house Rod and Laska walked a little way up the slope. They came to a small square enclosed by a low wall of masonry, the half-acre of the Norquay dead. A gate of grilled iron let them in. A red cedar rose in the middle of the plot like an enormous brown mast which had sprouted flat, feathery boughs that drooped as if tired with the weight of long-borne years, and cast a deep shadow over part of this burial ground. In this shaded portion uprose a number of grey granite slabs, the native rock every Norquay had used for such of his works as he wished to endure. Apart from these simple slabs stood a row of uniform design: a headstone four feet high, three feet wide; another, the width of the headstone and the length of a tall man, laid flat on the earth. Ornamentation there was none. Plain grey stone, worked to a smooth polish, briefly lettered — that was all. A few flower beds were let into the turf between. A simple, unpretentious place in which plain men could take their long sleep.

Rod stopped by the first of the larger headstones.

"This was the first of our family here," he said.

The girl looked down at the inscription.

RODERICK SYLVESTER NORQUAY

Born 1770

Died 1834

His eye was not dim

Nor his natural force abated

"This was his wife." Rod pointed. "The first white woman to live on the Pacific coast north of California. That was his youngest son. That was his eldest son, my great-grandfather. And that was *his* youngest son, who was killed by the Chilcotin Indians on their second raid. There's grandfather's wife, and a son and daughter. There is my mother's grave. And over there is my oldest brother, who died before I was born."

"How interesting," the girl murmured. "What an adventurous time these first people of yours must have had."

"Rather," Rod agreed, "when you think of some of the things they had to face. Still, by all accounts, they rather enjoyed themselves. It never seems to have occurred to them to go elsewhere. There were lots of men pioneered after Vancouver's first voyage, but all of them except old Roderick seem to have come here to make a fortune in the fur trade and go home to live on their gains. Old Roderick kept a journal all his life. It's a queer matter-of-fact account of what he did, mixed up with a lot of philosophic speculation on *why* he did it. It appears that from the first time he dropped anchor in Mermaid Bay to wait out a fair tide through the narrows, he had the feeling that right here was the place to make a stand. He says quite frankly in his journal that a few determined men could easily subdue the natives and possess great estates. He says further that shortly after letting go the anchor he saw a hawk fly from its nest in a great tree, and he thought to himself that, by the grace of God and his own resolution, he would some day build on this silent headland a stout nest in which many a brood of Norquays should be hatched.

"Imagine a man who had crossed the Atlantic and rounded Cape Horn in a hundred-ton sailing vessel on a fur-trading venture looking at a savage coast and planning to found a family!"

"He had vision," Laska supplied.

"He needed to have, those days," Rod grinned. "The North Pacific was a fur-trader's paradise, but it was several thousand miles from anything like civilization. Old Roderick knew that well enough. He knew a good deal about this region before he came here on his own hook, you see. He happened out here first when Captain George Vancouver made his voyage of exploration in 1792. He was a petty officer on the *Dis-*

covery. He had the journal habit, even in those days. He tells about the surveys they made that year and the next. The idea of this country — after he'd seen a lot of it — took such a hold of him that three or four years later he got out of the British navy, scraped up all the money he could beg and borrow, outfitted a barque called the *Hermes* and sailed for the Northwest to make a fortune trading beads and brass wire and Sheffield knives to the Indians for sea-otter skins.

"On that first voyage he got the idea of settling here. It evidently grew on him, because when he came out the second time — the first venture was a very profitable one — he brought a couple of dozen extra men, artisans of different trades, and set up a trading post here just as Captain John Meares tried to do at Nootka Sound a few years earlier — you'll find a very interesting account of Meares and his clash with the Spaniards over that post in Begg's *History of British Columbia*. Meares and Don Martinez between them very nearly got Spain and Great Britain into war. Vancouver came out here to look into that squabble as much as for anything else.

"But ancestor Norquay had this spot pretty much to himself. He bought Big Dent from a local chief for six sheets of copper, an old cutlass, and a pint of glass beads. Think of it! He built a blockhouse of logs with a sixteen-foot stockade. His men cultivated some land for vegetables. He had cattle and pigs and sheep — brought 'em out in the *Hermes*, like Noah with the animals aboard the Ark. But fur-trading was the chief business. He traded for sea otter as far north as Sitka. Here at home he got beaver, mink, marten, whatever the Indians brought in. The Northwest Fur Company claimed this territory. They were carrying on a big scrap with the Hudson's Bay Company at the time. Finally the Hudson's Bay swallowed the Northwest concern and got a free hand. They tried for years to make all North America their private fur preserve. But they didn't scare old Roderick off. Apparently he wasn't afraid of them. Too well-equipped, I suppose, to be driven off.

"On his fourth voyage in 1804 he took a cargo of twenty-two hundred sea otter which netted him fifty-six thousand dollars — so you can see what the fur trade meant in those times. On that trip he made off with the daughter of a country gentleman of Northumberland — he was Scotch himself, you know — an English girl named Dorothy Grosvenor. Her people considered him a low-class adventurer. So they took the bit in their teeth, boarded the *Hermes* and sailed away. Sounds quaint. They brought out three or four families with them. The men stationed here had mostly gotten Indian wives by that time. Dorothy sailed with great-great-grandfather wherever he went with the barque for three or four years. But their first child was born here on Big Dent in 1807.

"The next year the Chilcotins came down. They're a fighting tribe from the interior. They had a way of coming down a river to the head of Bute Inlet, killing as many coast Indians as they could, taking the loot and the young women back across the mountains. I suppose they had heard of this white man who had lots of goods. So they organized a surprise attack on Hawk's Nest, as it was already called.

"There was quite a scrimmage, by all accounts. The Chilcotins were beaten off. We lost six men in the fight. Those small headstones are for *them*." Rod indicated a compact row of graves.

"So the following year old Roderick, who had never given up for a moment the idea of making this his permanent home, started the stone house. He built one wing. His son added a wing. Grandfather can tell you how *he* built the last addition, and another storey, and how he put on a roof of tiles in 1860 after the Cariboo gold rush.

"The Chilcotins pulled off another surprise party in 1826, but they got such a hot reception they never tried again. By that time old Roderick had two sons and two daughters. The youngest son was the only man killed on our side. He led a party to destroy the Chilcotin canoes while they were attacking the house. He was killed by an arrow. But they smashed the canoes and only two Chilcotins out of forty got away. In fact, they were spared to go back and tell the rest of the tribe that it was bad medicine to molest the white men who lived at Hawk's Nest.

"They understood that, evidently, because they never came back. Although nearly twenty years later a brother of grandfather's was stuck full of arrows one evening right down where our boat landing is now. That killing was credited to the Chilcotins — in revenge. But it wasn't a fight. It was pure assassination. However, that was the last bloodshed here.

"The first fifty years of holding Hawk's Nest was altogether a pretty lively affair. But they kept right on the job. In '59 gold was found in the Cariboo and people rushed into B.C. by thousands. The Hudson's Bay monopoly was broken. B.C. became a Crown colony. We got title to our land. Grandfather began to operate in timber. Confederation with the Dominion took place in '71, in my father's time. There have been lots of changes in this country since old Roderick came. But we're still here."

"You can quite truthfully say that you belong to one of the first families, eh, Rod?" Laska bantered.

"Oh, well," he replied carelessly, "that's sheer accident. Nothing to be cocky about. I didn't have any hand in the big doings."

"Still, it's something to live up to, don't you think?" she inquired seriously.

"Perhaps. I don't know that it's on the cards for me to carry on any particular tradition. Neither myself nor Phil. We're superfluous, in a way. Of course we belong to the family, and all that sort of thing. But we're only younger sons, after all."

"I don't quite understand," Laska wrinkled her brows. "What difference does that make?"

"Quite a lot — to us," Rod grinned amiably. "You see, the original Roderick had certain notions about money and property. He laid down as a working principle for his heirs that the estate should never be divided and portioned out to each generation. He said that the bulk of it ought to remain compactly in one inheritance, for the benefit of everybody concerned. He made various suggestions as to how this should be carried out, but the main one is that the home place and the bulk of the holdings shall pass into control of the eldest son. We've proceeded always on that basis. Grandfather, in fact, when it came his turn, converted the estate into a corporation. The control is always vested in the eldest son. He owns the shares and carries on the management. Seventy per cent of the net income goes to him. The other thirty per cent of revenue is equally divided among the rest of the children, whether there's one or a dozen, and is paid to each for life as each attains his majority.

"Grandfather is really the king of the castle. He's eighty now and I don't suppose he can last much longer. The governor is the active manager. When the governor goes out, Grove takes over the whole works. He'll live here. His children will probably be born here, and *his* oldest son will be expected to carry on in the usual manner. It's a pretty well-established family custom."

"What do the younger sons do?" Laska inquired. "The girls naturally get married and go away with their husbands. But the younger sons?"

"Oh, we generally stick around," Rod said casually. "But once our schooling is completed, we are at liberty to do what we please. There's usually plenty of opportunity in connection with the family affairs. We own a lot of timber and land along the coast. But when a younger son wants to set up his own vine and fig tree he has to do it elsewhere."

"I see," Laska looked thoughtful. "It's something like the old English law of entail."

"Yes, except that it isn't a law. Merely a custom. You might call it a family tradition. Any generation could depart from it, if they wanted to."

They stood for a minute looking at the dull red of the tile roof showing through the trees.

"Shall we walk around a bit?" Rod asked. "Or shall we go and have a game of tennis before dinner?"

"Let's walk. I hate tennis when it's hot," she said frankly.

They closed the iron gate behind them and lounged along under the trees.

"What became of the *Hermes*?" Laska asked suddenly.

"Went to the boneyard long ago," Rod replied. "Next time you're up in the library look in that big glass case by the east wall. You'll see old Roderick's charts and navigating instruments, sextant, chronometers, so on. The binnacle and compass is on the *Haida* — some of the old metal fittings, too. The old *Hermes* was all oak, brass, copper and bronze. Her figurehead stands in a corner of the hall. You noticed it?"

"The wooden figure of a battered Neptune? I didn't know what it was," Laska confessed.

Across the lawn as they strolled, there came presently a man in flannels. When he came up to them it turned out to be Phil.

"The governor wants you, Rod," he said. "They're making medicine in the library. I'll look out for Miss Wall."

"You'd better look out for yourself," Rod answered with brotherly impudence.

If he had dreamed how close he came to the mark with this youthful attempt at repartee, Rod would assuredly have kept silence. If there were any one of his blood for whom Rod had a genuine unselfish affection, it was this tall brother who stood smiling down at Laska Wall. In the very nature of things Rod could not know that he had just placed in Laska's hands a weapon to be used — however unconsciously — against his brother, that anything he could say or do should conceivably tilt the uncertain scales of a woman's decision. So he grinned at his own sally and strode away toward the house, whistling "Hey, Johnny Cope" and wondering carelessly why "they" were making medicine and what his father could want of him so urgent that Phil had been sent to command his attendance. So far as Rod was concerned, his father's intentions and commands were usually conveyed in the most casual manner. In the Norquay establishment the authority of the head of the house was such that it never needed to be peremptory.

The wide porch facing seaward was deserted when he came there. He passed into a roomy hall, panelled in weathered oak to a ceiling crossed with massive beams. He took the broad stairway two steps at a bound, and turned more sedately into a big, low-ceilinged room where every inch of wall space was given over to loaded bookshelves.

When he saw what councillors composed Phil's cryptic "they," Rod felt for the first time a shadow of trouble in the offing.

His tutor, Mr. Arthur Spence, occupied one chair. Near him sat Grove, the eldest son of the house, a true Norquay in physique, long-limbed, wide-shouldered, with a more mature, slightly less engaging countenance than his brothers, although he had the same fresh colouring, the same reddish-brown hair and clear bluish-grey eyes. Norquay senior sat with his legs crossed, a bulky, well-preserved man. His years rode him lightly. He looked at his youngest son in silence. No one but Rod, perhaps, would have felt critical disapproval in that impersonal glance. None of the three understood how impressionable to a look, a tone, the nuances of personal atmosphere, an eighteen-year-old boy could be. Rod himself did not realize the lightning-like quality of his own perceptions where people were concerned. He had what he called "hunches." That they invariably proved correct never aroused in him more than a passing wonder.

"Sit down, Rod," his father indicated a chair.

The tutor and Grove arose, left the room. The fancy flitted across Rod's mind that they constituted a jury which had deliberated and given a verdict and now withdrew to permit the august judge to pronounce sentence. He racked his brain for a misdemeanor, a possible offence which merited paternal condemnation. He could recall none. Yet there was an air of suspended judgment in the slow puffing of his father's cigar, the judicial immobility of his manner, in the very silence of that pleasant room with its massive furniture and burdened shelves.

"I've decided it will be as well for you to enter McGill in the fall semester," he said dispassionately, fixing his eyes on his son with a slight obliquity of his brows. "Spence assures me you can easily qualify for entrance. You will go down to Vancouver day after tomorrow, get what clothes you need, then proceed to Montreal and stay with your Aunt Maida until the University opens. Give you a chance to meet a few people and get your bearings."

"Day after tomorrow!" Rod echoed.

"Yes," Norquay senior methodically deposited the ash from his cigar in a brass tray. "And in the meantime —" his even, mellow tone took on a slight acidity — "no more of this harebrained rapid-running with that Thorn girl in that gaudy barge of yours. It may amuse you, but it's hardly fair to the girl."

"Amuse me — well, it is good fun," Rod manifested a trace of bewilderment. He had never been attacked from such an angle. "But I don't see — unfair to Mary Thorn? D' you mean dangerous? We both swim like fish, and you can't sink a dugout. I know enough about swirly water not to run the rapids when it isn't safe."

"I wasn't thinking about the specific danger of drowning."

"What then?" Rod asked.

His father regarded him with a mild impatience.

"You're almost a man," he said impersonally. "It's time your taste in feminine associations rose a little above the half-wild daughter of a dreamy-eyed incompetent. Especially when it begins to attract attention. You seem to have forgotten, the last two or three days, that we have guests here."

"Oh, I see," Rod muttered. A flush crept up into his cheeks, as the implication of his father's words and attitude drove home. He was sophisticated enough to understand — and to resent — and to keep both understanding and resentment to himself. But he could not wholly conceal the small tempest that began to stir in him. He was dealing with a man accustomed to dealing with men, with personalities, and gauging them correctly for his own purposes. The boy's quick colour, the momentary flash in his eyes, brought an amused smile to the elder Norquay's face.

"That's all," he said. "Most youngsters seem to find it necessary to make asses of themselves about some sort of female sometime early in their careers. Don't be a common ass, Rod."

"I'll try not to, sir," Rod answered with as near an approach to sarcasm as he dared, "for the sake of the family."

With that he left the room, conscious of a quickly gathered frown on his father's face at this tonal shadow of irony. The Norquay characteristic, as Mr. Kipling once mentioned of colonials, was one of straight-flung words and few. This was not the first time Rod had manifested a variation from family type in his mode of expressing himself.

And as Rod strode down the hall to his own room he muttered to himself: "That's Grove. The governor never would have thought of such a rotten thing himself. Well, I may be an ass — but I'm not a damned cad."

He snicked the lock on his own door, flung himself moodily into a chair by the window. He felt a queer mixture of boyish anger and a touch of forlornness — as a colt that has had the run of wide pastures must feel when it is first haltered and thrust into a stall.

CHAPTER III

ROD HAD COME DOWN a hall that had, like everything about Hawk's Nest, a spacious air. It was high and broad. Dim light filtered into it through stained-glass windows, fell in mellow patches on carpet so thick and soft that he moved silent as an ancestral phantom — which, however, was no part of the Norquay tradition. Active, resourceful men, and beautiful, gracious women had lived and moved and had their being there. Those comfortable homelike rooms had seen their joys and minor tragedies, births and deaths, quarrels and affections. Some of them had left various monuments to their credit, chiefly in the upbuilding and sustaining of the Norquay fortunes. But none, the remembered and the forgotten, had ever returned in the spirit. It was as if having lived their span they were content to let their descendants have undisturbed possession.

Probably Rod was the only Norquay under that roof who had so clear a vision of all that had preceded him, and so faint a comprehension of his future. The normal youngster of that age is eagerly forward-looking.

He has no retrospect. He is full of impatient hopes, dreams, desires, whenever he lifts his eyes beyond the absorbing present. Rod deliberately refrained from lifting the curtain of the future. When he went beyond the engrossing moment, he looked backward over the history of his country and his family which were so closely knit — and he saw all the great adventures, the exciting struggles, the foundation-laying and the slow purposeful upbuilding, as something which had become a finished process before he was born.

He would spend hours mooning over his great-great-grandfather's journal and feel a pang of regret that he had not lived in those quickening days. They were gone. The land was tamed. The Chilcotins would never again come raiding. The sea otters were vanished along with the men who hunted them. The trading vessel, square-rigged or fore-and-after, had given way to the steam tramp. From Land's End to the Strait of Juan de Fuca was a twenty-day voyage instead of thirty weeks. Law, order, custom moulded men now. The frontiers were charted and surveyed.

What was the use of being born with a spirit that chafed against the dull certainties of a world in which everything was known, defined, reduced to a formula? The world that Rod knew was like the Norquay family — static! So he summed it up. All the great deeds done, or at any rate the necessity, the spur of doing removed beyond him. Those silent shores to which Roderick Sylvester Norquay sailed with Vancouver in 1792 were cluttered with grubby towns, marked off into private areas for individual exploitation. Those inland seas which they had explored and charted were speckled with vessels in the lumber trade, the coal trade, coastal transport, fisheries. The forests were falling under the axes of ten thousand loggers. There was only the adventure, the struggle, the arid business of making money. And no Norquay had a vital need of doing that. Their forefathers had attended shrewdly to the acquisition of land and timber when it could be had for the taking. The Norquays did not need to *make* money. They had it. It came rolling in to them. They could sit still or play; it was all one. Static! That was the term Rod used.

That a capacity for thinking about such things in such fashion was scarcely the normal intellectual equipment of an eighteen-year-old youth did not occur to Rod. He had the singularly unboyish quality of hoarding his thoughts, of living very much in a reflective world of his own, which he shared with no one; which indeed he sedulously masked from every one he knew, unless it was Mary Thorn. Even to Mary he permitted only shy, stray glimpses of what sometimes crowded his brain, as a concession to her confident belief in him, her conviction that the most fanciful thing he could utter was at least worth consideration merely because he saw fit to give it utterance. Whereas any groping effort to encase an abstraction in words served only to bring an amused look to the collective faces of his own people. His father would lift heavy eyebrows in polite surprise. Grove would laugh coarsely. Even Phil would look a little puzzled, a little bored. Rod knew. He seldom made such experiments in self-expression. But his mind would concentrate with burning eagerness on a great variety of things. And sometimes his conclusions saddened him without his knowing why.

This decree of banishment from Hawk's Nest in midsummer provoked him to sullen pondering in the quiet of his own room. He recognized authority. Obedience was an observed tradition in that house. It was not the fact of his being bundled off to a university that troubled Rod. He had looked forward to that as a necessary and perhaps delightful experience. It was the snap judgment which hastened the date of this mental discipline — as if it were a penalty inflicted on him for an offence — as if he were a small child caught with his fingers in the jam pot.

So Rod, sitting with his elbows on the windowsill looking out on the tiderace streaming full flood between Valdez and Big Dent, seeing the glassy green incline and the white flash of foam, wondered irritably why his father saw fit to penalize him, to warn him in that offensive, suggestive manner about Mary Thorn. There was no ground for that. Rod knew his father as a fair-minded man, not much given to moralizing, nor arbitrarily instructing his sons in ethical problems. He wouldn't have issued a fiat like that without someone stirring him up. Rod scowled. He could guess pretty well who had done the stirring; who, being not too nice in surreptitious amours himself, was inordinately jealous how the family dignity, the family honour fared in his brothers' hands. Which was a very precise summary of one phase of Mr. Grosvenor Sylvester Norquay. It wasn't a flattering estimate of character and Rod kept it strictly to himself. When he was small he had disliked Grove's high-handed style, his tendency to domineer, an occasional outcrop of a brutal streak. As Rod grew older that dislike became contempt, deep and abiding. A queer feeling to exist between brothers. Yet not so rare.

A warning bell brought Rod out of his absorption. He dressed and joined the others in the dining room.

It was a leisurely meal, unobtrusively ceremonial, after the conventional fashion of those who have gained the privilege of partaking of food as a pleasure, and not as a mere necessity. There was nothing lacking. To dine at Hawk's Nest was the equivalent of dining in the home of any cultivated person in New York, Paris, London — black broadcloth and planished shirt front, corsage that revealed gleaming shoulders; snowy linen, polished silver, cut flowers; conversation as an art; good food, wine, perfect service. A black-coated man hovered discreetly behind the chairs, silently anticipating every want.

Rod's eyes swept the table and came to rest on his grandfather. A lean old patriarch with a thatch of hair white as the table cover, a moustache waxed to spiky points, a thin curved nose between deep-set, faded blue eyes. He was past eighty. He could still relish a glass of port, find pleasure in sitting beside a pretty woman — upon whom he would bestow a blend of compliment and reminiscence. For now the old man lived almost wholly in the past. When he walked slowly about the grounds, leaning on his stick, he never spoke of what was to be, only of what had been. Rod looked at him and wondered if *he* would live as long and see so many changes. He was sitting beside Mrs. Wall, a plump well-groomed woman of forty-five. Above the murmur about the table Rod could hear him telling her of the gold rush to the Cariboo in '58. He had a crisp incisive manner of speech. He had been the first Norquay to attend McGill. He was an educated man, almost a scholarly one, in spite of an active life. He had built well and widely on the fur-trading foundation.

"He was the last of the constructive period," Rod mused. "The governor has merely stood pat. Grove will likely go backward. We're a rum lot."

He had to give over these inturning reflections and be polite. He was seated between Isabel Wall and a Miss Sherburne, a darkly handsome creature whose fascinations were too precious to waste on a mere youth. Miss Sherburne's profile slanted eagerly to the left, toward Phil. But Isabel had no such reservations. Rod was nearest her own age. He was fair game. He proceeded casually to divulge to Isabel such information as she sought about running the rapids in a canoe, about Mary Thorn. She appeared to have a considerable curiosity about Mary. Presently Rod began to wish her deaf and dumb. Outwardly he remained patiently courteous. It was a relief when coffee and cigarettes ended the meal.

It took him some time to escape from Isabel. Normally he would not have minded her chatter nor her appropriation of himself. But just now his mind held tenaciously to something which had been nagging him ever since that interview in the library. When he saw Phil give over a palpable attempt to segregate Laska and saunter off toward the float landing, he excused himself and followed.

They walked down the slope together, out on the slip, seated themselves on a bench.

"Give me a cigarette," Rod demanded abruptly, as his first utterance.

Phil handed over his case. Rod lit one.

"Getting real devilish," Phil bantered.

"Was Grove aboard the *Haida* when you came through the rapids this afternoon? I didn't see him."

"Down below, I suppose," Phil replied. "I didn't notice. But he was with us. Why?"

"I thought so. What a skunk he is. Yet in this family he's the little tin god on wheels. He thinks everybody is as rotten as himself, too."

"You shouldn't talk like that," Phil remonstrated mildly.

"It's true. You know it is."

For a second Phil said nothing to this.

"One can't go about shouting unpleasant truths," he observed then. "What's wrong, anyhow?"

"I'm to be packed off to McGill day after tomorrow."

"But the term doesn't begin for weeks yet."

"Oh, I'm to visit Aunt Maida and explore the historic city which has justified its existence by containing the seat of learning where my forefathers absorbed the knowledge and culture which has enabled them to lead such eminently successful and praiseworthy lives," Rod drawled.

"Well, that's no great grief," Phil replied. "Nothing to get fussed up over."

"It was generally understood I was to begin next year. I'm being packed off as a punishment. It seems the family dignity is being compromised by my running rapids in a dugout with a girl."

"Well?" Phil waited patiently.

"Grove put a bug in the governor's ear," Rod dropped allusion for plain facts. "The governor wouldn't have thought of disciplining me. Grove's a damned snob. He has his gang here. He thinks I ought to spend my time entertaining them. He imagines it is a reflection on *him* that I prefer to play with Mary Thorn. Out of his own messy mind he takes it for granted — the governor would never of his own accord have suggested that I was — that I might — oh, damn! I don't like Grove's filthy insinuations, Phil. And I couldn't talk back to the governor. If it weren't for all these people here, I'd beat Grove up for his pains."

"You're hardly up to that yet," Phil smiled indulgently.

"Don't you fool yourself," Rod declared hotly. "I weigh a hundred and fifty-five stripped. I'm as hard as a rock — and he's mush. You know it, Philip. He's lapped up too much hard liquor, and dallied too much with that woman he keeps in the Bute Street flat to — to stand the gaff very long."

"Good Lord; nothing gets by you," Phil grunted. "How do you know these things?

"I have eyes and ears," Rod answered. "And I'm not asleep when I'm in town. He had a little blonde in his harem last year. The latest, I understand, is a voluptuous brunette. He has more light loves than some people have servants. By jove, he's the last one that ought to hint to the pater that *I* need looking after."

"Maybe it was old Spence," Phil observed thoughtfully. "The three of them were confabbing when the governor asked me to find you. Old Spence is rather strait-laced, and you're his especial charge, you know."

"No, Spence is only an echo," Rod said scornfully. "An echo of other men's thoughts, books, history, languages. Old Spence is decent, and he considers me so. Besides, he wouldn't talk himself out of a job any sooner than he had to. There are no more Norquay children for him to cram with predigested mental fodder."

Phil laughed.

"You certainly have a piquant way of expressing yourself, kid," he smiled. "I don't think old Spence would let his job interfere with his sense of duty if it were aroused. I imagine, too, that he is slated for a pension after tutoring the three of us. I guess it was our beloved brother who put you in bad. Does it matter so much?"

"I suppose not," Rod said reflectively. "Still, it does make me sore to have him meddle like that. He's too fond of butting in and it's always his own axe that wants grinding. Or else just pure cussedness. I could run the rapids on every tide, and seduce a settler's daughter every six months for all he personally cares. He doesn't care a hoot what I do until some of his guests, I suppose, remark on my paddling around in a canoe with a girl who isn't anybody and who wears shabby clothes. Then he's all for class distinctions and a high degree of personal purity. Huh!"

Rod's snort was eloquent, and Phil grinned in sympathy. His grin faded with a suddenness that caused Rod to look up, curious as to what had brought that swift change and sobering fixity of gaze to his brother. Grove and Laska Wall had walked down to the top of the bank. They stood thirty feet above tidewater, sixty yards distant, the slanting sunbeams casting their shadows far across the grass. Grove had one hand thrust in his trousers pocket. With the other he gestured largely.

"Behold — these — my possessions," Rod interpreted sardonically. "Go up and cut him out, Phil. She's too nice a girl to —"

"I wonder why they fall for him the way they do?" Phil muttered under his breath; but Rod's keen ears heard.

"They don't know him, and we do," he said cynically. "He's there with the smooth talk, and the pleasing manner, and the good looks —

and don't forget the possessions. That counts a heap with most of the girls we know."

"Oh, shut up. You don't know what you're talking about," Phil said roughly. And when Rod turned in surprise at this outburst, Phil rose to his feet and stalked away up the gravel walk into the grounds.

Rod followed at a more leisurely gait. He bore no ill will. His dignity was touchy enough in respect of any affront from Grove. Phil was privileged to be as brusque as he liked. There was never any malice in what he said or did. Rod always gave Phil the benefit of the doubt. He was only a little puzzled as he gained the house and noiselessly made his way upstairs, to look over his fishing tackle and then read himself into drowsiness.

Rod's forenoons had been given over to study under Mr. Spence, M.A., B.Sc. He found himself, in view of his near departure for academic pastures, excused from this. He did not feel any particular gratitude for the exemption. Mr. Spence, in spite of certain classical prejudices, an insular sense of superiority to mere colonials which twenty-odd years' residence under the Norquay aegis had but slightly vitiated, had a faculty of making dry facts palatable and interesting matters completely absorbing. Rod had a mind like a sponge; Mr. Spence had supplied it rather deftly with choice liquids. So Rod had none of the schoolboy's exultation at seeing the last of his teacher. He merely wondered at a greater liberty bestowed upon him when the family seemed unduly exercised lest he plunge into mischief.

Thus having the whole day before him where he had counted only on the afternoon, he swallowed his breakfast — which was a go-as-you-please meal that kept the cook and butler busy from eight to ten-thirty — took his fishing kit and paddled the lurid dugout into the channel.

He glanced back at a piercing whistle from ashore. The distance was too great for words to carry, but not for Rod to make out the signaller as Grove. He waved a paddle and kept on.

"Probably wants to wish somebody on me to go fishing," Rod grunted. "He knows I'd much rather go alone. No chance, old cockatoo. This is *my* party."

He bounded light-footed as a cougar up the steps to a porch floor pricked full of innumerable tiny holes from the sharp caulks of logging boots, walked without ceremony into a rather bare front room, and when he found no one there to answer his casual "hello," passed on to the kitchen. Mary and her mother were cleaning up the breakfast things.

"I'm headed for the Granite Pool," he announced. "Can Mary come along, Mrs. Thorn?"

"I expect she can," the girl's mother answered placidly, "if she wants to."

But Mary shook her head. "You're too early. Lots of work to do yet."

"You can work when you can't do anything else," Rod said. "Come on. Don't be a piker. You're only in Mrs. Thorn's way. Isn't she, Mrs. Thorn? Isn't a girl a nuisance around a house? I'm sure you'd much rather have a boy."

"I don't know about that," Mrs. Thorn smiled gently. "Mary's about as good at most things as a boy. Isn't she?"

"Oh, sure — that's why I want her to go fishing," Rod grinned. "Come along, Mary."

"If you want to go, child, never mind the work," Mrs. Thorn encouraged in her soft, even voice. "There isn't enough to bother anyone."

"Perhaps Mr. Thorn will go, too."

Rod dropped his creel and vanished out the back door in search of the head of the house.

Mrs. Thorn looked down on her daughter's brown head. She was a tall woman, with more than a vestige of good looks, a certain grace of carriage. Her skin was fresh, unwrinkled. Her voice had a pleasant, throaty tone. An odd expression flitted across her face now, and Mary, glancing up, caught it; a wordless, sympathetic understanding. She rose on tiptoe to kiss her mother's cheek.

"Run on. Vacation will end soon enough. I don't suppose your father will go," Mrs. Thorn said. "Better put up a lunch. The chances are Rod didn't think of that."

"I thought of it," Rod came back in time to overhear, "but there was no time. I had to make a getaway."

"Playing hooky?" Mrs. Thorn teased.

"Yes. From our honoured guests. They can't do anything without being personally conducted. And as it isn't my show, I'd rather let someone else do the conducting."

In ten minutes they were swinging uphill from the narrows, on a path that rose steeply through heavy timber, turning aside here and there for great trees. They moved silently, saving their breath for the climb. High overhead rifts of blue sky showed through interlocked branches. Dew still clung to the bordering thickets. They walked in cool shadow, on ground the sun never touched except in narrow shafts because of that canopy of leaf and bough. They bore on up until they came out on a height of land bare of timber, where only moss carpeted the granite ridge. On their right Little Dent and Big Dent and the twin Gillards lay like dusky green blobs in the shining race of the tide. The red roof of Hawk's Nest was a flaming dot against paler green. The channel below was a still paler shade. The mainland receded to height after height, mountain after mountain, the farther peaks faint blue cones on a ragged horizon.

"What a look. Air's clear as crystal this morning."

Mary nodded. They walked a hundred yards along the open backbone. To the left blue-black water mirroring the shore trees, the distant hills, walled on three sides with bold, ravine-split cliffs, gleamed in a deep hollow. They plunged downward through dense thickets. The patch discovered itself anew to their hurrying feet. In ten minutes, panting a little with the speed of their descent, they stood on a rock shelf thrusting into the Granite Pool, a little lake hidden in the Valdez hills. There was neither inlet nor outlet. It was half a mile broad, mysteriously fed by hidden springs, full of cutthroat trout rarely disturbed in their aqueous heaven.

In the Granite Pool Rod Norquay and Mary Thorn had a special, proprietary interest, quite apart from the fact that one side of Oliver Thorn's land touched its shore, and elsewhere its cliffy borders were ringed about by the Norquay holdings. Their interest was not one of physical ownership. They had discovered it for themselves. They were the first, so far as they knew, to cast a line in those deep, still waters. They had given it a fitting name. Even the trail, cleverly blinded, had been the work of their hands, assisted by Mary's father. Except Indians and timber cruisers, a ubiquitous and taciturn clan, few people knew that such a lake nestled in the hills so close to the Euclataw. These two, who had haunted it through the summers of four years, kept their knowledge to themselves. The Granite Pool was their own; the way thereto and the angler's joy therein a secret they refused to share. Oliver Thorn humoured them in this; it pleased him that two children should have such a sanctuary. Rod evaded divulging the source of the baskets of trout he carried home — justifying himself by the sure knowledge that if all Hawk's Nest knew, vandal parties under Grove's leadership would invade trail and lake, make fish hogs of themselves in the Granite Pool, profaning its beautiful solitude in the name of sport.

A raft was moored to the shelving rock. They got aboard and cast loose, jointing up their rods as the raft drifted down on a patch of lily pads among which faint splashes sounded intermittently, followed by concentric ripples that spread away till they were lost on the surface of the dark water.

"They're still feeding, thank goodness," Rod observed.

Mary nodded, busy with her gear. She rose, flicked a Royal Coachman forty feet on her third cast and struck a twelve-inch trout. Whereupon they both became galvanized by that curious suppressed excitement which is a heritage from remote periods when man secured his daily food with his own hands, or went hungry.

At four in the afternoon they had taken their leave of the pool, climbed to the ridge, and were sitting on a down tree trunk, looking from that vantage at a steam tug far below with a great boom of logs trailing astern. She passed through the lower rapids in the brief slack. Rod's creel lay at his feet, heavy with their catch. He watched the raft of logs move slowly up the channel. Then his eyes turned to the girl, rested upon her with definite appraisal.

Rod had been looking at Mary Thorn more or less casually ever since he was a leggy boy in knickers and she a slim elf in abbreviated gingham dresses. But he had never been so conscious of her as now. So late as yesterday he had regarded her without personal awareness of sex. How was it, he wondered, that a few words from his father, a cryptic hint or two, could make everything different? Nothing had happened.

Yet he knew that a different quality had entered their companionship. A boy and a girl could play together without thinking of themselves as male and female. A man and a woman couldn't. His father had warned him that he was a man and should comport himself accordingly. As if a man's natural instinct was to run amuck! Perhaps that was the truth. Rod smiled uneasily at the notion. He was not precisely an unsophisticated youth, but he could scarcely comprehend that there is only a shadowy border between the frank, sexless affections of childhood and the uneasy glow of maturing passion. He had never nursed a libidinous thought about Mary Thorn. And yet —

His eyes rested on her with a new sort of gauge. She sat staring down Cardero Channel, her hands in her lap, not so much intent on some distant object as deep in one of those long, thoughtful silences into which she now and then retired — a characteristic that Rod liked because it was something he himself often did. Her hair was a brown smoothness about her head, tied back with a narrow ribbon. She was very pretty, Rod decided critically, prettier than any girl he knew. But something more than superficial prettiness attracted him. He didn't know what. It eluded him. She had a woman's bosom and neck. Her body was made up of harmonious contours. Her expression, absent, reflective, gave him the feeling that he looked at maturity and wisdom. It surprised him to think that such an aspect of her had never struck him before.

Looking at her, he suddenly felt a queer, constricted feeling in his breast. He desired all at once to touch her, to rest his fingers lightly on that delicately tinted skin. She would laugh at him. He wondered if she would. He wondered what she thought about, locked up in herself like that. What went on in her mind that brought tiny puckers of concentration in her forehead? Was she as suddenly acutely conscious of him, in a disturbing physical sense, as he was of her? And he wondered futilely why he should be troubled by such unaccustomed thoughts and sensations now, when so late as yesterday they two had sprawled together on the mossy benches of Little Dent, laughing and chattering like two boys bent on innocent adventure in the world of boyish action.

Now there was certainly a mischief working in his blood that was not innocent. He knew it. It made him quiver. There was a ferment in his mind as well as in his body. Was this what Spence meant when he discoursed solemnly on the arrival of youth at man's estate? The pitfalls of uncontrolled passion. The ineradicable animal in man. Spence always spoke of the most intimate relation between a man and a woman in guarded terms. He conveyed the idea that it should be a matter of rational choice — on the man's side. Spence never discussed the woman's part; he ignored the woman. The man, then, according to the Spencian ethic, carried on his sexual life according to his innate character. If he was inherently brutish he sought sexual satisfaction promiscuously. The ideal, sanctioned by society, therefore ethically sound, was love, matrimony, the ultimate family, achieved progressively with mature deliberation to balance emotion. Mr. Spence did not inform Rod that this ideal progression depended on a great many uncertain factors. Perhaps he did not know. But Rod had accepted his tutor for several years as an oracle on culture in general, as well as in its specific branches, and it was difficult for him to turn a deaf ear when the oracle spoke of ethics — in spite of the fact that Rod's own observation, the conclusions of a fairly acute if youthful mind, stirred doubts.

He granted that Phil might pass muster. Grove wouldn't. He could think of several men, young and old, within the Norquay orbit, who wouldn't. But Grove was the most outstanding, because he had the most intimate knowledge of Grove's personality and his surreptitious amours, which had been overlapping each other ever since Rod was old enough to understand such matters. If a reasonable state of personal purity were necessary to the Spencian image of a gentleman, Grove could not qualify. Yet Mr. Spence had as much respect for Grove Norquay as Grove's world in general — which was a great deal more than either of his brothers held for him. Grove was clever. He was handsome. He could be generous to his equals. His manner was beyond reproach. Yet outside of his own class women were to Grove a sporting proposition, to be pursued and captured for his sensual gratification.

No, there was something lacking in the wisdom Mr. Spence had attempted to impart. Mr. Spence distinguished sharply between love and lust. He had explained the difference without making the difference clear. Rod wondered which of the two had overtaken him all unexpectedly, sitting beside Mary Thorn on a log. Which was it that made his heart beat faster. Was it love — blooming precociously? Or was it the other thing, against which Spence had warned him to be strong?

Curious thoughts and reasoning. Strange shadows flitting through the corridors of Rod Norquay's mind; beautiful shapes and grotesquely distorted ones. What youth thinks and feels is a measure of what it will think and feel in maturity. A maple does not spring from a poplar seed. The pine sapling lacks a long lifetime of becoming a tree, but as a sapling it is still a pine.

"What are you thinking about so hard?" he asked Mary.

He was not so curious now about her thought. He was more intent upon his own. But he wanted her to turn her face. He wanted her to look at him. And when she did turn in a little wonder at the unaccustomed question, Rod took her face between his trembling hands and looked steadily into her grey, inquiring eyes for a second. Then he kissed her. She did not shrink as he looked. Nor when his lips touched hers lightly did she move or speak at first. Only the blood mounted up her neck, into her cheeks, flooded her face to the roots of her hair. Rod's hands dropped. She looked at him without reproach. He could read nothing beyond a mild wonder in her expression. He wondered at himself. It had been quite unpremeditated. But he was not sorry, nor ashamed.

"Now, you've spoiled things," Mary said at last. "I won't go with you anywhere if you're going to kiss me whenever you take a notion. I'm not a hug-and-kiss girl, and I didn't think you were going to be that kind of a boy."

"I'm not, on general principles," Rod said frankly. "I never kissed a girl before. I never really wanted to, until just now. Is it a crime?"

"No, I suppose not," Mary said. "I know girls and boys in town who are regular kissing-bugs. They don't seem to think any more of it than shaking hands."

"What rot," Rod snorted. "Messy lot. Must be."

"I don't think so," she said doubtfully. "They're not bad — just silly."

"Therefore I must be too," he caught her up quickly. "Why didn't you stop me? You could easily enough."

"I didn't want to," she said slowly. "That's the funny part of it. We shouldn't. I must be as silly as the rest. What's the matter with us, Rod? We shouldn't feel that way, you and I."

"Why not?" he asked. "We're no different from other people."

"We're just kids," she sighed, "halfway through school. We have no business playing at — at love."

She brought the word out with difficulty. It was what she meant to say, but the utterance seemed difficult.

Rod poked at the moss with his heel. He could see the force of her assertion. He was only a little surprised that her thought kept step with his own. And he voiced an observation which transcended his years and experience when he said:

"If you feel certain things, why, you feel them — whether you're sixteen or sixty."

Mary rose and picked up the rods.

"Come on. Let's go home," she said bluntly.

"Home," quoth he, as he slung the creel strap over his shoulder, "is nothing like this."

Whereat they both laughed and the tension seemed to snap, leaving them at ease again.

"Don't rush so," Rod complained, three hundred yards down the trail. "There's no hurry, and it's the last time we'll go anywhere together this year."

Mary stopped short, faced about.

"Why? Because of what I said?"

"No. The fact is, I'm being packed off East to school sooner than I expected. Going to town tomorrow. Then straight to Montreal. Be back Christmas, I suppose, but I may not have a chance to see you."

"But you'll be here next summer through the holidays," she said.

"No telling," Rod grumbled. "The governor might send me travelling in Europe. He did Phil. Part of our education, he says."

"I see," she breathed, and swinging about, went on down the trail. It was steep and narrow, the path bordered close by thickets. Rod could only walk at her heels. When he crowded close she quickened her pace, heedless of his protest. She did not look back. She went downhill light-footed as a fawn, at a speed beyond Rod's liking, until they came out on the flat near Thorn's house, where the trail widened and Rod drew up beside her. She stopped. There were little stains down her cheeks.

Rod put one arm across her shoulders.

"We've had lots of good times together," he said huskily. "We will again. I'll be back."

"Oh, yes, you'll come back." She looked at him wistfully. "You belong here. Of course, you'll come back. But it'll all be different."

"Why should it be different?" he demanded.

"I can't quite say. But I know it will. You'll see."

Rod puckered his brows over that last. He had an idea what she meant. Once or twice during this brief summer she had more or less haltingly said things that Rod scouted, dismissed with scarcely a thought. Two years in a city high school had taught Mary Thorn a great deal more than she learned in the classroom. She had gotten stray glimpses of the social wheels, the invisible walls that enclose the rich and powerful wherever they go. None of this had ever made any great impression on Rod. They were not things he had ever to reckon with as obstacles. But he was not obtuse. He could make deductions. He had broken bread times without number under Oliver Thorn's roof. No Thorn had ever crossed the threshold of Hawk's Nest. There was a gulf between the two houses deeper than the Euclataw Passage, less tangible than that streaming tide, but nevertheless a reality. Mary had grasped that salient feature. Rod could cross such a gulf; she could not.

He saw dimly what she meant. But even if it had been clear, it would have carried little weight just then. He was too quickly stirred by the warmth of her flesh through the sleeve of his shirt, where his arm still rested on her shoulders. The faint aromatic smell of her hair teased his nostrils.

"Stuff," he said. "We'll always be chums. Anyway, I'm glad I kissed you, Brownie."

"So am I," she whispered. "That was really goodbye, Rod. There'll be thousands of girls in Montreal."

"Oh, stuff," he answered roughly. "I won't be kissing *them*."

They walked on slowly toward the house.

CHAPTER IV

ROD HAD COME DOWN the path with a club bag in one hand, talking amiably with his father. He had seen his trunk put aboard the *Haida*. Mrs. Wall, Laska, Isabel, Miss Sherburne, Grove, and three or four other unattached young men and women who made up the house party were on the float to see him off. They filled the quiet upper bay with light talk and low laughter. Rod stood by the deck rail chaffering with them. But his eye missed one figure. He had not seen Phil since breakfast. Already the engineer was priming the big motor. He could hear the hissing of air through open petcocks. And old Phil hadn't come down to say "goodbye, kid."

Rod's glance wandered to Grove, standing by Laska Wall, a fine upright figure of a man in white flannels. And he wondered idly why this elder son of the house should be like flint to his brothers' steel without ever seeming aware of the hostile undercurrents he so often aroused. Or perhaps he simply did not care. Perhaps he felt such a complete assurance that the liking and loyalty of younger brothers was a negligible thing.

Then, as the first deep bark of the exhaust waked a hollow echo in Mermaid Bay, Phil came down with long, quick strides, dressed in a grey suit, a bag in his hand.

There was a quick exchange of casual exclamations, a shaking of hands. Phil stepped aboard.

"All right," he called to the deck hand. "Cast off."

The *Haida* backed clear, gathered way as she turned into the slackening tide. She slid past the Gillard light, lonely and untended on its steel pillar. The narrow gorge of a canoe pass opened behind the island. From a rocky point south of the pass and the light, a trail that Rod knew ran to Oliver Thorn's house. And as Rod's eyes swept the shore, he marked a figure on the highest point of this beach trail. He waved his hat. Something white fluttered like a pennant in answer. Then the cruiser's way cut off Gillard, the red roof of Hawk's Nest, and Mary Thorn on the trail. They vanished behind the low, timbered hills of Valdez, and Rod turned to his brother.

Phil sat on a skylight, his hands clasped over one knee, his eyes on the streaming wake. But Rod knew he was not looking at the bubbles in the wash, or at anything concretely visible. It was too much the concentrated look a man bestows upon things afar, remote, but vivid in the eye of the mind.

"Cheer up," he said abruptly. "The worst is yet to come."

"I wonder?" Phil replied absently. A faint smile replaced that set expression. "I suppose the worst always is ahead — only unseen."

"What's up?" Rod demanded. "Why this last minute dash, and the abstracted air?"

Phil stared at the deck.

"Do I show such outward signs of inner disturbance?" he inquired whimsically. "If I do it was a wise move to leave. I didn't think I gave myself away openly as a bad loser."

Rod said nothing. He waited. He knew his brother.

"Laska Wall's going to marry Grove," Phil said with a simulation of casualness that would have deceived anyone but Rod. "I had the pleasure of wishing her much happiness last night."

Rod could think of nothing appropriate to say. He seemed to understand quite clearly. And he couldn't feel anything but resentment against a girl who, having a choice between the two, preferred Grove. Laska fell a long way in his estimation in those few seconds.

"Well," he ventured at last, "I should worry. She's a nice girl. But there are plenty of nice girls."

"That's true enough," Phil sighed. "But the devil of it is, kid, that I wanted this particular girl. And I can't seem to be cheerful about someone else getting her. Maybe it sounds a bit crude, but I'd almost rather it had been any other man I know. Grove's — well, I pass him up. He doesn't play the game. But he gets by. I suppose he always will. Even the governor, who isn't exactly a fool, and who is decent, can't see our worthy brother as he seems to us. Well, that's another chapter. I'm not funking, but I think I'll get off the Norquay band wagon pretty soon. I don't imagine things will seem quite the same around the old place once Mrs. Grove is installed. New brooms, you know."

"Maybe. I don't know. I can easily see where we might begin to feel like intruders in our own home," Rod hazarded. "But what's the use of crossing bridges before you come to 'em?"

"I think," Phil returned, "I've come to a rather important one."

He fell into moody reflection again. Rod leaned against the rail, unwilling to break into this absorption. He knew Phil was smarting under a hurt the nature of which he could understand very well. And he was hotly on Phil's side, a position he took instinctively whenever Grove appeared as the protagonist.

That it was quite in order for Laska Wall to make her own choice probably carried much less weight with Rod than with Phil. Nor was Rod clearly aware that all his incipient clashes with Grove took root in profound differences of character, rather than in any definite invasion of his rights or Phil's by their elder brother.

There were crossed wires everywhere, he reflected. Why should Phil want Laska so badly, and why should Laska prefer by far the lesser man? These mysterious, passionate wants! Rod wandered idly if Mr. Spence, comfortable in a deck chair, his nose in a red-bound volume, could interpret these strange impulses of the flesh which could so sorely try the spirit? He decided Spence could not. Young as he was, Rod knew there were things in life that cannot be learned. They must be felt, suffered mostly. Lessons in the school of self-experience. Phil, he perceived, was getting a lesson, and taking it seriously. His own turn would come.

He shrugged his shoulders. There would be a different atmosphere about Hawk's Nest when he came home again. But Rod had already encountered the philosophic maxim that change was the only constant factor in a kaleidoscopic universe.

He went up forward, made himself comfortable in the bight of a coiled hawser, let his mind dwell on what "green fields and pastures new" four years on the Atlantic littoral might open to him.

While he pondered over the immediate future and what it might bring, the *Haida* plowed down Calm Channel, cleared the Redondas and stood into the open Gulf, reeling off her fourteen knots per hour. Before night he would be in Vancouver. In a week he would be in Montreal. Beyond that Rod could not see, nor, as the sun filled him with a drowsy lassitude, did he greatly care. For four years yet his life would be ordered, directed; he would be a human sponge soaking up knowledge, impressions, experiences common to a university career. After that —

Rod sleepily declined to transform himself into a seer.

CHAPTER V

WHEN THE DECK HANDS had dumped a trunk, a bag, a suitcase and sundry bundles on the float and the *Camosun* had backed into the stream, Rod still stood looking about him, trying to mark changes and finding none. He had been away almost two years. He might have been gone only overnight for all the external difference in what he saw. Time's scythe had mowed no grass, felled no trees, had left untouched the bold contours of his native hills, had neither added to nor taken away from the well-remembered tintings of sky and sea, the delicate shadings of the green forest which seemed to hold its own on every hand against the continuous onslaught of the logger. It was as if the puny axes and saws of man could no more than make tiny openings in that incredible stretch of coastal forest. Pygmies attacking a giant in the vast amphitheatre of the changeless hills!

Except for the stone house with a roof that gleamed like burnished copper in its setting of lawn against the deep olive of massed boughs, all that Rod Norquay could see by turning on his heel must have been bared to his eye much as it was bared to the gaze of his great-great-grandfather on the poop of the *Hermes* in 1797. Earth and water, air and sky. The changeless elements. Life was a flux, but the hills endured, and the sea. Man could ravage the forests in the name of industry. But the forest would grow again. Those high aloof mountains, with glaciers clinging on their shoulders, held out welcoming hands to Rod as they had seemed to welcome the first of his name a century before. They would be there, flinging vast shadows at sunrise and sundown, bearing their robes of dusky green and royal purple and virgin white long after he was gone.

Rod felt a keen, deeply personal appreciation of this background. He had looked at the Alps and the Pyrenees and the Highlands since he last saw The Needles looming over Bute Inlet. And he loved his own hills best. He did not care if that stamped him as a provincial. There was something here that stirred him. His native fir and cedar, the maples that flamed along the beaches in autumn, were dearer to him than English oaks. The grassed area about Hawk's Nest, with thick-trunked, lofty trees rooted in noble hundreds, was more beautiful to him that the Forest of Fontainebleau. He was home, and he had never imagined he would be so glad to get home. And he was quite aware that it was neither persons nor things that filled him with this keen satisfaction.

In four semesters he had listened to and taken part in many a sophomoric discussion where Art and Beauty went on the dissecting table. To himself he had once defined beauty as such perfection of form, tone, colour, expression, as touched human heartstrings to a responsive vibration. It did not matter, he sagely decided, whether this perfection lay in sculpture, architecture, painting, music, literature, in the everlasting hills or the shifting scroll of the sea. The sense of it, the response to it, wherever found, alone differentiated man from the animals. The attempt, more or less successful, to capture something of this beauty, to interpret it, to visualize it in marble, in colours, in words, he took to be the function of art. What art was he did not know. But beauty he could see and feel. He smiled to himself now, recalling bits of discussion between classmen about Art and Beauty. They could become so serious over abstractions. Here a man could forget abstractions. He was like his great-great-grandfather. *This* fitted him as a glove fits the hand.

He glanced across the channel. Oliver Thorn's weathered house stood blended with the forest, the west wind trailing a blue pennant from the chimney. Then he turned to meet Stagg, the butler, who had recognized the single debarkee and come down to welcome him and see about his things.

"Who's here, Stagg?" Rod inquired, as they walked up the path.

"Your grandfather, Mr. Rod, of course," Stagg answered. "Mrs. Wall, Miss Isabel, Miss Monty Deane, Miss Joe Richston, Mr. Sam Deane, Mr. Harold Collier of Seattle. Mr. Philip has taken them all down to Rock Bay on the *Haida*. We're expecting Mr. Grove and some people on his yacht for the weekend, sir."

Rod sought his grandfather in the library. He found the old man with his chair by a French window opening on a small balcony, his thin hands nursing a long-stemmed pipe.

Rod felt the firm pressure of his hand-clasp, wondered at the extraordinary vitality of the man. From this same vantage he had once fired a muzzle-loader at the painted Chilcotins. Down that same channel his eyes had beheld the historic *Beaver*, the first steamer to furrow the Pacific. He had seen the Anglo-Saxon and industry lay the firm foundation of a new commonwealth. He had seen steam supplant sail. And his eyes were keen yet, although he was eighty-three and walked slowly, leaning on a stick.

"You've filled out." The old man eyed him critically. "Did you get anything out of McGill besides girls and athletics? I understand you are being noticed in sport. I take the queening for granted."

"Why, gran'pere," Rod laughed, "does it run in the family? I haven't heard that the Norquays who attended McGill were outstanding cavaliers."

He made a mental reservation about Grove. Echoes of that young man's affairs still reverberated faintly along the St. Lawrence.

Grandfather Norquay smiled.

"In my day we were wild perhaps, but not wanton," he said. "I don't know the present generation very well, my boy. But it has curious aspects — what I see of it now and then."

"Are we much different from other generations, do you think?" Rod asked.

"In certain features," the old man answered slowly. "Yes. Very much. But I may be wrong — and it doesn't matter. I have seen a great deal of change. Some things go on unchanged. Others — my father, I recollect once —"

He went off upon a tangent of reminiscence. Rod listened, wondering if there would come a time when *he* would sit with snow-white hair and withered skin, telling his grandson of the now, which would then be fifty years under the horizon of time.

He went downstairs presently to have a bite of lunch, then outside to walk here and there. The warm June hush filled the parked spaces, that languorous stillness with an undertone of humming insects and — when one sat perfectly still to listen — the flutter and rustle of foraging birds. Under the drowsiness invisible growth, vegetable growth, responding vigorously to the warmth of sun on moist, fecund earth. One could almost hear the murmur of countless inorganic changes, expansions, all the old forms renewing themselves in the appointed way.

Rod went about from spot to spot, observing the lilacs, the rhododendrons, the bloom-hidden rockeries, all the fragrant beauty of the grounds and the sanctuary of the massed woods running back of Big Dent. He brought up at last on the float. He looked into a commodious boathouse. His dugout, the brilliant paint a trifle faded, sat on blocks, wide checks in the wood from long drouth. He shoved it into the water, let it fill to soak and swell tight. Then he took a rowboat and pushed out of the bay. A short run of tide made a slow current in the channel. He was well pleased to feel and smell salt water again, to have the sharp odour of kelp in his nostrils, to sniff the aromatic pungence wafted by faint airs out of the banked forest across the cool sea.

He had no particular purpose, no explicit destination. Perhaps for that reason, or lack of it, he landed an hour or so later at Oliver Thorn's float.

Your natural patrician is alone able to practice democracy without condescension, to meet his fellows on any common ground available. It made no difference to Rod Norquay that Oliver Thorn and his family were completely outside the Norquay orbit socially, financially, perhaps even intellectually — although the last count was highly debatable. It merely amused Rod to recall that Norquay senior had once frowned on Thorn as a "dreamy-eyed incompetent." Rod knew these people, no matter how or why. He knew them. He liked them. That was sufficient.

And there was Mary besides, a stimulus to his adolescent curiosity. He quite frankly wanted to see her again. She had been almost the only real playmate he could associate with the later and most important part of his youth. He had vivid and pleasant memories of her, which had not grown less by two years during which she might have died or married or gone to a far country, for all he knew. There had been one or two stiff little letters, then silence. Rod easily accounted for that. Too many things pressing in on them both. Too acute a self-consciousness. Rod never thought of the manner of their parting without a slight wonder at that queer surge of feeling. He supposed it was the same with Mary Thorn — a something that made for restraint between them, that could not be overcome by letters. He knew girls without number. He danced with them, rode with them, drove them about in motor cars. Two years of Montreal and three months in Europe had tremendously expanded his experience of femininity. And Mary stood out against this background of girls like an oil portrait among a group of half-tone prints.

Rod didn't attempt to account for this. He hadn't cast a sentimental halo about her. His pulse did not quicken when he thought of her. He simply remembered her vividly as a girl he knew and liked better than all the rest. The nearest he came to an analysis of the "why" was to wonder if it were not because he remembered Mary in her look and words, in her person and manner, as supremely natural. He had an ingrained dislike for the artificial. He had been born with that predisposition. So had Phil. He liked to think that was a Norquay characteristic. And the generation of girls and young women Rod knew seemed like exotic flowers, with their lipsticks and powder, their exaggeration of speech, their startling frankness. They were easy to admire. Upon occasion their provocative sex might trumpet a challenge. But in the main rouge and talcum, pert slang, the assurance of complete sophistication amused Rod without greatly interesting him.

He took it for granted Mary would be at home. But the Thorn world had moved as well as his own. He found Oliver Thorn sitting on the porch looking over a newspaper. They shook hands. Mrs. Thorn came out to greet him. And freshly she impressed Rod with a sense of serenity, of kindliness, of a motherly quality he could not remember in his own life.

"Where's Mary?" he asked.

"Still in town. She'll be home soon, though, I hope. She cut a year in high school and entered the U.B.C. last summer," Mrs. Thorn told him. "She's quite grown up, Rod. I don't believe you'd know her. She's changed, like you."

"But I don't think I've changed much," Rod demurred.

"Of course you wouldn't see it yourself, but I can," Mrs. Thorn smiled.

She went back into the house. Rod sat talking to Thorn. Trout-fishing, the salmon run, timber, matters current along the B.C. coast. Westward of the float a set of boomsticks enclosed a floating mass of fresh-cut cedar in four-foot lengths, split to a size — shingle bolts for the mills.

Oliver Thorn had owned for years a square mile of the finest timber on Valdez: magnificent fir close-ranked on the ridges, cool groves of cedar in shadowy lowlands. He held it indefeasibly, under a Crown grant. Rod knew that because he had once heard his father and Grove comment impatiently on the man's clear title, and wonder why in his circumstances he would neither sell nor cut the timber himself. Grove had observed caustically that someone had blundered. That particular stretch of woods was almost surrounded by the Norquay holdings. His father had merely shrugged his shoulders. Rod wondered idly now why a poor man did not turn those trees into useful cash. He uttered a modification of this thought.

Thorn smiled.

"I follow the wise course of greater folk," he said musingly. "Your people own miles and miles of timber, for instance. Yet they don't fill the woods with loggers and market every stick that can be cut. They log enough each year to bring in the necessary revenue. Isn't that about it?"

"Probably. I really don't know the family policy about timber, though."

"That's about it, I'd say," Thorn went on. "And mine, although it looks like a lazy man's tactics, is much the same. I bought this stretch of timber cheaply. By and by, when the time is ripe, I'll log it off or sell it to a logger. I'm doing just what the founder of your family did, Rod, and what your family continues to do. I'm holding property that will steadily increase in value."

He stopped to pick up his pipe and put a match to it. Then he continued in his slow, drawling voice.

"People have often thought me either a sluggard or a fool to sit tight here, as I've done. Some men would throw a crew of loggers in here, rip the heart out of this limit in a season, make twenty or thirty thousand dollars, and go somewhere else to do the same thing. Your pushing, bustling kind of man who doesn't see anything in the woods but so many thousand board feet per acre — that kind of man thinks I'm a damned fool.

"The fact is," he resumed, after a brief pause in this, the longest speech Rod ever heard him make, "I have no expensive social position to maintain, and I'm not keen to pile up a fortune. A reasonable amount of work is good for my liver. But working under pressure, driving other men, worrying over deals and prices and costs and contracts is not only distasteful to me, but I'm not good at it. I know because I did it for fifteen years. I not only didn't like it, but I didn't make money.

"You see," he turned to Rod, with a deprecating sort of smile, "men are born different. Some have a beak and claws to rend and tear, and they do rend and tear with the best. Some are bound to kick and gouge their way to the top of the dollar pile. For them that's the real object in life. Others have great foresight to grasp a great opportunity whenever it comes within reach. I imagine the first Norquay was that kind of man. And finally there's the fellow like me; more a dreamer than a doer; inclined to be contemplative rather than actively constructive — or destructive; more apt to take pleasure in seeing a tree grow than in cutting it down; able to work and plan and think clearly in respect of his individual acts, but somehow incapable of herding and driving and compelling other men to function for him. That's me. I pioneered in logging here on the coast. I was one of the first to introduce powerful machinery to handle this big timber. I made a little for myself now and then. But mostly I made money for someone else. And I got tired of going ahead under full steam. *My* wants are simple. My family's wants are simple. A reasonable amount of leisure. A reasonable amount of security. A chance to read and think. Freedom from hurry and worry. That seemed good enough for me. And this," he waved his hand toward the timber banked thick on the slopes behind his house, "has given it to me for several years. Each season I cut a few hundred dollars' worth of cedar — without making a dent in the total. Each year the value of the stand increases. There's twenty-two million feet on my ground. When I choose to sell, it will bring me enough for a decent living as long as I'm likely to live, and something left over for Mary. That's good enough."

Half an hour later Rod heard the *Haida* whistle far down channel. The tide had gone slack. He rowed back, a little keen to see Phil. And as he crossed he looked back at Oliver Thorn's timber and thought to himself that Thorn was doing precisely what the earlier Norquays had done. He had shrewdly based his material security on possession of a natural resource. There was no accident in Oliver Thorn's ownership. The man had a sound design that differed in scope but not in kind from the design whereby the Norquays had become what they were and held what they had.

This was the man Norquay senior had termed a dreamy-eyed incompetent.

Rod smiled. It wasn't like his father to make blunders in estimating men. Then he fell to thinking of Grove — and he was not so sure of the paternal judgment. Or was it that his own distaste for his elder brother blinded him to excellent qualities and abilities easily visible to a father's eye?

CHAPTER VI

"WHEN I WENT AWAY you were talking about going on your own," Rod said. "What kind of a twist have things taken here? You seem to be pretty much the whole works now."

"Only by proxy," Phil answered. "Somebody has to be on the job more or less. I don't mind so long as they give me a fairly free hand. Matters here have become secondary in the Norquay scheme of things, but they're still quite a handful for somebody."

"Loosen up," Rod commanded. "You weren't at all explicit in any of your letters, and the governor confined himself mostly to checks and a few casual admonitions. Has Grove quit Hawk's Nest for a career in business? What does this trust company thing amount to?"

"Lord knows. Did you go and see the plant?"

"I wasn't interested. Seeing the governor was away I only stayed in town overnight. I saw an electric sign in huge letters on a roof downtown."

"The sign of progress. The oriflamme of a budding financier, a comet flashing athwart the financial firmament," Phil intoned with ironic inflection. "That's Grove. Hawk's Nest and timber was too cramped a field for his vaulting ambition. He couldn't be satisfied with the one-horse show that was started here a century back. Our brother is by way of shedding a golden lustre on the name, Rod."

Rod snorted.

"What's he after?"

"That's what *I* ask," Phil replied. "Echo answers what? Money, is one's natural answer. But that doesn't follow. He could live here and run things in the same offhand manner that we're used to, and have more money than he would ever need. There's always been a surplus. Do you know what the income of this estate runs for the last twenty-five years?"

Rod shook his head.

"Over a hundred thousand on the average. It could be doubled, trebled, if one cared to go at the timber roughshod. So it isn't money," Phil continued. "The governor would have been perfectly satisfied to turn everything over to him as soon as he married. On the contrary, he persuaded the gov. to set him up in this blatant money-grabbing scheme. Personally, I think private banking and trust fund operations are just a glorified sort of pawnbroking. We've always made our money out of productive enterprises. I can understand Christ's indignation at the money changers. They're damned parasites. Grove, however, has no such peculiar ideas. He's become a man of affairs. The two years he spent in New York and London financial circles have turned his head, I think. Talks in millions. A wizard of finance. A wizard! Grove could always fool women. He never fooled a man of keen perception — outside of his own father. Grove's actually proud of this trust company thing, you know. Nailed our name to his financial flagpole. And he has associated with him five or six of the shrewdest business buccaneers on the coast — Deane, Arthur Richston, Mark Sherburne, and his father-in-law, John Wall. I don't like it, Rod."

"It's his funeral," Rod answered carelessly, "if they pluck him."

"I wasn't thinking about him," Phil drawled. "It's the rest of us. We wouldn't like a smash. Maybe I'm pessimistic."

"What does the pater think of it?"

"Oh, backs him stoutly. Keeps all his loose change in the Norquay Trust. Believes Grove is launched on a wonderful career. Maybe he is. But I don't think our beloved brother has the necessary grip for that sort of career. He loves power; he's the chesty sort. He revels in big affairs. And I don't think he really knows what power consists of, nor how skilfully and wisely to direct affairs."

"Did you ever like Grove, or trust him?" Rod asked bluntly. "Did you ever get on with him?"

"No." Phil answered as bluntly. "I wouldn't admit it to anyone but you, old kid. But I don't. I never did. I never will. We'll always be secretly at odds in everything."

"Same here. I wonder why?" Rod uttered reflectively. "Suppose we're subconsciously resentful — jealous because he's first and entitled to the lion's share?"

"No, no. Nothing so petty. It's fundamental. Grove looks like us. But he *isn't* like us, only outside. Inside he's different. They can talk all they damn please about heredity, environment, and cultural influences. They don't account for some people. Grove's a snob at heart. He's gross. He's a fairly clever — or cunning — good-looking healthy animal, with a purely animal psychology under a veneer of good manners. And I suppose one should view him with a degree of tolerance, because he was certainly born what he is. But one doesn't like that type of man as the chief representative of one's family."

"And you think the governor fondly imagines Grove is quite a decent sort and plays the game like a gentleman — a bit masterfully, but still according to Hoyle?" Rod mused.

"Absolutely." Phil frowned. "To me, that's the devil of it. He's honest, the governor is, and a bit old-fashioned in some notions. And he's fairly tolerant and pretty blind to certain obvious defects of character close to home. The fact is, old kid, he's rather proud of his three sons. He'd wink at almost anything one of us did — in reason. And Grove comes first. He simply can't see Grove with critical eyes. It's quite natural, Rod."

Rod would have pursued the subject further, but there now approached them in a body, where they sat dangling their legs over the

Haida's cabin, their male houseguests armed with gear for salmon fishing at the upper narrows.

That evening, as they drew clear of a nook in Stuart Island at slack water, a long, lean, cruising yacht, canopied, mahogany tenders shining in boat chocks on deck, her bow wave curling out with a hissing sound, swept by the *Haida*.

Young Deane's eyes followed her enviously.

"Classy packet that," he said to Rod. "I was out on her a couple of weekends. She's a dream inside. Fast, too; shows her heels to everything in Vancouver Harbour."

Rod smiled. Grove's yacht interested him less than the owner. Grove was expanding. Decidedly. Rod had a fanciful vision of his brother as a balloon, swelling and swelling to the ultimate overstrain and collapse. A whimsy, of course. Finance was profitable. Money bred money. Yet it seemed strange that a Norquay could turn his back on Hawk's Nest, its ordered comfort, its atmosphere of security, its leisure and its peaceful beauty, to sweat over making a barrel of money only to spend it on such costly toys. It was even more strange to think that their father abetted and encouraged Grove in this departure from the old accepted way.

"Makes this look like small potatoes, eh?" Rod found Phil grinning at his elbow as they rolled in the *Kowloon*'s wash.

"Must be money in trust companies," Rod observed sardonically. "That's bigger than the *Hermes,* which old R.S.N. sailed around the Horn."

"I wonder what *he'd* think of Grove?" Phil murmured.

"I wonder," Rod echoed.

He repeated that mordant query to himself in the course of the evening. Grove brought a dozen people on the *Kowloon,* a further installment of Deans and Richstons, and several young men and women whom Rod met for the first time, but whose names were familiar enough as people who were "somebody" in B.C. They had dinner aboard, but afterward they took possession of Hawk's Nest, hauled a piano outside and danced on the wide verandah or wandered over the grounds in pairs. Rod detected a livelier tempo than had been common to Hawk's Nest gatherings. They drank a little more freely than he remembered as the usual thing there. By eleven o'clock two or three of the men were quite comfortably "lit up." Rod noticed that, even before Laska drew his attention to them.

"Young Deane and Tommy Richston are tight," she said amusedly. "Look at their eyes. See how very solemn Tommy is."

They were sitting by an open window in the living room, watching the glide and dip and sway of the dancing couples.

"Yes, rather," he replied. "Time to turn off the tap when the guests get pickled."

"It won't hurt them," Laska remarked indifferently. "They generally behave well. Isn't it lovely here, Rod? So clean and fragrant with the woods all about and the sea at your door. I love this old place."

"You ought to," Rod smiled. "You belong to it now."

"Do I?" she said. "I hadn't thought of it in just that way."

It struck Rod that he might find it difficult to explain just what he meant. He *felt* that he belonged to this old grey house. Some indefinable bond existed between him and it, something woven about him by heredity, usage, affection, by the generations of his blood who had belonged there before him. Could anyone else feel that way about Hawk's Nest? He didn't know.

He looked at Laska with frank admiration. She was one of them now, in a special sense. One of the clan. She was a beautiful woman. Her hair was the colour of ripe wheat straw, her eyes a very dark blue, luminous, expressive. She had grace and dignity. Rod had a feeling that she must be innately kind and generous. He wondered why in the name of God such a woman preferred a man like Grove to a man like Phil.

"I hoped we'd live here," she said presently. "But Grove has to be in town."

"Has to be?"

Rod could not help the inflection. Laska looked more keenly at him.

"'Do you also disapprove of Grove?" she inquired.

"I also?" Rod countered. "I don't get you, sister-in-law."

"I don't really know you very well, Rod," she said softly. "But I'm quite sure you're not stupid."

She eyed him with a tantalizing smile that made Rod uncomfortable.

"You're just as well pleased we don't live here, aren't you now?" she went on. "And you aren't the only one with that attitude, are you?"

Rod considered a moment. He thought he understood her. And he retaliated, insofar as his breeding permitted him to retaliate. He had a retentive memory to draw on.

"I told you once that only the oldest son counted for much in this family," he replied, with a short laugh. "You drew the lucky number. Isn't that good enough?"

She sat silent for a few seconds.

"I am answered," she said briefly.

The subject ended there. Someone came to get Laska for a dance. Rod, who was tired of dancing, and a little bored with the high spirits which had originated chiefly in various decanters, betook himself upstairs to bed.

Something had gone wrong with Hawk's Nest. The old sense of cohesion, of the family as a unit, seemed lacking. Rod missed that atmosphere of solidarity. Until now he had in a vague fashion regarded his brothers, his father and grandfather, his sister Dorothy, the little groups of first and second cousins as links in a chain. There might possibly be a weak link or two — he considered Grove such a one — nevertheless it had been a chain forged of kinship, common aspirations, interests, traditions. For each of them and for all of the fairly numerous brood descended collaterally from that adventurous fur-trader, Hawk's Nest and the Norquay estate had formed a cherished background, a guarantee of certain rights and privileges, a sure wellspring of reasonable opportunity to make the best of the business of living.

Materially it was still that. But Rod had a curious impression of the old spirit having subtly withdrawn, of them all having become individualistic, separate entities with conflicting desires, ambitions, both active and potential — individual egos unleashed, clashing, bent headlong on each his own ends, without regard to the others.

He blamed Grove for this — and his father for letting Grove make it so. Grove was the disturbing element. He was turning everything inside out. Rod didn't like the people Grove surrounded himself with. He resented Hawk's Nest being subject at Grove's pleasure to an invasion by free-drinking, slang-slinging people, whose pursuit was not so much pleasure as excitement.

He grew drowsy in the midst of such reflections. After all, it didn't matter much. Especially to him. Probably this crowd was not much different from the general run of people who had money to spend and time to burn. He supposed that he was hypersensitive, too damned particular, finicky — too infernally quick on the hair trigger of an impression.

And so he fell asleep.

CHAPTER VII

GROVE'S GUESTS DANCED, drank, sang, tennised, gossiped and played cards during their waking intervals for forty-eight hours. Then the white yacht fled down the sea lanes to bring her owner to his mahogany desk on Monday morning rejuvenated by a quiet weekend at his country house, as the social page of the Vancouver *Province* duly chronicled.

Perhaps the item was correct enough in one particular. Possibly Mr. Grove Norquay was rejuvenated, or refreshed. Quietness would not so have restored his force. Next to display, Grove liked action. Whatever else he might lack, he was endowed with abundant energy. He was a big man, like most of the Norquays, handsome, with an engaging manner. It was scarcely correct for Phil to say that Grove never fooled men. If he did not fool them he had a faculty of influencing them favourably to himself. That faculty had made men like Arthur Richston and John P. Wall willing to let him stir the financial pot in which their money bubbled as well as his own. A young man in search of a career would not have commended himself to them simply by reason of his search. Even with the Norquay prestige behind him he would still need that indescribable quality which is called magnetism for lack of a more definite term — that personal power of suasion which successful motor-car salesmen and old-world diplomats alike exercise to secure signatures on the dotted line. Good men have that persuasiveness, that ability to compel confidence, and bad ones also. To which category Grove Norquay belonged it would be difficult to say. There is the blind power of circumstance to consider.

In this year of our Lord, 1911, Grove was a brilliantly successful young man in a city where success was most completely estimated by the noise a man and his money made. Grove was as well satisfied with himself as any young man could be whose career was assuming meteoric aspects. Everything he touched turned out well. The Norquay Trust Company seemed to exercise a hypnotic drawing power over investors with loose funds. There was a speculative movement in land rising to a climax in Vancouver, a something that was to assume gigantic proportions in the following eighteen months. Already shoe clerks were beginning to go without lunch to make payments on plots of land in distant suburbs, and to go about their duties dreaming of the quick turnover and the long profit.

All of which, when it occurs in a seaport in conjunction with the building of two transcontinental railway terminals, an expansion of shipping, an upturn in mining and timber, breeds that phenomenon of Western America, the "boom." Great is the confidence of the participants — and the entire community participates. For the time being it is forgotten that whatever goes up must come down. It is a great game while it lasts. Better than draw poker. Better than playing the ponies. It is legitimate, respectable, as well as thrilling. It isn't gambling. It isn't even speculation. It is investment.

Of course a trust company with a well-defined and legally restricted field of operations was not actively participating in this frenetic exchange of land titles, notes, mortgages, options and hand-to-hand agreements of sale. But the rapidity and number of such transactions created a business which Grove's company absorbed so thriftily that its growth shamed the furious beanstalk.

The Norquay Trust occupied the first two floors of a new building named after itself, on the roof of which rose a steel skeleton covered with incandescent bulbs, the sign Rod had marked on his return.

Here Mr. Grove Norquay appeared to feel that he moved at last in his proper sphere. He loved the sound and echo of huge sums, of complicated transactions, of facing men over a massive desk and deciding matters that involved much money. He liked noise, action — it gave him a sense of power, of irresistibility — just as he liked being master on his own yacht and host to a crowd of people who talked a little louder and faster and drank a little oftener and danced with a trifle more abandon than was really necessary. He could have a "whale of a time" with a lively crowd, whether the party was stag or mixed. On dead ones, either social or financial, Grove wasted no moment of his valuable time. A man with money and a sporting inclination, a women with any pretensions to youth and beauty, could be reasonably sure of Grove Norquay's consideration — at any rate for a time. He esteemed the good mixers as the salt of the earth. But they had to be the "right" sort of people. By his birth, training and antecedents Grove held himself duly qualified to judge of that beyond dispute.

He was attempting to convey the weight of this mature judgment to Rod one forenoon some days later. Rod and Phil had come down with the *Haida* to meet their father on his return from a trip south. A mild curiosity to see Grove's shop had led Rod into the Norquay Trust Building. Grove had shown him about and explained the scope of the undertaking with what interested Rod as ill-concealed pride.

"I believe you're all puffed up about this thing," he said amusedly, when they sat down at last in Grove's private office.

"Well, why not?" Grove conceded. "I organized it. It's a pretty big show, and it's my show."

"After all, it's only a money-making scheme, isn't it? You don't make anything or do anything, do you? You just handle sums of money and grab off a percentage. Eh?" Rod said innocently. He was thinking of Phil's phrase: glorified pawnbroking.

"Oh, tush — you don't understand." Grove dismissed that.

Then he proceeded to fraternal advice, slightly tinged with remonstrance.

"Didn't I see you walking along Beach Avenue with that Thorn girl after dinner last night? I understand she's down here going to school."

"Probably you did," Rod answered indifferently. Grove frowned.

"It's hardly the thing for you to cultivate her publicly," he observed. "A fellow can't carry on these country kid acquaintances in town. Aren't there girls enough in your own crowd for you to stroll along the beach with?"

"Look here," Rod challenged earnestly, "with your record in the female line you're barking up the wrong tree when you start advising me to keep within bounds. My own taste and judgment are quite as good as yours."

Grove eyed him coolly.

"My record in the female line," he murmured. "I didn't know I had one."

"No? You mean you didn't know I knew. Do you think I've been deaf, dumb and blind for the last six years? Even if I had been, you must remember you went to McGill before me. There are still a few lingering odours of you on the campus, and in some of the downtown joints."

"Well, well," Grove said cynically. "You aren't so slow as you seem, after all. So far as Mary Thorn is concerned, your taste is good enough but your judgment is damned poor. I always told the pater he kept you cloistered too much, Rod. If you have a crush on the Thorn person, go to it. But do keep her out of sight. Saves talk. These nobodies from nowhere always mess things up by trying to horn into your own crowd if they get half a chance. You understand?"

Rod looked at him soberly.

"You're a piggy sort of creature, d'ye know it, Grove?" he said with icy deliberation. "I sometimes wonder what induced Laska Wall to marry you."

A faint tinge of colour crept into Grove's face.

"I sometimes wonder myself," he said slowly, as if the thrust had set him thinking. "However, that's beside the point. If I made an ass of myself on certain occasions, that's no reason you should. Of course," he waxed sarcastic, "if you are like Phil, a youth of virginal purity, all I need to say is that it's advisable for you to seek your chemically pure companionship in your own class, on the streets or off."

"Your idea of virginal purity doesn't interest me," Rod said as he rose. "If Phil and I happen to have certain ideas about common decency which you can't understand, why, that's your misfortune. But if you want to get along with me, eldest brother, you'll leave my moral and social training alone. If you don't like my associates, you can ignore them. Keep your homiletics for your customers."

"All right, kiddo," Grove agreed ironically. "You're a Norquay and you can do no wrong. But I can tell you from experience, Roderick, old kid, that these poor men's daughters generally figure on getting something out of travelling with fellows like us. Believe me, they do."

Rod didn't answer. He was angry, both at Grove's advice and insinuation. In another second he would have been ready to blow up. So he walked to the door. In a square mirror let into a panel he got a glimpse of Grove, half-turned in his chair, looking after him with a slightly puzzled expression.

Laska had asked Rod to luncheon at the house. Grove lunched at his club. Phil had vanished about his own affairs after declining Laska's invitation. He wondered if Phil suffered from constancy; if love were a thing that endured beyond hope. He couldn't say. There was a difference in Phil. But there was a subtle sort of change manifest in everything Rod knew. At any rate he, himself, had no reason to find anything but pleasure in lunching with his sister-in-law.

So he went alone. He walked the twenty blocks that lay between the downtown traffic roar and Grove's home in the West End, thinking of his brother's cynical advice. Insofar as it bore upon Mary Thorn, Rod dismissed it contemptuously. He had met Mary by such chance as brings people together in any town. She was on her way to keep an engagement and he had walked with her the length of the beach along English Bay. But Rod had foresightedly provided himself with her telephone number. Now in a spirit closely akin to defiance he stopped at a pay station and called her up. Yes, she was free that afternoon. Yes, she would go for a walk with him.

Rod went on, more placidly. She was the same Mary Thorn who used to run the rapids with him, but a little taller. She had attained womanhood and bore herself accordingly. Rod had never been able to make invidious class distinctions between himself and her. He couldn't now. Along with Phil she had a place in his affection which she had pre-empted long before either was aware of sex. Rod's active and analytical mind had lately come to the conclusion that of all the people young and old in this land of his birth there were only two who could stir him to any warmth — Phil and Mary. That puzzled him. He supposed he must be an emotional freak. He had chums in Montreal. He knew men, women and girls by the score here in Vancouver. He regarded girls here and elsewhere with sophomoric condescension. He never missed them when they were absent. And he *had* missed Mary Thorn. How much he didn't realize until he met her again, after two years. It was very odd. The emotional and intellectual experience of twenty couldn't account for such facts.

Rod soon gave over trying. He found himself turning in at Grove's gate, and Laska coming forward in a hall to greet him.

Late June had ushered in a burst of heat. Their luncheon was served on a porch screened by wisteria. The purple clusters of bloom scented the cool shade. A seven-foot ivy-grown wall enclosed the grounds, shutting away everything but the neighbouring upper stories and the high, green timber of Stanley Park on the west. It was almost as quiet there as in the woods. The downtown rumble was a far surflike mutter that made a tonal background for the hum of bees foraging in the wisteria.

Laska talked at intervals. She had grown up in Montreal. She asked Rod about places and people there, grew briefly reminiscent about her childhood. Curled in a hammock after luncheon, she was silent for a time.

"Rod," she said abruptly, "when your father comes — he's due tomorrow, isn't he? — do something for me, will you?"

"Of course," Rod answered. "What shall it be?"

"Suggest to him that it would be pleasant to have me up at Hawk's Nest for a few weeks."

She regarded him thoughtfully, her lips slightly parted. Rod was puzzled. He hesitated.

"Will you, Rod?"

"Certainly. But — but why don't you just come? Simply say you want to — and come."

"It isn't quite so simple as that," she explained. "I couldn't go unless your father rather made a point of it to Grove. Grove's funny. He isn't at all keen on me going there, except when we cruise up on a week-end. And I'd like to go there and stay awhile, quietly. I'm fed up with Vancouver. I'm tired. I want to rest."

"You can't think what a giddy whirl we live in," she went on presently. "Dinner parties, general hilarity; just one thing after another. One has to go whether one feels up to it or not. One gets so weary of it. Get your father to have me come to Hawk's Nest, Rod dear."

Rod promised.

She went off on another tack after that. With a touch of malice she brightly recounted the quasi-scandal pertaining to certain people in their set, people Rod knew slightly. It seemed to afford her ironic amusement.

"But," Rod observed in comment on a rather piquant anecdote concerning a pretty widow and a man of family who cut a big figure in local industry, "that's pretty raw if it's true. And if it's just gossip, it's rotten nasty gossip."

"I shouldn't be surprised if it were quite true," she said indifferently. "Some people do what they like. Others have to toe the line. It's a queer, queer world, Rod."

He left about two-thirty. Striding up Robson Street to Mary's boarding place, he shook off a half-formed impression that Laska was bored and discontented, that she found the only world she knew a rather hollow affair. There was a vague fretfulness about her. It was just an impression. And it was not his concern. Mary Thorn was decidedly his concern, for that afternoon at least. Laska, Grove, the Norquay Trust vanished out of his mind at sight of Mary Thorn.

For, as he walked beside her along a street which led to the sandy foreshore and green reaches of Stanley Park, Rod found himself stirred by a strange procession of fancies. They trooped through his mind, quickened his blood. What was there about a girl (a pretty girl, but of no great beauty compared to other girls he knew) in a white organdy dress, with a rather immobile face shadowed under the floppy brim of a leghorn hat, to stir him so, to make him desire nearness to her and to find that nearness disturbing? Rod's brain registered flashes of himself holding her close, of her face smiling into his — unwelcome visions like that while his lips uttered sentences about Montreal, continental Europe, books, plays he had seen, such *pronunciamento* generally as the conversation required of a second-year university man who had been abroad.

"I wonder if this is the way a man starts in getting foolish over some particular girl?" Rod thought to himself. "Or am I just like Grove and some fellows I know?"

This while he told her of a quaint old place in Scotland, where he had visited a branch of distant kin, the summer before.

Mary listened, talked in her normal quiet way, turning to him occasionally with a smile that fluttered briefly across her face and made her eyes light up.

There was no provocative suggestion about her. It was nothing she did or said that stirred and puzzled Rod. It was merely herself, her presence, a pleasant-faced girl with a low, throaty note in her voice and a slender well-formed body which had a peculiar grace of movement. Magnetic? That overworked term to define the indefinable. What was there about her to stir a man so? Rod asked himself that after he had said goodbye to her at five o'clock.

And there flitted across his consciousness a faint, troublesome perception of dynamic forces in human relations of which a man must acquire knowledge empirically, concerning which all the textbooks are silent.

Rod spent the months of July and August very much as he had spent all the Julys and Augusts of earlier years. That is to say, he paddled a canoe, swam, sailed, fished trout and salmon, made himself agreeable to sundry guests, male and female. About Hawk's Nest no material change appeared, however Rod might vainly wrinkle his brows over a subtle transformation which he could not analyze, but which he felt as a blind man feels the nearness of some insensate mass. He was free from the tutorial direction. Mr. Spence had definitely retired into a pensioned leisure, having done his full duty by this generation of Norquays. Rod was twenty, his brain and his beard both in training for manhood. He could lounge or play as he elected, come and go as he desired.

Not so long before, measured by seasons, life had seemed to him the simplest sort of affair. One took it perforce as it came. Certain things were ordered, irrevocable; other things a matter of choice; a few, a very few transitory phases of existence, a matter of chance.

McGill, Mary Thorn, Grove, his grandfather, and the old, old journal of Roderick Sylvester Norquay began to make him question this definitely limited philosophy of living. The element of chance loomed larger. It even invaded the sacred precincts of choice.

He looked at Mary Thorn as they sat on the porch of her father's house, as they ate a pocket lunch beside the Granite Pool with their rods and creels beside them, as they slipped in the dugout alongshore with the open diapason of the rapids welling up, and he wondered by what necromancy of body or spirit she could so effortlessly set his blood racing, draw his flesh toward her as a magnet draws steel, until his resistance was stoutly tested. How? Why? Rod could explain it simply — but his explanation failed to satisfy. It rode his imagination as something that transcended mere fleshly instinct, which he understood well enough, of which in his sophisticated world he had observed sundry manifestations.

Rod had once said to himself that the family had become static. He had felt a regret for this grooved state; all the great adventuring done; all the great efforts and endurings and activities accomplished. Ease flowed about them in a wide stream. And Grove was the fine flower of it all — a comet flashing across the local heavens, with a tail of yachts, mistresses, vulgar display spreading luminously behind him.

Grandfather Norquay sat in his chair by a sunny window or walked with his stick slowly about the grounds — a tall, spare, silent old man, thinking his contained, regressive thoughts. Rod would look at him and wonder. He would look at Mary Thorn and wonder. He would look at Grove, when that kinetic gentleman marshaled his house parties down the *Kowloon*'s gangplank, and wonder. Then he would entrench in a library chair, fortified by cigarettes, and read the typed copy of his great-great-grandfather's journal, and his wonder —which was no more than the vital curiosity of an inquiring mind — would turn from the general to the particular.

He would lay down that hundred-year-old document, clasp his hands behind his head, and strive to construct imaginatively for himself a future based on the known factors of the present and the past. Strangely enough he always came out of these spells of daydreaming with a sense of futility, with an envy of his forbears, with a regretful sense of having been born too late. Romance might still be a lusty godlet but he moved beyond Rod's ken. He would visualize old Roderick on the poop of the *Hermes*, pistol in belt, peering out from under a three-cornered hat, one eye on the beauty of a mountainous, thick-forested coast, the other keenly on pelts of sea otter and the profitable risks of barter with savages. Battles with the sea, with a hostile environment, a fine courage, and a far, future-piercing vision. Rod saw the log stockade ringed about by painted Chilcotins, arrows flying, muskets cracking; the battle fought and the dead buried; life continuing in armed watchfulness; the slow weaving of the planned pattern.

"The old fellows had all this in mind," Rod murmured once. "Order and security and well-being. I wonder if they saw everything so firmly established that it has become rigid? That all the Norquays can do now is to live and die like gentlemen. I wonder if old Roderick would have been such a keen, far-sighted old blade if he could have seen the fifth generation as it is? Maybe he would regard us with pride. I wonder? Anyway, they had a whale of a time those days. The Trojans and Spartans had nothing on them. And there has been no Homer to write an *Odyssey*. No *Iliad* of the pioneers. The epic of fur and timber and the conquering of a wilderness peopled with savages. I wonder if I could?"

Rod nursed that idea from the fetal stage to a lusty infancy. He bore it, still in its swaddling clothes, back with him to the university when hot August wore into cool September, and the smoke haze of forest fires vanished before the autumn rains.

He would never become a financial generalissimo like Grove. Unlikely that he would ever be called upon to step into Phil's executive shoes. Unless he voluntarily embarked upon a voyage toward some material port, he would never have to buckle on armour and joust for dollars in the commercial tourney. But — if he were able, if he had the gift and the patience to develop it — he might do these adventuring progenitors a service by making them live again for their descendants — a generation, Rod held, deprived of romance and bold enterprise, limited and circumscribed and in danger of stifling spiritually in the midst of a material plenty.

This fascinating project in the field of creative effort he kept to himself — even from Mary Thorn, who had always aided and abetted him in fanciful undertakings, whose moods and reactions seemed mysteriously yet infallibly to keep step with his own.

CHAPTER VIII

TIME BRIDGES MANY A gap in the life of a man, periods that have no substance in them, no matter how occupied, how filled with minor incident; stretches of days, months, years flow as unctuously as syrup from a tilted spout, as straight and open as a white road across a level plain. Then all at once comes a divergence, a break in the flow, new vistas and compelling actions. Something leaps lancewise at the heart or brain out of the peaceful monotony. Something to be attained looms suddenly like a flame in the dark. Or he finds himself catapulted into some unforeseen clash, tingling to the shock of conflict.

Rod Norquay finished the formal education of a gentleman's son in the next two years. He acquitted himself according to the family tradition, escaping high honours without being plucked. He came home in 1913 with a B.A., a few lettered sweaters, a miscellaneous assortment of classical and scientific and philosophical odds and ends imprinted on a fairly retentive memory — and a half-formed doubt of the utility or advantage of formal education. Having been officially labelled as the finished product of the educational machine he supposed that he would somehow be expected to justify the pains and expense of the cultural process. But where or how he had no idea. He was finished with school. He was home again. Everything was as before. If he were trained for any specific purpose, that purpose was as yet hidden from him. The desire to write an epic novel scarcely qualified as a purpose. In the outwardly simple but internally complicated affairs of the Norquay establishment he was a superfluous unit. Apart from the family he was, as yet, of less consequence than any logger on the Norquay pay roll.

"What's the use of being brought into the world, fed, clothed, and educated, if you're of no use or consequence to anybody?" he observed to Mary Thorn. "Nobody needs me to help solve their problems. I have none of my own — none that amount to much. That was all attended to before I was born."

"You don't know how lucky you are," Mary retorted. "You can do whatever you want to do. You've got everything that most men have to struggle for all their lives — and then don't get."

"But I don't seem to want to do anything that amounts to a hill of beans," Rod replied. "It's like a football game against a third-rate team. No fun in a walkaway. I have the instincts of a — a — what shall I say? Buccaneer? Pioneer? Adventurer? I don't see much chance for anything but a money-making adventure. I don't need to do that, even if it were to my taste. I couldn't get much kick out of making two dollars grow where only one flourished. Can't you show me a windmill or two, Mary?" he ended whimsically. "I'll mount Rosinante and knock 'em over."

"Every avenue is open for you," Mary declared. "You can map out any sort of career you choose."

"What, for instance?" he inquired. "There has to be a motive. Most of 'em are financial. There's the law, and science, and the arts. I don't warm up to a career as a matter of duty. I've talked to the governor, seeking light in my darkness. He blandly observes, 'Suit yourself, my boy. There's really no hurry,' and goes on reading his book or paper, as the case may be. I'm inclined to believe the radicals at school were right. They claimed that economic urges lay at the root of all purposeful action in the world of affairs. Hence, I lack the strongest motive of all to *force* me to action."

"Haven't you any secret ambition of any sort whatever?" Mary inquired.

Rod reflected a second.

"Well, I won't commit myself," he replied. "Have you?"

"Yes," she answered demurely. "To be successful, beautiful and beloved."

"Successful — what do you define as success?"

"Act of succeeding; consequence, issue, outcome or result of an undertaking, whether good or bad," she laughed.

"Oh, hang Webster," he returned. "What's your real, honest-to-goodness idea of success? What do you want most of all? What do you want to do? What do you live for? What's your heart set on as an objective?"

And Mary, sobered a little by the sudden earnestness of his tone, could only shake her head.

"I'm not quite sure," she confessed. "There must be something over the hill — but I don't know what it is."

"Funny," he ruminated. "We're both in the same boat."

"How absurd," she protested instantly. "You give me a pain, Rod. Born to the purple and growling about it! In the same boat, indeed. The only point of similarity is that we're both dissatisfied with what — with what's in sight. You're sighing because no new worlds beckon you to conquer. Everything's at your hand. All you have to do is select your weapon and choose your field. All the prestige of wealth, good family, is at your back. You go somewhere, you want to do something; you mention your name; somebody says, 'Oh, one of the Norquays,' and the way is made easy."

"What's the use of an easy road if there's nothing at the end of it?" Rod asked impatiently.

"Oh, your breakfast must have disagreed with you," she flung back.

"I like a road that leads away to prospects bright and fair,
A road that is an ordered road, like a nun's evening prayer;
But best of all I love a road that leads to God knows where,"

Rod quoted. "Perhaps that expresses it best. If there is anything in heredity the original Roderick's restlessness has cropped out in me — without either his capacity or his opportunity for doing things. Think of the resolution, the spirit of that old fish, the vision. He saw far beyond himself. He must have had a dynamic energy. Whatever he wanted he went after, tooth and toenail. And look at the result — in the fifth generation — of his pains and planning. The governor's idea of life is as rigid as granite: good food, efficient service, genteel restraint in all things, taboos and forms of all sorts. Grove's a glorified shopkeeper, with all a vulgar shopkeeper's love of display. Phil's the official watchdog of the family's material interests. And I'm a negligible quantity. Rum lot. And I'm the only one who isn't perfectly satisfied with everything. Even old Phil would just grin if I talked to him the way I'm talking to you."

"He'd be right," the girl replied slowly. "You've got what everybody's after — ease, security, leisure. You aren't chafed by anything sordid. You ought to realize how fortunate you are and be satisfied. You find life pleasant. Isn't that good enough?"

"Why, yes, so far as it goes," Rod admitted. "Only nobody who gets beyond purely superficial thinking is ever satisfied with mere pleasantness. I'm not a cow to lie down in a clover field and chew my cud forever."

"I give you up," Mary said. "You're a discontented pendulum."

"It's the fault of my education," Rod returned with mock humility.

"Education is a mixed blessing sometimes," Mary said in a tone that brought him to surprised attention. "It shouldn't be bestowed indiscriminately on those who can't live up to it, who can't gratify any of the cravings and dreams that education breeds. Education, if it's thorough, destroys too many illusions — illusions that one must hold as realities, if one is poor, a nobody, and without a chance to be anything else."

"Good Lord," he exclaimed, "you don't feel that way about it, surely?"

"Now and then — not always," she murmured. "It's like loving a thing and hating it, too. There are times when Euripides, and Housman's lyrics, and Thomas Hardy don't fit in with cooking and cotton stockings — when poetic and artistic visions of what-might-be tantalize like glimpses of a cloud-hidden moon. Why should one sharpen one's perception of beauties that are beyond one's reach? I should have been trained in domestic science or nursing, or selling fripperies to rich women, instead of being put through the cultural hotbed of a university. They meant well. But unless a girl has a ready-made social background, or a decided talent, the so-called higher education is only a handicap."

"Oh, come now. Hardly," Rod protested.

"No? You don't know anything about people outside of your own comfortable, spoon-fed class, Rod. That's the trouble. I do. I know my own kind of people first-hand. Three years in the U.B.C. has taught me something about your kind. I've been an outsider — looking in. Money, clothes and manners. Manners are an asset; money is a necessity. If you've got both you can go anywhere, do anything. If you haven't, there's the deadline, and you can't cross. Pretty much everything that university training fits one for, especially a girl, is across that deadline. It's rather depressing — sometimes."

Rod was dumb for the moment — because he was not stupid, and he knew what she said was true. He had seen the working out of those unpleasant truths during his own university career. He knew youngsters at McGill sweating and scraping through — boys with steel-bright minds, struggling against the fearful handicap of poverty. He had an inkling now of what old Mark Sherburne meant when he ironically retorted to someone across a dinner table that he didn't need brains — he could buy 'em by the gross. Rod hated the idea of Mary Thorn being embraced in such a category. He reviewed in one panoramic flash her situation and his own. He compared her with girls he knew. Isabel Wall, for instance. Less mind — oh, much less. Isabel was a doll-like creature still. An impractical, useless young woman, even if highly ornamental. Clothes, dances, parties, sports, and men about comprised Isabel's desire of and knowledge of life. Yet she had everything money could buy. She had the entrée everywhere.

Mary had neither money nor more than a glancing acquaintance with those who had. He recalled with a touch of shame that although they had played together from childhood, despite the fact that they had lived within sight of each other for ten years, Mary had never set foot within Hawk's Nest. And he had a swift, disconcerting vision of how difficult it would be for her to get a foothold in the Norquay circle — or its equivalent.

It wasn't right. It wasn't fair. There was something rotten in such an arrangement. Insofar as this clear-eyed girl sitting beside him was concerned, Rod felt that he must do something about it. Why, he didn't pause to consider. He simply felt the compulsion to act, as he would have been impelled to act if some unfairness had been practiced toward himself.

They dropped that subject as if it were a live coal, as if they had both become suddenly wary of self-revelation. And as they continued to speak casually of other things, Rod mentally registered the fact that by some occult process they two, from their divergent poles, seemed to converge always. Six months, a year, two years: the separation in lapsed time didn't seem to matter. When they met again they did not so much begin where they left off, as at once find themselves on common ground, breathing a natural air of intimacy. Girls in Rod's experience were either provocative, kittenish, silly, or rare, lofty-minded creatures whose worship at the shrine of pure intellect was almost an affectation. He had been in the last four years so often between the devil of jazzy damozels and the deep sea of the female highbrow, alternating between amusement and impatience. Mary Thorn came nearest to qualifying as a chum, with the added factor of an elusive personal charm.

They were sitting on the caulk-punctured board steps of Oliver Thorn's house. For a minute or two Mary's gaze turned on the slope that ran up to the Granite Pool. Whenever Rod tried to analyze his liking for her, he stressed that quality of self-containedness. She could think her own thoughts as if he were not there. She was thinking them now. He wondered what they were. He had a retentive memory; he was tenacious of impressions. Looking at her, he wondered if she were thinking of the day they sat on the log watching the rapids boil in their pent channel; if she were thinking of that unpremeditated kiss. Recalling it, Rod felt his heart quicken. And, as if some invisible thread linked their minds for an instant, Mary's eyes turned to his with a reminiscent gleam. A faint flush tinted her cheeks. She looked away.

Rod covered her hand with his. She let it lie passive. The touch warmed his blood, filled him with a quick glow. For a moment all the world was shut away, all but himself and her and the hot sunlight on the shining channel water.

He shook off that swift rush of emotion, startled, astonished, a little dismayed. He sat testing the strength of his resolution, wondering at the thing that stirred him so deeply, trying to grasp its substance. Her hand was warm and soft. Faint tremors shook it slightly.

"What a damned shame things are so badly arranged," he said. "Let's fix 'em to suit ourselves, Mary."

She looked at him with a straight, unwinking gaze. Her mouth quivered, then shut tight, lips compressed. The flush that had tinged her creamy skin faded into a pallor on which tiny freckles stood out across the bridge of her nose in pinpoints of tan. She tried to withdraw her hand. Rod's grip tightened.

"No," he said. "You can't get away."

"Don't be silly," she whispered. "I hate sentimental men."

"Am I?"

"Well, you're manifesting symptoms."

The colour came back to her face with a rush.

"Perhaps you're right."

Rod's fingers relaxed. The words that hovered on the tip of his tongue failed of utterance. Sentimental. It was like cold water on him. He had rather prided himself on his freedom from sentimental episodes.

"Yes, perhaps you're right," he repeated. "I'd have been asking you to marry me in another breath. I have a mind to propose formally, just to see how ruthlessly you would turn me down."

"The ruthless turn-down would come from another source not from me," she answered sombrely.

"You'd be marrying *me,*" Rod repossessed himself of her hand, of both hands, "not my family or my acquaintances. They don't count so much as you think. We could have a whale of a time together, Mary. You're the only girl I know that's real, honest-to-God girl. You always were. I wonder if you have the same queer sort of feeling about me that I have for you?"

"I expect I have," she owned. "I'm not a fool, or a liar, or inclined to be evasive, Rod. I don't care for you in a cool, quiet, calculating fashion. I'm not made that way, any more than you are. But, oh, Rod, I've had a lot of unpleasant wisdom forced on me since you went away four years ago. It won't do. It won't do!"

"Why not?" Rod demanded. "If we choose to say it will, who's to stop us? We're ourselves, and living our lives is our own affair."

"Living our lives isn't just a matter of doing whatever a passionate impulse may urge us to do," she answered slowly. "What do you suppose your family would do and say when you announced your intention of playing King Cophetua to the beggar maid?"

"Whatever they jolly well pleased," Rod growled his defiance. "Besides I'm no king, neither are you a beggar. You exaggerate. Surely you haven't so humble an opinion of yourself?"

"It isn't humility. Far from it," the girl flashed back. "I may dislike the station in life in which it has pleased God to place me. But don't ever think I'm humble or diffident about it, or myself, or my people. Oh, no, Mr. Roderick Sylvester Norquay. But I don't wear blinkers. I see a lot of things I used to be unconscious of. One of them is that men like you are regarded as one class of beings, and girls like me quite another. Isn't it so?"

Rod sat silent. He was clear-sighted enough to see what she meant. His people — and by his "people" he embraced the whole category of his class — would say quite frankly and emphatically that Mary Thorn "wouldn't do." She wasn't anybody. She had never been anywhere or met anyone. In a courteous, matter-of-fact manner they would make an issue of that. They would never countenance and accept Mary Thorn without a tussle. He saw all that, but it did not seem to him vital or final. And he merely sat silent while he sought cogent reasons to show her why these harsh facts she mentioned did not matter so far as they two were concerned. Why should they be governed by exterior restraints, taboos, penalties, if they had a burning need of each other?

He tried to put that into words. But the devils of perversity had entered into Mary. He could not drive them out. He sat there holding her hands, persuading, reasoning, pleading. He had a conviction that emotionally some flame in her leaped to the passionate fire within himself, and that she resisted only by some intellectual force that was stronger than his own. He could master her heart but not her will.

"What do you want out of life that we can't get together better than if you go after it single-handed?" he demanded savagely. "Am I not man enough for you? Why drag in class and money and all that sort of thing. You know that doesn't count between us. We've got something — there's something in us — that pulls us together. It was there long ago when we were kids paddling around together. It's grown stronger, through four years of almost complete separation. The peculiar magic of that — whatever it is — begins to work as soon as we come together. We don't have to tell each other. We know. Don't we? Isn't it true?"

She nodded, lips parted, eyes bright, looking out over the channel as if she saw more there than the running tide.

"Then," he continued, "if it seems good to us to plan a future in which we shall be partners as well as lovers, why shouldn't we?"

"Too soon, for one thing," she said. "You're twenty-two, Rod; I'm nineteen. I have another year in school. How do we know that what we seem to want so badly today will satisfy us completely tomorrow? And even if *we* were sure, we can't dodge facts. You couldn't just by marrying me make me a Norquay, with all the rights, privileges, and standing of the clan. Neither your family nor your friends would accept me as one of themselves. Certainly not at first. Perhaps never. Look," she continued sadly, "I don't know anyone you know. Your people don't know my people — don't want to know them. It would be a struggle. You'd have to pull me up to your level, or be dragged down to mine. They'd say you were marrying out of your class, and they'd punish you in so many subtle ways. You knew Marty Graham, didn't you? Have you seen him and his wife since you came back?"

Rod shook his head.

"I heard he cut school to get married. What about him?"

"You see, it works automatically," Mary said. "He married a girl I knew rather well. She was a senior when I entered the U. They were very much in love. Are yet, for that matter. But they're not very happy about it. Marty's people accept her so grudgingly. His friends have dropped him more or less. Marty had always been used to plenty of money. His father gave him a job in the office at the regular beginner's salary and cut off his allowance. His pay is less than Grace herself is capable of earning. Marty's pride won't permit her to work. She *is* clever and ambitious, and probably has more real culture than some of the people who either patronize or snub her because she's a nobody — her people are poor as church mice and rather commonplace. The whole thing has got Marty's goat, and it's getting Grace's. Marty can't see why he should be deprived of everything he had been taught to regard as his right. Grace resents the way he's being penalized for marrying her. She is proud, too, and the invisible wall that's thrown up in her face hurts. I can see lots of breakers ahead for them. In fact, they're in them now."

"Marty Graham's a nut," Rod declared. "Can't a man make his own way without his people's backing, if he has to? You don't put me in Marty's class as a husband, I hope."

"He's a nice boy," she sighed. "He can't adjust himself to a way of living for which he had no training, that's all. After a while he'll begin to see so clearly what he's lost by marrying out of his class, as they say. Then the fat will be in the fire. They'll both suffer."

"But I tell you Graham's a nut. A footless ass. He always was," Rod protested earnestly. "Don't his actions prove it? Would I grieve if the family got rather miffed over me marrying the girl I wanted? Not much. I'm not quite so dependent financially as he is, anyhow. That's one of the good points about our affairs. There is no arbitrary cutting off of my small share in the inherited income. Even if there were, I'm quite sure we could play the game so they'd have to take us at our face value — which is quite good enough. Why, you chump," he tried to rally her, "is that all that worries you?"

"It doesn't worry me," Mary said straightforwardly, "because I'm not going to be tied or bound, or tie you, Rod. I don't know where I'm going, but I'm on my way — through school and whatever comes after. I don't know whether my destiny leads to a job or a profession, to art or dishwashing, but it must lead somewhere that I want to go, where I'm qualified to go. I have to find out where."

"It leads here," Rod drew her up close to him for one unresisting moment. "You know it does. I've often wondered if it did — but now I know."

He kissed her. She rested against him a second or two, her eyes shut, hot colour flooding her smooth cheeks. Then abruptly she pushed herself away, sat plucking with nervous fingers at the folds of cloth across her knees.

"It doesn't lead there yet," she said shakily. "Perhaps not at all."

She rose to her feet. Rod followed up across the porch, cornered her against the wall.

"You do love me?" he challenged.

"Yes."

"Then why don't you marry me?"

"Because I do love you, Rod," she whispered. "Can't you see? It won't do. Oh, I can't explain. I haven't the words. But the unanswerable logic of it is clear in my mind. I knew we'd come to this. I've dreaded it. We can't go any further. We'd both lose."

"That's not true. You know it isn't." He shook her roughly. "We're both thoroughbreds. It isn't class that counts. It's character. All the rest is just trimmings. If accident of birth made me a rich man's son, is that any reason why I shouldn't make my own way and my own place in the world if I have to choose between that and conforming to class prejudice in so important a thing as picking a wife? What sort of weak saphead do you think I am?"

"It's no good, Rod," she answered doggedly. "You simply don't understand. You've never had any experience of poverty, of struggle, of sordidness. You'd lose a lot that even money can't buy. And after a while you'd begin to wonder if it were worthwhile. The world well lost for love is a fine poetic fancy, but nothing more. I tell you quite frankly I'm afraid of love. It brings pain. It brings all sorts of bitter things to men and women, this mating passion. I have an instinct about these things. I won't marry you. I *won't* be carried away by any sort of feeling for you. I don't even want to see you again. What's the use? Oh, what's the use of our even thinking about it?"

She broke away from him with a wrench of her body. The door

slammed behind her. He heard the quick patter of her feet on the uncarpeted floor. Then silence. Rod had a clairvoyant vision of her flinging herself on her bed, of her shoulders shaking, of sobs strangled in her throat. And he stood bewildered. What had seemed so simple had become disastrously complex, bearing implications of grief and pain and loneliness beyond his comprehension.

But there seemed a note of finality in that scene. He could not break down her defences, tenuous as they were.

And so, his heart filled with a strange, heavy ache, Rod walked down to his canoe and put out into the channel. Across the way the red roof and grey gables of Hawk's Nest beckoned him home. Home — where there were no problems that could not be solved by the writing of a cheque, Rod thought sardonically.

The inevitable reaction set in. A passionate resentment against Mary Thorn began to burn in him. She was a fool, he said. He himself a greater fool to abase himself before her.

But neither abnegation nor self-bestowed epithets could rid him of that heavy feeling in his breast.

CHAPTER IX

ON AN AFTERNOON A week later Rod sat in the library nursing a book, a cigarette, and some curiously mixed reflections. A weekend party had come and gone, leaving Laska, her maid, and a friend at Hawk's Nest. Whereupon Phil had taken the *Haida* and departed for a point up the coast. The old restful quiet had succeeded that forty-eight hours of good-natured clamour, the laughter and drinking and dancing, in which Rod, morose and broody, seemed to detect an irritatingly hectic note. He was glad they were gone, glad to see the *Kowloon* clear of Mermaid Bay. Grove was getting beefier, more assertive, more arrogant. He was so cocksure, so frankly contemptuous of things and persons outside his own sphere.

Yet by all accounts Grove was becoming a reckonable power in the affairs of B.C. There was a dash and sweep about his operations that moved men to admiration. He had been tremendously successful in all he undertook, far more so than Rod had believed possible. The

Norquay Trust Company was a three-ring circus and Grove was the ringmaster. Lesser men and concerns leaped and curvetted when he cracked his whip. He was fond of cracking the whip, Rod cynically observed.

Rod eyed his father, sitting on the other side of a periodical-strewn table. He wondered what his father thought of Grove now. But he knew that his father was thinking of quite another matter — for which he was himself responsible. He continued to look at Norquay senior with a mildly expectant curiosity. The library was the council chamber of the family, the place chosen for edicts, discussions of policy, admonition. From childhood Rod and his brothers had, so to speak, taken their medicine in that pleasant book-lined room. His father now bent a placid eye, slightly quizzical, on his youngest son. Rod waited.

"I really don't see the necessity," Norquay senior remarked at last. "Of course a gentleman need not necessarily be a drone. On the other hand one doesn't need to do a labourer's work in order to acquire knowledge of labour. You've finished school, of course. You have seen a little of the world and as time passes you will undoubtedly see a great deal more. Still, if you're keen on this, I'll speak to Phil. He can give you charge of a camp."

"I don't want to take charge of a camp," Rod said. "I'm not competent, for one thing. I'd either make a hash of it, or leave it all to a foreman — which is not what I'm after. What I mean by going into the woods is to go in and work; take over jobs as I master them. I want to know all there is to be known about timber, from the standing tree to the finished product."

His father continued to eye him.

"What's the idea for such thoroughness — this starting in at the bottom and getting blisters and experience together?"

The root of this expressed resolve lay in a folio of notepaper on a stool beside Rod's chair. But it was not a matter he could make clear, or even discuss with his father. At least, that was how he felt.

"I want to see the wheels go round," he answered lightly.

"Very well," his father agreed. "You shall. I'll speak to Phil. He'll see that you get a job. I take it that's what you want."

"The job's incidental," Rod replied. "I've been thinking about this for some time. I'm not dull. I have an idea I'll pick things up quickly. I want to know something about timber, about methods of handling it, about the men who actually do the handling. I want to get it first-hand. Even a university training should be an advantage in that."

"No doubt." Norquay senior permitted himself an indulgent smile. "If you're so interested in timber, it's a wonder you didn't take a forestry course. The Lord knows we need forestry experts in B.C."

"Why?" Rod inquired. It had no bearing on his purpose, but the remark aroused his curiosity.

"To teach them how to get one prime stick to the booming ground without destroying twice as much more," his father snorted. "To inaugurate a campaign of necessary reforestation. Outside of two or three concerns, logging in B.C. today is an orgy of waste. They're skimming the cream of the forest, spilling half of it. Kicking the milkpail over now and then, refusing to feed the cow they milk. However, *we* don't do that. I can show you limits we logged when I was a young man that will bear merchantable timber by the time your children are grown, my boy. But to get back to our sheep. You surprise me. If you'd gone in for wild-eyed art, it would have seemed more natural. I never could make you out, my son. You were always a bit dreamy. Sure this isn't just a whim? Want to see what makes the wheels go round, eh?"

"Precisely," Rod agreed. It was as far as he would go.

"Well, it won't do you any harm," his father rambled on, "and you may acquire a useful technique. We are expanding more or less, in spite of a conservative policy. Phil would undoubtedly appreciate a second-in-command before long. He has his hands pretty full. On the whole, I'm rather glad you've taken this notion. I won't last forever, and I'd like to see you and Phil solidly established before my mantle descends on Grove. Timber and land are good, solid foundations."

"What about finance?" Rod asked idly. "That seems pretty gorgeously productive, pater. Does it ever strike you that Grove may outgrow the regulation Norquay mantle?"

"If he does, it will be because he has made a more capacious one for himself." Norquay senior smiled complacently. "I imagine Grove's well able to run his own show and live up to the Norquay tradition, too. He *has* a genius for affairs."

"So it seems," Rod commented dryly — and the "affairs" he was thinking of were not the ones his father had in mind. "I wouldn't fancy it myself."

"As a matter of fact, no youngster knows quite what he fancies," his father drawled. "I had a fancy for the law and politics. Two years of reading Blackstone and a term in the Legislature cured me of both. Take your Uncle Mark. He was past thirty before he found his real bent. Follow your natural bent, Rod, whatever it is. You have plenty of time and backing. This beginning on the ground floor may work out. Knowledge of any sort never comes amiss."

So that was settled.

When his father presently left the room Rod picked up and opened the folio. He read over forty or fifty closely written sheets, knitting his smooth young brow over the phrasing.

"Won't do — only in spots. It's dead. I've got to breathe the breath of life into these people. And I don't seem to know how."

He sprang to his feet, paced the floor.

"All I know is what somebody has told me, what I've read in books," he grumbled. "Cobwebby stuff. Pretty — lots of it — moving — but no substance. All I got out of school was a mass of unclassified facts. I'm crammed with 'em. I know what a lot of great men did — but not how they did it — *why* they did it. And language. What's the good of a 'steen-thousand-word vocabulary if you've got no peg to hang it on, only the old pegs other people have used till they're all worn and shiny? I'm like a man with a craving to paint beautiful things he can see, with a whole box of colour-tubes, and no idea how to apply his colours to get the effects he wants. Or a finely made steam engine all ready to run, greased and oiled and water in the boilers, but no fuel to make steam. I don't know people, humanity, only one kind. I don't know life; only one comfortable groove of it. I don't know anything that really counts, except that I don't know much. I wouldn't be stuck with this, if I did." He faced about, frowning on the pile of written sheets. "I'd be able to make a thing go the way I wanted it, whether it was a story or a girl. I can't do either. I don't know how — and I've got to find out how. As long as I stay in a nice, fenced pasture I never will find out. It's all too cut and dried. Too many taboos. Too many fences. I've got to break through. I'm too much like the pea in the pod — I am green, the pod is green, all the world is green."

He sat down in a chair, clasped his hands behind his head, and lost himself in concentrated thought.

The history of Rod's family was part of the history of his native land, insofar as Anglo-Saxon occupancy had made history. The Norquay foothold had been the first individual one established by a white man on the Pacific between Spain to the south and Russia to the north. That century and more of far-seeing purposeful struggle had culminated in the possession of every material benefit men live and work and sometimes vainly die to grasp. Blood had been spilled, storms braved, great risks faced to win that security. To Rod, ever since he could remember, these things had been real, vividly coloured episodes enacted under the auspices of the high gods of adventure.

He was imaginative, creatively imaginative. Old Roderick Sylvester, the barque *Hermes,* the sea-otter trading, the bride who fled her English home to fare into strange seas for love, the Chilcotins on their bloody forays, the wooden blockhouse, the first course of masonry, the vast influx of gold-seekers in the Cariboo rush of '58, the completion of Hawk's Nest in all its comfortable permanence — these were not simply things he knew as part of his antecedents. They were realities, as if they had happened but yesterday under his own eyes. They moved him strangely, deeply. He could reconstruct in his mind all that crowded century. In his mind's eye all the men and women whose bones lay underground about the great red cedar lived and moved and had being once more. He could see them as clearly as he saw Phil and his father and Laska or Mary Thorn.

He had been trying to capture those visions, those personalities, those old stirring times so crowded with pregnant action. He had been trying more or less earnestly for a year and a half. And he had failed. He was aware of his failure. The human equation somehow evaded him when he put pen to paper. He couldn't put his finger with surety on the well-spring of human motive. He hadn't the key to character. Rod had more than a casual acquaintance with literature in two languages. He knew Balzac and O Henry alike, Homer and George Ade, De Maupassant and the Brontes, Flaubert and Anatole France, Ibsen and Tolstoi and Gorky, Kipling and Hardy and Dickens and Poe. He read these writers, and he saw that they created men and women, creatures of pain and passion, even as God created them. He perceived that they did it, that with deft strokes they clothed their skeletons with flesh and blood and breathed the breath of life into them, so that they strutted and sighed and fought with an emotion-compelling intensity. But he could not do it himself. And he passionately desired to catch and transfix those gorgeous pictures his brain evoked from that pioneering past.

It could be done. It wanted doing. Rod had always wanted to do it. Unconsciously he had been preparing for the task. He had meant to do something like that ever since a day when he had laid down his book and told his tutor that *someone* ought to write the *Iliad* of the pioneers, an epic of the men and women who with vision and high courage had tamed a wild land for their children's children, those bold spirits who shrank from nothing by land or sea that promised a reward for enterprise.

Rod thought he knew why there was no magic in his pen, why these magnificent visions eluded capture. It was not a reasoned conviction. He felt his lack instinctively. The first faint labour pains of creative effort apprised him of his need: to plunge into the agitated pool of life instead of viewing it from a distant eminence. That was how the manner of life he had led from childhood struck him now — as a view from afar. Rod was sophisticated enough to realize that his world was one exclusively occupied by a limited number of fortunate people, holding their pre-eminence largely by sheer inertia. Statistics, observation, his university delving in economics and sociology, had informed him that for one very wealthy family there were a hundred subsisting in various degrees of comfort, a thousand but a step beyond poverty. Accident of birth, or inherent superiority? How was he to know? How could he know unless he got outside the fences, inhibitions, the unyielding rigidity of his own class? It *was* rigid, Rod perceived, although that perception had only become clear to him through Mary Thorn's eyes. It had a fetish of superiority which might or might not be valid. Even aside from that, how could he fathom things that were universal above and apart from class and even race — men's hopes and fears and aspirations — unless he established a contact with men? And Rod's instinct, the wise, fundamental instinct of an unwarped nature, urged him to make that contact first among the lowly, where the sweat and strain was greatest. There was the raw material. The Norquays — a little more perhaps than any of their circle — were the finished product. Rod wanted to know the process — and the by-products.

That was why he chose the woods. It might be well to know timber. But it was better to know men. And the way to know men was to live among them, to work with them, to stand with them — if such a thing were possible — upon a common ground. Afterward — he would know what he knew.

So for himself Rod, at the age of twenty-two, defined the approach to knowledge: through experience — plus imagination. And to him it seemed that with the first rebuff life had dealt him, it had also given him a clarified purpose, a definite mark to shoot at.

CHAPTER X

ROD FOUND WORK IN a logging camp, a thing that tried his vigorous young body to the utmost until he hardened somewhat to the task and learned what every manual labourer must learn — to strike a gait he could hold all day and not one that sapped his energy in two hours. He found a relief he had not expected in physical exertion. He could stop thinking about Mary Thorn. He took to work as some men take to whiskey when a dumb ache oppresses them or some haunting memory will not let them be. And Mary Thorn did haunt him so long as he could look across from Hawk's Nest at that weathered cedar house. He told himself that he was a fool to feel that way. But logic had nothing to do with feeling. Irrational or not, it existed. Something in him had burned up full flame. Love, the mating instinct, whatever it was, had settled upon an object and refused to be directed elsewhere. There was more than sex involved. He did not know precisely what else, but he was sure of something above and beyond the urge of the flesh, however strong that might be. Because he couldn't say to himself that there were other girls and be consoled. Another girl wouldn't do.

He couldn't rid himself of the notion that he and Mary Thorn were made for each other. His mind went questing forward and backward and verified the emotional prompting. They had been shaping their own destiny for years. Or was it being shaped for them? He couldn't decide. But he could trace some indefinable influence drawing them together since childhood. There had always been a subtle pleasure in being together, a community of personal interest, a flowing of thoughts and feelings along the same channel that transcended the material factors in their lives. The material factors were prying them apart now. Rod saw that. He knew Mary's inflexibility once she determined on a given course. He had beaten his will against that in simple, childish matters. She would not be driven. She would walk her own road. She had always been a silently determined, lovable little devil, Rod told himself sadly. She was herself uniquely, neither a pattern nor an echo, and he would have loved her for that alone in a world where girls were very largely patterns or echoes, armed for conquest in the arena of men with the sole weapon of their sex.

Rod would say to himself that she was wrong, that money and caste and social privilege made no difference. But his mind was too acute not to see that she was right. Where he differed from her, what he resented most was her conviction of the importance of these things to him. That resentment kept him away from Mary Thorn as much as her positive refusal. He was too much the youthful egotist not to believe he could ultimately break that down. But he did not wish to coerce her, even through her own affection, until he saw a breach in the Norquay wall through which they could walk together.

Meantime he sweated through the last of a hot July. Phil had obligingly supplied him with a "job."

"This working up from the bottom doesn't strike *my* fancy," Phil had observed. "But if you're keen on it, old kid, have your way. They're apt to give you a rather rough time, though."

Rod grinned at that. He stood now five foot eleven in his socks. One hundred and seventy pounds of bone, muscle and nerves perfectly coordinated. He had made every team in school that he tried for, and he knew what it was to undergo discipline, to withstand punishment. It only amused him (when it did not irritate) this solicitude for his comfort as if he were something to be marked "fragile," "handle with care," whenever he stepped outside his own well-ordered environment, where rights and privileges and precedence were so clearly defined they went unquestioned. His father's admonitions, Grove's unsolicited counsel about girls, Phil's prudent objection to his getting down to a logger's level. It was the first and only time Rod heard Phil voice the old caste shibboleth. It surprised him, but he made no comment. He had his own program. He did not mind what they said so long as they did not actively oppose. And if the loggers undertook to give him a "rough" time because he happened to be the owner's son, he expected both to learn and teach in the process.

His work began in a camp fifty miles northwest of the Euclataws, on Hardwicke Island. For a month he worked as a bucker, following up a falling crew to saw the felled trees into standard length logs. He pulled all day on the end of a crosscut saw. The woods about him resounded with the clink of axes, the whine of steel cable in iron blocks, the shrill tooting of donkey whistles, the shudder and thrash of great machines spooling up half a mile of twisted steel rope on revolving drums, dragging enormous logs as if they were toothpicks on a thread, shooting them down to salt water, whence by raft and towline they passed to the hungry saws of the town mills.

Rod loved the cool green forest. It made him a little sad sometimes to see it so ravished. Wherever the logger went with his axes and saws and donkey engines he left behind a desolation of stumps and broken saplings and torn earth. But Rod was no sentimentalist. He knew that humanity does not survive by beauty alone. Timber is a utility. It must serve its turn. Nevertheless the artist in him suffered now and then at the havoc — as a sensitive man turned butcher may perhaps occasionally revolt at his killing trade, despite the fact that man is a meat-eating animal.

In this first month Rod found little of note beyond hard work and monotony. The camp was well-established, well-equipped, moving along an efficient routine. The crew was disciplined and orderly. They let Rod alone. Insensibly they seemed to realize that while he was among them he was not of them, and they neither rode him nor made him one of themselves. In this camp he learned something of logging operations, but little or nothing of the logger that was new.

With the dog days, however, Phil transferred him to a new camp nearer home, a new operation — lock, stock, and barrel — from the grey-moustached logging boss to the cookhouse flunkys. They were mustered on the Valdez shore a mile below Little Dent when Rod joined. A hundred men, half a dozen donkey engines on floats, drums and drums of flexible steel cable, scow-loads of lumber, tools, all the machinery and personnel gathered for a raid on the fir and cedar spreading over that hillside to the Granite Pool and beyond.

"You can get all the dope you want on logging here, and be at home too," Phil pointed out. "This camp will run for years. We may have to put in a railroad to reach the farther limits."

"Are you going to cut all this Valdez timber?" Rod asked.

"That's the idea, I believe."

"We seem to be speeding up all around for some reason," he remarked, after a little. "I don't see why we should, but we are. This show very near doubles our force."

Nor could Rod see why, but he suspected Grove's financial expansion as the cause. Grove was shooting at millions. He talked quite casually now of major and minor operations, as if he were treating the body of commerce like a surgeon. The Norquay Trust was getting its fingers into every industrial pie from which a money plum could be extracted. Before the new camp had cut a stick Rod learned that ground was being broken in Phillips Arm for a pulp mill capitalized at two million. The Norquay Trust was helping to finance the thing, handling the pulp company's bonds. It was to furnish an outlet for low-grade timber — cheaply made newsprint. To Rod it seemed chiefly an excuse for some financial juggling and to strip a lovely valley of timber, to pollute a beautiful stretch of sea-floored inlet with waste from sulphurous acid bleaching vats.

It was all one to Rod, a part of the inevitability of things. He would have preferred to let Phillips Arm retain its beauty and solitude, its forested valley a home for deer and bear and coveys of grouse, its shining river the highway of salmon to their spawning grounds. He would have cut the Valdez timber last of all, because he liked to look south from Hawk's Nest on a slope of unbroken green. But he had no voice in the matter. If they chose to strip the granite ribs of the earth to their primal nakedness, not of necessity but for an ambitious man's profit, he could only shrug his shoulders. He had his own row to hoe. Rod was beginning to suspect that if Grove were a throwback to some coarse, high-handed animalistic type, he himself was something of a variation from the true Norquay strain. Like did not always produce like.

Here about him work went forward with a swing. A dozen carpenters wrought marvels of construction on shore, transforming raw lumber into bunk houses, cook shacks, office, blacksmith shop, commissary. The falling gangs kept intermittent shudders running through the hillsides above, where they threw down their daily score of great trees. The donkey engines hitched cables to stumps ashore, slid off their floats, hauled themselves puffing and grunting into the shadowy woods, black-bellied mechanical spiders drawing themselves along by a thread of twisted steel wire. A pile-driver crew with a two-ton steam hammer drove rows of sticks alongshore to enclose a booming ground. Another crew built a chute from tidewater to the first benchland. Men and powerful machinery directed with skill and energy wrought this transformation. In two weeks logs were plunging down the chute — one hundred thousand board feet per diem.

It was all new: machinery from Washington shops — steel cable from England — tools from Welland Vale — a logging boss from Oregon — men from every corner of the earth. To Rod there was a dual advantage in this. He saw the technique of preparation pass through every stage, emerge from apparent confusion to orderly, foreseen results. On the personal side he was merely one man in a crew. There were no old hands to make it easier or harder for him because he was a Norquay. The logging boss was a man with a reputation for getting out timber. It was almost a religion with him. Rod marked him shrewdly. If Jim Handy had any hopes or ambitions beyond so many thousand feet per day brought to tidewater Rod never learned what they were. The man was a human logging machine. Other men commended themselves to him only insofar as they were efficient in the woods. To Handy, owners and owners' sons were subordinate to the job itself. He was the most perfect example of a single-track mind Rod Norquay had ever encountered.

But the crew as a whole had no such limitations. Rod fitted among them easily, discovering in himself new phases of adaptability, finding in the conglomerate mass as many angles of human interest as there are facets on a diamond. They were literate and illiterate, talkative and silent, coarse and fine. The bunkhouse echoed with everything from downright obscenity to analytical discussions of the entire social order. One didn't, he perceived with some surprise, have to graduate from a university to have ideas, to express them comprehensively, to examine life critically in its spiritual as well as in its material aspects. And out of the few who stood intellectually head and shoulders above the non-thinking ruck Rod came to know best and to like genuinely a man but two or three years older than himself.

Andy Hall was a high-rigger, an expert on steel cable, the manner of its placing, splicing, its capacity for strain, and its life in the humming blocks. He was short and compactly muscular with sandy hair and a clear blue eye that could be both quizzical and cold. His work was his work. He was paid to rig cable, and he did so, and did it well. But he was what he termed a class-conscious proletarian. Andy flew no red flags. He kept his nose between the covers of a book when he was through his work. But whosoever dragged him into discussion was apt to encounter the deluge. He had convictions which he voiced in unequivocal terms. His vocabulary was equally rich in terse colloquialisms and pure English.

"Where did you go to school, Andy?" Rod asked him one Sunday morning. They were lounging in the shade of a branchy maple left standing beside the bunk house. Rod had been listening to Andy outline the theory of evolution to an argumentative Swede with a Lutheran complex.

Andy grinned.

"School of experience," said he. "University of life and books. Never graduated. Never will. Always be a student — gettin' plucked now and then. No," he hunched up his knees and smiled amiably at Rod, "I never had the advantage of being formally labelled as an educated man. You're a McGill man, I understand. Find it helps much on the job?"

"Not on the job as a job," Rod answered. "Still, it helps to give me a certain slant at things which pertain to the job. For sheer physical labour you might say a university training is waste. At the same time —"

"What are you doing on the job, anyway?" Andy inquired with blunt directness, although good-naturedly. "You don't have to. Why don't you go play with the rest of the butterflies?"

"I want to see what makes the wheels go round," Rod repeated the only reason he ever gave.

The high-rigger jolted him with his reply.

"We do," he said calmly. "Me and old Jim Handy, and the Christian Swede, and Blackstrap Collins on the boom, and all these Danes and Norskys and old rivermen from Michigan. We make the wheels go round and the master class — to which you belong — lives soft off the proceeds. It must be great to ride always on the bandwagon, and to feel the conviction that you are ordained by God to do so, eh? To pop your whip and make the plug lean hard against the collar. What would happen to you if they all balked?"

Rod clasped his hands behind his head and leaned back against the maple trunk. He had finished a creditable week under an exacting hook-tender. It was good just to rest, to look lazily up at a blue September sky through quivering leaves. Sufficient unto the day —

"I don't know," he said unperturbed, "and right now I don't care a hoot. Master class and serving class is all one to me at this particular moment. However, I don't want to ride on the back of the working class — as you put it, as the parlour radicals at school used to declaim — without paying for my ride. I'm not quite so sure of these economic fetishes as some of you fellows. A man can sell his labour, if that's all he has to sell, without selling his soul to the buyer. And that's what counts most. You can hire somebody to cook your food and make your clothes and keep your house in order. But you can't hire anybody to live your life for you, to suffer your pains and dream your dreams. Rich or poor, a man must live his own life. Maybe you fellows are right about the intensity of the class struggle, about the importance of the economic basis being better adjusted. But the fact remains that a man's existence is as much a matter of purely individual longings and visions and strivings as it is of getting his daily bread. It isn't all a matter of material interests, Andy. You can't perfectly adjust human society on a purely material basis. We're all egoists, most of us thoroughgoing egotists as well. We all want to do and be for ourselves. That seems to be fundamental. We can't help it. We're made that way. And there is one thing the altruists and social reformers seem to overlook, so far as the class struggle within any national group is concerned: the crowd that has the greatest driving force, the most cohesion, will always be in the saddle. It doesn't matter whether we like this conclusion or not. If there is anything in evolution, in the whole history of mankind, that is a fact."

"Good enough — you got something in the old bean, after all," Andy smiled. "You will have light in your darkness when some of your crowd are fumbling around bewildered, wondering what has happened to them. Yes, you're dead right, Norquay. You put it very well. The group with the greatest cohesion, the greatest driving force — it isn't a question of moral judgments — it's a question of power. But the real power lies in the men who do the world's work and the brains that are hired by capital to direct the work. Only they lack cohesion. If they ever learn the value of cooperation, of community of interest — look out! Your crowd learned that lesson long ago. It's a scream when you look at it cold-blooded. We cut down trees and saw them into lumber and build houses — and you own the houses. We build motor cars — but the men who build 'em seldom have one to ride in. You know," he laughed amusedly, "when I look at our industrial system in its entirety, it seems to me like a huge, unwieldy machine that we've built up hit-and-miss, and the damned thing is operating *us* instead of us operating it. Even the men who are supposed to control it aren't sure they have the thing in hand. Some day this machine will become so complicated it won't work at all. You can hear friction squeaks in a good many of the joints now. It's liable to break down."

"Then what?" Rod prompted.

"Then we'll have to devise a new industrial mechanism that will be the servant of society and not society's master."

"How will you do it?" Rod asked.

"I don't know," Hall answered. "So far as America is concerned, the present machine seems good for many generations — with a little patching and lubrication. But sometime it will have to be done. It will not be done by the group in the saddle. They're only interested in maintaining the status quo. If it is done at all it will be forced along by visionaries, damn fools like me, who dream of a perfect, harmonious society of mankind — and get called names because we talk about our dreams. Ain't it queer," his tone became tinged with contempt, "that the man who has beautiful visions and translates 'em in terms of sculpture or music or painting or literature is hailed as an artist, while the fellow who has an equally beautiful vision of a human society strong and healthy, purged of poverty and dirt and injustice, is frowned upon as a dangerous agitator? It's a giddy world when you stand off and look. Eh?"

Rod nodded. He was more interested in Andy Hall than in Andy's theories. Yet there was a bone in the meat of Andy's statement that Rod's mind chewed on long after Andy had gone into the bunkhouse to shave and take his Sunday bath in a washtub by the creek.

The man with a vision and a dream was never so comfortable as the man who merely had an objective. But he had more within him to stay his soul in the time of stress, Rod believed. Also it was a trifle surprising to find so nimble-minded a youth as the high-rigger working for a daily wage in a logging camp. True, his wage was six dollars *per diem*, which was equal to the stipend of some professors Rod knew. Nevertheless Rod considered that Andy, with his obvious intellectual ability, was misplaced at manual labour, even labour that called for a high degree of skill. He rather admired Andy's radicalism. There was a stout honesty of conviction in him. Rod was not so sure himself that all was for the best in the best of possible worlds — that comfortable illusion which sustains so many worthy people.

When he pondered Andy's simile of the complex machine gradually getting out of hand, proceeding to the ultimate smash, he couldn't help thinking of Grove's accelerated pace. That was merely a casual impression. Probably Grove had the levers firmly in hand.

He had half a notion to go fishing, to wet a line in the Granite Pool. Or walk over the hill to Oliver Thorn's. Mary had probably gone back to town now. Still — it was very pleasant to lie there under the maple, to rest his body, to let his nostrils be titillated by a smell of doughnuts frying in the cook house. He ought to drop down on the slack and see Phil.

Thus Rod, resting against the earth, two days' growth of beard on his chin, caulked logger's boots on his feet, a gaudy Mackinaw folded behind his head, cogitated idly, drowsily, until at last he fell into a doze from which the noon meal gong awakened him.

CHAPTER XI

THE QUALITY OF PERSISTENCE in the face of difficulties is one that men are variously endowed with. Hope revives in some breasts sooner than in others. To some the spur of a desire, a need, a conviction, never ceases wholly to rowel them into action. They cannot for long accept defeat or frustration as final. For such, the line of least resistance is closed. Reason, logic, all the chances of success may be against them, but they strive with infinite patience and unflagging courage toward a given end.

Rod Norquay had quite clearly defined Mary Thorn as a given end. Sometimes in analytical mood he took stock of his feelings about her and marvelled at the depth and intensity, the consistent urge of this desire. A flare of impatience would burn up. He would be angry with Mary awhile, then sorry for himself. It was, he held, a strange way for a woman to feel — to love a man, to admit frankly that he satisfied her ideal of a man, that her flesh yearned to his after the law of nature —

yet to fear, to hold back from the decisive step because of — what? Social differences? Rod dismissed them with a gesture. They existed, but they did not matter. What then? An unexplained reluctance to give up her freedom? Some undivulged ambition? A secret desire to try her own individual wings before they were clipped by marriage?

"You have some queer ideas about the business of living," he said to her impatiently, one day. He had blazed a trail from the upper workings on Valdez to join the path that ran from the Granite Pool to Oliver Thorn's. He had made several journeys over that ridge before Mary went back to town, sometimes in the evening, sometimes of a Sunday afternoon. It was pleasant to see the momentary glow in her eyes when he came in.

"I like you in Mackinaw and caulked boots, Rod," she said irrelevantly. "Are you going to make a profession of logging?"

"I said you have some queer ideas about this business of living," he persisted.

"No, you only think them queer," she said. "They're sound enough. I don't want to make a blunder."

"You think marrying me might be a blunder?" he asked a little stiffly.

"I don't want to marry anybody, Rod," she repeated, a statement that never failed to anger him. "Is it so important that one should marry?"

"It's important to me," he said.

"Are you the only one whose will or desire counts?" she inquired. "It isn't like you to take that position about anything."

"Mary, Mary, you know what I mean," he exclaimed. "Life doesn't seem more than half-complete without you in the picture. When we were kids playing together we lived from day to day. But we can't do that now. I can't, anyway. I've either got to be sure of you, or give up all idea of you. All this stuff that seems to stick you — my people and money, and what they'll do to me in disapproval, and all that — it doesn't really amount to anything. If I didn't know how you feel about me I'd say it wasn't worthwhile combatting such fool impressions."

"Ah. If you found yourself cut off from a great many things you unconsciously value; deprived of things you've accepted as your birthright, you'd begin to change your tune, I think. You wouldn't be human if you didn't," Mary commented. "Anyway, that isn't all, and you know it isn't, Rod," she broke out with unexpected heat. "I'm not so sure as you are that marriage is an end in itself. It's just a step. Probably instinct tends to drive a man and a woman into each other's arms. It seems so. But I can see things ahead of us in such a step that I rather shrink from. And what is just as important, I happen also to see things ahead of me that I rather anticipate, things I want to try and do. I want — oh, what's the use, Rod? We don't get anywhere talking about this. Why can't we just be friends and let it go at that?"

"Could you be just friends with me now?" he challenged.

And when the girl's fundamental truthfulness brought a thoughtful look and a touch of colour to her face Rod was answered without words.

It was like swimming upstream, he thought to himself, halting on his way to look down on the tide roaring and foaming through its narrow passage by Little Dent. Manhood wasn't proving quite the careless easy way of his youthful fancy. It had sometimes seemed to him then, with preternatural vision for a boy, that for well-born people the chief trouble lay not in getting things they wanted, but in wanting anything much. His life had seemed to him then a matter of absolute certainties.

And it wasn't. Not by a long shot. He wanted Mary Thorn. He wanted very much to write brilliantly and acceptably about his native land, which he loved for its bigness and rugged beauty as well as for what it had so generously bestowed on him and his. He could neither have one nor accomplish the other. But he would! Oh, yes. He pursed his lips and set his teeth upon that determination, as he lingered on the ridge where the old trail pitched down to the Granite Pool on one side and the new one slanted to the camp at tidewater.

The autumn haze hung like a diaphanous veil over mountains and waterways. Vine maple and alder shone brick-red and pale gold in the low ground. Hawk's Nest lifted its flaming roof across the channel. He wondered if there were a weekend party there. He wondered how they would look at him, these sons and daughters of the well-to-do, if he came stalking up the porch steps in caulked boots and Mackinaw shirt. Rod smiled. Even Phil considered him a little too thoroughgoing in his logging career. To the rest, to Grove's crowd, it would simply be a joke. They all believed in work — in getting it done, not in doing it — and most of them were a little tainted with the idea that labour, especially such labour as is hard and poorly paid, was the exclusive privilege of the labouring class. Rod, who had learned a great many astonishing things in two months among men who were not in the least dismayed by sweat and dust and noise, found himself for the moment viewing Grove, the fast crowd Grove travelled with, very much from the logger's point of view.

"If you neither feed yourself, nor clothe yourself, nor direct the production of anything useful, nor create anything beautiful, what the hell justification have you for existing?" Andy Hall had once attacked the idea of a leisure class. He had outlined a theory of the leisure class very much in the manner of Veblen. Then he proceeded to attack it, first on moral grounds, then on the basis of its social utility.

Rod found himself half in agreement just then. There was not and had never been in his mind any doubt of the courage, energy, and usefulness of the first Norquays. The original Roderick had reaped for himself and his followers the reward of enterprise initiated by himself. He had handed on his winnings. So far as Rod could see, there was no great virtue in merely standing pat and holding on — resting on dead men's accomplishments. That was a bog he determined his feet should never sink into. Grove, for instance, was not standing pat. Yet curiously, he had always thought of Grove and the Norquay Trust as a dubious undertaking — dubious in character and uncertain as to outcome. By all the conventional signs and tokens he was wrong. Grove was certainly moving with purposeful intent. He was a dynamo for energy. Already he was credited with stupendous achievements. But to Rod that seemed a great deal worse than the gentlemanly *laissez faire* which his father had set as a standard.

"Oh, damn, I wish it were spring again," Rod muttered as he strode down the hill.

Spring was at hand almost before he realized that the vernal equinox had come and gone. But winter had to precede spring. In October the fall rains broke in bitter earnest. The sodden drip of eaves lulled him to sleep at night and greeted him on awakening. He went to work in the morning with his fellows and trudged back at night soaked through heavy clothing. The bunkhouse reeked with steam from sodden garments festooned above a red-hot stove. Day and night, for weeks on end, grey clouds and drifting mist hovered above the trees. Every gully discharged a stream seaward. To step through a clump of brush meant a shower bath. Everything a man touched, tools, gear, timber, was damp and clammy cold. The thin soil squashed into mud under their boots. The moss was saturated. The great firs dripped like weeping giants. Even the old hands on the coast began to remark profanely that there had never been such rains.

Yet the logs came down. The falling gangs went grumbling into the wet thickets about the base of the trees they must fell. The rigging-slingers and hook tenders cursed as they fumbled the slippery cables. Donkey engineers scowled from beneath the tin shelter over each machine. And Jim Handy prowled in oilskins from gang to gang, silent, eagle-eyed, on the job. Rain or shine the timber came log by log to the booming ground, the boom men with their pikes arranged it in sections, and when the sections grew to a thirty-swifter raft, a tug hauled in, hooked on her towline and the cedar and fir of Valdez began its journey to the mills.

During those sodden weeks Rod Norquay put by all that he had ever been. His work, that opus which had led him to forswear, however briefly, the ease and comfort of Hawk's Nest, was laid away. Not forgotten. He sat sometimes in the evening, dreaming. He had wanted to see what made the wheels go round, to know how and why men laboured and endured privation, to see what life was like in the raw. And he was getting insight with a vengeance. He saw men throw down their tools in a passion and quit at a word. He saw new men reel drunkenly down a steamer's gangplank and go to work next morning with aching heads and bloodshot eyes. He saw a snap phrase bring a blow, a fight to a finish. The whole panorama of the timber, trees, men, machinery, shifted before his eyes that winter, gave him food for thought as well as sometimes a flash of something that stirred his pulse. For there were heroic moments, risks, long chances taken and skilfully avoided. A flying limb, a snapped cable, a rolling log. A man had to be alert. It was no place for a dullard. The logger had his pride of calling. It was borne in upon Rod that only tried men followed the woods. It was something of a satisfaction that he qualified as one of them on the job.

It was not so regarded in the family circle, he discovered to his secret amusement. Grove openly disliked the idea of any Norquay mixing with the men. Norquay senior observed dryly that Rod need not make quite so close a contact with logging and loggers. Phil frankly invited him on different occasions to come in out of the wet.

At the Christmas shutdown, foregathered at Grove's house in town, Rod noted the growing concern on his behalf. There was a hint of protest in the jocular remarks about his devotion to logging as a vocation. Grove's thinly veiled contempt, Laska's mild wonder that he should go in for "that sort of thing" nettled Rod.

He sat back, appraising his father, his brothers, the friends of the family, the train of people who came within range of his observation, all well-to-do, all thoroughly insulated against material discomfort, able to command and have their commands obeyed without question. They were as supreme in their respective positions as Jim Handy was on the Valdez job — more so, because Handy's power was only delegated to him, and these people Rod knew, wealthy merchants, financiers, propertied magnates of various sorts, held their power in their own individual right.

He wondered if they knew their power and how far the roots of such power penetrated the social soil, if they had grasped it with clear purpose and sure intent; and if they would have the resource and determination to keep it when they were challenged by what they called the "rabble"? Rod wondered. There might never be such a challenge. Andy Hall doubted the possibility within several generations. But Rod himself was not so sure. He had none of the purblind middle-class hatred of and contempt for labour agitators, those sometimes sincere and sometimes hypocritical mouthpieces of the muddled aspirations of the wage-workers. Rod had a working knowledge of economics, a trained understanding of cause and effect in the world of industry, in the field of production and distribution. He was without prejudice, and he knew what he knew. Men like Andy Hall, when they did not claw up out of the class where they originated, remained within it and festered. They could never be servilely contented. They had too much force, too positive a character. Their perception was too keen.

It amused Rod to speculate on how his father and Grove, the Deanes, Walls, Richstons, *et al* would fare if they were ever faced with a situation in which they would have to black their own boots, prepare and serve their own food, wear overalls instead of tailored clothes. They couldn't. That was his cynical conclusion. They wouldn't know how. And they had an attitude which could only be translated as contempt for those who did know how. Somehow, by the grace of God, or chance, or skilful management, they had become entrenched behind material fortifications, their hands grasping the strings of an ample purse. And from behind these fortifications they looked out with narrowed eyes upon lesser folk.

That, it struck Rod all in a heap, was the thing that confronted Mary Thorn when he talked to her of love and marriage. She had grasped the essence of class distinctions. She doubted his — their — power to overcome an *idée fixe*.

Whereupon he straightway hunted up the place where she boarded and haled her forth to a show and afterward to supper in the Exeter Grill, where he was most likely to encounter some of his own crowd. His cogitations had put him in a defiant mood. He would show them.

He looked across the table into her eyes and wondered if she had always been as keenly aware of the invisible fences about him as he was fast becoming himself. Well, he promised himself lightly, some of those fences were due to be smashed.

CHAPTER XII

ISABEL WALL, THE PERT and pretty sister-in-law of Mr. Grove Norquay, became at last the cause of Rod's first definite breach in the fences.

When summer full-blown came tripping on the heels of spring, Rod left the Valdez camp for good. It had been a wholesome experience. One year in the woods had shown him quite fully the technique of big timber operations. It had shed an unreckoned light, moreover, upon the nature and mental processes of the men who handled the timber, which Rod was sure seldom appeared to the owners of the woods as a matter of any particular importance. He knew himself duly qualified as a practical logger. He was egotist enough to believe himself more capable of getting results without friction than most logging bosses. But he had not set out to qualify in timber so much as to get outside the shell of his class and see how and why man in general functioned both in and out of industry. He had covered the first phase that occurred to him. His own individual job, his book, began to nag him again, to assume form, proportion, to cry out for embodiment. So he laid aside caulked boots and Mackinaws for canvas shoes and flannels, and took up the pleasant ways of Hawk's Nest when June brought the first coho salmon into the rapids and a chair in the shade was a comfortable thing.

Perhaps, as Phil put it in fraternal raillery, Isabel thought that if one Norquay in the Wall family was a good thing, two would be better. The truth is that Isabel suddenly became aware of Rod as a man and characteristically sought to annex him by the usual methods. She had finished her education in a presumably fashionable school on the Atlantic seaboard that spring, coincident with Mary Thorn's graduation from the University of B.C. Isabel's social experience had been judicially expanded in the intervals of education. She was twenty now, a sophisticated young person, accustomed to associating with other sophisticated young persons of both sexes. She had seen little of Rod except during summer vacations. For a year she had not seen him at all. Now she seemed to discover him anew and to mark him for her own.

Rod granted her uncommon charm. She was pretty and petite and modish, and she spoke the current lingo with effortless facility. But while she pleased his eye she failed to stir his blood. There was a sufficient reason for Rod's immunity, which of course Isabel did not know.

It became obvious that Isabel was in deadly earnest. And when it became equally obvious to Rod that both families were complacently agreeable to Isabel's manoeuverings he grinned first, then grew sober as the remedies he used to cure Isabel merely aggravated the disease.

It wasn't a simple flirtatious liking Isabel had for him. Rod was too keen to make such a mistake. It seemed that this dainty doll-like creature was capable of intense feeling and not too sure in her control of the emotional disturbance. Rod began by being amused. Then he felt sorry. In the end he grew a little alarmed over the net result of being sympathetic. It is highly discomforting to a young man to have a girl weep spontaneously on his chest, unless he conceives it to be his special mission and blessed privilege to soothe this particular damsel's tears. Isabel did that one evening in the shadow of a hoary old cedar in Hawk's Nest grounds. She couldn't help it, she said, after a long embarrassed silence during which she dabbed the tears away. She was a fool and she knew it, but it couldn't be helped. One wasn't responsible for one's feelings, was one?

And Rod, with a little ache in his breast, a great deal of wordless sympathy for Isabel, because he had for a long time suffered that queer state of stifled longing that seemed sometimes as if it would drive him mad, agreed that one was not. They let it go at that.

Rod sat with elbows on the sill of his bedroom window late that night, staring out over a moon-bathed landscape, silver barred with black, where the shadows of great trees lay across the lawn. He looked down a shimmering moon-path that seemed to offer a bright highway across the channel where Mary Thorn lay sleeping — if indeed she slept. Rod wondered if something in her breast ever drove her to a window to stare across the tide and think of him. She was home now. He had his own sources of information. Tomorrow he would see her. Tonight the querulous imps that make a man question his destiny and desire bade him consider if he did well to let his heart abide so constantly with Mary Thorn when there were other desirable women to be had for the asking. Isabel, for instance? All clear sailing. No questions asked or answered. The dual family blessing, and any little material wants cheerfully attended to. On the personal side — well, he was flesh and blood, sexual tinder. When Isabel put her face against his breast and sobbed in that stifled, choking fashion he had been deeply moved, thrilled, conscious of her physical nearness, the sweet fragrant odour of her tousled hair, the trembling of her small, soft body. Wasn't that good enough? What did a man want of a woman when he took her to wife?

Rod shook himself impatiently. What rot he had been thinking. Whatever it was in Mary Thorn that so imperatively promised to fulfil his every need, it didn't reside in Isabel Wall. He was sure of that. He could let himself slide into a temporary infatuation with Isabel — perhaps. He could conceive of possessing her. But he couldn't behold her down a long vista of years playing the game fairly and bravely, taking the cards dealt from the deck of life, good, bad and indifferent, with courage and fortitude. He couldn't picture Isabel doing that any more than he could picture her, *aetat* sixteen, shooting the Euclataw

Rapids in a dugout, eyes shining in sheer ecstasy of swift movement, hair streaming in the wind. Isabel would either have been frightened or wildly, dangerously excited.

That was as far as Rod carried his analogy. It was sufficient. He had not tried his hand at creative fiction without a sense of character, of form, proportion. He egotistically assumed that he could accurately gauge personal values, that he did it intuitively as well as rationally. If his prescience did not clearly account for the depth and tenacity of his affection for Mary Thorn it quickly and thoroughly disposed of Isabel as a substitute.

A light flashed from a window in Oliver Thorn's house. Rod rested his chin on cupped palms. Unrest, longing blew through the spaces of his being like a hot wind. The bright moon and the dusky woods beckoned him into their restful silences, and the light across the channel seemed to blink a message. It drew him like a magnet. Over there his heart lay. If Isabel's unheralded breakdown had served no other purpose, it had filled him with a wild impatience, revived a fever that burned him. The madness of a lover's moon! The coursing blood of youth clamouring for the fulfilment of life's promise — life that promises so much and often gives so little. The impulse to translate dreams into realities. *Quien sabe?*

He rose and went softly downstairs and out a side door to the pale emptiness of the lawn crossed with inky bands of shadow, and so sauntering, head bowed and hands sunk deep in his pockets, presently brought up on the float. The *Haida* lay moored on one side, the *Kowloon* on the other. A profusion of canoes and rowboats lay hauled out on the planks.

Rod stood awhile, like a man in two minds. His eyes lingered on the moon-path. His ears took note of the lessening monotone between the Gillard Islands on the east and the choked westward passage inside Little Dent. A still night and a slackening tide.

He got into a dinghy, shipped the oars, rowed slowly out into the channel. Halfway, an eddy setting toward the Valdez shore took him in its sweep. He let the oars rest and lighted a cigarette, gazing at the tranquil, silvery beauty.

"What a night," he whispered. "What a night for fairies and mermaids — and lovers."

Then the current slid him into the deep shadow cast by the high forested ridge behind Oliver Thorn's house, and as his boat touched the float and he sat in a moment of indecision, a voice spoke softly:

"Hello, Rod."

He looked sharply over the float. The shadow of the hills lay on it like folds of crêpe. But in a moment he made out a dim figure. He went over, still holding the painter in his hand. It was Mary, wrapped in a grey coat, sitting on a box.

"I thought you'd be in your little trundle bed," he greeted her.

"Then why did you come?" she asked.

"I don't quite know. Just on the chance. I was restless. Moon madness, maybe."

He sat down beside her. One hand shone white in the gloom where it stretched on her knee. Rod possessed himself of that. He bent, peering into her face. Her eyes glowed at him.

"All by your lonesome out here in the dark," he murmured. "How come, Brownie? Did you sit yourself down here to put the come-hither on me?"

She shook her head.

"Well, I came."

He put his arms around her, drew her close, felt her settle against him unresistingly.

"Glad?"

She nodded.

A solitary loon lifted his harsh, complaining cry somewhere in the shining channel.

"Calling his mate. And I've found mine. Or have I?"

He knew, or thought he knew. There was an attitude of surrender, unmistakable, complete, that filled him with a strange delight. But he wanted the verification of that voiceless pledge.

"I don't know. How can one account for a mood, a longing? I came down here to sit in the moonlight. It was so radiant. Then after a little the shadow crept out from shore, and it was just as if something black and gloomy had settled over me. I felt small and forlorn and lonely. And all at once I wanted you, Rod. I wished you were here. I wanted you. And you're here. That's all."

"It's enough," he said tenderly.

CHAPTER XIII

THE DAY FOLLOWING ROD drew his father into the library and bluntly announced his engagement to Mary Thorn, also that the date of their marriage was set for the first week in July, exactly one month ahead.

Norquay senior sat down, lighted a cigar. He did not precisely lose his poise, but he was slightly staggered.

"Well," he said at last, "the younger generation is supposed to be speedy but I didn't imagine *you* would ever step on the accelerator like this. Why the mad haste? Can't you at least give us a chance to get acquainted with the young woman?"

"We've had plenty of opportunities for acquaintance," Rod could not forbear saying, "since she is a close neighbour, so to speak. Besides, the family isn't marrying Miss Thorn, pater. I am. And I have known her for several years."

"I suppose she's pretty," his father observed grimly. "Has she any manners? Education? Ever been anywhere?"

Rod looked at him soberly.

"Are you trying to get my goat?" he asked. "If you want me to blow up, polite insult is as good a way as any. I'm of age and a little more. You took pains to educate me. You've granted at various times that I have good taste in many things. I should be qualified to choose a wife with — with the ordinary essentials."

"Perhaps I didn't put it very well," Norquay senior replied. "I don't mean to adopt a toplofty hypercritical attitude. I may seem unduly impertinent, my son, but marriage *is* important — in this family, and to this family. A wife isn't something to be put aside if she doesn't happen to suit. Remember, I've had no warning of this. Therefore, naturally, the first questions that occur to me are these: Is the girl such as we can accept into the family as one of us? Is she a person our friends can meet as one of themselves? Have you asked yourself this, Rod?"

"Yes," Rod answered. "Contrary to the general notion of what an infatuated youngster does in such circumstances, I have. Or at least I should certainly have done so if there had been any doubt in the matter. To be quite candid, Mary Thorn has equally as good manners and as much — if not a good deal more — education as any girl I know. And about fifty per cent more discrimination in most things. If the family and the family's set refuse to accept her at her face value, that will be the privilege of snobbery. It won't make any difference to me."

"Quite sure about that?"

"I meant it wouldn't make me hesitate. Of course, it would make a difference," Rod amended. "I'm not a fool. But this girl means more to me than merely pleasing my family and friends by what *they* regard as a suitable match."

"You're fully determined on this?"

"Absolutely," Rod confirmed.

Norquay senior half-turned in his chair to look out the window. His gaze crossed the channel, rested without change of expression on Oliver Thorn's house.

"I can scarcely conceive of a suitable mate for a Norquay arising out of such surroundings," he said gravely, "nor from such antecedents."

"I wonder if you know what you really mean by antecedents," Rod said patiently. He had to force himself to be patient. He had warned himself that he would have to encounter just such prejudice. It grated on him, but he kept his temper in hand and his wits alert. "For instance, you accepted Laska Wall as being quite worthy of the most important of your three sons. And I am sure Laska is. But you must know, pater, that if John P. Wall didn't have scads of money you would never have tolerated the Walls. Mrs. Wall herself is only passable. Wall is simply a keen, able money-grabber. His people were nobodys — petty tradesmen. Wall's father kept a little two-by-four shop in Toronto for twenty years. I learned that quite by accident. And it is nothing against them. It simply happens that in our more or less democratic West, Wall's daughters, having enjoyed every advantage of easily and quickly acquired wealth, go everywhere and are accepted. That being so, antecedents don't seem to carry so much weight as you infer. I believe myself that they do; but not in the way you mean. And though you may not credit it, Mary Thorn's people are as good, able, pioneering stock as we are. Except that they didn't take permanent root and acquire wealth."

"Acquisitive ability is a pretty good test of character, Rod," his father commented. "It takes brains, initiative, determination, sterling qualities to amass wealth and hold it. Your prospective father-in-law doesn't exhibit those traits."

"No? You've tried to buy his timber holdings, haven't you? I heard you confess irritably that you couldn't see why he would neither log it off nor sell. Perhaps it never occurred to you that he is doing precisely what we've done — on a smaller scale — acquire a natural source of wealth and hold it, benefiting by the sure increase in value. He has seventy thousand dollars' worth of timber there. He makes it produce a reasonable living. When he lets it go, he will have a moderate competence. He has managed to give his daughter a university education. If he hasn't luxury, he has something he values more — independence. That rather argues character, doesn't it?"

"The argument is yours, Rod. Special pleading. You'd have made an excellent advocate. But suppose the worst. Suppose you find you can't mix oil and water — you know what I mean — what then?"

"Well, then I won't be the first younger son of this house to break away, to go on his own and make the best of things as he finds them. Will I?" Rod asked.

"I'd be sorry to see you do that. It's so unnecessary. There's room and plenty for all of us here. Of course, if you should elect to do that, you have your inalienable income from the estate. But I'd much prefer to see you and Phil together carrying on the upcoast end of our affairs. I don't want to see my boys scattered. I may have a selfish interest in keeping the family together. I should find myself very lonely here with all my children gone."

"And you're afraid I'll ball things up by marrying a girl nobody knows, and to whom people may not take kindly, eh?"

"That's about it, my son."

"Well, it's coming off on schedule, you may be sure of that," Rod said tartly. "I think I love Hawk's Nest as dearly as any of us. I have a pretty keen sense of what's due the family. I am perhaps a little proud of belonging to it. I'd a little rather be a great-great-grandson of that adventurous old fur trader than anything I know. But I have only one life to live, and I propose to live it according to my lights. I am not going to do anything that will reflect on us. I merely intend to marry a poor man's daughter because she seems to me the most perfect woman I know."

"You are quite determined?" his father asked again. Rod answered him with a simple "Yes."

"At any rate there is no need for such haste, is there?" Norquay senior continued, with a hint of petulance. "Next month is absurd. Give us a chance to meet your fiancée, to get acquainted with her. If she is to become one of the family, let's have a show at making her feel that she'll be welcome. Incidentally, it will give you time to think. A month's engagement is positively indecent."

"Time to think, pater?" Rod echoed. "I've had a solid year of thinking it over. It has taken me a year to persuade Mary Thorn it's the only thing to do. You want us to think it over — after twelve months of thrashing it out from every conceivable angle. No. One month from today. And there aren't going to be any frills. If you are at all dubious about countenancing me in this, just say so and I'll make my own arrangements. I'd be delighted to have you meet Mary, and I'm sure you'll like her immensely, but if you have any idea of adopting a 'to-be-examined-on-approval' attitude with her, why I'll introduce her as my wife and we'll make the necessary adjustments afterward."

Norquay senior smiled at his son's vehemence.

"I didn't dream you had so headlong a temperament, Rod," he said. "Speaking for myself, I wish you had chosen differently. Still, I concede you are well within your rights, and I am anxious to meet this unexpected choice of yours. I'll be courteous and cordial. You know that. But I can't promise that every one else will."

"If they aren't —" Rod shrugged his shoulders. "Well, I don't think people will be downright stupid."

"If they aren't," his father continued judicially, "you can't browbeat them into being so."

Rod agreed that this was obvious.

"In which case," his father said slowly, "I shan't be able to do much. If people won't receive your wife, Rod, on terms of equality, you can't shove her down their throats."

"You needn't be alarmed," Rod assured him stiffly. "I shan't try."

CHAPTER XIV

ON THE WHOLE ROD considered that he came off very well in the matter of breaking this news to the family. Laska, who was staying awhile at Hawk's Nest, having a clear understanding of the situation, bundled Isabel off to town at once and gallantly proposed that she, herself, take Mary under her wing for the remaining four weeks. Rod promptly vetoed this.

"Won't work," he said frankly. "You've never even met the girl. She's much too clever to be fussed up by a burst of family interest all at once. I'm not going to have you pitchfork her into a giddy round before she has time to get her bearings. When we're married and come home, I'll take it kindly if you will all be as casual as if I'd married some girl we'd all known for years. No special efforts at gaiety, please, at this stage of the game."

Laska agreed that might be good policy. She was frankly curious about this girl Rod was going to marry. She was also well aware that the slangy fast-stepping crowd which occasionally descended on Hawk's Nest might make it difficult for a rank outsider thrown in their way. As Rod's wife, Mary would partake of the family dignity. As a mere fiancée she would be fair game, especially for the younger women.

So matters stood as they were. The circumstances were fortuitous enough. Grove was the one fly in the ointment — an uncertainty as to what he might do or say. And Grove had just betaken himself across the Atlantic, cooking up some financial stew in London. Grove was very jealous of his dignity. He was more arrogant than ever. Rod anticipated a certain amount of minor trouble with Grove. Hence he was as well satisfied that Grove was not present to inject the virus of his distaste into the already dubious mind of their father. Phil merely grinned and wished him luck.

"I don't know that I'd have had it turn out just this way if I'd been the arbiter of destiny," Oliver Thorn said to him. "I hope you and Mary will never be sorry. It's natural, I suppose — but natural evolution sometimes has its pains and disasters. Why do you want to go outside your own class to fall in love and marry?"

"Because I can't find what I want in my own crowd," Rod responded blithely. "Neither can Mary," he added as an afterthought.

Old Thorn reflected on this.

"Maybe you're right," he admitted soberly. "I never thought of it just that way before."

"And when it comes down to brass tacks," Rod went on, "the only fundamental difference between my family and yours is a matter of money. It's hardly right to classify us as belonging to a different order."

"True enough," Thorn agreed. "Mary's people, her mother's and mine, have had advantages, as they say. We didn't somehow manage to retain a stranglehold on the sources of wealth, that's all. We've been a restless lot. We've helped open up new territory from the Alleghanies west. We've always been independent. But we never took root for long. There are certain inherent advantages in taking root in the right sort of soil," his gaze rested on the red roof beyond the channel, "in taking hold and hanging on. With the prestige that goes with money — pshaw!" he made an impatient gesture. "When I let go this timber

I'll have plenty to give two old people of simple tastes a comfortable living as long as they live. I never thought about money in connection with Mary before. Maybe she'll have a tussle with some of your crowd. Still — give her a wardrobe and a background — she has everything else — they'd all kowtow."

"My idea," Rod agreed blandly. "They will."

"Perhaps," Oliver Thorn sighed. "Still, she's got a handicap. If the going gets rough, don't blame Mary. Blame me. I should have foreseen something like this — and made preparation."

"Oh dammit," Rod said carelessly, "there isn't going to be any blame. Mary has real class. You know it. I know it. If there are poor simps on our visiting list who won't recognize it, why I'll just mark 'em off the list."

And so they were married.

Various people have various ideas about marriage — ideas which sometimes do and sometimes do not coincide with facts. Love is as old as humanity. Marriage is an institution. Were this simply a mendacious tale of romantic youth, one might close it here with a sigh and the simple statement that they lived happily ever after. One could leave the rest to imagination.

And so they were married — married!

Well, what of it? People do not cease to live after marriage. To most it is only the beginning of their real being. So, one would say, it should have been for Rod Norquay and Mary Thorn. One would be right. They were possibly more fortunate than most. Home, friends, the invisible aura of wealth, established position, lay to their hand. They had nothing to face beyond the inevitable process of adaptation to the intimacies of matrimony, to each other's individual moods and tenses. This seemed no problem, since neither they nor any other young man or woman passionately in love ever recognized such a problem. Instinct triumphs; mutual taste smooths the way for compromises in the clash of their separate personalities.

Poverty, unremitting struggle for an economic foothold, unwelcome babies and frowsy domesticity withers many a fine flower of romantic passion when it should still be brightly blooming. Rod and Mary had before them no toilsome effort to keep the wolf from the door. Their place in the sun was made and provided. They had but to eat, drink, and be merry. Where could lie in wait for them the elements of clash and struggle, of fear and hope, of stifled griefs and aching disappointments — all the sad travail and hard-won victories bestowed upon men and women through the long procession of the years?

Go to, you say. Considering the circumstances they marry and live happy ever after. That is the accepted formula.

Quite simple. But life is not an affair of formula. The simple tends to become the complex. So the findings of science indicate. So from time to time philosophers inform us. We don't pay much attention, by and large, to either scientific or philosophic fulminations. But occasionally one or the other, or both, utters a workable truth. The dictum that even the simplest thing contains within itself all the elements of the profoundly complex is one of these basic truths.

Fate, Destiny, God, Chance, whoever or whatever rolls the dice of events did not decree that Rod and his wife should come to their full estate by way of teas and tennis, the secure comfort of Hawk's Nest and the full social life open to the Norquays in town when they chose to avail themselves of town. It didn't elect for Mary an absorption into the younger matrons' set, immediate luxury and alternate boredom and excitement. Nor for Rod a mixture of gentlemanly leisure, casual attention to estate affairs and dilettante efforts at writing a prose epic of pioneering times. No. Before they were born, forces were shaping to jostle them out of this pleasant groove. Or was it merely a careless roll of the dice? Who can say?

They returned from a brief honeymoon quite frankly absorbed in each other, in the confirmation of the dreams and glamour of love, exultingly triumphant in having achieved a perfect union of the spirit as well as the flesh. They were welcomed to Hawk's Nest by a handpicked group of the family and intimates. Laska, Phil, their father, their sister Dorothy from Victoria with two chubby sons, two cousins from Montreal, an old school chum of Phil's with his wife.

For the time it seemed to Rod that his childish impression of family solidarity, of complete and intimate understanding and support, which had made so fine an atmosphere of home about the place, had been restored in full force. As if the Norquay Trust Company and Grove's hectic yachting parties, jazz and restlessness, the slow disintegration of their unity had vanished into some place remote.

It was very pleasant for a week or so. Rod watched with mingled pride and amusement the first cordial effort to be kind to his wife, merely because she was his wife, evolve into a relieved acceptance of her as quite one of themselves.

"One would think," he reflected, "that they had half expected her to eat spinach with a knife."

Rod, of course, knew quite well that Mary's adaptation to this more luxurious mode of living, a more elaborate manner, was no more difficult for her than his own ready fitting-in to the life of a logging crew. He had long ago learned that rubbing elbows with people is the surest cure for self-consciousness; that the fundamentals of good breeding are simple. There were a great many people of his own kind who believed that good manners must necessarily be the exclusive possession of the well-to-do. It had never occurred to him before so strongly, but he saw now that most of his own family and many of his friends took it for granted that to be poor — as they defined poverty — meant that one had never been anywhere, knew nothing, murdered the King's English, committed every conceivable *faux pas,* and was naturally an impossible sort of person.

It was a narrow creed, one that filled Rod with impatience. Those who held to it most rigidly were least qualified to pass rational judgment on any man or woman. Their knowledge of life was as limited as that of the people they regarded as inferior.

"'Fess up," he bantered Dorothy, one day. "You were all very dubious about the new Mrs. Norquay, weren't you?"

"Well, what do you expect?" his sister replied. "One doesn't anticipate a combination of brains, beauty, and deportment from such a source?"

"Why not?" he inquired innocently.

"Well, one doesn't," she replied. "I don't understand it yet. Mary's a dear. She has never had any advantages, so to speak, yet she fits in here as if she belonged. That's all I know about it."

"The fact of the matter is, Dot," Rod gave his own opinion, "that girls like Mary Thorn are rare birds in any class, top or bottom. It takes more than clothes and manners to make a real woman."

On the whole, Rod had every reason to be satisfied. It was not the family custom to be demonstrative. They liked Mary. Perceiving that she was a normal young woman of good taste and sound sense, they took her to their bosom, figuratively speaking, without more ado. There was a formal welcoming dinner to which Oliver Thorn and his wife were asked as a matter of courtesy, and to which they came and acquitted themselves with credit. Grandfather Norquay remarked afterward that Mrs. Thorn was a very fine type of woman. Rod's father conceded that Oliver Thorn was a more intelligent, better-informed man than he had imagined. All of which was duly gratifying to Rod.

But this satisfactory state of affairs was broken into by Mr. Grosvenor Sylvester Norquay in his most characteristic manner. He came back from England in due course and steamed straight to Hawk's Nest on the *Kowloon.* Contrary to his custom, he came alone, and he arrived for some inscrutable reason in his worst temper and his most disagreeable manner.

"Well," he said to Rod at the first opening, "you made a hash of things for fair, didn't you? By Jove, I used to think you had taste if not judgment. I perceive you have neither."

"Are you referring to my marriage?" Rod asked.

"Excellent guesser. You don't imagine I'm referring to the price of logs or foreign exchange, do you?"

"Those are about the only matters you're qualified to pass on, and I'm doubtful about even that," Rod said quietly. "That'll be about all in that vein, elder brother. I know you don't like it — although it's none of your business. I daresay you're going to cut up as rough as you can on general principles. But another break like that and I'll smash you. You may be the big noise in the Norquay Trust, but dictatorial trust company methods won't work in the family. So you'd better be a good dog and not growl or show your teeth. I'll whip you if you do. I'm quite competent to do the job. If you think I'm not, just go ahead and be insulting and act the snob and get critical and sneer: the whole bag of tricks you put on when you want to hurt anybody's feelings. I may not be able to prevent you. But I can make you sorry. And I surely will. How would you like to go back to town with two black eyes and your classical nose a bit off centre?"

Rod told him all this in an ordinary conversational tone. And when he issued such a direct challenge, he was not merely letting a little steam off his youthful chest. He had a feeling that the only way to deal with Grove was to defy him — to act first. The threat of personal chastisement was perhaps Rod's only concession to a personal animus. He meant precisely what he said. There was a definite limit to what he would permit Grove to do and say, where Mary was concerned. A dozen times in his life his hands had doubled into fists against Grove — an involuntary action. He was — or he had been — a little ashamed of this eagerness to do bodily damage to his brother. Once, long ago, Grove's domineering tactics had roused Phil out of his placidity, and Rod had felt his heart uplifted at sight of Grove knocked sprawling with a single hearty punch. Not that Grove lacked the fighting heart; he would have fought Phil to a finish then and there, but for their father's scandalized interference. Grove couldn't stand long in a losing fight; he couldn't take punishment; that was a weakness both his brothers had fathomed long before.

And Rod had never forgotten that for weeks thereafter Grove was politic, to say the least, in his invasions of Phil's territory. Nor had Rod ever quite rid himself of the feeling that it would be a pleasure to repeat such a chastisement with his own hands. They were blood-brothers. There was even a profound physical likeness, except that Grove ran slightly to beef. But they didn't think, or act, or feel alike. They were antagonistic at every point where their lives touched. And Rod did not mean, if he could help it, to let this scowling elder duplicate of himself put a single spoke in the wheel which promised to revolve so smoothly for Mary and himself.

It was *so* childish, Rod said to himself impatiently, when Grove left him with an inarticulate growl, for him to take it that way. What difference need it make to Grove whom his brother married? Grove was the biggest toad in a puddle where big toads were common.

But it was the nature of the man to restrict the splashing to such as he approved, if it were in his power. It was also the nature of the man to be greedy of power, to exercise it arbitrarily if he could, regardless of justice or even common sense.

For the class of people out of which Mary Thorn had sprung Grove Norquay had only a disdainful recognition. They were the material upon which such as he were ordained to thrive. Rod knew Grove and Grove's crowd. Grove's dignity would suffer at their hands. Grove would be maddened by jocular references to his new sister-in-law. A hand-logger's daughter! How quaint of Rod! Grove would be as disagreeable to Mary as he dared, as vindictive as he could. He was made that way — more vindictive over trifles than he would be over a deadly wrong.

Rod wondered why their father had never been able to see the weakness of this his son. Phil did. Phil had frankly expected a debacle in Grove's financial operations. It hadn't come. He throve, waxed great. Nevertheless, quoth Phil, in a moment of pessimism, a man may successfully direct a great profit-making enterprise and still be a poor specimen of manhood, a gross, self-centred, unstable egotist. Rod agreed.

Mr. Grove Norquay tarried only two hours at Hawk's Nest. His visage and manner were at no time genial. He acknowledged his introduction to Mary in about as distant a fashion as he could effect. And having had a wide experience in freezing undesirables, Grove could be appallingly glacial when he tried. His iciness was wasted on Mary. She merely smiled, gazed at him with bland unconcern. She was fairly good at that. Thereafter, during a brief, general conversation Grove took pains neither to address her nor to look at her, except for an occasional appraising glance.

He exploded a small bomb in the vicinity of his wife after luncheon.

"We're going back within the hour," he said. His tone was brusque, snappy.

"Must you go back so soon?" Laska inquired amiably. "It was hardly worth the long run."

"I said '*we*,'" Grove bore hard on the pronoun. "If you have any things to take, better have them got ready."

"But, good heavens, Grove, must I go back to town on such short notice? Has anything extraordinary happened?"

Laska was frankly astonished.

"Nothing has happened. But I'm afraid you must. I came especially for you."

Laska looked thoughtful for a moment.

"Of course," she said dryly, "when one has promised to love, honour, and *obey*, one hasn't much choice. I'll have my bags sent aboard. Give a whoop when you're ready to leave."

She rose. Her gaze swept the faces of the others, came back to Grove. It seemed to Rod that her glance flashed hostility at her husband, although she was smiling. And in the same breath he caught a queer flicker of expression on Phil's usually immobile face. Undercurrents. Veiled swirls of feeling. Rod sensed them all about him, as if a state of tension had been set up. That, he thought irritably, was Grove's usual effect. If he were crossed, ever so slightly, he proceeded at once to generate an atmosphere.

"He had to get at somebody so he takes it out on Laska," Rod said to himself. "Snarly beast. If she'd been keen on going to town, he'd have insisted on her staying here. Phil's sore. I wonder if the old boy's still a little tender about Laska?"

The answer to that came within half an hour, when Rod had forgotten the passing thought. He had gone out on the porch to smoke. There was a recess behind a bulging window. There Rod found a chair. He sat deep in his own mixed reflections. Phil turned a corner and stood by a pillar, hands deep in his pockets. Just as Rod was about to speak, Laska came out. She was hatted and gloved, carrying a small bag.

"Goodbye, old scout," she said whimsically. "It's been very pleasant here the last few days. I thought I was going to get acquainted with you all over again. But the oracle decrees otherwise. Will you come and see me in town?"

Phil shook his head.

"Why not?"

"Always too busy," he said briefly.

"Of course," she agreed, after a pause. "How stupid of me to forget that. Well, goodbye."

They shook hands. Laska vanished around the house. Rod saw her appear on the gravel walk, joined by Mary, Dorothy and the others. He didn't need to ask why Phil was not with them to speed the departing guest. The expression on Phil's face as he stood looking after Laska told its own story. Rod understood. He was streaked with the same vein of constancy to an affection, an ideal, a conviction. He was supremely sorry for Phil — for them both.

"Five years," he thought, "and it hurts him yet. Laska knows it, too. And she hasn't a shred of an illusion about Grove. Poor devils. And they have to go right on playing the game."

There was a different sort of game afoot, however, the petty malice of which was presently disclosed to Rod.

CHAPTER XV

WITHIN THE MONTH, EVENTS marched one upon the heels of the other as if set in motion by some unseen intelligence working to an inscrutable plan.

Dorothy left for her home in Victoria. Phil's chum and his wife departed. The cousins returned to Montreal. Norquay senior betook himself to town. Rod and Mary had Hawk's Nest largely to themselves, with Phil coming and going on the *Haida*, his fingers lightly on the pulse of the Norquay activities in the woods. And there was Grandfather Norquay, who never left Hawk's Nest now, who sometimes kept his room for days at a stretch, appearing only occasionally at table for a meal. He was growing feebler, Rod noted. He walked abroad now with two sticks instead of one.

So for a matter of ten days Rod and his wife were left pretty much to their own devices. Time rested lightly on their hands. They were still too engrossed in each other to count hours or days.

Then the *Kowloon* slid into the landing one mid-afternoon. If Rod's father had hand-picked a few people to welcome Rod and Mary home, so Grove had selected his weekend guests for a purpose. If he had not openly primed them, he must have indicated his attitude.

Rod got that impression at once. By dark, when they began to dance on the roomy porch, this impression had grown to a certainty. Laska hadn't come. With the lot Rod had only a casual acquaintance. They were all someone or the children of someone, and like most of Grove's friends, they were accustomed to a speedy pace.

Rod perceived that there was a compact to ignore Mary. It was too pointed to be accidental. The women simply didn't see her. The men were perfunctory. They were not rude. They were much too finished a product for that. They simply didn't include Rod's wife in anything that was said or done. But that was quite enough. A rapier in skilled hands is as deadly as a spear.

Through that first evening Rod simmered. It was his home, the home of his fathers. As matters stood, his rights and privileges there were equal to Grove's. He knew he was under fire — platoon fire from skilful ambush. And he couldn't shoot back. It didn't injure him. But it did enrage him. It was so petty. Cheap malice. And stupid, useless — because Rod knew that Grove and Grove's friends could neither make nor mar him socially or any other way. These people, with their wealth, their modishness, their perfect assurance, were after all only a certain clique. That portion of the Norquay family which counted most had accepted Mary Thorn, at first out of common courtesy and thereafter because they found her well worth acceptance. The outer fringe of the Norquay connection would follow suit, and all who knew them would be governed thereby.

But that knowledge did not lessen Rod's growing anger at such tactics, nor still a little fear of the effect on Mary. This — this sort of thing precisely — was what she had foreseen and feared and shrunk from. It was only a passing phase, Rod knew. But he could see that it rankled. She bore herself stoutly, as impassive as a Chinese mandarin. No more than Rod himself would she or did she retreat under fire. She did her duty as a hostess in a difficult situation. But when they withdrew to their own rooms, at the end of an interminable evening, she lay back in a chair silent and thoughtful, while Rod spilled a vessel of wrath on his brother's head.

"Don't get fussed up about it, Rod," she said at last. "It doesn't matter much, does it? If what I've seen of these people this afternoon and evening is a fair sample of their normal behaviour, I wouldn't get on with them even if they wanted me to. I've overheard more suggestive things and double-edged remarks in the last few hours than I ever heard in all my life put together. If that's smartness, I'll never be smart. I don't feel as if I'd been slighted. I'm glad they didn't fall on my neck. I don't like them."

"Nor I," Rod growled. "Grove always did prefer damaged goods. But I don't like them trying to put over anything like that on me — on us. That's all. It's dirty."

"You can't do anything," Mary pointed out. "You can't challenge the assembled company to bestow courteous attention on your wife under pain of — what? If you even notice it, you'll only amuse them — make yourself ridiculous."

"Certainly. That's why it's so damned annoying."

"Forget it." She smiled. "Come and sit down by me. What does it matter?"

"I'll lock horns with him yet," Rod muttered.

Then, sitting on a hassock beside her with Mary's fingers weaving tangles in his hair, Rod forgot his irritation.

It returned the following day. Grove moved about among his guests, bland, courteous, engaging. He was at home in the polite raillery that passes for wit in such gatherings, where open homage is paid chiefly to the social trinity of food, liquor and dancing, and where sex is no shrinking violet. Whenever his eyes met Rod's, Rod detected a malicious sparkle. Grove was enjoying the situation. And Rod yearned to make him smart for his petty, useless triumph. His exasperation grew with his helplessness.

"Come on," he said to his wife at four in the afternoon. "You can leave the dinner arrangements to Stagg. Let's go across the channel and get the taste out of our mouths."

They had dinner at Oliver Thorn's.

"Funny," Rod thought, as he sat on the caulk-splintered porch steps watching the smoke curl and weave from the end of a cigarette. "Funny what an atmosphere can do to you. 'Better a dinner of herbs where love is than a stalled ox and hatred therewith.' The ancient wisdom is still wisdom. If Grove can pull off that sort of thing whenever he likes, we'll have to leave Hawk's Nest. There's no defence against it."

They rowed home at dusk. Phil had come back. The three of them sat out on the porch and observed the merriment quickening to a livelier tempo as the evening wore on. Phil made no comment for a long time.

"One would imagine," he observed at last, rather dryly, "that we three were taboo. We don't seem to be very popular with this crowd."

"There's been about thirty hours of this semi-glacial period," Rod informed him. "It's getting old with me."

"What about you?" Phil turned to Mary.

She shrugged her shoulders.

"I'm like the minister when he was kicked by the mule. I consider the source," she said.

"Proper attitude," Phil said. "I've been taking notice. I know our elder brother's pleasing little tricks. I wouldn't let it annoy me, sister Mary. Grove often starts things he can't finish. I didn't think he was quite stupid enough for this."

The *Kowloon* departed early Monday morning. Thinking it over as he watched her whip around the Gillard light, Rod decided that honours were easy for the time being. But he very nearly determined to force an open clash if Grove tried to carry it off again.

This clash, which Rod foresaw, and which he perhaps subconsciously welcomed, was nearly due. They had Hawk's Nest to themselves, its cool quiet rooms and corridors, the pleasant porches and grounds bright with flowers and scented shrubs, its sweep of velvet lawn and rolling acres of parked forest, where the great trees lifted plumed heads to the sun. Into that blended atmosphere of peace and permanence and beauty no jarring note came until another weekend brought back the *Kowloon*. This time Norquay senior was home. Rod sat back to see if

Grove meant to carry on with his design of making Mary's road as rough as lay in his power — and also to see how their father would take such obvious malice, if it were shown.

But Norquay senior missed all the calculated slights Grove and his guests adroitly managed to put on Rod and his wife. It seemed to Rod that they played up to Grove's lead with accomplished skill. It was a new sort of game and Mary Norquay was " It." They found it amusing. Or was it only that they were an ill-bred lot? Rod was not sure of Grove's company, but he was sure of Grove. Grove saw to it, subtly, that Rod should understand what he was driving at. Grove enjoyed the situation. Rod's self-control didn't deceive him. He knew that Rod was fuming inside, and he let Rod know that he knew.

But something more fundamental brought matters to a head. Lacking that, Rod would probably have ended by complete indifference to what Grove and his friends did or said.

The *Kowloon* was due to leave Monday afternoon. At ten in the morning, Rod sat reading in the library. Phil was writing letters at a desk in one corner. Norquay senior was walking in the grounds with Mary. From his seat Rod could see the tall tweed-clad figure sauntering beside his wife. His ill-humour vanished. That was answer enough to Grove and his clique. He glanced indifferently up at Grove's entrance. That gentleman didn't seem so gay and festive this morning. He bit off a cigar end with unnecessary force and sat smoking. He scowled. His eyes were a trifle glassy, the lids reddened. Faint shadows showed beneath the lower lids.

"The morning after the night before sits heavier on him than it used to," Rod thought cynically. "The pace is beginning to tell. Damn fool."

He resumed his reading.

The butler came in.

"The foreman of the Valdez camp and two men want to see you, sir," he addressed Phil.

"Send 'em here," Phil replied, without looking up.

Rod continued to read. There was nothing unusual in men from the camps coming to Hawk's Nest with complaints or for instructions. Disputes between men and logging bosses had been threshed out times without number in that pleasant, book-lined room. The Norquay policy had always been patriarchal.

Stagg ushered in Jim Handy and two men. One was Andy Hall. He nodded to Rod with a genial grin. Handy looked fretful. His short, white moustache stood out at the aggressive angle it always took when things went wrong. All three had shed their caulked boots and working garments. They wore their town clothes. Above clean white collars their faces were burned to the brown of weathered oak by summer sun and hot winds.

"I got a strike on my hands," Handy announced to Phil. "They want fifty cents a day raise all round. They want bathtubs. I expect maybe they want regular hotel waiters to sling hash for 'em, too," Handy permitted himself a logger's witticism. "These two guys represent the crew."

Phil turned to the loggers.

"Striking is rather a new kink in the logging business," he said casually. "If you don't like the job, why don't you quit?"

"Quitting wouldn't change things," Andy Hall replied. "You want to get out timber because it is profitable. We want to work because we have to work for somebody. But we would like better working conditions. Seems more reasonable to ask for 'em on the job than to quit the job."

"Are you two a self-appointed committee?" Phil inquired.

"No," Hall assured him. "We were picked by the crowd to act as spokesmen. A hundred and forty men can't all talk to a boss at once. You can take it for granted we speak for the entire crew."

"All right, we'll take it for granted," Phil returned. "Just step out into the hall for a minute or two. After I've had a word with Handy you can state your case."

"You're foolish to waste time discussing anything whatever with these fellows," Grove remarked, as the door closed on them. "I'd pay off the works and have a new crew sent up. The bird that spoke is too smooth-tongued for a logger. He's got agitator written all over him."

"Best high-rigger I ever saw," Jim Handy growled. "All loggers agitates now and then."

Phil paid no attention to his brother's comment. He addressed Handy.

"When did they pull this strike?"

"This mornin'. They chewed the fat till midnight in the bunkhouse. After breakfast not a man turned out. They wouldn't talk. They said these two would talk for 'em. I've told you what they want. Fifty cents a day raise. Six bathtubs."

"Bathtubs!" Grove snorted disdainfully.

"Short notice," Phil ruminated. "H'm. Have they been kicking?"

"Loggers always kicks," Handy grumbled. "They've been growlin' some. I've told 'em they always got the privilege of quittin'. I've fired three or four of the mouthy ones. When they all laid down at once, I reckoned I'd better put it up to you."

"What do you think about it yourself?" Phil asked him. "Can you get another crew together and go ahead?"

Handy shifted uneasily.

"I hear men's scarce in town," he said. "If I can dig up a crew, of course I can go ahead. But no pick-up crew will get out as much timber. Not for a month or two anyhow. Most of this bunch has been on the job since the camp opened."

"We're paying standard wages," Phil observed. "If it were left to you, Handy, would you give them the raise?"

"I don't know but I would," the logging boss brightened. "Cheapest. One or two of the big Island camps have tilted wages. This crew can sure get out timber. Breakin' in new men costs money."

"Just what have you told them?" Phil inquired. "If you haven't stirred them up, I may be able to talk them out of it."

Handy grinned.

"I was darn careful not to stir 'em up. I know loggers. I'm a logger myself. I didn't say much of anything. When I seen they was set, I just said, 'Well we'll put it up to headquarters. I hire and fire, but the owners sign the paycheques.'"

"All right. Send those two in as you go out," Phil said finally. "I'll see you down on the float after I get through."

Andy Hall and his companion entered.

"Tell me what you want," Phil said briefly, "and why you consider yourselves entitled to it."

"We ask for fifty cents a day raise for every outside worker on the job, from whistle-punks to hook-tenders," Wright voiced their demands. "We ask for you to put in at least half a dozen baths, tubs, or showers; showers would suit us best and they're easily installed. That's all."

"Why go on strike at snap notice? Phil complained. "Why didn't you ask for these things? Does it seem to you that the way to get your claims considered is to disorganize the work first and then make your demands?"

Wright motioned to Andy Hall.

"You tell him."

"Mr. Norquay," Hall began quietly, "if you'd ever worked as a logger in a logging camp you'd know that asking for changes doesn't bring them about. There are a hundred and forty men in your woods on Valdez. We are, if I say so myself, as *skookum* a logging crew as ever was got together on the B.C. coast. And we *have* been asking for these things. Jim Handy is your representative on the job. We haven't anything against old Jim. He's as fair as the average woods boss. But he has exactly the same idea as most employers — keep wages down and prices up — get all the work possible out of the men. His own job as foreman depends on getting results. For the last month every time anybody has tried to talk to him about wages or camp conditions, somebody has got fired. This particular crew is tired of a take-it-or-leave-it basis of employment. That's why there's a show-down. Neither of the things we ask for is unreasonable. It is unreasonable to fire a man for wanting to talk about his wages and the conditions under which he must live."

Phil eyed Andy Hall searchingly for a second or two. Grove had twisted sidewise in his chair and glared at the logger with visible displeasure.

"Let's take up the matter of the bathtubs," Phil resumed. "Why should we supply casual labour with baths when there is a running stream through the camp and the sea is at the door?"

Rod shifted in his seat. It sounded rather callous. He thought of the unction with which he had heard worthy people declare that cleanliness is next to godliness.

Andy shrugged his shoulders.

"I could easily justify bathing facilities on moral and sanitary grounds," he said impassively. "I'll simply put it this way. Most men prefer to be clean. If it's impossible for them to be reasonably clean, they'll be uncomfortable. A man who is uncomfortable gets discontented. A discontented workman is a poor investment. There are a hundred and forty men coming out of your woods every night, stinking with sweat and dust in the summer, plastered with mud in the winter. There is one shallow wooden trough with tin washbasins and a half-inch tap. We make shift with the creek and the salt-chuck in summer. But a man who has done ten hours' hard labour in the woods can't stand naked outdoors and bathe in cold weather."

"I never before heard of bathing as an issue in a logging camp." Phil smiled. "Well, we'll concede the bathing facilities. We'll agree to build a bathroom and install pipe showers with a hot-water supply."

"Now this raise in wages," he continued judicially, after a brief pause. "I really don't believe we can go that far. We're paying the standard wages — a fairly liberal scale, it seems to me. I suggest that you go back and get the crew out to work on the understanding that we'll adjust this claim for wages between now and next payday. This strike is too much in the nature of a holdup. Wage questions can't be settled offhand. Don't you think that would be the most amiable way of ending the tie-up? The shower-bath matter will be attended to at once."

Andy Hall shook his head.

"I'd like to be polite and agreeable," he said. "But I'm not acting for myself as an individual, you must remember. The men threshed this out pretty well before they took action. They won't move a stick unless they get this raise. They've tried to talk to Handy, and Jim simply grinned and fired the men who insisted on talking. The point is this. There is no such thing as a standard wage in the logging industry. You are paying as much as most camps, more than some, less than others. The International, on Vancouver Island, employing over four hundred men, is paying what we ask. So are two or three smaller concerns."

"And," Hall continued without heat, as deliberate as if he were intoning a column of figures, "we are working under a foreman who is a driver. That's nothing against Jim Handy. We're not sore on him. A logging boss holds a boss's job by virtue of ability to get out logs. But old Jim keeps a crew on its toes. If a man isn't up and coming, he doesn't work long for Handy. We're putting more timber per man per day into the booming ground than any crew on the coast."

"How do you know that?" Phil demanded sharply.

"We have made it our business to find out," Hall answered imperturbably. "You know it's so — if you keep tab on your business. That's why we want more money. We're earning it. We're entitled to it."

"And," Wright put in, "if we don't get it, we're through. Nobody wants to work on a job where he knows he's getting too much the worst of the deal."

"We can, I suppose you know, pay you all off and get another crew," Phil reminded.

"And we can get other jobs," Hall replied unruffled. "But we'd both be losers. No, that wouldn't benefit either party to this dispute. You have a reputation for being fair, as fairness is reckoned in logging camps. That's why you have efficient crews and a minimum of labour trouble. We know we are entitled to what we ask. If we don't get it, we'll be good and sure it isn't a question of the Norquay Estate being unable to pay such wages and still show a profit. We'll know the refusal is purely on the grounds of policy. And if a logger's frank opinion is anything to you, you'll find it damned poor policy."

Phil sat tapping his pencil on the desk, smiling a little to himself.

"Go down to the landing and wait for me there," he said. "I'll give you a definite answer inside of half an hour."

The door closed on the two loggers. The three brothers looked at each other.

"Cattle!" Grove broke out with quite unnecessary heat. "A mob like that attempting to dictate to us."

"I'd hardly call two men a mob," Phil commented dryly. "It is scarcely dictating for men to state the conditions under which they are willing to work."

"Are you going to let them stick you up like that?" Grove demanded unpleasantly.

"Your way of putting it is offensive, but I know what you mean," Phil maintained his placidity. "I rather think I shall. I'm considering. We can certainly afford to give them a raise. Handy is a driver. He does get out —

"It isn't a question of affording it," Grove broke in. "It's a question of principle. You simply cannot afford to allow a crew of dissatisfied loggers to imagine for a minute that they can tell you how you're to run your business."

"Handy, as I said," Phil went on unheeding, "does get out timber."

"You mean," Rod supplemented, on the spur of an impulse, "he has the faculty of keeping a crew going at top speed, and they get out timber. Well, I can vouch for that, after twelve months under him. If these fellows were paid on the basis of production, they'd get bigger wages than they're asking. I made some calculations myself from time to time before I left the camp. Hall's figures are conservative. I got cost figures from the town office and reckoned the output. That Valdez camp for six months straight put out twenty percent more timber per man than Hardwicke Island. I suppose you know that?"

Phil nodded.

"That high-rigger is almost too clever to be a logger," he observed. "Know anything about him, Rod? Notice the beggar's language? Most reasoned and unemotional presentment of a case I ever heard a logger make."

"He's a good man on the job. He has been there since the camp opened." Rod prudently refrained from mentioning Andy's economic heresies. He liked Andy Hall and he foresaw Andy marked as an "agitator," that abused term which once tagged to a working man makes him anathema to most employers. "In fact, I'd say old Jim has a crew it would be a pity to break up — if getting out timber efficiently is any object — for so small a matter as fifty cents a day and bathtubs."

"They never bathe," Grove sneered. "They don't look as if they did. I never got close enough to smell 'em, but I suppose they don't mind it themselves."

Rod sat silent. It struck him that Grove was thrusting at him. And it struck him, too, how little either of his brothers knew about the men they were discussing. They didn't discuss them as men, so much as material — a commodity, a necessary part of the producing machinery which had the inconvenient quality of voicing its wants. As if a donkey engine should protest against an overload. Rod himself had got under the logger's skin. He would never be able to think of them except as men, to deal with them otherwise. They had their vices and virtues, but they were not impersonal machines. He could not impart this knowledge, convey such an attitude and feeling, to his brothers.

"First time I ever heard 'em kicking for baths," Phil grinned. "Did you start a movement for cleanliness while you were among them, Rod?"

"It wasn't necessary," Rod assured him. "Most loggers like to be clean if there's a chance. I bathed in the creek like the rest. I've scrubbed myself off in a hand-basin in the winter. I didn't think much of the inconvenience. I suppose because I knew I could get away from it any time I wanted to. They can't. I'm for plenty of baths, in every camp we run. It's only common decency."

"That's simple. I expect, on the whole, we'd better give them what they ask without quibbling. I've always found it pays to keep 'em reasonably satisfied."

"You'd better consult the governor before you commit yourself," Grove said meaningly. "I'm opposed to it myself."

"My dearest elder brother," Phil shot back instantly with exaggerated, icy politeness, "when you elected to pursue a career in finance, the direction of the timber operations of the Norquay Estate devolved on me. So long as I have the authority I shall use my *own* judgment. Yours not to reason why — yours but to reap the profits that accrue. You try putting your fingers in this pie and you'll get them pinched. Do you get me?

"You know," he went on sarcastically, after a brief silence, in which Grove's face reddened perceptibly, "you really aren't in any condition to give an impartial opinion on anything so early this morning. Too heavy a hangover. Too many cocktails. Too much of a muchness. You can't stand the pace the way you used to. You come out of your morning bath grouching instead of singing. So leave the loggers and logging to me. I have about decided to concede them both points."

"*I* would," Rod impulsively put himself on record. "Not only as a matter of policy, but as a matter of simple justice."

"Oh, you," Grove turned on him. In his voice repressed fury and utter contempt seemed to struggle for mastery. "One would naturally expect *you* to support any extravagant claim from such a source. You fraternized with them. No doubt you find yourself quite comfortable on terms of equality with them. Particularly since you went the length of picking up a wife from among them. I have had about —"

Rod got to his feet. Something in his face cut short Grove's sentence.

"What you've had is not a patch to what you'll get," Rod said. "You yellow dog!"

The open palm of his hand popped with a dull smacking sound on his brother's mouth.

But characterizing a man as a yellow dog does not necessarily make him one. Grove spat out the crushed cigar and bitter ashes and lunged at Rod. He missed. While he was off balance, Rod knocked him down.

He rose, stood one hesitant moment, hands up like a boxer, head hunched between his shoulders. But when he rushed it was not to strike, only to grasp.

"Don't let him get hold of you," Phil warned sharply.

Rod didn't need the warning. He knew Grove's strength, was aware of his purpose. In school, Grove had been a hammer thrower, a putter of the shot. He had never been beaten at his weight as a wrestler. And though he was ten years past those athletics, he was dangerous still at grips. Rod twisted aside, evaded his reach, struck and dodged, struck and dodged again, quick sharp punishing blows that jerked Grove's hands defensively up to guard his face. When he did that, Rod put all his weight into a blow that would have ended the scrimmage if it had reached Grove's jaw. It was deflected by his forearm, smashed his ear. But it staggered him against a bookcase so that broken glass fell with a tinkle. Rod followed up his advantage, and Grove went down again.

Phil had his back against the door.

"It's locked," he announced calmly, in the brief time it took Grove to rise. "May the best man win."

"The best man *will* win," Rod panted.

He tingled. A fine exultant feeling that he dealt justice in the only adequate manner uplifted him. He had seldom fought in the twenty-three years of his existence. He had never imagined it would give him so keen a satisfaction to knock a man down. Yet it didn't surprise him. He knew in that moment that for years he had been longing to punish Grove as he intended to punish him now. Even in that stress of passion his brain, the rational, critical part of him, found time to wonder why so brutal an action seemed so eminently fit, so natural, such a pleasure.

Grove came at him again, striking wild, blood trickling from his mouth, from his nostrils. In the shift and exchange he trapped Rod against a heavy chair. They grappled, went to the floor with a crash. Grove's arm pinned him by the neck. Rod felt the other seeking a crotch hold. He made a violent effort, broke loose, thrust himself clear, bounded to his feet.

He had matched strength for strength and beaten Grove at his own strong man's game. There was a thrill in that. He could break any hold Grove could put on him. When he realized that, he dropped all defence. He crowded within the scope of Grove's arms and struck as hard and quickly as he could drive his arms, fists thudding against Grove's body, over his heart, on his face — until Grove's legs buckled under him and he sank on all fours.

Rod stepped back, dropped his hands.

"Enough?" he asked briefly.

Grove nodded, voiceless. His face was an unsightly mess.

And as Rod opened his mouth to speak further, the library door rattled, an imperative knock sounded. The voice of Norquay senior demanded testily to know why the door was locked. Phil flashed a look of mild dismay at Rod and turned the key. Their father walked in.

CHAPTER XVI

FROM A FOLDING CHAIR on the afterdeck of the *Haida* Rod looked back at Hawk's Nest. The cruiser's screw churned up bubbles and foam astern. Dent Island and the grey stone house with its red roof, the pale green of grass and the duskier hue of the woods behind were receding fast. They vanished altogether as they rounded the Gillard light and stood away south.

"I was born there," Rod said simply. "I never went home but I was glad to be there. I never left it before without being sorry to go."

"Aren't you sorry now?" Mary asked.

"No. Are you?"

"No," she said frankly. "It was lovely — it *is* lovely. Everybody was good to me. I was quite happy there until —"

"Precisely. It's Grove's bailiwick when it comes to a show-down. That being so, it's no place for us. I'm glad to be on the wing. I'd rather paddle my own canoe than be a guest on somebody's ship. It won't perhaps be quite so pleasant for you, old thing."

"The only unpleasantness I dread," Mary rejoined, "is your beginning to wonder if it was worthwhile, after all. A lot of people aren't going to be able to see me with a microscope, Rod. You don't seem to get that yet. I can't play the game the way they do. They're so chesty and cocksure. All their lives they've lived well, dressed well, gone where they chose with perfect assurance, accepted by their equals and deferred to by their inferiors. They have me at a disadvantage. I don't speak their favorite shibboleths, or see life from the same angle. I'm not sure," she hesitated wistfully, "that I will ever want to. But it would be dreadful if you found that you were being severely penalized for marrying out of your class, as they probably put it. That's the only thing I have any reason to dread. All the other possibilities," she made a quick inclusive gesture, "being poor, making the most of a little, longing for the unattainable, a great effort for a few simple pleasures — I know them all. They aren't so very terrible. They don't frighten me. But for you, because of me, to cut loose from everything and every one that has made up your life and then begin to chafe under it — that does."

Rod glanced over his shoulder. The deck was empty. He put one arm around her, shook her gently.

"I'll pull some caveman stuff on you," he threatened tenderly, "if I ever hear you talk like that again. In the first place, you mean more to me than anything or anybody. In the second place, nobody is going to penalize me. They won't try. There's no real reason they should. You'll see. While the governor is horribly annoyed about what he calls a disgraceful quarrel, he doesn't even dream of blaming you. He lays it to his sons' fiery tempers and shameful lack of self-control. He'll cool off. And having known you, he'd never dream of following Grove's lead. I know him. He's fair. If we should happen to live in Vancouver this winter, and we care to go out, you'll see that most of these high-flying friends of Grove's will conveniently forget, and be very nice to us — because we are what we are. There are enough people of some consequence to accept us as such and the rest will follow suit. Oh, I know them. They're just like sheep. That's a side issue. It can't make any difference to us."

Mary snuggled her hand in his.

"I hope not," she murmured.

"It can't," he declared. "It wouldn't make much difference if it worked out the other way. No," he grew reflective, "I'm like you. I don't see things from the same angle as most of the sleek, comfortably insulated people I know, nor do I want to. I want to know where I'm going, and *why.* It isn't just enough to eat, drink and be merry. I'm lucky in a material way, perhaps. I happened to be well-born, and I've had security wrapped about me like a blanket. Still, I doubt the value and permanence of a lot of things that many people — my own people included — take for granted. I run true to form, just as Grove does. Only I think his form is rotten. That's why we don't hitch. I know we should have come to an open break sometime, if you had never been a factor. I despise him because he is what he is and does what he does. And he hates me, because he's impressionable enough to feel that contempt. Anybody or anything that Grove can't dominate he dislikes. You know, I have a fancy that he sometimes feels he's shoddy, and tries to bolster himself up with the high-and-mighty pose. But after all that doesn't matter, either. I'm what I am and I shouldn't be cocky about it, I suppose."

Rod sat silent, recalling that scene in the library. All the hot anger had evaporated long ago. He was not sorry. No. But he was sobered. It had given him food for thought. His mind was so made that it fed upon, digested for good or evil, every crisis, each outstanding event, the significance of whatever stirred him deeply. Certain phases of a conversation with his father kept recurring to him. Certain things had been said — some calmly enough — some with a touch of passion. Rod thought again with impatience that his father had a blind spot where Grove was concerned. But it didn't matter much now. He had taken the only reasonable course open to him after that encounter with Grove, the simplest, most dignified solution. He could not remain at Hawk's Nest and preserve peace and dignity. He recognized that there lurked in him an eagerness to clash with Grove on almost any provocation. They were fundamentally antagonistic; they had always been. The gulf between them grew wider as they matured; the deep-rooted distrust and dislike of motive and action became more profound.

"It's as well the break came," he said aloud. "It was bound to come over something. I've simply been marking time. Now I can do — whatever I *can* do. Both of us. We don't have to follow copy any more. We can make our own copy. I rather like the idea."

"It sounds good to me," Mary said gayly. And they smiled in understanding.

"For the first time in my life I feel like a free man," Rod said abruptly. "Isn't that queer? Free in the sense that I am absolutely at liberty to work out my own destiny, insofar as any man can do that."

Phil came up from below. He sat on the low cabin roof, dangling his long legs.

"Well, children," he said cheerfully, "what's your program? Going to stay in town awhile?"

"Not long," Rod answered. "We're going to resume our interrupted honeymoon. For a month or so. After that — well, I'm not making any cast-iron plans."

"When you get ready to do something, let me know," Phil remarked. "This blow-up has sort of opened my eyes. It made me realize that our family solidarity is badly shot. Grove feels his oats more and more. If I weren't more or less passive, and if I didn't get a certain amount of satisfaction out of carrying on the show — and there's the governor to consider; he *is* a good sort — I'd quit. I may have to by and by. I won't stand interference. If I have to drop the reins, I'd like to take a whirl at something that might grow. We could make a go of it in timber, I think. We both know our ground there. I've got some money put aside. Think it over, Rod."

"I surely will. Only, as I said, I've no cast-iron plan. If you want to make money, why not try finance? *À la* Grove. That seems to be gorgeously productive."

"Finance. Huh!" Phil snorted. "I'd rather play poker. I don't want so much to get something as to *do* something."

"Andy Hall said to me once that the fundamental principle of modern business is to do everybody and do 'em first," Rod drawled. "That ought to give you scope enough."

They laughed. It was a quaint notion. As such it amused them.

Rod's expressed intention of resuming their honeymoon was based on an impulse with which, when he defined it, he found Mary in complete accord. She was no echo. So that with her interest assured he proceeded to act.

A week later they disembarked from a coastwise steamer on a float landing before a logging camp halfway up Bute Inlet. They had doubled on their course and come back to a point within thirty miles of Hawk's Nest to go on a voyage of exploration and discovery, as Rod whimsically defined their object. It was indeed a whim, based soundly on appreciation of natural beauty, of dusky still forests, of the sound of running water, the indefinable charm of wooded loveliness in which they could move untrammelled together, that had brought them here with a sturdy rowboat, a tent and bedding, fishing tackle and a supply of food. Campfires and wood smoke at twilight amid these cathedral stillnesses that filled the untouched forest. This was what they desired, for the time.

A fisherman's motor boat carried them across the inlet for a sum, towing their loaded skiff astern.

"That's the place." Rod pointed. "Let us off here."

The fisherman chugged away. They sat in the boat, oars in hand, gazing up at cliffy slopes where the forest opened about mossy knolls, where ledges of bare rock barred the hillside, rising up and up from a short reach of gravelly shore where tiny wavelets broke at spaced intervals. The inlet ran northwest, curved away among high mountains. Far above and on either side of this great arm of the sea, low hills rose to cliffs, cliffs ran up to precipices, and a jumble of cliff, gorge, precipice, and virgin forest lifted far above to high, aloof peaks, domed with snow and studded with glaciers. The afternoon wind was but a sigh. All that sweep of sea and mountain range brooded in the sun as voiceless and changeless as when the first Norquay sailed the *Hermes* to Dent Island more than a century before.

"This is something like, eh?" Rod murmured.

Mary nodded. "It makes me *feel*," she said. "I can't quite express it. I might if I had wings."

"I have a feeling too," Rod confessed. "But it's mostly one of emptiness in my tummy. Let's get ashore and make a pot of tea. The Hiding Place is just around the corner. Give way, men! I'll show you a sight."

They turned a jutting point and met a slow outsetting current. Against this Rod made his way straight for a cliff which, as they drew near, opened like a great window chiselled in solid granite. Through this the stream flowed, sluggish, deep, a pale-green translucence between high, damp walls. Somewhere within rose the monotone of a waterfall. The square framed broad-leaved maple tops. Higher up the pointed crests of cedar and the tufted plumes of fir stood sharp against the sky.

They rowed into the cleft, worked upstream between high, flood-scoured walls. In that chasm the sun touched only for an hour at noon. It was dark and cool. Mosses and maidenhair fern lightened black crevices with streaks and clusters of green. There was a beauty about this gloomy cleft floored with liquid emerald, but it was not a beauty one wished to embrace or linger with too long — too cavernous, a little grim. Mary drew closer to Rod in that hundred-yard passage. But she clapped her hands when the boat drew clear. They came out into sunlight. They had passed through the canyon as if it were a door which led to a tiny flat cupped in the hills, all clear of dense forest, almost free from thickets, clothed with bracken. The creek wimpled between low, gravelly banks. Between two maples on one side stood a small cabin of split cedar. Fireweed lifted blazing heads in a mass on one bank. A small grassy plot surrounded the cabin and the two trees. Rod sidled the boat in to the bank.

"Isn't this some little retreat?" he asked. "I came in here once long ago when we were cruising up the Inlet. Only had half an hour or so to spare. The crowd was in a hurry. I've always wanted to come back and camp awhile. This creek comes out of a lake in the woods about two miles inland. They say it's a gem. A trapper built the cabin. He's supposed to have made a blazed line to the lake."

"Lovely, lovely," his wife murmured. "And this country of ours has so many of these beauty spots. Sometimes I think we were so fortunate to be born here, Rod. If one could paint this. If one were a combination of Corot and Turner."

"Maybe one is," Rod commented genially. "How do we know what we can do? We've never had a chance to try. But you'd have to splash this 'on a seven-league canvas with brushes of comet's hair.' There are some things man can't reduce to his own dimensions; can't reproduce in miniature. How could you get the effect of this? Lofty heights. Sweeping distances. Big forests of big trees. It's all too — too superlative. Nature was in the mood for a grand gesture when she fashioned this part of the world, Mary mine."

They made camp under the maples after a look at the mouldy cabin interior. The stars came out to speckle a cloudless sky as they sat over their evening fire. Before they turned into blankets spread on a layer of fern and hemlock boughs, a moon sailed up from behind the Coast range. It touched all the hills with a silver glow, filled every hollow with ebony shade. They fell asleep to the lullaby of falling water and wakened with the sun on their faces.

They had no definite object beyond an impulse to be alone, to live awhile in those peaceful solitudes, to fish or loaf or climb as the spirit moved them. But that eagerness of spirit which has sent men alike to the Poles and into equatorial jungles to look on the face of new lands touched them both. They spent a day setting their camp to rights after the fashion of the woodwise. Then they sought and found the trapper's blazed line. It led them by dim marks through dense thickets, across lowlands where cedars stood like brown columns supporting the sky itself, their feet planted in thick mosses and sunless shade, over fir-clad ridges where a west wind made a faint sighing among branches a hundred feet above their heads, and brought them at last out on the shore of the lake.

The numerous lakes bordering close on the heavily wooded, mountainous coast of British Columbia have two characteristic features. They lie in granite pockets with steep-to, rocky shores. Or they spread in low basins shrouded in dense forest, and the margins of such lakes are a marshy jungle. In either case they are difficult of approach. One must clamber over jagged rocks, or work up through crabapple, devil's club, and sedgy grass.

The Granite Pool on Valdez was one exception. This nameless lake proved another. Rod and Mary came to it through a heavy stand of cedar, massive old trees which had killed all the lesser growth in their centuries of possession. No sapling grew there, or bush or fern or vine.

The level ground was carpeted with moss, which alone could thrive in that sunless place. Over this soft footing Rod and his wife walked by the little creek, flowing with faint murmurs in its bed of worn pebbles, till they stepped suddenly out of that semi-gloom into the brightness of open water rippling in the sun.

A low, gravelly beach at their feet; wooded points jutting into the lake; an island lifting a green mound of trees a little distance offshore; the lake itself bending away out of sight behind the base of a great mountain five miles distant — this they saw.

"You never know what you're going to find back in these hills." Rod sat down on the gravel. "Let's sit and look. It's worth a look."

"If we just had a boat up here," Mary observed, after a little.

"We'll have one," Rod answered promptly. "I have an axe. There are plenty of cedars. I can make a dugout of some sort in three or four days. Let's move camp up here. There'll be trout umpty-inches long in here, and I would like to see what's behind that mountain. We'll certainly explore *this*."

He made good his word, in sweat and strain. It was not a light task to shoulder-pack their food, bedding and tent over that pathless two miles. Nor was the shaping of a rude canoe from a cedar log and the hollowing of it by axe and fire so easy and simple as it seemed. But they accomplished these things. And having done so, they viewed their works with sinful pride, blessing the wilderness for what it bestowed upon them.

They meant to stay two or three weeks. Their food was reckoned on that basis. But they had been liberal in their estimate of supplies. There were trout in lake and stream. The blue grouse hooted on every hillside, and when they wanted meat they hunted these toothsome birds. Three weeks lengthened to four, to five — six. It became an amiable contest, a matter of achievement, to see how long they could live off the wilderness. They were completely happy there. It was as if some invisible barrier stood between them and the world of their fellows, where griefs and pains and irritations, hopes and fears and joys and ambitions ran their course. They did not know what went on beyond the rampart of their seclusion. And they did not care. They were too absorbed in what each day might bring forth as it passed. They experienced deep, ecstatic satisfactions in the simplest things. Rod began to work on his book again, in the intervals of hunting, fishing, exploring. He would lift his head, stirred out of concentration on imaginary things, at the sound of Mary singing as she moved about certain tasks. And he would smile. It was good; it was what he wanted. Peace to dream, to catch and transfix incident, character, a colourful background for heroic undertakings, as they mysteriously took form in his brain. To love and be loved; to get something more out of life than just a leisurely existence; to create something of worth above the measure of money.

He was aware that this was just an interlude. They would have to go back to the business of living along more conventional lines. They were both too much the normal product of society even to wish complete withdrawal from their kind. That would only be an evasion. But it was an experience they found to their liking. They promised themselves to repeat it often.

"We're barbarians at heart," Mary said once. "Our so-called culture is only skin-deep. Otherwise we couldn't sit over a campfire and be content. Nor lie in the sun on a mossy rock and feel that blissful sense of complete well-being. People with instincts like those should survive more or less complacently almost anything but loss of freedom. What do shops and streetcars, cities and frontiers mean to us here?" She waved a hand at the ring of mountains, the enclosing forest. "People handicap themselves when they grow too civilized."

"I wonder if they do?" Rod mused. "Perhaps. I know people who would be very uncomfortable here — where we have been quite at our ease. It seems to be instinctive with us. We get quite a kick out of it too. Maybe we're throwbacks. Why shouldn't hereditary impressions crop out?"

"Maybe," Mary said reflectively. "By all accounts Roderick the first was a man who didn't mind long journeys or isolation. He must have felt at home here, or he wouldn't have made his home in a savage country. Certainly it wasn't compulsory with him. You don't have to throw back very far, Rod, to the self-sufficient type."

"And my people," she continued presently. "They were originally

New York — upstate, not Manhattan — before the Boston Tea Party. Then they went across the Alleghenies. Then they went to Illinois. Then to Minnesota. Both my grandfathers fought in the Civil War. When they came back from that, Minnesota was too crowded for them. With half a dozen other families they trekked across the plains — in '67. They drove their stakes in southern Idaho on the banks of the Snake. Always restless. Always striking out into new territory. Wanting elbow room. Determined to have it. Never taking root for more than one generation. They went into virgin country with their cattle and horses, their tools and rifles, and made homes where there had never been homes. They didn't get rich, but they were always independent, always competent to fend for themselves. Why shouldn't we have an instinct for this, Rod? It's in our blood."

"Well, we'll do it again," Rod prophesied. "This is a good retreat. We'll come back."

With that as a mark to shoot at when summer came again, they left the Hiding Place one cool September morning. By the coasting schedule Rod knew a steamer should touch at the logging camp across the inlet that afternoon. They were leaving reluctantly. Their supplies had stretched to the elastic limit, but the limit had been reached. Time had accelerated his pace. It seemed but yesterday that they had come, in burning July. Now the mornings were touched with autumn chill. The vine maples showed glints of russet, streaks of burnished copper. The alders were growing yellow. Frost touched the leaves at night. New snow had fallen on the high peaks. Rain threatened. It was time to go.

They rowed across the inlet and tied up to the logger's landing. Two men worked on the floating logs, making up a tow. Far in the woods, in a deep valley, they could hear the toot of donkey engines. A train rumbled out on a trestle, dumped five cars of logs with a terrific splash. A clutter of raw, unpainted buildings stood about the shore end of the trestle.

"I'll go see if the storekeeper knows what time the steamer's due," Rod said. "May be able to get a newspaper. Funny. So long as we were in there, I never thought about papers. Old habits revive."

He walked the trestle ashore, disappeared among the buildings.

Presently he came into view again, walking slowly, an opened news sheet in his hands, reading as he stepped from timber to timber. Midway, still two hundred yards from the float, he sat down on an abutting platform, and remained there, the paper before his face, until the minutes lengthened to half an hour and Mary grew impatient.

She left the float. She neared her husband without him giving a sign, so deep was his absorption. He only looked up when she spoke. There was a strange bewilderment on his face, a look of mingled anger and incredulity.

"Why, Rod," she exclaimed. "What is it?"

He thrust another paper at her.

"Read," he said. "The world's gone crazy. There's a war. There's been war in Europe since early August. And we're in it up to our necks. Read."

CHAPTER XVII

THEY SAT SIDE BY SIDE in the autumn sunshine, reading of places drenched with blood — Liege, Louvain, Charleroi, Mons, Cambrai, Namur. The battle of the Marne was over. The prolonged battle of the Aisne was at its height. Rod had commandeered every paper in the camp. Page by page, column by column, they conned that incredible account, piecing it out by inference, filling the terrible gaps by vivid conjecture. There remained the primal fact that all Europe was in arms, that men perished by thousands daily, that their own countrymen were crossing the seas to fight.

"Phil's gone," Rod broke a long silence. "Says so here. He left for Valcartier the other day."

He looked out over the inlet's benign face.

"He'd do that," he said absently. "They'd give him a command at once. He's trained — went to Kingston."

He sat with hands clasped over his knees, silent, absent-eyed. And

Mary looked at him with a catch in her throat, filled with intuitive foreboding. Words, of which each had a better command than falls to most, failed them. They sat there wandering in the maze of their own thoughts until the shrill whistle of the approaching steamer woke an echo in the hills.

A day and a night on this slow-footed vessel brought them to Vancouver. They passed through the Narrows at dusk, cleared Brockton Point and stood up to the dusky wharves ranged below a vast haze of reflected light. Roof signs twinkled in all the coloured extravagance electrical sign experts could devise. Looming high on a square office building stood Grove's heraldry:

THE NORQUAY TRUST

Rod's upper lip drew in a curl. He could not exactly say why. It was involuntary, instinctive. That sign offended him. The taxi that wheeled them to the Vancouver Hotel passed the place, and Rod's lip curled again at sight of the chaste illumination upon richly polished mahogany revealed through immense windows of plate glass. Again in their room that curious distaste for his brother's works came over him at an advertisement of the Norquay Trust Company in one of the evening papers he bought. It ran thusly:

Your country calls you. Before you go overseas
put your affairs in the capable hands of

THE NORQUAY TRUST COMPANY

Then he turned to the war news.

Wherever he went in the city for the next two days the war topic hovered on men's lips. The streets wore the panoply of war in the recruiting aspect. Troops drilled in parks, on playgrounds. Bands marched abroad to stir men's blood. There was an edge of expectancy in the air, for the *Leipzig*, the *Dresden*, the *Nuremberg*, and two unknown battleships were loose in the Pacific. No one knew what truth lay in the rumour that any hour might see their shells dropping in the downtown section. There was nothing to stop them. They out-steamed and outgunned any British squadron in those waters.

Amid this ferment Rod walked the streets, bodily restless, uneasy in his mind. For he had somehow none of the illusions about war that carried many a young man lightly along the line of least resistance in those hectic days. There was no glamour for him in a purely military adventure.

He loved his native country. He was proud of it. It had bestowed upon him a splendid heritage. He did not question a matter of duty. With his temperament and traditions such a questioning was impossible. But he revolted against being a pawn in the European game. He could not muster up an excited, voluble hate of the enemy. He did not respond so readily as some to the propaganda already loosed so effectively. He wondered a little at the execration and exhortation and invective that poured from the press, the pulpit, the fulminations from every public speaker, the vixenish resolutions of the women's societies. It was as if they were urging each other on to a task for which few had much stomach. It perplexed Rod. If one's country was at war, one must fight. That was plain to him as two plus two. Why should all these non-combatants lash themselves into such a fury over a European frontier, over the ancient feud between the Teuton and the Gaul? It amounted to this in his mind: we must fight because our statesmen have committed us to the task; but we will not whip the German by foaming at the mouth. That's childish.

He met Andy Hall the second day. Before the *Province* office on Hastings Street there was always a crowd reading the bulletins posted from time to time, studying the war map on which the positions of the opposing armies were kept up to date by little flag-headed pins. The curbstone Boards of Strategy functioned there. Knots of men held heated discussion, or stood silently digesting news. There was a sprinkling of the indifferent, the merely curious.

A man at Rod's elbow broke out:

"I'll go. Damn right I'll go — in the ranks of a regiment made up of bankers, bond owners, and politicians. But I don't see them breakin' their necks to sign up. Why should I? I never had nothin' but a job, and poor ones at that. I ain't goin' to fight just for a job."

"Maybe you'll fight for *that*?" a voice taunted — and with the words came the sound of a blow, and then a scuffle and oaths. Rod turned to look. The bystanders were parting two struggling men. Andy Hall's freckled face glowed genially beside him.

"Even in these times the dissenter is with us." Andy indicated the brawlers. "How are you?"

"So, so." Rod shook hands with the high-rigger. "Still working for us? How did the strike pan out?"

"Oh, they got what they asked. I got fired as soon as old Handy thought things had settled down. About two weeks later. I guess he was afraid I might rib them up to ask for something else." Andy smiled amiably.

"Oh, that was rotten," Rod sympathized.

"Fortunes of war," Hall observed lightly. "Don't do to criticize your master's methods; not if you make your criticism so effective that it costs them money. Then they say you're an agitator and they can you off the job. The working man is mostly a sheep. The bosses know that. When a fellow like me — who isn't a sheep, but who understands and pities the sheep — sets out to show 'em how to get better pasture, he either gets taken into the fold and becomes a minor boss or he gets outlawed. Perfectly simple. You must not disorganize a profitable industry by demanding better pay. Industry doesn't like that."

"What do you think of this fracas across the pond?" Rod changed the subject to one that was for him personally, at that moment, much more important.

"Come and have a drink, and I'll tell you," Andy suggested.

They walked west to the Strand bar. Rod looked at his companion as they stood ordering their liquor. The Strand was a far cry from the usual haunt of the logger. He flourished in what Andy called the "slave market" down on Cordova Street, a region of Semitic clothing stores, cheap hotels, employment agencies where the woodsmen flocked in hundreds, gathered in groups along the sidewalk, rioted in the bars, or sought a job with empty pockets.

And Andy Hall was a logger from his head to his heels. That was his trade, the only means of livelihood he ever practiced. But he did not look the typical logger now. Apparently he did not follow the average logger's cycle of a red-hot time in town as a reaction from intensive labour in the woods.

"This fracas interests me more than you'd think, maybe," Andy proceeded over his glass. "In the first place it was inevitable as the result of the constant extension of spheres of influence — which is merely a euphemism for control of certain markets. The world's getting too small for the competitive system. Commercial interests are bound to clash. Armies are the policemen of trade."

Rod smiled. It was not a new nor in any way revolutionary statement. He had heard the same interpretation of world affairs, more subtly expressed, in university classrooms.

"What's the navy?"

"The water patrol," Andy bantered.

> "'Oh, the liner she's a lady
>   An' she never looks nor 'eeds.
> The man o' war's 'er 'usband —'

"Out of the mouth of the greatest drum-beater in English letters I answer you."

"It's a wonder you aren't away," Hall changed his tone abruptly. "Your brother's gone. Or have you got better sense?"

"Sense? Is there any sense in a war?" Rod countered. "But we're in it. If fellows like me won't go, who will?"

"You've said something," Andy replied quietly. "Leaving aside the sordid causes of war, war itself is the most senseless pastime any nation can engage in. There's a confusion of sentiments, a queer mixture of anger and defiance, vindictive cravings for retaliation, and hatreds that civilized men should have outgrown. An ingrowing fever to see your own side win. Once the first gun pops, it doesn't seem to matter *why* — any more than it matters to two men scrapping what the scrap started over. What each wants is to whip the other. But this particular war — commerce is at the bottom of it. You know it. You're too wise not to know. Struggle for commercial supremacy has started every war since the Crusades, and a few of the dynastic rumpuses. This is a row over property rights, real or potential. And as a member of the propertied class you have a vital interest in it. The bird who started that fuss in front of the *Province* wasn't so far wrong. He has nothing to fight for — nothing worth fighting for. You have."

"From a purely material point of view, certainly," Rod answered. "But can't you see any more in it than that?"

"Should I?" Andy asked musingly. "Can there be an obligation of service to one's country without one's country assuming some obligation in return? And does one's country assume any obligation toward such men as me? If it does I don't know what it consists of. The man with nothing but his hands has few rights and no privileges. What does the casual worker, the completely propertyless man receive from his country that he should gladly cross the seas to die for it on foreign soil? Can you tell me? I don't think you can. In that sense one doesn't mean one's country geographically. These mountains we call ours will stand unchanged, the forests will grow, the rivers run to the sea, the salmon go up to the spawning grounds, the birds will mate and sing, whether we win or the Germans, or if both sides fight to the last man and the two races expire. So that really one's country means Bill Jones and Sam Smith and Jack Robinson — human society — the national unit. If Sam Smith, by skilful exercise of the acquisitive instinct, acquires ownership of the hills and the forest, and permits me and Bill Jones and Jack Robinson to work for him whenever he can profitably use our labour, and has no responsibility for our welfare at such times as he can't employ and pay us wages, why should we shoot and kill, and be ourselves shot and killed in defence of his hills and forests?

"That," Andy went on in his low, deliberate voice, "is one way of looking at it, one way of putting it. I'm what they call a common worker. So far as I know, my people have never been anything else but workers, tied to a job because they knew nothing else. I've never had anything but a job myself. I've dug up quite a lot of assorted facts and a variety of knowledge out of books between hours on the job. I've done quite a bit of thinking about what I've seen, and heard and read. Every dollar

I've ever had, the food I've eaten, the clothes on my back — since I was nine years old I've earned 'em all by sweat and aching flesh. By way of illustration I'll cite the fact — with no personal reflection, you understand — that the Norquay estate employed last year on its timber operations upward of three hundred men. The net profits for the year run over two hundred thousand dollars. That's what your country means to *you.* But that means nothing to *me.* I have only myself, my energy, the strength of my arms and a certain skill to sell. And you don't employ me because I'm hungry or need clothes, or because I'm ambitious to better *my* condition. Oh, no. You don't recognize me as having the slightest claim on you for subsistence. You will only hire me at a wage where my labour can be transformed into cash at a profit to yourself. In slack times I can starve. It doesn't make any difference to you. That attitude and practice is typical of the industrial system of every civilized nation. I present you with the case of the intelligent worker, when he analyzes his situation in and relation to society. I ask you if we, who are the have-nots, should be proud and glad — as they tell us we should be — to die for the perpetuation of this state of affairs?"

Rod had an uncomfortable impression of the perfectly ordered and smoothly moving world he knew being critically examined and condemned by a dispassionate, impartial, and very acute intelligence. As Andy Hall put it, there seemed no bond of common interest, of sentiment, even of common justice to bind them together. Andy did not ask on behalf of his class, nor of himself as an individual, "What is there in it for us?" He only asked in moody accents, "Why should we, who have only the shadow, sacrifice ourselves for those who have the substance?"

Only a sophist could make other than one reply. And Rod was no sophist. He was only an earnest and troubled youngster reacting to the day and hour, according to the best traditions of the best of his class. He felt that there was more to be said on the subject than a laconic answer to Andy's "why?" There *must* be, or his world was a sham, thriving on social usury, and patriotism was a farce. It did not seem to Rod this could be possible. But he could not voice the thing that was in him. It was an emotional certainty, not a reasoned conviction. And he knew that as an impulsion to act the first was by far the greatest driving force in all men.

"I don't know. A man — each man — must answer that for himself," he spluttered. "It's like this. We're all in the same boat. If everybody stands on his rights and demands a readjustment of a faulty arrangement of things before he will make a single defensive move — we'll be whipped out of hand. In fact, it looks as if the Germans had us staggering now. And I daresay two thirds of their armies are made up of the working class of Germany — who seem to be quite in accord with their masters' policy of conquest, or they wouldn't put up such a corking fight. If you fellows as a class refuse to meet them at their own game —" he threw out his hands in an eloquent gesture.

"Hell, you think I'm so thick-headed I can't see both sides of the fence?" Andy grunted. "I wasn't speaking for my own class. It's speaking for itself every day — to the recruiting sergeant. I'm speaking to you as a thinking, feeling individual who sees himself being sucked into a whirlpool. I'm trying to point out to you in the most rational manner possible what the *real* situation is. You can't deny it. It exists. Why, if the bulk, even a working majority of the damn fools that call themselves men, had a few glimmerings of social and economic wisdom there wouldn't be any German or French or Russian or British armies in the field. Only a few handfuls of atavistic adventurers. I'm not by nature a humble, peaceful toiler. I'd just as soon as not fight for anything that's worth fighting for — and all the hard fighting isn't done with guns, either. All my life I've seen the show run by arrogant, power-proud people who aren't nearly so clever as they seem to be. They make a mess of things too often to be really clever. And the rest of us growl and knuckle down to our jobs. We're slaves, not so much to our masters, as to our own inertia, our own lack of intelligence, slaves to the common, well-nourished illusion that to get something for nothing is the solution for all our difficulties. We merit contempt. No one among the well-fed and the cultured who have never soiled their hands with common work has more impatience with the bovine mass than some of us who are of the mass. We lose faith in ourselves and our own kind — but our masters never lose faith in us — in our docility to fetch and carry. They know how to use us without our knowing how it's done. They tell us now that the Germans threaten our lives, our freedom, our country and its cherished institutions. That's true enough. But we risk our lives daily in industry with very much less freedom of choice in the matter than even primitive man had in pursuing his food, clothing, and shelter. What cherished institutions of ours are threatened that we should go five thousand miles to fight in a quarrel between Russians, Germans, and French?

"And still," Andy drummed on the polished bar with his fingertips, "in spite of my reasoned convictions I find myself as much of a herd animal as the rest. Logic tells me this row is the same old thing on a larger scale — an affair in which the have-nots will do the fighting as they do the work. But logic doesn't help me where I live, inside of me, when I see fellows I know, fellows I like, getting ready to go. The old tribal instincts that are stronger and deeper than civilization and industry keep stirring up in me, nagging at me. The flag — it's only a symbol. Patriotism, patriotic duty has only a hollow sound when I hear the phrase used. And still — something gets me — I don't know quite what it is but it's there.

"It's a queer pass for me to come to," he finished whimsically. "Wouldn't it be? Me to go and fight for things and people that I don't believe in? Why should a man find his rational conclusions upset by an emotion he can't define? I stood looking at the Gulf the other day, and I thought how easy it would be for those German cruisers that are reported off the west coast to start slinging shells in here. And the picture of 'em potting at us made me sort of swell up and get all hot and angry inside. It's illogical and and absurd for me to feel that way about what's going on in Europe. And still — there it is. Some of these days I'll find myself in the army headed overseas. And I'll be wondering how in hell I got there. How, I ask you, can a man who thinks as I do, *feel* the way I do, about this?"

But that was as difficult to answer as Andy's other question — and Rod was too deeply involved in a personal problem of his own, a conflict between two powerful sets of feelings, to consider Andy's psychological *impasse.* They had another drink and went about their separate affairs.

For another forty-eight hours Rod stirred uneasily about the town. He met his father by chance, talked with him briefly. He spent a little time each day in one or the other of two clubs in which he held membership. He and Mary went once to dinner at the home of a classmate, married now and frankly unsettled by the war cloud. He met other young men he knew. He missed a great many others, but he knew where they were. He heard the one thing discussed in clubs, in hotels, on the streets. People lived the war in public and private. Rod wondered if they dreamed about it in their sleep, as he sometimes did.

Between himself and Mary a singular constraint had arisen. It was as if some impalpable substance enfolded them, sealing their lips upon things they both felt and feared but could not embody in speech. Where the unspoken thought had scarcely needed words, so perfect an accord of mind had they attained, now each was locked in a separate chamber of his soul, brooding inscrutably, wordlessly even when they sat knee to knee by their room window or lay wide-eyed in the night, flesh touching flesh, mute in the face of an ache to speak and be understood.

Rod came in one evening after dusk. Mary had begun to dress for dinner. She sat on the edge of their bed, hair down, a silver slipper hanging idly from one hand. She looked at Rod when he came in, a silent question, almost an appeal, and then her eyes dropped to the floor.

"Dorothy is over from Victoria," she said tonelessly. "She telephoned half an hour ago. Charlie has been offered a commission. She's planning to go east with him and later across to London."

Rod sat down beside her, put his arms about her. His fingers stroked her thick, soft hair.

"I have to go," he said quietly. "I've hammered it out for myself. I can't keep out of it."

She laid her face against his breast. Her arms pressed tightly about him. A little shudder shook her.

"Oh, Rod, Rod," she whispered. "I can't bear it. I've seen it coming. We've just begun to live. And I'm going to have a baby."

He sat holding her close. She did not cry. She clung to him silently. The slow heave of her bosom, the occasional shiver, that desperate struggle for calmness, made him ache.

And he thought, with a slowly rising tide of bewilderment, of the wholly inadequate preparation that had been bestowed upon them for such a bitter sip of life's cup. For her a lonely childhood, an education frugally achieved, and marriage. For him eighteen years of a sheltered, tutored existence, four years of college, twelve months in a logging camp, three months of inconceivable happiness — and the war.

The Great War — which in five years was to bestow upon his country, at the price of many lives and outpoured treasure, such priceless victories as a scramble for oil and a squabble over debts!

CHAPTER XVIII

WHEN MEN WALK OFTEN in the shadow of death they rise superior to its dread aspect, or they become indifferent to it, or they succumb to its ghastly presence and welcome it as a relief from unendurable suspense. Upon these emotional reagents all the heroism and endurance and cowardice of humanity in war is based. And when the shouting and the tumult dies the survivors sometimes find themselves incredible of their survival in a world excitedly muttering the shibboleths of peace — peace, where there is only a truce. For the dumb clods, led or driven, and the high-spirited adventurers did not alone comprise the armies which the nations lately sent forth. Willy-nilly, by outward compulsion or inner sense of duty, the sensitive, the lovers of beauty, the humanitarian, the altruist, those strange souls to whom disorder is an evil, justice a passionately cherished dream, freedom the birthright of every man — they too wore khaki and were deafened by the guns.

Upon them, and they are no inconsiderable portion of this our country's manhood, the war has left its mark. Not so much in the scars on their bodies — for those are things men forget as easily as women forget the pangs of childbirth but in the more tenuous fabric of their souls, in the processes of their intellect. Many question the value of the ordeal — judged by its results.

It was a questioning of this nature that troubled Rod Norquay on an evening in January, A.D. 1919. He sat among civilians in a Canadian Pacific smoking car while the Imperial Limited rolled westward through a rainy night. He was on familiar ground again, the soil where five generations of his blood had been nourished. The Coast Range was far behind the train. On his right the Fraser River made a pale shimmer in the darkness, with here and there the glowworm running lights, the yellow window squares of a river boat. It was good to be back, back to life that could be lived fully and freely, not simply endured.

But it was not good for him, in those last homeward miles, to listen to the talk that ran in the smoker. It was pitched to the same key as had fretted him in Paris, in London, all the way across North America — boundaries, coal and iron, concessions, indemnities, reparations. Europe, Asia, and Africa, the islands of the Pacific, had been rearranged, parcelled out, in Rod's hearing in hotel lobbys, in ship saloons, in railway coaches, day after day, by sleek, middle-aged civilians, clever successful fellows who knew what was what. He was sick of it. Was that the reality behind the war to end war?

"Loot," he said to himself scornfully. "They can call it what they like, but that's what they mean."

In the field even Fritz shot his looters when he caught them red-handed. But in civil life, behind the rampart of a victorious army, they had their eye on the loot. They couldn't see much else that was worth consideration. This group in the smoker — he had been in the enforced physical intimacy of railway travel with them for four days. They had been a trifle backward about approaching this moody young man in a London-tailored uniform of the C.E.F. with three thin gold stripes on his sleeve. They had respected his reserved silence. But they had talked for his benefit. Short of stuffing his ears with cotton he could not avoid hearing. And they talked voluminously, sagely, on the political and economic aspects of the war, and the peace that was in the making. Rod grew to hate them. In his own mind he called them buzzards. Which is a measure of his state of mind, for he was naturally courteous and tolerant toward his fellow men.

He welcomed the dim turreted and domed outlines of Hastings Park. He recalled the mustering and drilling there, the housing of men by thousands in buildings designed for show cattle. By a curious association of ideas he reflected that many of those men had been butchered less mercifully than the stall-fed beeves once shown in those barn-like structures, every time a battalion went up the line, wherever bombing squadrons could locate trench or billet, whenever enemy field guns could get the range.

Well, it was over. As the train slowed into the eastern portion of the yards, creeping between the docks and the city, he had a momentary, fantastic impression of having passed through a vivid nightmare of four years' duration. Because all this was the same. The Europe he knew had been torn to pieces, disfigured to strange aspects. Here the North Vancouver ferries, the self-same vessels he had ridden on, were scurrying back and forth across the inlet, passing each other in midstream. Masts and funnels of deep-sea ships rose beside well-known docks. The rumble of downtown traffic; the chaste pyramidic roof of the Provincial Courthouse pricked out with ten thousand incandescent bulbs; the Moorish pile of the Vancouver Hotel; the white monolith of the Burns Block; the arching crown of the *World* Building, all these were adumbrated in the thin hovering haze of light reflected from a million windows, thousands of arc lights, batteries of electric signs. Here were things he knew, greeting his eyes as if he had been gone merely overnight.

He took a final stare, before the coach slid under the long platform roof, at one familiar, flamboyant sign:

THE NORQUAY TRUST

Letters of fire, six foot high. He had never been able to look at that glowing emblem of Grove's career without a touch of scorn. It had been the last thing his eyes marked from the rear of a departing troop train. That, like this, had been on a wet, windy night.

His lip curled now. But his physical inertia, his moroseness, that appallingly critical inturning of his mind, vanished with the final clutch of the brakes. Something flowed through him, warming him like strong brandy. He relinquished his bags to a porter, passed eagerly to the vestibule. He was no stray dog of war now, wistful and lonely. Through the car window he had caught a glimpse of Mary's face, upturned in the glare of a light. Beside her stood his father, a tall, erect figure in a belted overcoat — both smiling, expectant. This was something like! The old things, the things that mattered.

It was worth something to come home like this — to this — he thought as his wife's arms closed about his neck, and he cut off her glad, little cry with his lips. His father threw dignity, reserve, to the winds and pounded him on the back, while a score of familiar faces pressed about him and hands reached for his.

Then the reaction — the unmistakable warning from a body too greatly abused.

"Let's get home," he said to Mary. "I'm getting wobbly. Good night, everybody. See you all again soon." He waved to the welcoming group. "Come on. I have to move. I must."

Mary slipped one arm through his, peering up anxiously. Rod's face was white, strained, in the station glare.

"Never mind the bags. Well, we can tell a red-cap to send them out by an expressman," he muttered. "Give me your arm, pater."

"What is it, Rod?" Mary asked anxiously.

"Tell you later. Keep walking — slow. Can't talk. Walk."

His voice sounded dull and heavy. Three abreast they moved across the platform, stood a few seconds in an elevator, passed out over a tiled floor and between the high fluted columns of the main entrance, to a street where pools of water glistened, where the wet asphalt shone black, and the air was full of rain lines driving before a southeast gale. Norquay senior guided him through scurrying people bent under umbrellas.

"Here's the motor," he said.

"All right. Got my wind back now." Rod smiled.

"Been sick?" his father inquired solicitously.

"No. Just a temporary let-down after being more or less keyed up. You'll see lots of fellows coming home like that, soon. Something lets go now and then."

He lay back on the upholstering between them, happy to feel Mary's hand pressed warmly close in his. In a few minutes the machine turned in a short, curved driveway, stopped under a portico.

Norquay senior kept his seat.

"I'll see you tomorrow, Rod," he said. "Good night. Pleasant dreams to both of you."

The house was strange to Rod. He knew, of course, the street and number, but nothing more of the place where Mary had made her home for more than two years. He followed her into a living room where a fireplace glowed cheerfully, a simple, comfortable room. And they stood in the middle of it for a few seconds with their arms about each other, careless of their damp clothes, of Mary's hat tilted askew, of all but the fact that they were together after being long apart.

"Did you miss me?"

"Are you glad to be home?"

Needless questions. Fond and foolish questions. They laughed and stood apart, threw off their heavy coats. "Kid's asleep, of course," Rod said.

"Yes. Come, look."

She drew him through a short passage into a bedroom. A small tousled brown head rested on a pillow. One hand clutched a dilapidated woolly dog with luminous glass eyes, the other was thrown straight out on the white counterpane, the chubby fingers relaxed.

"How the little beggar has grown," Rod whispered. "He looks like you, Mary."

"Everybody says he's a perfect Norquay," she replied demurely. "So there you are."

"We've been very lucky," Rod said quietly. "If I'd known the situation was so critical at sea, I shouldn't have let you come home when you did. The place you had in Chelsea — I went out to see it before I left — for old times' sake. I hadn't been there since you came home. There's a new house — at least, the upper storey's all new. I made inquiries. A

Gotha dropped high explosives on it about six weeks after you left."

Mary shuddered.

"Well, it's over," she murmured. "I cried all Armistice night after the joy-whoopings. Silly thing for me to do. Everybody here went mad. Where were you?"

"Mopping up," he said grimly. "We didn't believe it at first. Then we sat down and smoked cigarettes and drank tea, and wondered how soon we could get home. God damn the war — and the war-makers!"

His voice choked with passion.

"Ss-sh, Rod," she warned, and drew him out of the room, back to a chair by the fire.

"I can't help it. That's the way I feel," he broke out again. "And I feel that way like other men who've been through the big show, because of the things we saw done and had to do ourselves. The beastliness — the uselessness of it! And you don't realize the uselessness of it until you come back into civil life and notice the glib way people think and talk about it all; what the papers print, and the preachers preach, and politicians cooking up their little messes, and a group of white-whiskered old men at Versailles politely quarrelling over the distribution of the plunder. Only there isn't going to be much plunder. They can't realize that. And they go on threatening and haranguing and wrangling over coal and iron and oil and indemnities, as if that was what we fought for. If it had been — I wonder if it was? When I feel that it was I have to curse.

"I'm home." He put his face in his hands. "But I know so many that won't come — good fellows — lots of 'em just kids — the pick of the bunch — Phil, and Bill Fraser and Dan Hale — dozens of fellows I went to school with — scores out of my own company. People prattle about the supreme sacrifice, as if that were a reward in itself. Damn them, they don't know what it means. I'm sick of all the saccharine tosh I hear about the war. It may have been necessary, and necessary jobs have to be done. But if the war-glorifiers at home were taken out and given a sniff of gas and a dose of cooties, and left lying about here and there for a few hours with part of one leg blown off, they might change their minds about the soul-uplifting part of it."

He lay back in his chair, eyes smouldering, fingers locked together for a minute. Then he smiled wanly.

"Listen to me rave," he said. "You mustn't mind. I get that way now and then. You do, in the army. You have to bottle up so much. I *am* glad the row's over, and I'm glad to be here, and I'd like to go up to the Hiding Place with you and the kid and camp out till I forgot I ever was in a war. I expect in time it will get hazy. Only I have spells of thinking that Andy Hall was right. I wonder what became of Andy."

"Who was he?"

"A logger who worked for us. Clever chap. Thought his own thoughts about things, which isn't characteristic of loggers — or men in general, I'm beginning to believe. By the way, your father and mother are looking uncommonly well. But it struck me that the governor had aged a lot. Notice it? Did it knock him all of a heap when Phil went West?"

"No, he was rather quiet and sad for a while, but with the casualties running so high we'd all schooled ourselves to expect bad news of you both any time," Mary said quietly. "Something *has* worried him lately. He's here a good bit. Takes Roddy out for a walk or drive nearly every day. He's well, I think, but lately he's been moody."

"See anything of Laska?"

She shook her head.

"Very little. I don't see a great deal of people, Rod. Every one has been lovely to me. But — I don't fit into the giddy pace. You know, if you don't flutter prettily and with all your heart, you don't make a hit with the butterflies. Since I came back from London I've — I've just put in the time. You know — oh, we're a pair of softies — but it is good to be together. We *have* played the game."

A Chinese boy brought in tea and cakes. Rod and Mary toasted their feet at the blaze and sipped tea and talked. The windows that gave seaward over English Bay shivered in their casings under the gusty puffs of the storm wind. A chime struck ten.

"Is there a bedroom upstairs? " Rod roused himself out of a silence to ask.

"Two. But neither is completely furnished. There are two nice ones on the ground floor, which is plenty for us so long as we have no guests. Why?"

"I would much rather sleep upstairs."

"Why?" Mary repeated.

"Doctor's orders," he answered lightly. "High altitude advised. Oh, it's just a notion of mine. You'll have to humour me."

"It's easily arranged," she said. "I'll have Yick make up a bed. You *are* whimsical, though, Rod. What's back of the notion?"

He laughed it off. An hour later, feeling himself sink into sleep with a delicious, pervasive sensation of contentment, his last conscious reflection was a hope that he would never have to explain what lay back of the notion. He felt Mary's arm resting across him. Surely body and soul could be at peace henceforth.

Well on in the night he wakened with a familiar apprehension tugging at his consciousness. His brain was quite clear. He knew what was happening. It had overtaken him before. The thinking, reasoning part of him, or perhaps the purely intuitive, urged that he rise and fight off a paralyzing numbness that seized his feet, his hands, that crept slowly upward and inward, chilling his flesh. Curious, he thought, to die like that, to stand by and watch himself run down like an unwound clock. He could hear the slow regular breathing of his wife beside him. He could feel the even beat of her heart where her breast pressed against his shoulder. His own heart had stopped — fluttered and stopped as he awoke. Would it begin again? He lay waiting, feeling that numbness seize his limbs, feeling his breathing grow more difficult.

He remembered what he must do. His will — that strange, detached segment of his being that was cognizant of and superior to his flesh, commanded him to rise at once if he would ever rise again. And by some supreme effort of a body dying if not already dead he twisted himself sidewise, set his feet on the floor, hauled himself erect by a bedpost. Three steps to the door. Three steps from door to staircase. He moved in blind obedience to the will to live, moved with that clear, fantastic conviction of being already on the threshold of death. No pulse, scarcely a breath, speechless. He could not utter a sound. Only motor muscles moving obedient to that imperative will, and that crystalline awareness of what was happening. He had a reluctant shrinking from that picture. To escape all that war could dart at him — and to die of a cardiac failure on the night of his homecoming. No, by God! Not if he could reach those stairs!

He reached them. Felt with a torpid foot for the top step, held to the balustrade with two unfeeling hands, went down *stamp, stamp,* heavily, jarringly from step to step. His head swam. He suffocated. But he moved. His mind functioned. His body obeyed his will. All but his heart. That stood still, lay inert in his breast — until he was within four steps of the bottom. Then it fluttered, feebly at first, tumultuously after a second, so that his breath came in quick gasps and long sobbing sighs.

As he realized with a rush of thankfulness that he had won against long odds, a switch clicked above, light flooded stair and landing, and Mary came hurrying after him.

"What is it, Rod? What's wrong?" she whispered. He found words to answer while he kept on *stamp, stamp*, to the bottom. Those dead hands; blood congealed in them. He began to clap them together. He stamped with his feet on the hall floor like a horse in the treadmill.

"Heart stopped," he said weakly. "Been giving me trouble. Nothing the matter with it. Just flutters and slows down. This time it stopped. Had to get up and jog it on the stairs. That's why I have to sleep upstairs. Been warned."

"I'll send for a doctor," Mary cried.

"Doctor — hell!" Rod's strength was coming back. The blood pounded in his temples. He could breathe, speak without effort, although weakly. "I've had the best men in Paris and London at me. They don't know what's the matter. They say there's nothing the matter. Heart's organically perfect but functionally weak."

He repeated it ironically to himself, that phrase of the medical men — when he had got back to normal and was able slowly to ascend the stairs with her help — repeated it silently while Mary sat wrapped in a bathrobe, looking at him with troubled, anxious eyes.

He made light of it. It was nothing much. Very soon he would be quite all right. He had been warned that he might have a recurrence, and that he must when possible be on an upper floor when he slept, because to move jarringly was imperative and he would not have strength to climb. He stepped heavily from step to step and so joggled his circulation back to normal. But that would soon wear off. She was not to worry.

Thus he lied gently to ease her mind. He did not want to die like that. He did not want death in any form to overtake him. No. The possibility was sufficient to stir him deeply. He had seen death at his elbow a hundred times in four years. He had done his part, expecting that soon or late his turn would come. It was part of the game. Life came to have little significance to men whose occupation was destroying life and being themselves destroyed. It would have been a simple matter to die in action; merely a moment of surprise, of incredulity, then oblivion.

He had escaped death; he had escaped marring. Suffering he could not escape, nor the sight of suffering that wrung him as deeply as his own. He had never been able to steel himself against the sights and sounds of pain. He had never been able to look indifferently on other men's agony. And he *had* grown indifferent to death. Men are seldom afraid to die, to risk death. Yet with the acceptance of death as an imminent chance there still flourishes the deep, instinctive desire to live.

Rod wanted to live more than he had ever wanted to before. He had come through the storm of war to this haven where he knew there was for him peace and security and affection beyond most men's lot.

Yet it was touch and go. The nervous man, the keenly strung, sensitive man, the thoroughbred will fight; he can die on his nerve. But there is a breaking strain beyond which he cannot endure. Before the continual impact of pain, death, horror, and disgust, the sight and knowledge of merciless destruction, of blind and calculated killing, of flesh and blood ground up and poured into a bottomless pit to narrow a salient or test a military theory, Rod had sometimes wondered if something in his heart would burst; if something in his brain would crack from that inner ache, a quivering sensitiveness that drew his nerves tight as fiddle-strings, a going on by sheer will, with his heart burning in hatred of the bloody muddle that engulfed him and his fellows. His heart had been strained until it weakened somewhere. That was all. He had not known what it was that changed the nervous heart into a weak heart.

Some time before the Armistice he noticed the difference — a slowing-down under excitement instead of a quickening of his pulse. A feeling of discomfort at night. A desire to get up, to walk about, to fight off a weakening sensation.

Then the Armistice. And a night in a Paris hotel when he was a dead man if it had not been for that imperative command of a mind that willed a body to defy dissolution. He had stirred somehow that sluggish heart into beating again, and he had called a doctor. Later he consulted specialists.

They could tell him little; they could do less. His heart was organically perfect but functionally weak. They all agreed on that. It might stop any time. Nothing could be done. He would either die very suddenly, or slowly his heart would strengthen, build new tissue, be strong again.

He coaxed Mary to settle down. He lay there beside her in the dusky room, where feeble shadows from arc lights swung by the roaring wind made flickering patterns on the wall, and he thought something like this:

Heart failure is failure of the heart to pulsate. Pulsation of the heart keeps the blood circulating (mechanics applied to the body) and the passage of the blood in and out of the heart keeps it pulsating. When the heart stops beating the blood stops moving. Hence start the blood moving and it must pass through the heart. The heart being organically perfect would pulsate mechanically — until — or unless —

Would he ever dare sleep again? Over and over that polysyllabic phrase repeated itself until he grew weary and his eyes closed in the sleep he would have denied if he could.

Organically perfect but functionally weak!

CHAPTER XIX

AT BREAKFAST ROD WAS introduced to his son, Roderick Thorn Norquay, who lacked a few weeks of being four years old. Born in London, hurried home in 1917 when every unnecessary mouth England had to feed brought her so much nearer want, Roderick junior had no memory of his father. Rod marvelled that two years could change a toddler into a sturdy boy in knickers who could be tentatively intrigued by gold braid, red tabs, and a shiny brown belt. They were both self-conscious enough to afford Mary a smile at their guarded approach to each other.

"It's funny to see you two," she said, when the youngster had marched away in care of a nurse girl. "You're like boxers — sparring for an opening."

"I suppose so," Rod returned. "I don't see the joke myself."

"Don't be so touchy, old dear," she wheedled. "You know what I mean."

"Not touchy." He smiled. "Just a bit off-colour. We've missed such a devil of a lot that we can't catch up with. Having to present myself cautiously to my own kid reminds me of that. Four years wasted — worse than wasted. And we're only two out of millions."

"Wasted?"

"Absolutely."

"Then you don't think it was worth the fight? Belgium, destroying an arrogant militarism, saving the world for democracy, making further wars impossible — all those high ideals?"

Rod looked at her. Her face was placid as a shaded pool, expressionless. Her tone had been without accent — no key to her faith in those matters.

"Just phrases. Useful phrases that served their turn. Who is so naive as to believe that now? Do you?" he asked without heat.

Mary smiled.

"No. But a great many people do. Or they say they do. They've gone about mouthing those catch phrases so long they repeat them as a sort of liturgic response whenever the war is mentioned. They respond to all questioning, all criticism, with that formula."

"I daresay," Rod mused. "But nobody in the army has any such illusions. I haven't had much chance to observe personally, but I don't know any place where democracy is in good working order. We certainly put a crimp in German militarism, but our own militarists are in a very flourishing condition, especially in France. In fact, a lot of men, from battalion commanders down to ranks, are beginning to ask what we *did* fight for. The few weeks I've been in civil life haven't enlightened *me.* After passing through that long trance of dirt, danger and drudgery, men do want to know. Some people, quite a lot, regard it as some sort of spectacular game at which our side won. They seem to be rather eager for the distribution of prizes. And there aren't any prizes. I don't think there will be. Nothing but bigger taxes, higher prices — a hell of a struggle to pay the bill — labour demanding to know *why*, after having fought a war and won it, they must come home and get to work and pay the bill. Oh, we won the war right enough, but it's a Pyrrhic victory. The significance of that long-drawn wrangle at Versailles doesn't seem obvious to many people."

"People — people in the mass," Mary said scornfully, "are just sheep. One big sheep says 'Baa!' and all the lesser sheep chorus 'Baa!' defiantly or plaintively, as the case may be."

Rod laughed. He got up from his chair.

"Where's that club bag? Oh, I see it. That sheep thing reminds me. I heard Andy Hall use that simile once, and I came across the same observation in a book I bought on the train."

He came back to his wife with a volume in his hand.

"Have you seen this novel?" he asked. "If not you must read it. Someone who knows this country and loves it and understands it has been putting a lot of things very clearly and sympathetically in a book. Some of it is real enough to have happened, and some of the characters seem like people I know. There's truth and power in the thing. There's a man or two in it who feels about the war and political flapdoodle and tricky manipulation of affairs and a lot of current skulduggery, very much as a good many able men I know feel about it all. There is some corking good description, some fine characterization, and some almost brilliant writing. Part of the scene is laid on the B.C. coast. It's so vivid it made me homesick. Have you seen it?"

He handed her the book. Mary opened it, let the leaves riffle through her fingers, turned back to the title page.

"*The Swirl*," she read. "A trifle reminiscent of Gissing's *The Whirlpool* but none the worse for that, I daresay. By Margaret Pierce. Yes, I've read it," she said soberly, "read it over and over till my eyes ached, and it seemed like words, words, words. You see this happens to be my book, Rod."

"Eh?" he looked blankly at her.

"I wrote it," she explained. "Mary — diminutive of Margaret. Pierce — what is the purpose of a thorn? Hence Mary Thorn — Margaret Pierce. I didn't particularly like to camouflage my identity. But I wanted to say a lot of things which coming from Margaret Pierce would be considered on their merits, and which coming from Mrs. Roderick Sylvester Norquay might arouse local misconceptions. I wanted to be unhampered by family considerations. I wanted to express my inner convictions about various aspects of life as it has been unfolding to me for a long time. So I hoisted a *nom de plume*. It would be strange if you didn't find a resemblance to persons and things and people you know. Yet there isn't a photograph there — just traits and habits of thought, inhibitions and passions that are common to humanity in general. I'm not a propagandist. I don't know that this book, or any other books I may write, has a message, unless it is the oblique inference that stupidity and ignorance and intolerance are more fatal than guns. I'm not so much concerned with isms as I am with — well, with what Joseph Conrad meant when he wrote: 'Fashions in monsters do change; but the truth of humanity goes on forever, unchangeable and inexhaustible in the variety of its disclosures.' You really think," she ended a bit hurriedly, "it's good?"

"Good?" Rod echoed. He sat down on the arm of her chair. "Of course it's good. Didn't I come lugging it home as a find?"

He looked down at the imprint.

"New York, eh? Did you have any trouble placing it?"

"Well, yes — and no," she said. "One publisher wrote me saying that it was work of a high order but he felt sure the time was scarcely opportune for its publication — unless I cared to modify certain passages which seemed to cast a doubt on the great moral forces underlying the war. That's almost verbatim. Another said that he personally enjoyed reading it very much, but was sure it would fail to get a hearing in view of the present demand for tales completely devoid of war atmosphere.

"It is amusing sometimes to try and trace motive and action," Mary smiled. "A publisher wants to publish books that will sell. Nearly every one is affected directly and indirectly by the war. Therefore the publisher concludes people want to ignore the war, or that they will uniformly recoil from a given aspect of the war, even if it is an individual attempt to interpret some obscure phase. War isn't the theme of this book. It's incidental, just as the war is incidental, one of humanity's growing pains. Anyway, I found a publisher. And it's getting a hearing, he tells me. People *are* reading it."

"You've found yourself," Rod said a little wistfully. "You've got the vision, and the power to embody your vision so that it stands out clear. I couldn't get it. I tried; I wanted to capture the spaciousness, the drama, the unquenchable spirit of the pioneers. And I couldn't. What I wanted to do seems mere inconsequential romancing beside the vivid reality you've achieved. How did you do it, wonder-woman? How do you know with such certainty what men think and feel, and how they can be beasts and heroes, groping blindly toward certain ends? Where did you get the astonishing grasp of those obscure motives which so often actuate people?

"You ought to write the history of the Norquay family, Mary. There's a theme for a novel. First the pioneer adventurer, courageous, determined, resourceful, infinitely patient about his foundation laying, seeing clearly what he was about. Then his son following in his father's footsteps. The grandson expanding upon the solidly laid groundwork, elaborating the original plan, acquiring land and timber, increasing the tradition of permanence. Then a generation that stands pat on its hereditary past, accepting wealth and culture as a birthright, things irrevocably bestowed upon a superior class, as a condition fixed and final for all time. Last of all a generation where the eldest son and heir is only a passionate, superficially glossed animal, who expends his fierce energy on women and financial undertakings, proving eminently successful with both. The second son, the well-balanced, sound-minded one, killed in the war. The youngest, a dreamy, sensitive youth, coming back from the war with a cracked heart and most of his romantic illusions about great men, great nations, and great idealistic undertakings knocked into a cocked hat with no task ahead of him worth an effort, with his keenest consciousness that of a world where all stability has gone by the board; a tired, disillusioned man who wants only to sit and think, and to be grateful that if everything else seems pinchbeck there's still a woman who is eighteen-carat gold to him. I don't quite see how you would make a pattern out of such a snarl — but —"

He didn't finish the sentence. Mary's arms drew him down to her with a fierce, protecting pressure. She held him, whispering tensely:

"What have they done to you? I can't bear to hear you talk like that. It isn't true. Life hasn't gone sour. We mustn't let it. We can make it good — we *must.* One daren't falter. One must *not* brood. We're over the top of a long hill that has tried us both. Well, then — 'Courage, the devil is dead!' Eh, Roderick Dhu? Love's *something* to hold fast by, isn't it?"

CHAPTER XX

FOR A FEW DAYS ROD went about a little, picking up threads of old acquaintance with places and people. The uneasy consciousness of a heart which might fail him at any moment troubled him now and then. Once or twice he felt that strange faltering. But it did not stop — not quite. He wondered if he had passed a crisis that first night at home when he felt himself locked in a grapple with death itself. And so he was very careful. It was easy to be apathetic, to be completely acquiescent. Nothing, he thought, would ever again make his heart swell with such repressed passion as the sights and sounds of the western front, the carnival of non-combatants in Paris and London, the bitterness with which for so long he had seen the agonies and endurances and destructiveness of war as sheer waste — blind, blundering waste, the offspring of cupidity wedded to arrogant ignorance.

He wanted to forget what could not be changed. Here it was easy to forget, at least to thrust it all into the background, now that he was home. For a time he would rest. When his heart strengthened he would take stock of his resources and move with determined purpose in some direction, toward some as yet indefinite goal.

In the meantime, free from military discipline, interminable parades, orders, red tape that fettered the hands of initiative and bound up a man's mouth so that he needed only two phrases in his vocabulary, "Yes, sir" and "No, sir," he went about in his native city observing, noting, listening in clubs, homes, on the streets, in hotel lobbies where he went to meet other men who had just come back.

If the landscape endured and the outstanding architectural features, many things had changed, contrary to his first glad impression, were still changing at an accelerated pace in this winter of 1919. In four years and a half his native city, when he came to examine it closely, presented a transformed physiognomy. Its lifeblood, people and money, flowed in a heavier stream through complicated arteries. Vancouver was bigger and better, he heard on every hand. New industries, shipyards, shipping, more elaborate affairs. The war had done a great deal for British Columbia, an elderly banker naïvely remarked to him.

Rod conceded that it probably had. But it had also done something "to" British Columbia. He couldn't say just what. It wasn't clear enough in his mind. But he could feel it. Or perhaps it was only himself. He could not be sure. He could dimly apprehend a difference. *His* world was changed. Phil was dead. Grandfather Norquay took his long sleep beside other dead Norquays in the plot at Hawk's Nest. Grove flourished largely, a scintillating comet, streaming across the moneyed spaces.

Rod sometimes paused after dark in some distant part of the city to look at the flamboyant sign with a speculative interest, without the old resentment, but with a shade of disapproval. Grove had become a big man — Rod couldn't escape that conclusion — a big man in his chosen field. Scarcely a day but some newspaper quoted him. He figured in local print co-equal with the Peace Conference and the latest authentic report of Lenin's death. Nearly nine years now of waxing great in the financial firmament. Grove bade fair to win greater fame and fortune than that old forbear of his who beat around the Horn to found a family in the wilderness because the land filled his eyes with pleasure and his soul with peace.

Would old Roderick have found pleasure and profit in discounting notes, clipping coupons at so much per cent, buying and selling bonds and mortgages, squeezing little debtors and bolstering up big ones for a consideration? Rod smiled at the quaint notion.

But he had evidently underestimated Grove's capacity. Grove had his community behind him. His finger was in every pie. His skill at extracting plums was envied and admired.

"He's what they mean when they talk about the greatness of our country," Rod thought cynically. "That sort of thing."

Oliver Thorn had sold his timber to the Norquay Estate and retired to live in a cottage on the Capilano slope fronting on the city, where he could, as he told Rod, spend his last years seeing the sun rise from behind the Coast range and set behind the far, blue rampart of Vancouver Island. John P. Wall, Grove's father-in-law, had made a fortune in building wooden ships and another in airplane spruce. Wall's youngest son had been killed overseas, but his eldest had been too precious an asset to the community to risk his life in war. Isabel was a beauty, still unmarried. (It seemed to Rod an astonishing thing when Mary told him Isabel was her dearest friend.) The Deanes and Richstons flourished, with one or two gaps in the younger ranks. They had grown richer with the war, vastly more sure of themselves, setting a pace in the social parade that lesser folk found hard to follow.

There were two avenues open along which Rod could saunter to exercise this detached observance of his own people: the homes which automatically opened to him, and brief daily contacts with men downtown. Socially things seemed a little more feverish, people just a trifle keener in the futile pursuit of futile diversion, the dancing just a little more frankly sensuous, the drinking a little freer, the talk looser. If one couldn't or wouldn't keep the pace one was "slow." It amused Rod and it vaguely troubled him. These people seemed so remote from so many things of importance that pressed close on them, matters that constituted both a warning and a threat. Downtown it was worse. Uptown rested on downtown. The economic link — the strongest link in the invisible chain — shackled them together whether they knew it or not.

And downtown was frankly on the make, with the most shrewd and far-seeing already privately dubious about a let-down in the swift flow of affairs that followed the close of European hostilities. Perhaps it had always been the same. He had not been aware how consistently material, how harshly practical, the world of commerce must be. But he couldn't get used to hearing them tot up Canada's share in the reparations, the gloating on what enlarged African and Asiatic possession meant to trade, their chesty pride in having swept the Hun from the seas (as if *they* had done it in their office chairs). He couldn't get used to that, because it was invariably accompanied by an undertone of growling about confiscatory taxation, enormous pension bills.

Here and there some elderly hardshell solemnly viewed with alarm three items debited to the war: first, the growing demand of labour for shorter hours, increased pay, and a voice in the conduct of industries for which they furnished the motive power; second, the Bolshevik upheaval in Russia which constituted a horrific menace to the sacred rights of private property; third, the military strength and insistent demands of France.

The war as a business proposition! Rod got up and walked away from a group of men in a club who rather vindictively discussed these important phases of the European debacle. If that were all — commerce — shipping — iron — coal — territory — indemnities. If that were all! His heart wouldn't stand his talking to those bankers and merchants and manufacturers and brokers as he wished to talk. He left them. What was held as piracy and brigandage for the individual became somehow the unchallenged privilege of a nation, if only the scale of operations were large enough. The Barbary corsairs were at least open in their deeds. They flew the Jolly Roger and their victims walked the plank without ado. Nor did the pirates get their fighting done by proxy and then grumble because they found it expensive.

Yes the world, his world, had changed. Of all that he had known through youth and early manhood only his wife — like the sea and the mountains — remained steadfast, a desirable reality. Now, more than ever, he was filled with gratitude and wonder that she had stood loyal, devoted, staunch as a rock in the bewildering flux of a period that seemed to him, in occasional sombre moods, to have quickened the disintegration of men and the cherished works of men to a degree that made him apprehensive.

This couldn't be the reality of things, he assured himself. He had somehow got them twisted. His vision and his understanding must be askew. He had to stop pondering about it all. It was difficult for him to do this. He had always been a thinking being. That faculty had cursed him in France. On duty in trenches, in action, in long lonely vigils, his mind had hammered him with insistent questions and speculations on the why and the wherefore of human activities. Many an answer that came like the answer to a sum saddened him. One should not see too clearly.

He found it so now. But at least he, as an individual, was not too deeply involved to stand clear of all this feverish hurrying and scurrying to nowhere after nothing. There must be something a man could do in the world that would bring him dividends in satisfaction of accomplishment, as well as dollars. For him, because his forbears had been both adventurous and far-seeing, there was no immediate economic pressure. He had no great responsibilities, beyond himself and Mary and their boy. If he needed more than the minor share which he held in the Norquay estate, he could surely get it without bowing his head and twisting his moral sense awry before the Moloch of commerce.

The more he saw of town the more he desired to turn his back on it. Not because it was town but because for so long he had had his fill of noise and motion. To sit amid a great silence, the strange, restful hush of a forest, in the shadow of great mountains — that calm, secure peace; to hear only the sighing of wind in high interlaced branches, the muted song of running water, the whistle of birds' wings — that was his wish.

Practical wisdom forbade. There was really one place where he longed to be with Mary and his son, and they could not go there. Hawk's Nest was no longer his home. It was Grove's. His road and Grove's diverged too sharply for him to go there even as a guest. Elsewhere they could not find comfort at that season. It was a winter of sleet and snow, of alternate frosts and rains. A half-sick man couldn't go camping like a pioneer with a woman and a child. And it was not camping as such that Rod longed for but the spacious background and comfortable security of his birthplace.

Whereupon, as a sensible man eschews the unattainable, he put it out of his mind. In the spring — he and Mary lay awake nights planning what they would do in the spring.

He came home from one of these desultory excursions abroad a little before dinner one evening.

"Your father has phoned twice since five o'clock," Mary told him. "He asked to have you call him up when you came in."

Rod got his connection.

"You telephoned, pater," he said. "Was it anything of importance?"

"Well, yes. Can you come down to the club after dinner, Rod? If not tonight, then by nine in the morning?"

"I'll come tonight. Say eight o'clock."

He hung up the receiver. As he got ready for dinner his mind was divided between the playful squeals of his son romping in the living room and the almost plaintive note in his father's voice over the wire. Norquay senior had changed with everything else. He had aged. Losing Phil had been a blow. But he was a proud man — and he had two sons left. That grief had not put care lines in his face, or caused the abstracted brooding into which he sometimes relapsed. Rod understood, of course, that the war had completed the break-up of the old family life at Hawk's Nest which Grove's embarkation on a career had begun, or Grove's personality had begun. His father admitted that he no longer cared to live at Hawk's Nest.

"One doesn't like to be alone all the time," he had put it quite simply. "Too many ghosts haunt those corridors for an old man. And at one's age one doesn't care to set up an establishment in town. When any of the others find occasion in summer, I go to Hawk's Nest. Otherwise I live at the club."

Yet the place was kept up. Stagg, the butler, his wife who ranked as housekeeper, a cook, two maids, and two gardeners held a sinecure. One could, Rod assumed, step in and find Hawk's Nest quite as of old.

He came back to his father. What bothered him? It couldn't be money or affairs. The Norquay estate was rock-ribbed. Timber, land, gilt-edged securities. It must simply be that he was getting old and lonely. When a man is past sixty and all his life has been spent in a well-appointed home, surrounded by a fairly numerous family and still more numerous relatives, he can hardly reconcile himself to the empty shell of a house, or the artificial atmosphere of even the most elaborately appointed club. Rod felt sorry for him. But if Grove hadn't failed to carry on the family tradition, Hawk's Nest would still be the year-around rendezvous of the clan, as it had always been. No effect without a cause. Rod put aside the thought that his elder brother could be blamed for a great deal if one chose to be critical.

His father sat smoking a cigar in a chair that commanded the club entrance, and he led the way to his rooms as soon as Rod appeared.

He took some papers off a table and sat fussing with them. He didn't seem inclined to talk at first, beyond a few casual remarks. Rod waited. He knew his father. He felt that something was coming — something that rested with a great weight on the elder man's mind. Since Rod came home there seemed to have arisen between them a more keenly sympathetic understanding than had ever existed before. It wasn't a matter of words. It was a feeling. Rod divined intuitively that his father had some deep trouble to share with him. He could not have defined any reason for this belief. It existed as a belief. In that conviction he waited.

"Five years ago," Norquay senior began abruptly, "I looked forward to sitting back with a pipe and slippers and a book while my sons carried on in the old way. For a hundred and thirty years, to speak precisely, we have gone ahead solidifying our position, doing well by ourselves and all connected with us. We seemed — as a family — to have acquired a permanence, a solidarity, beyond that of any family in this province. We have become a sort of institution. We were here first. Of the exploring adventurers, we were the first to take root. You know the family history. We have helped to make this country what it is. We have acquired a great deal of material power, yet I do not recall that we have ever abused it. In each generation we have had a lot of faithful service, and we have had it because we have scrupulously observed some form of obligation to those who served us. Men have trusted us as being persons entirely trustworthy. We have not been Shylocks. We have not been arrogant. We have never been greedy for more."

Five years earlier Rod would have assented, as a matter of course. Now he stirred slightly in his chair, as his father paused, and observed dispassionately:

"Would you include Grove in that last?"

"I am coming to Grove," Norquay senior answered. "To arrive at Grove by a logical sequence is the reason for this summing-up of ourselves. A few weeks before your grandfather died he said to me, '*My* father once prophesied that Hawk's Nest would some day hatch out an eagle. What's the last hatching? Sparrows. Sparrows! Quite apropos of nothing. We hadn't even been talking. He grew very uncertain in his mind at the last. A great age, Rod. Nearly ninety. He scarcely comprehended the war. Grove was there with a house party. I think their high spirits annoyed him. Sparrows!"

He contemplated the rug with a fixed frown.

"I wonder if he were right," he said at last.

"I must confess," he continued, "that I have spent my life in a state of inertia compared to his, and to the energy his father worked with. They were actively constructive. Looking back, I seem to have done nothing but maintain a sort of status quo. Indeed, lacking any necessity or any great personal ambition, with a disinclination for politics, a distaste for anything in the way of business outside of estate affairs, there seemed nothing upon which to expend great energy. I've moved along pleasant lines of least resistance. Looking back, it doesn't seem so satisfactory. Avoiding boredom, keeping up a moderate revenue without being a taskmaster to labour — that about expresses it.

"It seemed to me, however, that my sons must inherit some of the abounding energy, the creativeness, that I somehow lacked. Your eldest brother, whom you were named after, was a vigorous, high-spirited boy. That venturesomeness resulted in his death at an early age. That left Grove next in line. For many years I watched the three of you develop from sturdy youngsters into young men. Phil, it seemed to me, was something like myself. You were always a puzzle, an odd sort of boy, somewhat given to precocious remarks and unexpected actions. Lovable, but erratic, probably brilliant but not entirely dependable, I used sometimes to say to myself: How wide one can go of the mark.

"So you see it was natural that Grove, being the eldest, should be looked to for able carrying on of that which has become a tradition since old Roderick outlined his plan to hold compactly for the entire family that which he had built up out of nothing himself.

"It is a good plan. I have no fault to find with it. The stability, the working power of a large fortune is always depleted by being broken into fragments by division among each generation. The Norquay estate, as he outlined it in his journal, would be a tree ample enough to shelter all under its branches, so long as the trunk was kept intact.

"And it seemed to me Grove had all the qualifications to carry on with honour and profit. He had personality. He had energy and resource. He had ambition, which determined him on a career. I took his ability for granted; his character as a sure inheritance. His faults I conceded as the faults of lusty young manhood, minor failings to be put away in the face of responsibility.

"Yet you and Phil never had such convictions about your brother. Why?"

He paused on the interrogation.

"His weaknesses seemed fundamental. To us some of the things he did were despicable. He did things we would have been ashamed to do. Where his appetites and passions and desires were concerned, he had no consideration for any one or anything, nor any scruple about what he did if it suited him to do it and it was in his power. That was very clear to both Phil and myself. That was how he seemed to us. We used to wonder why you never had any inkling of what we considered his real character — or lack of it."

Rod was in no mood to be charitable, to mince words, to evade a frank answer to the direct question.

His father pondered briefly.

"You were right and I was wrong," he observed sadly. "All wrong. Phil put himself on record before he went overseas. He warned me not to trust Grove too far. It angered me at the time. It made our parting cool. That's one of my keenest regrets. He was right; you were both right. How can a man make such a blunder in reading his own son? Perhaps because he was his son. I have prided myself on a knowledge of men, too. Ah, well."

He nursed his chin in one palm.

"The Norquay Trust is insolvent," he announced presently. "Gutted, looted from within. It is about to topple over with a resounding crash. I have an outline of the position here." He ruffled the papers in his hand. "It seems incredible, but it is true."

"You're involved? The estate is involved, eh?" Rod asked calmly. It seemed nowise incredible to him. It seemed, in fact, an entirely logical outcome — unlimited power in uncertain hands, increasing momentum, a grand smash. There was not a single element of the unexpected. He had anticipated such a finale. So had Phil.

"Not technically. Not yet."

"Very well. Let it smash," Rod said indifferently. "Let him pick himself up out the debris and take stock of himself. May do him good."

"If that were all. But it isn't so simple," his father sighed. "Don't you see, Rod? Our name, the prestige of the family, the confidence of the public in us as well-known, wealthy people has been the chief foundation on which this tottering Colossus was built. A great many people of whom we never heard, as well as our friends and families to whom we are related by blood and marriage, have put their money into this. It means loss to all, complete ruin to many, I'm afraid. If it were merely a question of Grove —"

He made a gesture of dismissal.

"But it isn't," he went on. "In the public eye and mind we stand or fall as a family. We have a reputation for integrity. If one of the family trades on that, the rest of us can't escape the consequences of his acts. I gave Grove his head and encouraged him, and I can't shirk my individual responsibility. I have no knowledge of a Norquay ever shirking an obligation. I'm an old man. I may not have many years left. I'll admit self-interest. I feel that I must straighten this thing out so that no one will ever say with an angry sneer that we saved our own skins after making a mess of theirs. The reason I asked you to come and see me tonight was to know if you will stand by me and help me see it through? It's got to be done."

"There's only one answer to that, isn't there, pater?" Rod said slowly. "I've outgrown any active antagonism toward Grove. It was more contempt than antagonism, except for the time he went out of his way to annoy my wife. At the same time I wouldn't lift a finger to save *him* from ever so hard a cropper. Only if you put it as something to be done for the family reputation — that probably means as much to me as it does to you. I'm willing to undertake anything I can handle. No use banking on me too strong, though. I don't know either business or finance."

"Half our wealth is in standing timber," his father replied, "and you know timber. Phil told me that you knew more of logging and loggers than he would ever learn. The woods will have to be our salvation. That will be your job, Rod. You've been through a hard mill. I wish you could have had a long rest. But this matter won't delay. I know law and I know something of affairs. I have had accountants checking up this infernal mess. Dorothy's husband has agreed to take charge. It will take nearly all our available capital to plug holes. The important end, the producing end, must be our timber. That I'll leave to you. We must begin operations at the first break in the weather. You'll have an absolutely free hand."

The ghost of a smile flitted across Rod's face. A free hand to ravage and destroy the forest to make money which would be poured like sand into a rathole! And he uncertain of any definite tenure on life. What of his heart? That overstrained, vital part of him — which was organically perfect but functionally weak. A heart that was slacking up now, so that he rose and paced back and forth across the floor to stir it up.

"Well," he said at last, halting in his stride. "That's understood."

His father nodded.

"It may not be so bad as it seems," he said, with the first hopeful note Rod had heard him utter. "Though I'm doubtful of quarrelling with figures. Grove hasn't been dishonest. That's the only redeeming feature of the nasty mess. But his associates have. I didn't think it of them. But I have moral if not legal proof of their crookedness — cunning financial piracy on a considerable scale. I may be able to make 'em disgorge, and I may not. They've feathered their nests and left Grove, the poor fool, holding the empty sack. The intent is to throw the thing into a receiver's hands. But I'm prepared to checkmate that. There's to be a directors' meeting tomorrow at ten-thirty. I'd like you to go with me. You may find it illuminating. Suppose I pick you up on my way?"

"Why not drive out and have breakfast with us at eight or half-past?" Rod suggested.

"Better still. I'll do that, thanks."

He had never been a demonstrative man. But he shook hands at the door, and Rod's fingers were still tingling with the grip when he walked down the stairs.

As the wheels of the retreating taxi crunched the gravel on his driveway, Rod stood a moment with his foot on the first step. The night was clear, tinged with frost. Above the city roofs that curious lucence from a million lights dimmed the stars. And as his gaze embraced the downtown silhouette he marked for the first time from the house in which he lived the blazing sign of the Norquay Trust, as if it were something from which he could not escape — and for a moment he was tempted to a childish shaking of his fist at that glowing emblem of a corroded and tottering edifice.

CHAPTER XXI

ROD FOLLOWED HIS FATHER along a strip of thick carpet laid over a floor tiled in precise geometric patterns, looking about him at the dukes and duchesses of the counting room administering their high estate of correspondence and ledgers. Delicately fingered typewriters and computing machines woke faint, staccato tappings in that lofty room. He passed a row of ground-glass partitioned cubicles, each gilt-lettered with the name of some petty satrap of higher degree than those without such privacy. There was a decorous stir, an air of activity, persons moving about from desk to desk, discreet consultation. If, as an institution, it was moribund, coma had not set in. Or perhaps the stir and bustle was but the accentuated flutter of a financial heart struggling to force impoverished blood through a body approaching dissolution. He smiled at the fancy.

The directors' room, specially fitted up for deliberate and august discussion, opened off a mezzanine floor overlooking the main body of the offices. Norquay senior led the way. They left their hats and coats in a cloak room. Without ceremony, Mr. Norquay pushed open a door and entered.

They were a few minutes early, but they were not first. Grove sat at one end of a huge oval table, a massive creation of mahogany surrounded by a dozen equally massive chairs. He was flanked by his father-in-law and Arthur Deane.

The capacity for imagining a man in relation to his circumstances and surroundings was one which neither war, wounds, nor the passage of time had atrophied in Rod. This had given him a mental picture of his brother as a haggard man facing ruin with some degree of trepidation. He saw at once that this was a misconception. He perceived the well-remembered features. A cigar out-thrust from one corner of Grove's mouth. There were faint, pouchy discolourations under his eyes. He was older, and he showed his age. Otherwise he had changed less than Rod expected. He had simply become a thicker-bodied edition of his earlier self. Rod marked the familiar malicious flicker in his eyes upon recognition, and wondered with an inner sardonic amusement how Grove would take this invasion of his holy of holies by a younger brother whose parting act had been to inflict the severest bodily punishment Grove had ever suffered in his life.

But Grove merely nodded with a casual "how d'do, pater," and a careless "Hello, Rod," and motioned them to chairs. Thereafter he sat quiescent. Only the too-frequent puffing at his cigar, an occasional aimless movement of the hand resting on the table, heralded a strain. Beside him John Wall sat with hands clasped over his rotund paunch, impassive as a Chinaman. Deane pencilled interminable figures on a pad.

At intervals other men came in. A hushed atmosphere seemed the most outstanding quality of the high-ceilinged, beautifully panelled room. Voices sank to discreet murmurings there.

A moon-faced clock against the north wall struck a soft, silvery chime. Grove straightened up.

"Meeting'll come to order," he slurred the words. "This, as you know, is a special meeting called to consider a difficult position. I have a report and some figures for which I desire your attention."

He paused a moment to glance about the ring of faces — faces with bushy eyebrows and heavy jowls and many lines about the eyes, faces ruddy, saturnine, bearded, moustached. Hard and watchful faces converted by long practice into serviceable masks to hide feeling. Save Rod and his brother, not one was under fifty. Wary old birds, Rod thought, hard — hard as nails.

They represented collectively a sum in excess of ten millions.

Grove looked finally at Rod, then at his father. The tip of his tongue flicked across his full lips.

"This is a directors' meeting," he said. "It is slightly irregular for outsiders to be present. I —"

"If you can think of nothing more irregular than that, you may proceed," Norquay senior broke in. "I desire my son to be present."

John P. Wall rumbled deep in his broad chest.

"'S all right. 'S all in the family, Grove. Go ahead."

Grove began to read from a cluster of typed sheets. Ponderous phrases, heavy with the special terminology, the many-syllabled terms in which commerce and finance wraps its meaning when it seeks formal expression. Phrasing as difficult to the uninitiate as *The Critique of Pure Reason* is to the average freshman. Fundings, refundings, liquid assets, unrealizable commitments, debit and credit balances, mingled with references to the European situation, the New York situation, exchange, debentures, interminable strings of figures. It created a hopeless confusion in Rod's mind. There was so much language and so many figures. It was not a living, colourful language such as he cared for, such as could move him by its subtlety or vigour. He gave over trying to follow Grove through the maze and watched the faces of these men of affairs. Evidently it was clear enough to them. He observed slight liftings of eyebrows, communicative glances, fixed unwavering attention, comprehending nods. But their faces remained Sphinxlike.

Grove finished. He leaned back in his chair. For a moment his guard dropped.

"There it is," he snarled at them.

A short, full-bodied man at the lower end of the table said in a pained tone: "There is really nothing in that statement that we don't know, that we haven't discussed. As a result of mismanagement and unfortunate circumstances, the Norquay Trust Company is insolvent. The question is, what are we, the board of directors, going to do about it?"

"Liquidate — liquidate, I say," rumbled a man whom Rod recognized as the head of a well-known wholesale firm, a well-known man about town — a gentleman with a taste for old, very old Scotch whiskey, and a penchant for young, very young women. "Liquidate and be done with it," he repeated ponderously.

"How are you going to liquidate a two-million-dollar liability with assets of a million or less?" Arthur Deane inquired in his cold, precise voice.

An old man across the table, with horn-rimmed glasses low on the bridge of his nose, leaned forward.

"Is it as bad as that?" he inquired indifferently. "I wasn't sure."

"A careful analysis of the statement shows about that," Deane answered.

"We've got to get out from under, that's all," Bartley Richston broke into speech for the first time. He was quite unmoved, matter of fact. "No use blinking facts. As a going concern the Norquay Trust is on its last legs. How long," he demanded of Grove, "can you carry on as you are? Suppose it got about that you're shaky and all these four per cent depositors demand their money? How long would you last?"

"About half a day," Grove answered sullenly. "We can't stand a run. Damn it, you know that, Richston. I've told you a dozen times in the last month."

"Then a receivership is the only solution. A receivership and a winding-up."

Grove sprang to his feet.

"By the Lord," he cried in a passion, and his fist struck the table with a thud, "you shan't sink me like that. I tell you this thing can be pulled through. You've all made a fat thing out of it. You've got to back me up now. No use saying you can't. I know what your cash balances are in bank — every one of you. I know what Victory bonds you hold. This slump won't last. You've *got* to come through."

"Be sensible, Norquay," Arthur Deane put in. "No use throwing good money after bad. The war's over. The reaction's set in. The day of the quick turn and the long profit is past. It is unfortunate but other concerns have gone bankrupt. It is not exceptional."

Burrows, the short, stout man at the lower end of the table, grunted audibly.

"I make a motion," he said, "that our solicitors be authorized to appear in court and ask for a winding-up order."

"Second the motion," Richston snapped.

"You shan't," Grove declared hoarsely. Tiny sweat-beads began to stand out on his forehead. "What's got into the lot of you? You're running to cover like a lot of whipped dogs. All the thing needs is fifty or sixty thousand from each of us to carry on until the assets that we hold recover value. What if the war is over? Timber and mining and pulp and transportation go on. This isn't a corner grocery to be closed up as soon as business slacks off."

"You are wrong," Richston informed him. "This business does not differ essentially from the corner grocery — except in scope. It was undertaken to make money. It no longer does so. Considering the state its affairs have arrived in, it can never be made to do so. Therefore let it be wound up — at once. We waste time in useless talk. Let us agree on the motion, and act."

"Oh, yes, you're willing," Grove flung at him. "You've had a good many slices out of the melon. What about our trust accounts? What about our depositors?"

"Circumstances are too strong for us," Richston replied imperturbably. "We can see now that accepting deposits was a mistake. We should never have undertaken private banking. It's unfortunate, I'll admit. I suppose there'll be a noise in the papers and all that sort of thing. But it isn't criminal to fail in business. Be sensible, Norquay. Step out of it as gracefully as possible. *You're* not faced with ruin. No more are we. It *would* be folly for us to get more deeply involved than we already are. Let it go. What's the Limited Liability Act for?"

Sagacious nods animated the several heads. Grove towered above them impotent, his face red with anger, shadowed by a trace of fear, his look indicating momentary bewilderment at attack from an unexpected quarter. There lifted a low confusion of voices. Several speaking at once. Querulous complaining. Rumbles of mismanagement, muttered disclaimers of responsibility.

Rod's father rose slowly to his feet. His thin, smooth-shaven face betrayed no particular feeling. Only Rod, who knew the faintest indication of his every mood, saw that his eyes burned, that there was a repressed disgust and scorn in them. He rapped on the table with his knuckles.

"Before you prematurely explode this well-laid mine," he enunciated clearly, "I wish to make a brief statement. My son, whom you evince a tendency to blame, is a heavy stockholder. I myself hold a limited interest, but between us we do have control. I do not wish to offer excuses for Mr. Grove Norquay. He bears his own responsibility. I am aware, however, that there is other responsibility for the insolvency of this concern. I have perfunctorily attended but few directors' meetings. But I have my own sources of information. For some weeks I have foreseen this move. It is just such an action as might be expected of a group of men like yourselves. Yourselves" — a bitter gibing note crept into his voice — "most of you liars, and half of you thieves."

The masks dropped. Those various elderly, respectable gentlemen gasped and rose to the attack. Their old voices, some thin and reedy, some thick with indignation, were levelled at him. They demanded apologies. They thumped the table. Their voices created a hubbub.

"I will not be insulted."

"I demand a retraction."

"Anybody who says I'm a thief is a damned liar!" Etc., etc.

Rod sat back, an onlooker at this minor Bedlam. He was an outsider, and looking in from the outside it made him, figuratively speaking, just a little bit sick. If this sort of thing was the accompaniment of big business and finance when it fell on evil days — He felt a mild sort of disgust with these yammering old men. He perceived that most of them were intent only on saving their financial hides. That they were callously indifferent to what happened, so long as it did not happen to them.

He marked also that Richston manifested no resentment at his father's personal thrust. Deane muttered to himself. His face was flushed. Richston only sneered, leaning back in his chair. Of them all John P. Wall remained unperturbed, his hands folded over his abdomen, blandly inert. And Norquay senior rested his fingertips on the table and looked at the sputtering, the gesticulations, the commotion he had aroused.

They subsided into mutterings. All but Burrows. He rose on his stodgy legs.

"I shall not remain here to be insulted," he announced with a ludicrous simulation of dignity.

"Sit down," Norquay senior's voice popped like a whiplash. And Burrows, after an uncertain glance about him for moral support, resumed his chair.

"I have not finished," Rod's father continued. "I am not going to reason with you. I am going to talk to you in the only language such men as you can understand, and be moved by. It is nothing to you that a thousand innocent people may be partially or wholly ruined by your manipulations. But it happens that my name is involved in this as well as my son and my money. I tell you flatly that if you proceed to sink this financial galleon which you built and launched and sailed on profitable voyages, and now propose to scuttle since there is no more chance for loot — I tell you if you do this, that three of you sitting at this table face the penitentiary. And, by God, I'll see that you go there!"

He stopped. A chilly silence, in which Rod could hear the sharp intake and slow exhalation of breath, seemed to hold them all fast.

"There has been mismanagement. Yes. There have also been illegal transactions, criminal acts. They were well covered, but I dug them up. I have had able men looking into the affairs of this corporation for some time. I repeat, if you throw it into involuntary liquidation, I will put at least three of you behind the bars."

To Rod it was like having a box seat at a melodrama. Again the masks failed these men. His father had stung them twice. First with an insult, then with a threat. They looked furtive; they seemed apprehensive. They remained silent, glancing sidelong at each other. All but John P. Wall. He took out a cigar, lit it very deliberately after biting off the end, while his gaze travelled slowly about the circle of perturbed faces. His own remained placid.

"What do you propose then, Norquay?" he asked casually.

"That we assess ourselves proportionately to replace the funds which have been — dissipated. Appoint a new manager. Replace this board of directors and carry on until such time as this concern can be wound up with every obligation discharged."

Wall shook his head.

"No," he said calmly. "Far as I'm concerned — not a bean. I'm through. Let 'er crash."

Sheeplike they followed his lead. They seemed to gather courage. Their money was their lifeblood. They would not spill it lightly. Other people's money, perhaps. Not their own.

They gathered voice. They protested that no sensible man would try to bolster up a tottering business. Why should *they* risk large sums when they could avoid risk by merely stepping aside?

"I can't step aside," Norquay senior answered them quietly. "You wouldn't understand if I told you why. So you refuse, then? Very well. I have told you what will follow an enforced receivership. I stand on that."

He kept the same position, fingertips resting on the polished wood, staring at them with open hostility, frank contempt. He remained silent after reaching this impasse.

"We are no more anxious for a receivership and a public outcry over a whopping failure than you are," Bartley Richston declared. "But neither are we to be stampeded into sinking more money. It would be lunacy. Most of us see clearly that to go ahead simply means a bigger smash later on. This is no matter for sentiment. We are practical men and we see no sound reason for making tremendous sacrifices. As an alternative I would suggest — since you seem to think, contrary to our judgment, that the Norquay Trust can be resuscitated — that you take it over, lock, stock and barrel, yourself. You can have my interest. I'm satisfied my shares aren't worth the paper they're printed on. Then you can use your own resources to bolster it up, and if you succeed any profit or glory will be your own."

"Very well," Norquay senior agreed, very gently and — to Rod — quite unexpectedly. "I will accept your shares, and your resignations. In the usual manner you will elect in your places such men as I name. Not tomorrow, nor next week, but now — at once. It is quarter to eleven. There are clerks and telephones. I shall be back at a quarter to twelve.

"Remember," he concluded harshly, "I am a wealthy man and not given to idle threats. If any of you at any time now or in the future takes a step by word or deed to precipitate a crisis which I am trying to avoid — then I step aside. The funds I propose to use in clearing up this mess of your making I shall then devote to seeing that such of you as I can reach shall get your just deserts for certain disbursements in connection with this trust company."

He turned his back on them. Rod followed him out to the cloakroom. They put on their coats in silence, walked out to the street where a closed motor car waited at the curb.

"The Western Club," Mr. Norquay told the chauffeur.

"I need a drink badly," he said to Rod, "to take the taste out of my mouth. Well, we're committed to a devil of an undertaking, Rod. You'll have to begin ripping the heart out of our timber as soon as there's a break in the weather. It is our only salvation. I have turned everything else into cash the last few weeks against this emergency. I never believed we should ever get into so tight a corner. We've got a fighting chance. That's all."

"I wonder," Rod's mind envisaged certain passages in his great-great-grandfather's journal, "if it's as tight a corner as the Chilcotins had us in once or twice? There have been tight corners in the past, pater. Do you suppose we have lost our capacity for hard fighting? Gone soft? Eh?"

His father glanced at him. "God forbid," he said quietly, and relapsed into silence.

"It is my fault," he sighed. "I should have fathomed Grove long ago. Blind, blind! He's eaten up with vanity. Fancies himself a Napoleon on the field of affairs. They've played shrewdly on that. I can see it now. He doesn't realize yet what they've done to him, nor how. He's been bewildered for weeks — and still confident that if he could get enough money he could carry it off. A fool and his money! Power in weak hands. They made a tool of him, a common tool. And we've got to pay through the nose. There's no choice — unless we get down to their level and run to cover like jackals."

"If you have proof of criminal acts, why don't you club them with that; *make* them disgorge?" Rod asked.

The older man shook his head.

"Only as a last resort. I'm not really sure I could. Moral certainty is not legal proof. There are moneys loaned to companies that are really dummies. It's rather complicated, and they are very clever. I hardly expected to make them contribute funds. The most I hoped for was to frighten them away from a receivership, force them out of the thing quietly. I shrink from a public scandal. They wouldn't, if they felt personally safe. They could make Grove a proper scapegoat. No, I've done the best that can be done."

The machine stopped before the club entrance. They went up to Norquay senior's rooms, and he produced a decanter and glasses and a siphon of soda.

He drained his glass and set it down. He leaned forward in his chair, his elbows on his knees, his face in his hands.

"I have a strange feeling of some crisis at hand," he said gloomily. "I have taken the ultimate precaution. Their game is stopped, I'm sure. Still — I have that uneasy feeling. I'm not a fanciful man. I never took much stock in premonitions. Childish. Nevertheless — I can depend on you absolutely, Rod? Eh? If anything happens to me you'll see this thing through? Because there's no one else — you understand how I feel about it, don't you?"

"Yes, pater," Rod said quietly. "I understand. But nothing's going to happen to *you*."

"I'm an old man," his father said. "I can't stand much strain. What's the time? We'd better be getting back."

Sometime during the luncheon hour the original shareholders and directors of the Norquay Trust Company completed the last task they would ever perform in that capacity at that great table. They took their scowling faces one by one from the room. The final exit was made by John P. Wall, rotund-bellied, imperturbable, unmoved to the last.

He paused in the doorway to relight his cigar.

"Well, Norquay senior," he said casually, "I have to admire your nerve — but your judgment is damn poor. A man may lose his money. Only a bloomin' idiot gives it away."

CHAPTER XXII

THE THREE, FATHER and two sons, remained seated at the table without speaking for a few seconds after Wall's parting shot.

Then Grove heaved a sigh.

"Well, that's finished," he said with a return of his old briskness. "I can't say that I like the idea of draining the estate to protect this concern. But it won't take me long to pull it out of the hole. It's really better to have it entirely in our own hands. I didn't believe that crowd would ever get cold feet and leave me in the lurch. Good riddance."

"No," his father answered slowly, "it is not finished. I want your formal resignation as president. I want an assignment of your entire holding in this corporation. At once. When you have done that, it will be finished, so far as you're concerned."

"Pater! For God's sake! Have you gone mad?" Grove's eyes bulged. His mouth opened roundly. "You're not going to put me out?"

"That is precisely my intention."

"But you can't. Nobody knows this thing as I do. It won't run without me. I made it, I tell you. The complexity of —"

"You made it!" his father said wearily. "What have you made of it? A hash. A shaky, unwieldy thing that will fall to pieces if I don't plaster it up with money. Listen to me, Grove."

He leaned forward, pointing an index finger pistol fashion, and Rod had an impression of hearing sentence passed on a delinquent, a sentence from which there could be no appeal. He had never thought of his father as a harsh, merciless man. He was harsh now. There was an acid bitterness in his tone.

"Listen to me," he repeated. "You have had your head for nine years. You have sunk a sizable fortune in this, and it is nothing but a gutted shell. You have not only wasted your own money, allowed these men to filch it from you, but you have taken the money of people who trusted you and put it in jeopardy. Not because you were a crook or a thief — but because you associated with crooks and thieves without recognizing them as such. You should have known what constitutes business integrity. You have disregarded the highest obligation of a public trust. So you can't remain in control here. You should never have been in control. That was my mistake — for which we must all pay — all of us, do you hear? I should have seen through you long ago. Your private life is a scandal and your public life a sham. You're morally as well as financially bankrupt. You've misled me. I've had to learn for myself about things. You can be of no service in clearing up the mess you've made. I can't trust you. I have no confidence in you. So you must step aside."

Grove's chin sank on his breast.

"You ought to give me a chance," he mumbled. "I've made mistakes. Everybody does. But nobody can handle this thing without me."

Rod marvelled at the fixity of this idea.

"No," his father repeated inflexibly. "From now on you make your own chances. Charlie Hale will take full charge here. You will be at hand for a few days to give him such information as he requires. But you will have no authority. I want this attended to this afternoon. At once. See that you do it immediately."

Grove rose. He slouched through the doorway, all the sprightliness gone out of him. Rod felt a sudden twinge of pity. Grove had been broken on his own wheel. Norquay senior sat staring blankly at the table. A wistful sadness shadowed his face. It pained Rod. He was an old man and Grove was his son — and he had been proud of him. Rod understood.

"Don't take it to heart so, pater," he tried to cheer him. "It'll come out all right."

"The limits of human folly are only exceeded by human blindness," his father answered moodily, "and sometimes it is a little difficult to adjust one's vision to a merciless flash of light."

He sat tapping his fingertips on the polished wood.

"I really wanted you with me for moral support this afternoon, I think, Rod," he confessed, with a faint smile. "I'm sure it has been illuminating, if somewhat disagreeable. I think all the fireworks are touched off. Now I shall be here all afternoon with my solicitor attending to dry business matters. So I won't keep you. There are certain things I want to talk over with you, but tomorrow or another day will do as well."

Rod left the Trust building and walked along Hastings Street without a definite aim. There was an uncomfortable heaviness in his breast, a physical discomfort, which drove him to motion. And his brain was busy in a detached impersonal fashion. All the battles were not fought with guns and poison gas. Struggle seemed inherent in the very process of living, no matter how one lived, what precautions one took. Struggle was all very well — until it became edged with pain and bitterness. Prides, ambitions, frantic strivings for this and that — and defeats, reprisals, disasters close in their wake. He wondered what Grove would do now. He wondered if this unstable edifice of Grove's creation would go down in spite of all effort and bury the Norquay family in its collapse. He ruminated upon Grove's eagerly pursued career, slipping away now into sordid futility. A matter of dollars. No question of honour or duty, no sacrifice for anything resembling an ideal, no vision of usefulness to his family, his friends, or his country had illuminated Grove's headlong way. Grove had made a bid for neither respect nor affection in all his dealings with men. Only power, the purely material aspect of power, was a thing he valued. He had lost it. What would he do without it? A brigadier reduced to a K.P.

Rod's most conscious desire, as he moved along a street sodden with a drizzle of cold rain, was to be on the porch at Hawk's Nest, looking at high, aloof mountains deep in winter snow, hiding their heads in wisps of frost-fog, hearing the voice of the rapids lift up its ancient song. He craved rest and quiet, a surcease of incessant street noise, which was to him a faint echo of the sound and fury of the Western Front. He wanted freedom from clash and struggle until he could at least draw his breath and give his heart a chance. He believed he was past a physical crisis, that his heart would strengthen if he could withdraw from crowds and noise, from the swirl of acquisitiveness which bred the mean passions of which he had that day seen some manifestation. He didn't want to be chewed up in the machine which had got beyond Grove's control. He wanted no hand on those levers. Yet he seemed to see obscure forces thrusting upon him tasks he shrank from.

On the surface it was simple enough. They couldn't let a smash come. That was clear. To brace up that swaying structure unlimited funds must be created out of the raw material they controlled, that which had been the backbone of the Norquay estate — those lordly firs which clothed granite ridges and mountainsides, those ancient cedars that masked gorge and hollow and swamp. That would be his job. One well enough to his liking. Even the destruction of a thing Rod loved as he did his native forest could have an element of the constructive, too, if it were not dictated by a necessity born of human folly and greed. Still, that couldn't be helped now.

It was a curious feeling of the Norquay Trust Company looming over his personal life as it loomed over the adjacent buildings that depressed Rod most. It seemed rather fantastic to imagine that as threatening his peace and welfare, but the feeling was real.

He drifted along the street. People passed him singly, in groups, in pairs, in little droves, hurrying or sauntering, rich and poor, men, women and children, an endlessly flowing stream of humanity. A sprinkling of khaki showed among them. The majority were the last sweepings of the draft not yet demobilized. Others, he saw at a glance, were returned men. He wondered what they thought of it all now they were back.

He was to have that question partially answered before long. Within a block of the *Province* office where he had last met him Rod encountered Andy Hall. From the hand which grasped Rod's extended one the index and second fingers were missing. He wore a lieutenant's uniform; four wound stripes marked one sleeve. His freckled face had lost some of the old ruddy colour, but his eyes flickered as brightly quizzical as in those days when he rigged high-lead spars in the Valdez camp. Rod took this all in at a glance.

Where were you? What division? When did you get back? How many times over the length and breadth of North America were those questions being asked and answered in 1919?

"Months ago — last of September," Andy said. "The idea was that I should bear a hand getting draftees into shape at Hastings Park, since I was classified as unfit for front-line service. But I haven't done much. Flu knocked me out in November. They'll can me pretty soon, I hope. It's easy to get into the army, but hell to get out, even when they don't need you any longer."

"The tribal instinct won out, eh?" Rod smiled. "For a downright rebel you seem to have got on in the army."

"I'm still a rebel," Andy returned. "The war would have made me one if I hadn't been before. Still, when you are fool enough to volunteer for a job, you can't very well lie down on it. There were times when I felt like it, though. It was a dirty job, eh?"

"Rather," Rod agreed. "Remember the time we had a drink in the Strand and talked about the big show?"

Andy nodded.

"I was thinking about that as I came past the *Province*," he drawled. "If it were worthwhile expressing an opinion, I'd say the same — only more so."

"Let's stroll up to the Vancouver and sit down and gas awhile?" Rod suggested.

They found comfortable chairs in a quiet corner of the great hotel. Their talk covered Europe, politics, certain phases of trench fighting, and came back at last from generalities tinged with pessimism to the particular, to themselves.

"What are you going to do after you're demobilized?" Rod asked. It was not, on his part, an idle question.

"I don't know." Andy shook his head. "I'll never sling cable again, that's sure. You need all your fingers for that."

His eyes rested speculatively on the mutilated hand.

"Long before I lost my fingers," he continued, "I used to say to myself that if I got out of it alive, I'd never work for any man again — I'd never have anybody's collar round my neck. The army put that into me. It jarred my old idea of men voluntarily cooperating for the common good or any other purpose. The army — all the armies — were made up of picked men. Eighty per cent of 'em fell into two categories; they had to be led, or they had to be driven. If there was no one to lead or drive, they ran round in circles when anything happened. So I made up my mind to be a leader or a driver — to play the game the way the rest do, who manage to beat the game. I was so damned sick of orders and discipline. Orders that were stupid, or vicious, or simply issued as an exhibition of authority. Discipline that went beyond its logical purpose of securing cohesive action and became merely a whip to lash a lot of tired unhappy men. Nobody minded the actual fighting so much. That's what you were there for; you expected it; you got used to it. You took your chances without making a fuss, even if now and then your stomach sort of turned. No, the dirt and drudgery were worse than the danger. And to a fellow like me the sight and sound of fussy brass hats laying more stress on recognition of their rank and dignity, the unanimity with which they implied that they were *It* —hell, *you* know how everybody below the rank of a battalion commander felt about that. They could do anything they liked to you, say the worst they could think, punish you for somebody else's mistakes. And you couldn't say a damned word. You couldn't even look sour. That was insubordination. No. I didn't mind the war so much — it was the army — the whole fabric of the military system.

"I passed up a chance at a commission in '15 — because I was still too class-conscious. But I grabbed the next chance. That's what I'm going to do in civil life — grab chances. I don't know how, yet. I don't think much. I'm still in the army, and in the army you're not supposed to think. But I didn't run wild in France, except for brief spells, so I've saved most of my pay. And I hear talk of a gratuity to us heroes." He smiled broadly. "I'll probably come out with a couple of thousand dollars. After that — well, you see before you a man who has had a bayonet stuck through his leg, his carcass lightly punctured with shrapnel, one or two faint whiffs of gas. None of which did him more harm than to give him long spells of lying still and thinking. And he thought himself into a condition of mind that will prevent him from ever again working hard — for other people. No, Norquay, I will never again labour faithfully to make two dollars grow — for someone else — where only one grew before. I don't believe I could feel the slightest obligation toward a job again, or an atom of pride in doing a job well. You see, I can't lose sight of the job-owners — I don't like 'em. I despise 'em. They got us all into this mix-up. They called us to arms in the name of all the old gods that man has been taught to reverence. And then they laid down on us, and went to making money out of our necessities. No, whenever a man offers me a job, I'll think of war contracts, of seventeen prices for clothes and food, of the bonds they've salted away, of shoddy boots and defective ammunition — and the fact that some of them are secretly sorry the war is over and the big, easy money at an end. No, I couldn't be loyal to a job, with all that in my mind."

"Fiddlesticks," Rod answered this last. "If I had a stand of timber and I said to you, 'Here's a crew and machinery — go to it; you've got a free hand,' you'd get it out for me as if you were getting it out for yourself."

"Well," Andy hesitated, "if you bring yourself into it, that's different. You don't come in any of the categories I mentioned, or I'm very much mistaken. Operating a real job for a man you could like and respect. That is different."

"You see, you haven't lost a capacity for loyalty," Rod pointed out. "It's only been deflected. I understand that. Psychologically I've travelled pretty much the same road you have. All that you say is true.

Only it isn't all the truth, Andy. Just one side of the shield; the side that's turned to us; that's hard for us to get our eyes off. Fellows like you and me are a little up in the air right now. We feel like tramping savagely on the toes of a lot of smug, comfortable persons. That wouldn't get us anywhere. Nor would it change them — because they simply don't understand. What we'll probably get down to after a while — those of us who have a sense of order and any touch of creativeness — will be some sort of activity that won't set the world on fire or turn it into a Bedlam, but that will possibly do some little good in the immediate radius of our own activity. *Sabe*? A man has to do what he can, before he can do what he wants."

"A man," Andy observed thoughtfully, "generally has to solve his material problems before he can tackle spiritual ones. Yet the two are interwoven. It's very difficult. I'm a rampant individualist, by nature. Man is. But if you didn't have some check on individualism the world would be a regular Kilkenny. Rampageous individualism in big affairs is what started the big scrap. The same thing will start another. It may even start hellish struggles between individual exploiters here at home and the masses they're keen to exploit. You can't have order and peace and security in a society where everybody is straining every nerve to get what he wants, and to hell with the other fellow. I'm no Utopian any longer, but I do know that if evolution doesn't speed up the process of industrial reorganization, there are going to be some corking rows, and a lot of material and spiritual uncertainty for everybody. I may not seem very consistent in what I say or do, but I'm consistent in my perception of certain things. We've built up a complex mechanism of affairs. The machine is our master instead of our servant."

Rod thought of the Norquay Trust Company as a vast creaking mechanism exacting unrewarded service, sacrifice, claiming the vital substance of himself, his father, the estate. Grove's Frankenstein creation!

"It may be so," he conceded. "But we are not yet automatons."

They continued to talk until the dusk of the short winter's day closed in. When the lights began to blink along the street they separated, Andy to his barracks, Rod to his home.

A taxi stand fronted the hotel, looking across Georgia Street. Rod crossed the way. As he did so a newsboy passed crying "ex-x-x-truh" in a shrill treble. In the distance he could hear other voices wailing the same cry. The Peace Conference, a fresh outbreak in Europe. Anything was possible in that welter of political, racial, and economic antagonisms across the Atlantic. He beckoned the boy.

In the glare of a white-globed light standard he read the headlines:

PRESIDENT NORQUAY TRUST INSTANTLY
KILLED
SHOTGUN ACCIDENTALLY DISCHARGED

CHAPTER XXIII

A NORTHWEST GALE RATTLED a loose window in the library at Hawk's Nest. Beyond that the house stood solid to the blasts, as solid as a mountain mass of the granite that formed its walls. In the surrounding woods branchy cedar and tall, plumed firs bent before that gusty wind like bowed giants, giants that sighed in mournful cadences. Rod stuffed a folded bit of paper between sash and frame to silence the tremulous chatter of the wood.

He flattened his face against the pane for a few seconds. In the dark where the wind lashed at everything as if the Borean gods were in a towering passion, he could see faint, shifting flecks of white — wind-whipped seas breaking in the channel. In brief lulls he could hear the rapids grumbling at full flood, the deep roar of agitated waters softened by distance. He could mark under that black canopy of sky a silver streak where straight current met back eddy in a foaming line, and the devil's dishpans spun about deep vortices.

He went back to his chair before a glowing fireplace. It was near midnight, and he was wakeful, his brain a simmering pot. A succession of images trooped by; he couldn't stop them. Thoughts, fancies, realities leaped out of nothingness, loomed before him, vanished before the crowding army of their fellows, as if he were engaged upon a review of the past and a projection of the future. He could no more stop that procession than he could check the tide roaring through the Euclataw Passage. It was as if he stood aside and watched the entity that was himself performing this and that action — a single thread tracing a formless pattern in the warp and woof of persons and things. He could see it all very clearly up to the present. Beyond that the images were uncertain, tentative, sometimes blurred.

His youthful sense of the family as a permanent, imperishable force, in relation to which he as an individual was negligible, had been wiped out of his mind. The colossal stature of the Norquays had shrunk to his own dimension. The solid had become fluid, ready to trickle through his fingers if he did not have a care.

Five years ago tonight he had been at Hawk's Nest in a breathing spell from the Valdez camp. Out of all the permanences that surrounded him then, he was now only sure of one — Mary, his wife. His grandfather was dead. Phil was dead, and Grove. Their father was dying here tonight, while the northwester swept the coast. Materially, their hold was now uncertain on all that had served to make them what they were.

In a little while there would be only himself to make decisions, to take action, to bear a responsibility for matters which no longer involved merely himself or his immediate family but embraced people he had never seen, would never know. Their welfare, resting in his hands, burdened him with an oppressive weight.

Why should he shoulder this burden. He began to understand why men here and there evade responsibility, or break down under it, when the shadow of such responsibility loomed darkly over himself.

He had had no preparation for responsibility. He had lived — he smiled at the platitude — a sheltered life. Except in one or two isolated instances, such as his marriage, he had never been compelled to make a momentous decision. His youth, with its romantic dreaming, its fastidiousness which had made him shun such physical grossness as Grove's, had been ordered and directed. So had his more formal education. Even his four years in the army, except in unimportant details, had never taken him into the realm of plan and execution. He had simply been a cog in the military machine, obeying orders, reissuing those orders to men bound to obey him, as he was himself bound to obey others. Responsibility rested always in other hands. He had been aware of that and fairly content to have it so.

But that was at an end. Very soon now, a matter of hours, when the unconscious old man in a room down the hallway breathed out his tired life he, Rod Norquay, would become the fulcrum and lever which should move enormous weights. He would be faced by a necessity to take up a task which offered little hope of reward save a sense of duty performed. Other men's welfare, other men's money, other men's sins. He could draw back from this, or see it through. He could evade it or grapple it stoutly. But there it was, waiting for him to decide.

Grove had evaded, when he faced the incontrovertible result of his handiwork. Or had he? No one would ever know. He had gone in mid-afternoon from the Norquay Trust office to his home. He had telephoned a friend to join him in a duck hunt at a gun club on the Ladner flats, had arranged to pick up his friend. He had come out from the house to the garage, bearing a shotgun, a bag and a shooting coat, whistling as he came. He spoke to the chauffeur genially. While the man attended to some detail of his machine the shotgun cracked and Grove Norquay fell against the running-board. He was dead before the man could cry for help.

And whether it was sheer accident, or whether he had killed himself in a moment of despair at the muddle he had wrought, Rod could not say. Publicly it went as a sad accident. But he knew what his father thought. He knew, too, what rumours ran like sly foxes in the street, rumours which did not have their origin in mere conjecture, but which nevertheless would have brought Grove's financial castle tumbling about their ears if his father had not been prepared.

Rod would never forget the crowd of people in the street an hour before the Norquay Trust Company opened its doors. People well and ill-dressed, shopclerks, businessmen, middle-aged women, people whose motors were parked at the curb. They strove and pushed and jostled for advantage, eager to be first, until policemen came and herded them into line — a line that extended a block and curved around a corner up a side street like the tail of an uneasy, muttering serpent.

All that forenoon and well past the luncheon hour they filed past the paying tellers, presented checks, passbooks, demanding their money, withdrawing accounts. As the cash boxes of the Norquay Trust emptied into pockets that departed hastily through the front door they were replenished by sheafs of Norquay estate currency withdrawn from other banks in hundred-thousand-dollar lots.

From behind bronze grillwork Rod watched this scene. He marked the nervous eagerness of these people over their money. They were frightened, watchful, uneasy, until they had it in their hands. The air was charged with hostile currents, with a tension that communicated itself to department managers, the ledgerkeepers, the tellers. One man made a five-hundred-dollar mistake — and broke under the strain. He sat in his cage and wept, and a murmuring that was like a growl swept through the lofty, pillared room until he was led away and another man took up his work of handing out cash.

Once Rod's father came to sit by him for a minute. He looked out at the anxious faces, the people crowding forward, pressing eagerly up to the wickets. After a little he said to Rod in a low, tense whisper:

"The coward. The damned coward! He couldn't face the music."

About one-thirty the run tapered off. Every certificate of deposit, every demand was met promptly, courteously. Human nature asserted itself. An institution that could disgorge an enormous total and still exhibit great bales of currency and gold behind each teller *couldn't* be shaky. Who peddled the story that the Norquay Trust was broke, anyhow? Some damn fool. It was a false alarm. Fellow that started it ought to be shot — scaring people like that — making so much trouble. The Norquay estate's backing it. No chance of a concern like that being in the hole. What you think? Eh?

They stood out on the curb, repeating things like that. Men turned back at the very wickets. Some returned shamefacedly to redeposit their money, only to be told politely that the Norquay Trust declined to reopen closed accounts.

The ordinary cash depositors ceased from troubling long before the closing hour.

"That's that," Charlie Hale grunted. "We've pretty well disposed of the small fry. Fortunately a few big accounts can be met. And none of the trust accounts are at our heads like a pistol."

That was the end of a salient demonstration. Routine resumed its placid groove. Time and effort Norquay senior declared and his son-in-law, whose profession was accountancy, agreed, would bring order out of the chaos Grove had wrought.

Yes, he had somehow blundered into chaos. And no matter how many other clutching fingers might have been dipped into the trust coffers, Grove had failed to feather his own nest. His personal estate included only his house and his yacht. There was no record of his having ever withdrawn a dollar from trust funds, of receiving more than a liberal salary. His assets didn't include enough cash to bury him. Where, then, did the money go?

"Ask Wall, Richston, Deane — that crowd," Charlie Hale muttered, when Rod put the question. "I may be able to tell you after a while. A few things look very, very fishy. The fact remains that half the so-called assets are junk. There's no mistake about the liabilities. If I can follow certain leads far enough, we may be able to make somebody disgorge. But they're pretty clever. They seem to have got Grove coming and going."

"You will have to get crews together soon," his father had told him after Grove's funeral. "I'd put the first crew in on that Horn limit. It's beautiful timber and easy logging. Also start up the old Valdez camp. There are two or three limits on Hardwicke yet, as well. In fact, timber's all we have left. I've hypothecated everything else. I'll look after the town end. The woods will be your field. The weather ought to break soon."

The weather had not permitted woods work. But the turn of affairs had sent Rod and his wife and boy almost immediately to Hawk's Nest. The elder Norquay urged them to go.

"That's the place for you," he said. "It's our home. It has always been our home. It will be yours, Rod. You can consider it yours now. When I feel my time coming, I shall want to be there too."

And his time had come, perhaps a little sooner than he expected, perhaps not sooner than he wished.

"My life has been a failure," he said to Rod one day. "I might have made a different man of Grove, if I hadn't been so comfortably secure in the egotistic belief that to be my son was guarantee enough. Oh, I've been blind with the sort of pride that goes before a fall. And I was too harsh. He was proud too. I killed him myself, Rod."

He would talk like that, full of grief. And he would go on to speak of expiation, of the obligation upon them to give a steward's account of their trust.

"You see," he would repeat, "it was not simply Grove, but what Grove represented, what he sprang from, that bred people's confidence. No casual promoter, no fly-by-night financier could have induced that simple trust on such a scale. People looked beyond him and they saw something that was solid as a rock, that couldn't fail. We must live up to that, somehow."

The library door opened. Mary beckoned silently.

"He wants to speak to you," she said in the hall.

But the momentary flash of consciousness lapsed before Rod reached the bedside. He had been sinking for days. He was going out now, like a guttering candle. A nurse stood at the foot of the bed. A doctor stood, watch in hand, his fingers on the faint pulse. Rod looked a question. The man shook his head. Rod sat down beside the bed. To his quickened imagination the room seemed full of the flutter of sable wings.

An hour later his father died.

CHAPTER XXIV

"I HAVE SEEN SOME financial muddles in my time and some manipulation that was on the borderline of pure theft," Charlie Hale said to Rod, "but this is the worst mess I have ever had to deal with."

They were going over the situation in Hale's private office, which had once been Grove's sanctum, sitting by the same table upon which Grove had leaned his elbows long ago, when he remonstrated with Rod for walking Beach Avenue with Mary Thorn. Beyond its walls the faint murmur of voices arose, and the remote tapping of typewriters.

"Take this Spruce Supplies Limited for an example," Hale continued. "One of the apparently honest failures that left the Norquay Trust in the lurch. Spruce Supplies was organized by Richston and Wall. There were other stockholders — all dummies. Once incorporated, Wall and Richston apparently dispose of all interest in the company. Then Spruce Supplies proceeds to issue three hundred thousand dollars' worth of five-year, seven per cent bonds against their holdings, which consist of timber limits, camp equipment, and logging machinery, valued at seven hundred thousand dollars. The Norquay Trust takes these bonds as security for a loan of three hundred thousand, recommended and authorized by Wall, Richston, etc., in their capacity as directors. The concern is supposed to create a sinking fund to retire these bonds at maturity. They begin timber operations with a flourish. For two years they pay the bond interest. But after two years they cease payments. In the fullness of time the Norquay Trust forecloses and acquires all the assets. But, in my investigation of these assets, I discover that Spruce Supplies operated on a tremendous scale while they did work. The timber is practically all cut, the equipment is pretty well worn out. The men who cruised the limits for me estimate seven or eight hundred thousand dollars' worth of timber removed — prices went rocketing for airplane spruce, you know. A liberal estimate of what we have to show for three hundred thousand cash is less than sixty thousand in real value.

"There were seven shareholders. Five owned two shares apiece. Two are clerks who disappeared in the draft. Three are bond salesmen — forty-dollar-a-week men. The two who owned the bulk of the stock — well, one's a sort of confidential man in Richston's office. The other was for ten years in Wall's employment. They're both out of the country; with a few thousand dollars apiece, I imagine. Dummies — pure and simple. You can guess who got the money. But you can't prove anything. I doubt if you could take legal action against those foxy old birds if you had proof that the pair of them looted Spruce Supplies. It was ostensibly a legal transaction. The Norquay Trust Company should have protected itself, you see."

"And that's only one of several such," Hale concluded. "They made a milk cow of this business. They saw that funds were invested where they would do the most good — for them. They simply made a goat of Grove."

Rod stared at the figures on a sheet of paper before him.

"Liabilities practically four hundred thousand in excess of available assets," he murmured. "That's a hump to get over. How long can we reasonably expect to go on — I mean how much grace will we have to meet everything without going into forced liquidation?"

"With a fair amount of revenue from some outside source — say eighty or a hundred thousand every six months — we can go right along as usual," Hale replied. "There's no immediate call for funds. All the pressing obligations your father provided funds to meet. There's only a dead loss that this concern can't shake off by its own efforts. We can — we have — cut operating expenses to the bone. But as a trust company we can't — legitimately — make money fast enough ever to get even."

"There's only one outside source of revenue available, you know," Rod reminded.

"Is it wise to go any further?" Hale shifted uneasily. "You'll beggar yourself."

"Between beggaring myself and beggaring other people, there doesn't seem to be much choice."

"Do you consider yourself personally responsible for Grove's actions?" Hale asked earnestly.

"You know what the governor's idea was," Rod answered. "Grove put this over pretty much on the strength of the family standing. So we were tacitly involved. We'll be a public stink if we sit back. We aren't legally responsible; we are morally. That was his idea. I'm inclined to agree."

"That's drawing it pretty fine," Hale responded. "Grove was his son. Individually you are not to blame at all. It's easy to make a grand gesture and go down. Heroic sort of thing. But once you're down everybody'll walk on you."

"What are you getting at?" Rod demanded impatiently. "Do you want me to cut and run with the swag — like a burglar? It amounts to pretty much the same. I keep the estate intact, and these people all lose their money. I don't quite see why you should try to dissuade me."

"I'm rather anxious to know just how far you will go with it," Hale returned. "Suppose you change your mind when the going gets rough? I've got involved in this myself through connection by marriage."

"What would you do if you were in my place?" Rod asked softly.

"I don't know," Hale twisted uneasily in his seat. "I'd hate to be faced with such a decision, Rod. Your family has cut quite a figure in this country for a long time. Hate to see it peter out. Money *is* essential.

Without money," he made a gesture of dismissal. "I went over the whole thing with your father. Probably take your last dollar to see it through."

"Are you thinking about Dorothy's share of the estate?" Rod asked his brother-in-law point-blank.

Hale didn't resent the question. He answered frankly.

"Well, yes and no. I wasn't a rich man to begin with and four years in the army didn't improve my finances. Still, I can get by comfortably on my profession. I didn't marry Dot for her income. It would be convenient to have it continue. But that is not what disturbs me. I don't like to think of the family fortune all shot to pieces, the old place up the coast passing into the hands of some damned profiteer — some pot-bellied swab who made a barrel of money building useless ships or selling bacon to the government. The rallying point of the whole clan will be gone. You'll be like a feudal baron without a castle, without a single man-at-arms."

"Still, you see my position, don't you?" Rod persisted.

"Surely," Hale admitted. "I'm not dense — or unsympathetic. *Noblesse oblige.* Only it's a pity. People won't care one way or the other a year after it's over. Everybody's too busy whipping his own particular devil around the stump. When your wife has to wear cotton stockings and do her own cooking, the very people you're protecting will only think of you with contemptuous pity."

"I would rather incur their contempt than my own," Rod answered that: the last had stung him a little. "Well, I'll keep in touch. So long."

He went home, back to the rented house which they kept on for convenience. Six weeks at Hawk's Nest had revived the old feeling of its being the only place he could ever truly regard as home. That fierce possessive pride rose stronger than ever in his breast when he walked about the grounds, when he stood among those massive trees rising in brown-trunked ranks over Big Dent, when he lay in his bed at night and looked drowsily up at the high, beamed ceiling. It was as permanent as the hills — or it should be made so. And it was his, his own, to keep and pass on to another generation of Norquays — if he could. If he could? There had never been a question of that nature to harass a

Norquay since the cornerstone was levered into place in 1809. If he could!

Why shouldn't he? It was simply assured. He had only to stand back with his hands in his pockets, aloof, unmoved, while Grove's white elephant died for lack of the nourishment he alone could supply. Hadn't his father done enough? The figures had staggered Rod at the time. Although every active productive undertaking of the estate had stopped for the duration of the war, yet their fortune had not shrunk appreciably. Not until Rod's father began to pour it into those looted coffers. Every liquid asset, bonds, gilt-edged securities, real estate — all hypothecated to raise funds.

Hopeless to think of ever redeeming them. But there was still timber which with labour and machinery he could transform into money. He owned that clear of all encumbrance, thousands of acres of it, the finest virgin timber on the Pacific coast. With Hawk's Nest and standing timber he still had firm grasp of the old, comfortable security for himself and all the collateral branches of the Norquay clan.

Why should he voluntarily give that up?

To organize his forces, to live under the pressure of a struggle for more and more revenue, to drive labour, to watch markets and prices with a feverish intensity, to live and breathe and think in terms of money and more money was hateful to him. To whip up a sick heart day after day. Suppose it laid down on him? Who would carry on?

He looked back from his own doorstep at the square roof and the skeleton sign of the Norquay Trust looming on the jagged downtown skyline. It was like an inverted pyramid resting on his shoulders, crushing him.

He walked through the living room with a glance. He knew Mary would be upstairs where she had arranged a workshop for herself with a desk, a shelf of books, a typewriter. She sat there making aimless marks on the margin of a pad on which she had written a few sentences.

He had explained the situation to her roughly long ago. Now he sat down to explain in detail, to outline his personal relation to an inherited problem.

"There it is," he concluded. "What do you think? I can go through with it, or I can let it go. It may beat me even if I do my best. At most we'll only have Hawk's Nest and some machinery. I can hardly hope to salvage more than that."

She looked at him for a second with an enigmatical smile.

"Why ask me, Rod?" she said finally. "You're going to do what one would naturally expect you to do. You've made up your mind. You don't really consider that you have much choice, do you?"

"No," he admitted. "I can't see that I have. I hate the job. I don't like cutting my own throat. I don't like paying for a dead horse that somebody else killed. But I simply can't do the other thing."

"I don't like poverty," Mary said presently. "I've known comparative poverty, though, and I'm not much the worse for it. I'm quite confident that between us we could manage very well if we had nothing but the clothes we stand in. One can sometimes turn dreams into dollars. No, I'm not much afraid of anything the world can do to us. Rod junior will manage to grow up into something of a man on considerably less than 'steen thousand a year. If you feel that something more vital to you than money is involved in this — . One has to be guided in such matters by one's convictions. A profound conviction, right or wrong, is a tremendous driving force. If you throttle it to grasp a material advantage — people do sometimes. And they suffer for it."

She sat tapping the pad with her pencil.

"Queer complications crop up over such a question," she said at last. "I wonder if you know that practically all my father's money is in the Norquay Trust. The few thousands that are to keep him and mamma in comfort while they live — all he saved out of a lifetime of work."

"Good Lord, no, I didn't know that," Rod said. "He didn't get it out when the scramble was on?"

She shook her head.

"He laughed when I asked him. I did. I telephoned him when you told me what was happening downtown. He hasn't even thought of revoking the trust. You see," she explained, "he made a trust fund of it and draws only the income. He said that people could make damned fools of themselves on the strength of a rumour, but that he was sure anything the Norquay family backed was as solid as Gibraltar."

"Well, you have there the key to why Grove shot himself, and to why my father died of grief as much as of the flu," he said quietly. "It may be a sinful pride, but by God it's a reality I have to abide by. If we go down, we go down with our flag flying."

"But we won't go down," she said cheerfully. She came and put her arms encouragingly about him. "We may lose materially, but there are precious things that can't be taken away from us. Only you'll have to be careful of yourself. You'll have to relax. You've been strung up for weeks, brooding over this mess. I don't like that. You mustn't. We'll play the cards we hold, and if we lose, why we'll have played without cheating. Eh? Smile, Roderick Dhu."

"You're a jewel," Rod whispered. "I won't brood any more. Won't have time. I'm going to get under way. May I have a man in to dinner if I can get hold of him?"

"Half a dozen, if you like," Mary smiled.

They went downstairs. Rod called a regimental headquarters at Hastings Park. He got some information there, and called another number. Yes, Mr. Hall was in. In another minute Rod had him on the wire. Yes, he could come out to the house.

In the broad mirror of Rod's imagination, as he sat waiting, there stood forth successive images of what he meant to accomplish and how. His mind had a faculty of projecting ways and means, not as skeleton ideas, but as extraordinarily vivid pictures of the actual proceeding. He meant to make Andy Hall a commanding officer, the chief of his labour staff. His program took form in flashes, glimpses of men, machinery, stretches of forest, booming grounds — all energized, dynamic. There was a simplicity that he appreciated in such an undertaking. It was not a matter of finessing, of juggling with pawns and tokens on the commercial chessboard. It was not an affair or stratagems and artifice and cunning. It was honest productive effort, men and machinery moving purposefully under a directing force to supply human needs. He liked that aspect of what he meant to do.

Hall was ushered in by Yick Sing. He was in civilian clothes, a small bronze button in his left lapel. Rod led him upstairs to Mary's den.

"How long since you were demobbed?"

"About two weeks," Hall answered.

"Good. I'm going to start a pretty extensive logging show. Will you help me organize it?"

"Why pick on me?" Andy inquired languidly.

"I know you," Rod replied. "You know logging and loggers. I want a man who will understand what I'm driving at, a man I can trust."

"How do you know you can trust me?"

"I don't know it. I feel it."

A queer expression flickered across Andy's face.

"A rebel like me?" he said. "You know what I think about your class — you masters of my class. You people who have control of all the sources of power. Who give us jobs or take them away, according to the dictates of your interest. You understand and believe in class distinctions, don't you?"

"I understand them, yes. But character is more important than class."

"What is character?" Hall demanded.

"Indefinable, in most cases. But it's recognizable. Whatever your situation in life, without this thing we call character you're a dud. It exists independent of class. A leisured environment, quickened intelligence, liberal education, a tradition of uprightness, is supposed to form it. But it crops out, regardless of all these things. It's inherent in some people. It's an individual quality, not a class hallmark. But I'm getting away from the point. Your social and economic theories have very little to do with your individual function in society as it stands. You don't imagine there's a working-class movement for general betterment on foot in this country that will be imperilled by your working for me as a well-paid assistant in a job I'm undertaking? Do you?"

Andy grinned broadly.

"Hardly. So long as industry supplies jobs at living wages, everything'll be lovely. Give 'em jobs. That's all they want. They're uncomfortable in their minds unless there's somebody to tell 'em what to do. Tchk!"

He shrugged his shoulders.

"A soggy lump of dough," he grumbled. "Still, such as they are, I belong to 'em. I know what they're up against better than they do. And I'm sorry for 'em, without being able to change things."

"You find your people, the workers," Rod said, "a soggy lump of dough that the active brains of the world rather ruthlessly knead into such shapes as they require. And I find greediness, thoughtlessness, arrogance, and waste outstanding features among a considerable portion of my own class, which we agree controls and directs industry. Neither of us likes the prospect, but what can we do about it? Not much. We didn't create this state of affairs. But our actions are shaped by it. Even if a certain humane instinct in us revolts at being mixed up in an unseemly scramble where everybody is grabbing what he can, we have to accept that condition. If we have to fight for what we want — whether it's merely to exist or to pursue an ideal — why not fight with the best weapon that offers? I'm offering you a commission in industry insteady of enlistment in the ranks. It's neither philanthropy, nor a bribe on my part."

"You pay me a compliment," Andy said gravely. "It's true I know logging and loggers. But I don't know that I'd make a good boss — from the employer's point of view. It would not be possible for me to drive men."

"I don't want to drive men," Rod broke out impulsively. "I want to lead 'em, if it can be done. If I can give men just a little more security in their jobs, a little better conditions under which to work, a little more return in wages, that's more to them than all the theory in a thousand books. So long as men must work for wages they'll choose to work where they get the most for their effort. That's the sort of condition I want to create. Circumstances compel me to log for a profit like every other logger. But I'm neither a hog nor a parasite. I'm willing to share profits with the men who make them for me."

"All right, I'm your man," Andy said abruptly. "I never intended to look at a paycheque again. I can be a free and unfettered beachcomber and make a living and still be my own boss. But this looks interesting to me. If you don't like my style, or I yours, I can quit on short notice."

"Yes," Rod smiled. "That's where you have the best of the bargain. You can quit. I can't."

"That's rather stretching it a bit," Andy observed dryly. "I can't see that."

"You will presently," Rod informed him.

He sketched for Andy's benefit the situation in which he stood, the necessity for creating revenue, the obligation which he felt to rest heavily upon him.

"If I can pull out in a couple of years with Hawk's Nest, some machinery and a well-organized crew, I'll be lucky," he said. "If I can do that, men and machinery is all I need to build up a permanent structure of industry that will take care of my wants and the wants of every man in the organization."

"Your own crowd will be saying what a damned fool you are," Andy mused. "You're an idealist, Norquay. And I didn't think there were any left. I didn't believe idealism existed as a practical working force in any possible employer's mind. I'd got so lately that I didn't think there was anybody left in the world to whom a square deal meant anything but a convenient phrase. After all, that's what you're after, isn't it? Trying to live up to your notion of what constitutes a square deal?"

"Yes, I think that's about it," Rod agreed.

"Well, if you don't find the going too hard, if too many practical difficulties don't trip you," Andy prophesied, "I'll say that if you tackle the logging game in the same spirit you'll go a long way. It's a damned scarce sort of spirit. The stupidest husky in the woods can *sabe* a square deal. This is going to be very interesting. When do I start in, and what's the program?"

"I want you to begin tomorrow looking up a woods' boss and getting together a crew. We'll shoot 'em up to the old Valdez camp, start the falling gangs, and begin overhauling the machinery that's stored at the old camp. There's a watchman in charge, and everything's in good shape. We'll have to frame up a wage schedule. There will have to be some renovating on the camp. All sorts of details arranged. If you can meet me at the office in the Pacific Building about nine in the morning, we'll tackle the first arrangements."

"I'll be there," Andy promised.

"Meantime," said Rod, "let's go downstairs where it's more comfortable. If you have no other engagement you may as well stay to dinner."

"Thanks, I will," Andy accepted. "You won't mind, I suppose, having the cook serve square peas for me?"

They chuckled and so managed to dissipate the last trace of stiffness between them. Rod considered that he had won a minor victory. He knew that Andy Hall was one of those occasional beings who sprang from obscure sources with brains, courage, a pertinacious diligence in whatever he undertook, with infinite capacities for loyalty to either a person or an idea: the sort of man who leads forlorn proletarian hopes and is sometimes crucified by his own kind for fighting their battles. He could trust Andy Hall. Rod would have found it difficult to say, offhand, just why. But he knew that he could. And he had to have about him men whom he could trust, men who could understand that he was not simply another exploiter seeking ruthlessly his own advantage.

It was easy for men like Hall to lubricate the wheels of industry, or to set up frictions that produced minor disasters. Men like Andy thought in terms beyond themselves, beyond their personal ends. They rose up out of the low ground of their origins, looming above the common ruck like tall trees above a thicket. Rod was very glad to have Andy Hall's paid services. But he appreciated even more Andy's instant grasp of a difficult situation met in the only possible fashion.

A murmur of voices sounded in the living room. Rod was a trifle surprised to see Isabel Wall's piquant face turn to him over the back of a Chesterfield. She had been in the south all winter. Almost five years had left Isabel unchanged in appearance, except that her fair hair was thicker and bobbed in the prevailing mode so that it stood out around her head like a fluffy aureole, making her seem, with her big blue eyes and delicate pink-and-white skin, more like a charming doll than ever. Rod's mind revived that embarrassing scene under a high moon among the great tree shadows on Big Dent. He had not seen Isabel since. She put out her hand now with frank friendliness. It was all a little unexpected. Isabel so patently belonged in the camp of the enemy. Yet she seemed very sure of her ground here in his house, very much at home.

He introduced Andy to his wife, to Isabel, to a plump matron with two chins and a positive, not to say emphatic manner of speaking, a Mrs. Emmert whom Rod vaguely remembered.

He fell into conversation with Isabel, or rather Isabel talked and he listened. Isabel prattled as of old. Rod lost himself in speculation as to how any one could possibly talk so much and say so little. It was an art. He came out of this semi-absorption. Isabel ceased talking. Her face turned aside with a new quality of fixed attention. Rod looked and became aware that Andy was speaking to Mrs. Emmert with a bitter, gibing note in his usually pleasant voice. The whimsical, good-natured expression of his face had vanished. His face had hardened; his eyes had narrowed.

"You may consider it a notable distinction," he was saying. "But possibly your son has his doubts."

The lady made a sound in the nature of a gasp.

"You see," Andy continued in that frozen tone, "people whose knowledge of war is based on what they read in the papers don't know anything about war at all. The front-line men do. Most of 'em don't care to talk much about it. Being a person of no discrimination, I do talk about it. There is no glory in war — particularly this war — for the men who actually carry on the war. All the benefits of this ruction (if there are any benefits, which I doubt) are derived by people who stayed at home and did their patriotic duty by knitting socks and buying bonds and selling supplies to the War Department. You can't tell a soldier that it was anything but a dirty, dangerous job which he hated."

"That's the most unpatriotic thing I ever heard," Mrs. Emmert sputtered.

"I paid two fingers and a hole in one leg for the privilege of saying things like that," Andy observed tartly. "They're true. Your attitude is common enough. You've got one of these hermetically sealed minds that conceives of war as some sort of international game played by young men with guns, a game in which your son distinguished himself by winning a medal. A medal!" he snorted — and plunged his good hand into an inner pocket.

"Look, madam," he said ironically. "Three of 'em, Military Medal, Military Cross, *Croix de Guerre.* They don't give you these trinkets for looking wise and talking about other people's patriotic duty. They give them to you for killing men, as a rule. That's all war is, just killing. For the stunt by which I earned this French thing I should be execrated in any civilized community. And I didn't do it to earn a decoration, nor in any spirit of heroism, I can assure you. I was caught like a rat in a trap. I was responsible for the lives of other men. I was frantic with rage and fear. I won't shock you by describing what I did. It made me sick afterward. I tell you I have a strong stomach and it made me sick to think about it. And they gave me a medal. Pah!" he snorted contemptuously. "People like you talking about the great privilege of having participated in the war. You're as bad as the Germans. Go to some slaughterhouse and watch pigs and sheep die with squeals and bleats and blood spurting out of their throats. Substitute men for pigs and sheep, and you have war. Of course, if you have a butcher's instincts, you take to it as a pastime."

Mrs. Emmert was evidently making one of those formal calls which do not permit the visiting female to lay aside her wraps. She rose now, fully caparisoned in her furs and her dignity.

"I have never been so insulted in my life," she declared. "I consider your remarks to be positively seditious."

And with that she swept majestically to the door — not, however, without a sidelong glance at Isabel Wall. That young lady, to Rod's surprise, merely smiled, shook her head, and murmured:

"Sorry. But it doesn't arouse *my* righteous indignation."

The door closed with a slam. Mary, who had risen, resumed her seat and smiled. Andy Hall stood up. He pocketed the decorations. His face was slightly flushed.

"I expect," he said, "I'd better be on my way. You see, when I come across such persons, I blow up. I can't help it. I'm on one side of the fence. People like that are on the other. When some silk-upholstered fool starts drooling sentimental tosh about the war and mouthing intellectual a b c's as positive wisdom, I simply get red-eyed. I don't really belong on your side of the fence, and I'm just bone-headed enough to be glad I don't, if many people like that graze in your pastures."

"Sit down, Andy, and be calm," Rod laughed. "There isn't any fence so far as we're concerned. Sit down and have a cigarette. Dinner will be ready soon. Forget the fat woman. She doesn't know any better."

"Room for one more at the festive board?" Isabel inquired.

"Of course," Mary replied. "There always is."

"I wonder," Isabel turned her bland, childlike prettiness on Andy Hall. "I wonder if Mr. Hall knows how fierce he looks when he is angry? Is that an expression you cultivate in the army, Mr. Hall?"

"No." Andy replied with unexpected acidity. "I cultivated it to protect myself against idiotic questioning by London flappers."

"Entirely useless here," Isabel said sweetly. "This isn't London, and I'm not a flapper. Or at least, I'm a sort of a graduate flapper, if anything."

Andy stared at her in some slight puzzlement.

"I'm afraid," he said more politely, "that I don't quite get your drift."

"Oh, you will presently," she assured him with mock gravity. "It's really important that you should. You see, you certainly did browbeat Mrs. Emmert. And when I find a man browbeating my sex, I consider it my duty to subjugate him."

"You speak a language I don't understand," Andy retorted — but he said it with a smile.

"I'd be pleased to teach you," Isabel replied demurely. "I'm sure you wouldn't be a backward pupil."

Rod leaned over the back of a chair silent, amused. Mary sat on a low stool, her hands clasped over her knees, egging them on with brief sentences. And the other two, who had never seen each other before, whose orbits were as diverse as the separate paths of the Dog Star and Halley's comet, turned upon each other batteries of light-hearted chaffing. They ended up on the chesterfield together, comparing their favourite drinks, dances, and cigarettes, in all three of which they seemed to have had a comprehensive experience. They were at any rate congenial in banter. Mary drew her husband out of the room on some pretext.

"Is that your revolutionary rigging-slinger?" she asked.

"Yes. He is going to be my superintendent of works."

"I like him," Mary said. "Apparently so does Isabel."

"Everybody who knows Andy Hall likes him," Rod informed her. "But that little feather-brain is only interested in him as a new specimen. She probably never encountered anybody quite like him."

"Feather-brain? You don't know Isabel," Mary declared.

"I know her better than you do."

"Oh, no," Mary smiled. "You may have known her longer. But not better. Isabel outgrew the fluffy-ruffles stage while you were away at the war."

CHAPTER XXV

ACROSS THE CHANNEL, in the green bank of timber bisected by the path that ran from Oliver Thorn's old house to the Granite Pool, rose white puffs of steam, intermittent, like sporadic geysers. Those were donkey engines at work. They tooted shrill responses to the signal pull. The woods were full of prodigious shudderings and rumblings. The powerful machines snaked fallen trees, sawn to lengths, from where they were felled to the last splashing plunge into the tidal booming ground close by a group of new camp buildings not far from Oliver Thorn's abandoned house. A "sky line" lifted its long, aerial cable far up that hill. Down this logs came at the rate of two hundred a day. The shore was lined with floating logs, new cut, exhaling the odour of pitch, a pleasant pungent smell. The Granite Pool itself echoed the clack of axes and the thin twanging of saws, and mirrored the downward swoop of great trees. The falling crews were stripping the shores about the Pool, destroying its seclusion, shattering its restful silence, obliterating its cool shade. Farther east the Valdez camp, in which Rod had served his apprenticeship, bit deep into these heavy woods. Three hundred and fifty men, a dozen donkey engines, a logging railway in the making, miles of steel cable were chewing the heart out of the forest. Far beyond sight and sound of Hawk's Nest another crew slashed at the last of their timber on Hardwicke Island.

There was no picking of prime trees and care to conserve the younger growth, nor far-sighted culling of the forest crop. It was complete destruction. Within the boundaries of each limit the earth was stripped to its primal nakedness. Sky-line and high-lead gear ripped strings of logs over the surface, plowing deep furrows in the scant soil, tearing up saplings, shouldering aside rotten trunks and small boulders, bursting into dusty clouds the dead snags in the way. When the loggers shifted to a fresh stand they left desolation behind. Timber great and small was money. Every stick landed in tidewater went for something; number one export, number two, the broken cedar for shingles, the poorer grades of spruce and hemlock for pulpwood that the mills chewed up and spat forth in tons of newsprint.

Rod sat over his breakfast at Hawk's Nest one morning in early summer of '19. The far, faint sounds of the machinery he had set in motion reached now and then into that quiet room. But he was not thinking particularly of this organized effort which filled the woods over there with crashings and rumblings and whining cable. He was watching the tall, somewhat stooped figure of the butler who had served in that house ever since Rod could remember, and he was thinking that in connection with this man he faced another of the many disagreeable tasks he must perform.

He rose, walked to the door, turned back. It was no great matter, and still — like a modern Atropos he must go on snipping threads. If the hand that held the shears shook a little now and then, it could not for that reason be stayed. He had not much choice. He was too deeply committed.

"Come up to the library in a few minutes, Stagg," he said.

"Yes, sir."

Rod sat down by a window that overlooked Mermaid Bay. A Kern tug lay against one shore beside a million board feet of Norquay cedar, waiting for the fierce tiderace to go slack before she eased her boom through the south narrows for the long Gulf tow. In a little while she would pass out, dragging astern a brown comet's tail of slaughtered trees.

His eyes turned back to the interior of the room, came to rest on a portrait of his great-grandfather — the Norquay who had prophesied that Hawk's Nest would some day hatch out an eagle.

"Even an eagle could hardly hold his own against a flock of buzzards," Rod muttered.

No. One slip was sufficient to invalidate, even to destroy such families as his, in this day and age. Perhaps there had been a time when people of the equivalent class would have seen in the Norquay difficulty something besides a chance to participate in the loot. Out of his intimate knowledge of the family history as revealed in sundry documents and half-recalled conversations, Rod knew that every Norquay, from the original Roderick down to his father, had put out his hand and opened his purse to save other men from ruin, sometimes out of friendship, sometimes out of generosity, often from a clear sense of class interest. At least friendship and social intimacy had bred something more than mere lip-fealty. Other generations did not break bread and drink wine under each others' roofs to go forth planning how they could filch each others' possessions. The generation to which his father belonged would have understood quite clearly the Norquay obligation in regard to Grove's blundering.

His, Rod's generation, didn't understand. At least, if it understood, it cynically denied his code. It laughed at him behind his back, looked with disbelief on the course he was taking. It was, they held, purely quixotic to sacrifice so much, to risk all in repairing a misguided man's folly. Childishness. What were bankruptcy laws for? Why had sound commercial brains devised the Limited Liability Act if not to save the enterprising bourgeois from loss when one of his undertakings failed? What simpleton would unhesitatingly accept a moral responsibility when no legal compulsion existed?

Rod smiled grimly. He had become more closely acquainted with the ethics of modern business. It struck him that if corporations were in the nature of things soulless and dehumanized in matters of money, that attribute tended to spread to individuals. He wondered if that were possible. It was a disagreeable conclusion, one he hesitated to accept. But he knew this: that both his father and himself had aroused a strange combination of antagonism and contempt by merely doing what they felt in honour bound to do.

The antagonism was the fiercer for being grounded in cupidity. It smoldered under the surface, ready to blaze out if he left an opening. There were those who would like to pick his bones. He was aware of this attitude. It burgeoned forth in many aspects of his affairs.

If he had looted the Norquay Trust within the law and let the plucked victims pick themselves bewildered out of the ruin, while he sat back with his share of the plunder and the great Norquay estate still firm in his grasp, these contemporaries of his would have esteemed him as a clever man, almost a great man, certainly a man with a genius for affairs. A man of affairs, a man who could safely and expeditiously get possession of large sums of money. What was the difference?

He might have been execrated by some who lost their money. The losers, they said cynically, always squeal. But if he had shrugged his shoulders and stood aside, his own class would have backed him to a man. They would have rallied round his standard. They would have upheld him in the press, socially, by every means within their power. Their admiration would have been tinctured with envy. They would have understood so clearly that genuine greatness was involved in making such a coup and getting clear when the crash came. His own people — no, by God, the Walls and Deanes and Richstons were not his kind of people, not one of the whole pushing caravan, the petty tradesmen swollen to greatness with one generation of a rich country's development, grown greater with exorbitant profits derived from a war which had been fought for them but not by them. They were Grove's kind of people. And Grove had been a — a —

Well, he didn't like to ponder on Grove. There was no encouragement in that. He found his brother's memory depressing. Grove reminded him of a joyous diver plunging headfirst into the troubled waters of life and coming up, not with a pearl but with a handful of slimy ooze. Grove, he reflected, would probably not have given a second thought to discharging Stagg. And he was compelled to give several regretful thoughts to that unfortunate necessity.

Stagg knocked and entered, stood waiting. Rod motioned him to a chair.

"How long have you and Mrs. Stagg been with us?" he asked.

"Twenty-seven years next November, sir."

The man was proud of his length of service. It showed in his tone. Twenty-seven years. Rod looked at him. He had been an infant in arms when this man entered his father's service. For twenty-seven years Stagg had waited on them and theirs, arranging their tables, polishing their silver, serving their food, ministering deftly to their every want, expressed or implied.

"Have you saved any money?" Rod pursued. He had no false delicacy about asking such a question. He had to know whether he was about to chuck a penniless man out into a world that would be far harsher to William Stagg than Hawk's Nest had ever been, even in its most exacting moments. Rod had been taught, not as a lesson but as a principle of living, that faithful service begets an obligation. It seemed to him a natural corollary. His instincts inherited, acquired, however he came by them were more or less patriarchal.

"We've saved a good bit, sir."

"That's fortunate," Rod continued. "Because I shall have to close this house. I shall have to let everybody go."

"Yes, sir," Stagg murmured. He clasped his fingers across his knees and stared at the rug.

"I hate to do it," Rod went on. "But the way things stand, keeping up this place is more of a drain than I can afford. For a time I'm only a — a sort of steward of the Norquay estate. If I get out of the hole with anything left, you shall certainly have the pension to which you are entitled, Stagg. I'm acting under a very disagreeable necessity."

"Yes, sir," the man nodded. "I've been hoping it wouldn't be necessary, sir. Still, I've expected it."

"Oh, you have? How's that?"

"There's been talk, sir. It gets up here, sir, from town."

"Servants' talk?" Rod inquired.

"The kind of talk servants hears, sir," Stagg replied. "People are saying that you are a fool to ruin yourself over the Norquay Trust Company."

"I don't agree with them," Rod, said impassively. "But they may be right. What do you think about it yourself, Stagg?"

"I had eleven thousand dollars on deposit in the Norquay Trust, sir," Stagg returned calmly. "About all we've saved in a lifetime of work, the missus and me. You can fancy what I think, Mr. Rod."

"Eh? Well, I hope you got it out while the getting was good, although it's reasonably safe if you didn't," Rod smiled. "Unless the heavens fall or some such catastrophe occurs, the Norquay Trust will pay interest and principal in full on every account before I close its doors — which I intend to do as soon as I can turn our timber into cash."

"I feel safe enough," Stagg assured him. "But you can imagine how I would have felt if the Company'd failed, sir. So I'm bound to be prejudiced in your favour. If you'll excuse me, sir, I've known the Norquay family a long time, and it wouldn't have seemed natural for it to let a thing like that happen. People like you, Mr. Rod, may get in a hole, but you can't be kept there. You always get up somehow. I'll be awfully sorry to leave. I really will. This place is like home to me. I'll hope to come back as soon as you get things straightened out, Mr. Rod."

Rod sat thinking for a few seconds.

"Thank you, Stagg," he said then, very gently. "I appreciate what you have said. You seem to understand quite well some things that other people, who should, don't see at all. Now," he continued, after a pause, "I want you to put everything in order this week. Cover the furniture and put away china and silver and linen and so on. Fix the house properly. It never was closed before, but you will know what should be done. When you're finished I'll pay you all off. Cook, I understand, has relatives living on the other side of Valdez. The gardeners can work for me in the woods, if they wish. The housemaids are flappers who haven't had time to get attached either to us or the place. That'll be all, Stagg. Thanks."

The man got up. He seemed to hesitate, took a step or two, stopped.

"May I ask if you're going to sell Hawk's Nest, sir?" he finally blurted out.

Rod shook his head.

"No, Stagg. They may take it away from me eventually. But it is not for sale."

"Thank you, sir. I couldn't believe you'd think of selling Hawk's Nest, sir."

Stagg bowed and closed the door softly behind him.

CHAPTER XXVI

SOMETIMES ROD'S HEART troubled him so that he would turn in his ascent of a hill to some part of the works and go down again, *stamp, stamp*, joggling it from that enfeebled flutter back to its normal beat. And afterward he would sit on a log for a while, struggling against a wave of depression. So much depended on him alone. He was the mainspring. If he broke or ran down, the job must go unfinished; people, his own people and many others, must suffer. And yet, when he faced the prospect of going on and on like that, flogging a weak heart to its work, keeping his brain alert to direct a big undertaking and the mass of detail involved, making money and more money and pouring it like water into an endless pipe, he felt a profound weariness, an unutterable distaste for this game of profit-creating which other men played with such gusto.

The sum that passed through his hands in any calendar month of 1919 would have been sufficient to give him everything he wanted for years to come. He lived no better than his loggers. He was separated from Mary most of the time. He became a peripatetic. Something always required his presence in a camp, and immediately thereafter in town — some new phase of the timber market or the Norquay Trust affairs.

"I'm almost a widow," Mary said to him once. "It's as bad as the war. About all we get a chance to say to each other these days is 'Hello' and 'Goodbye.'"

Some day there would be an end to that, of course. A clean slate and a chance to draw his breath, to sit idly, contentedly, on the beach while Rod junior hunted crabs among the rocks, to talk with Mary about things that were not measured in money values.

He had never been hungry to grasp material substance out of life so much as to understand life, the absorbing spectacle of the universe, to fathom its strange manifestations of beauty and terror. All his life he had loved the sight and smell of forests, the sound of running water, the majesty of the hills. He had loved peace and beauty and harmony. He loved them more than ever, but the beloved trinity had vanished out of his days. He was become an engineer, his hand on the levers, his ears full of the roar and grind of machinery. Only for a few hours now and then in the privacy of his own home could he achieve rest and content; or when for a moment he could stand forgetful and look up at the mainland palisades, rising tier on tier to far heights behind Little Dent and the Euclataws.

Yet in spite of struggling with a formidable task, irritating problems, planning, directing, moving with sure purpose to an end the value of which he sometimes doubted, he began to get little glows of satisfaction when he was not too tired, more especially as that first year closed and he knew that the heart which had been organically perfect but functionally weak was regaining strength, slowly attaining functional perfection once more. Perhaps that lessened his moodiness, made him quicker to respond to external stimulus. He had gone for a year on his nerve. He had followed a light that sometimes seemed no more than a will-o'-the-wisp. With bodily soundness he began to feel a touch of pride in the work of his hands and brain.

He had made no costly mistakes, either in men or tactics. It was odd, he reflected sometimes, as he went about the workings, that other men, corporations, were carrying on various private wars with labour, and that he should be free of those clashes that arose so often and so unexpectedly in the years following the war. It was even more odd that he should be regarded with suspicion by these other men and corporation heads for maintaining production without strikes, disputes, clashes, antagonisms.

They had years of experience. He had started with more theory than experience. He was beating them at their own game; largely, he believed, because he came to it with a fresher point of view, a policy based on an understanding, partly reasoned, partly intuitive, of how the logger working for a day's pay feels about his work and the man he works for.

For years before the war, loggers in B.C. coast camps had lived and worked under conditions they were powerless to change. Any sort of accommodation, any sort of food, the lowest wages they could be compelled to accept; that was the logger's portion. The Norquay camps had been better than most, but Rod knew they were bad enough. The logger was hardy, strong, patient, skilful, by a process of elimination.

The war changed conditions without changing the logger's essential qualities. With labour scarce, with timber production a military as well as an economic necessity, with organization in the air, the B.C. logger took the whip hand. His memory was tenacious of old wrongs. He did not ask, he demanded, and his demands were grudgingly conceded because his employers were taking huge profits in airplane spruce, in exportable fir and cedar, in shipbuilding material. And although the timber market took little count of the Armistice, the employers did. With the first demobilization, with the first infiltration of discharged soldiers into the labour market, industrial war was secretly declared. They set out to tame the militant logger who thought that he was entitled to bathtubs, clean sleeping quarters, grapefruit for breakfast if he desired it, and the maximum wage for an eight-hour day.

But the logger did not tame easily. Individually he was a wide-shouldered person with language and spirit to match the muscles developed in the woods. He did not submit without a struggle. Collectively he was organized to fight, and he fought with the only weapons available. The season of 1919 was a period of disputes, grievances, abortive wage cuts, strikes, sabotage, all that goes with a labour war — a war that in 1919 and well into the next year was a series of lost battles for the employers and corresponding bitterness on their part.

Into this troubled arena Rod Norquay had stepped with his pressing need of continuous operation. He was wise, and generous impulses went with his wisdom. He believed that the logger was a simple man who could be led where no man could drive him save under the sharp spur of acute need. He had believed that the logger was a man and not a mechanism long before he took a year in the woods himself to see what made the common man laugh, weep, fight, play, drink to debauchery, and rise sometimes to heroic proportion under stress. He had learned then that man is not so completely the perfect product of class and environment as he superficially seems. Mary Thorn had unconsciously shown him that first. This one and that — Andy Hall, Oliver Thorn, old Jim Handy the logging boss, even Grove before the war and after, and the crucible of war itself — had taught him that however the human unit is outwardly shaped by place and circumstance, each is flesh and desire and a creature of passion.

So that it was impossible for him ever to regard his men as so many tools to be used or laid aside as he willed. He was free of the curious detachment of the captains of industry from the lesser ranks. He neither locked himself in the ivory tower of the contemplative spirit, nor fortified himself behind the golden wall of material security. He remained a man in a man's world, directing and shaping the cutting edge of his human tools without once forgetting their essential humanity — so that they admired him for his deftness of touch.

He had been fortunate in his choice of Andy Hall. Even old Oliver Thorn voluntarily came out of his retirement and directed one part of his operations. Rod did not always know by what occult process he judged men, but he made no mistakes in men. And men are always the prime levers. Machines, powerful, complex, will not operate themselves. They do not create themselves. If mechanism seems to overshadow men, it is only because of a distorted sense of proportion. Hands and brains come first; everything else in the world of men is a by-product. The energy of hand and brain is as necessary as directive force; without that energy, however rude, uncouth, unskilled, there would be nothing to direct; and its reward should be liberal and ungrudging, a right, not a concession. Until Utopia comes in the millennial dawn men must exist under a social and industrial system that is not the creation of a class or a period, but is the slow growth of centuries. Under it the strong, the acquisitive, the self-disciplined, the men of force and character somehow get to the top. But having got to the top, being secure in their power, if they were wise they neither despised nor trampled on those at the bottom.

That was a creed which Rod Norquay, Andy Hall, and Oliver Thorn held in common. These diverse men — Andy, a fiery proletarian rebel, whose steel-trap logic picked fallacies and blunders wholesale in the modern economic system, yet whose inherited instincts drove him to fight with the clan when the clan went to war, and from which he had returned with a touch of bitterness and a tinge of cynicism; Rod himself, a patrician by birth, training, environment, a gentleman in the amplest meaning of that much-abused term; Oliver Thorn, the gentle, contemplative, kindly, shrewd old man — they shared that conviction. It was more than a conviction; it was an article of faith.

"I may be wrong. If I am it will break me instead of getting me what I want," Rod had said to Andy in the beginning. "But this is my idea: men will work faithfully if they are even reasonably satisfied with their job. Men are still capable of loyalty even to a boss and a job, although a lot of propaganda denies it, and the intellectual radicals say it's a slave attitude. I don't mean to fall back on the insincere platitude that the interests of the employer and employee are identical. But I, as well as the men who will work for me, will be faced with a condition, as somebody put it, and not a theory. So long as they must work for a wage and I must make a profit to keep them employed, anything that will reduce possible friction is worth considering on its merits. So we start on this basis; we forestall agitation for better conditions by setting an example in the way of conditions. We provide first-class living quarters. We serve the best food available. We pay top wages, with the added inducement of a bonus based on production. No man is to be fired for any sort of economic heresy. They are free to do their own thinking, to express their individual opinions about the outfit, about working conditions, about industry in general. They can agitate and discuss any social theory whatever without risking discharge. I don't care whether they are Reds, Syndicalists, Socialists, Free Thinkers, Single Taxers, theorists of any description whatever — so long as they will devote their working hours to doing the work. That's a general policy. I think it will go. The surest way to breed fantastic theories is to muzzle men through fear. The surest way to make men dissatisfied is to be arbitrary over trifles. The cooperative commonwealth may be a million miles away, but cooperation on the job with benefit to us both is not an impossibility. I think that will work."

It did work. It had an effect beyond mere efficiency on the job. It did away with inhibitions that bred sullenness. When a man was well-fed, well-housed, well-paid, where it was easy for him to see that he was regarded as a human being with certain rights and privileges, an atmosphere of good feeling soon developed.

It became a mark of distinction to work for the Norquay estate. Rod's fallers, buckers, loaders, his minor bosses, his donkey engineers, began to take an active pride in what they did. They boasted of what they could do, and made good their boasts. They walked with a swagger. A good many of them called him by name when he went among them. It dawned upon Rod finally that they liked him, that they were working for him as no other logging crews on the B.C. coast worked in those uncertain days when the union organizations of wartime were fighting tooth and toenail to hold their own against organizations of reactionary employers, who affected tremblingly to see in the struggle for wages and hours the horrid spectre of Bolshevism.

In so much he gained success. Sometimes he would feel a profound resentment because there loomed always the possibility of failure, of collapse, of material ruin. With the estate intact he could have tested, experimented in a field that interested him. He had no illusions about industry, about the competitive scramble. He had no visionary schemes for speedy remodelling of the economic structure. But with the means to work, he could have worked with a sense of security; he was quite sure that he could effect a change for the better in a field he knew and force others to follow his lead.

It was not, he saw, political power or vengeance on a class that labour cried out for. It was security of livelihood, a recognition of their rights as human beings — two things that were everywhere acknowledged in theory but frequently disregarded in practice. If political power, direct action, accentuated class struggle were the only ways to secure these two essentials, as some held, then the industrial clashes must go on, must grow more bitter. Rod not only believed that society should, in its own interest, guarantee labour a decent livelihood as its rightful share in mass production, but he believed it could be done — he believed he could do it himself — he believed it could be done in any industry — he believed that sometime it must be done to avoid a greater evil.

The test of anything is its workability. Rod's policy worked, with almost four hundred men on his pay roll. And if he had not been compelled to pour his profits into that moribund Trust Company he could have built up a reserve strong enough to carry his working force over any possible non-productive period. At the worst now, he could square the Norquay account with the world at large. But a little thing might leave him with no resources whatever. And he regretted that. He knew what he could do, if he once had a free hand.

That uncertainty bore on him hard. He was doing his best. His men were doing their best. Logs came down to tidewater in a marvellous flow, as if the trees were handled by intelligent automatons with legs and fingers of steel. He had no labour difficulty that was not solved on such occasions as it arose by a half-hour's dispassionate talk over a table with the spokesmen of his crews. The walking delegates of the Logger's Union approached him as confidently as if he had been a member of the union.

But there was always that cursed pit into which he was flinging his trees. It yawned bottomless. It loomed before him distressingly, an Augean stable that he must clean. He had his weak moments, his hours of utter discouragement. But he could neither stop nor turn aside. Sometimes in the streets of Vancouver, after a checking up with Charlie Hale in the Norquay Trust office, he would have the morbid fancy that the deep traffic roar of the city was like the roar of the rapids by Little Dent, and that he was in a frail craft shooting that fierce economic tiderace to disaster in the financial whirlpools.

What a price to pay for one man's purblind ambition! He would look back at the chaste white square of the Norquay Trust Building, at the black iron skeleton of the great electric sign, and his lips would mutter a curse.

CHAPTER XXVII

LATE SUMMER OF 1920 pricked to utter collapse the prosperity balloon which had been deflating ever since the Armistice. Europe still stewed in the choice juices of local punitive expeditions, reparation snarls, gyrating exchange, so that North American commerce lagged by the way with heavy feet. Here and there industry somehow kept going. It couldn't stop altogether, even lacking foreign markets. Crops were sowed and reaped; people were fed; life went on. But capital ventured timidly. Wages fell, even though commodities seemed reluctant to cheapen. The stress came particularly hard on the Pacific Coast. The bottom dropped out of the lumber market. A thousand loggers walked the streets of Vancouver, hungry, bewildered, as soon as their savings gave out. Only here and there a few companies and individuals, fortunately situated, well-managed, or filled with bowels of compassion for their men, were enabled to continue. They could log cheaply. They were willing to risk a little loss rather than disband crews and let machinery rust; and they hoped for the upturn, the revival of "confidence,"

that talisman which commends itself to Boards of Trade and Chambers of Commerce.

Rod owned his timber. He neither leased, paid royalty, stumpage, nor interest on borrowed capital. It was choice timber, picked long ago when his forefathers had the cream of coastal forests to choose from. If a tree could be cut and sold at a profit by anyone, he was the one. So long as he could operate without loss, he meant to keep on. He had to keep on, until the cost of production overtook the market price.

And because he kept on along the lines he had laid down in the beginning, he found himself in disfavour with people who had once considered it a privilege to know a Norquay. He did not suffer from that. They could not hurt him. If he had not been deeply troubled because he saw the nearing end of his own rope, he would have been amused.

To know that there were men who damned him heartily for paying labour so much a day when labour could be had for less. To be aware that a certain clique looked forward to the weight of the Norquay Trust crushing him, and that there might be pickings on the bones, because he was young and inexperienced in business. To be regarded as a quixotic fool. To have certain men freeze up when he met them in clubs, hotels, on coastwise steamers. To have others draw him aside for earnest remonstrance. It was strange what an interest they took in his welfare; how eager they were to point out that he was hurting himself and demoralizing the labour market, making it hard for them to readjust their business to changed conditions, to deflate properly. Labour *had* to come down off its high horse and his tactics delayed the unseating. And so forth. None of it troubled Rod.

He did not want their friendship. He set no store by their opinions. He had been a solitary animal all his life, too self-contained for superficial friendships. He had dreamed in and out of books as a youngster while some of these others were already up and doing. As a man he played a lone hand, acted with resolution, brooded over his own problems, disregarded the non-essential.

He had his wife and his son. He had a given task to accomplish. He had a friend or two to lean on if he needed to lean, Andy Hall, Oliver Thorn, his brother-in-law who wrestled with the Norquay Trust as the angel of the Lord wrestled with Apollyon. In the city office he had two men he could rely on, two heirlooms, two old, very wise, white-moustached men who had handled accounts, costs, sales, during his father's regime and Phil's. And there was Stagg, the butler, and his wife, who elected to remain at Hawk's Nest for the sake of house room and a sentiment Rod understood, valued, was moved by. They were, Stagg said, too old to go into service elsewhere. They had a bit of money put by. Enough to live rent free, but not enough to cope with the cost of town living. They would like to stay at Hawk's Nest and keep it aired and dry, to care for such part of the grounds as Stagg could keep from going to rack. Rod thanked them and let them have their wish. It gave himself and Mary a room always ready when they wanted to spend a day or two there, which they did at times. It was pleasant to sit on those wide porches in blazing August, to watch Rod junior prance across the lawn astride a stick. Hawk's Nest was home in a very dear and intimate sense, even if it could no longer be maintained in the old opulent state. Rod never passed down the channel in the *Haida* about his business without a lingering, regretful look at that red roof glowing against a background of green timber and great mountains.

There remained only one link — apart from his sister Dorothy who came to Hawk's Nest each summer for a month, and in whose Vancouver home the diminished Norquay clan gathered at Christmas — between Rod and the numerous folk who had haunted that place in the old days, the girls he had danced with, the young fellows who had been his contemporaries. That link was Isabel Wall.

It seemed a strange friendship. He had always regarded Isabel with a feeling of patient tolerance. She had fallen in love with him once, in her doll-like fashion, to his great embarrassment. She appeared to have no recollection of that episode. She seemed firmly attached to Mary. Between them, diverse as they were, there did exist an intimacy, an understanding, an affection that Rod was slow to fathom, which he did not fathom at all until he began to take serious stock of Isabel and discovered that for all her unchanged pink-and-white prettiness, this diminutive person was really not at all the Isabel Wall of his original conception.

It seemed to him in the beginning to be incongruous that his wife's greatest, almost her only intimate, should be the frivolous daughter of a man who, next to Grove Norquay, was chiefly responsible for the evil days upon which the Norquay family had fallen. But because his faith in his wife's judgment was a vital thing, he let that pass. If at first glance it seemed incomprehensible it was an accomplished fact. Isabel lived in his house as much as she did her own. She seemed absolute mistress of her comings and goings. If she had once had no mark to shoot at save dress and parties and men, she did not seem to care greatly now whether she danced and played and flirted. Yet she seldom uttered a serious thought. She remained a charming irresponsible, given to slang and cigarettes. She descended upon them in town, at the Euclataws, whether they were at Hawk's Nest or in the logging camp on Valdez, when the mood took her. She was always welcome. Isabel was a gloom-dispeller. Rod used to wonder at first if she did not come chiefly for the joy she got in devilling the life out of Andy Hall. But presently he found himself with a sneaking fondness for Isabel and her quaint pertness. And when he reached that stage and admitted it, Mary laughed.

"Isabel's a jewel, Rod. She's sound and sweet and true as steel. She's been pampered and petted all her life. Yet it hasn't spoiled her in any of the various ways in which that sort of thing does spoil girls. She sticks to us because she says we're about the only real people she knows. That tiny blonde head contains some very sound wisdom. She hasn't many illusions left, and still she hasn't got cynical or hard and calculating. Laska made a hash of her life and has reacted accordingly. Their mother's hopelessly society-mad. Her idea of heaven is to be presented at Court sometime. Bob drinks like a fish and goes on the loose just as Grove used to do. Her father knows only the money game and plays that to the exclusion of everything else. The poor kid's only chance in the world, she says herself, is to find and marry a man who can stand on his own feet."

Shortly after that conversation Rod went in search of a logging boss, thinking, as he walked beside a chute in which hummed a steel "main line" that quivered under the strain of a heavy load, of Isabel and her astonishing metamorphosis. Or was it merely a cropping out of something latent? Undeniably that did happen. By all the rules of the game, Isabel should continue as she had begun, a butterfly, a dainty parasitical creature who had never toiled, spun, or concerned herself with anything but each day's pleasure as it came her way. He hadn't credited Isabel with perception to fathom the futility of the pursuit of pleasure as a life work, without duties, responsibilities, or any creative passion. But he could understand her instinctive revolt. He wondered what John P. Wall thought of this daughter who found dissatisfaction in a life that was all pleasure and no purpose.

His errand took him far up into the workings. The daily routine of a logging boss is an active one. The man Rod sought moved always ahead of him, giving his overseeing eye to various spots where separate gangs of men busied themselves with powerful and noisy machinery, devoted to localized and violent struggle with logs of enormous tonnage. A stranger to logging as it proceeds in the forests of the Pacific Coast invariably gets a first impression of desperate effort and grave danger in his approach to a donkey engine at work. The black, round-bellied monster shudders and strains on anchored skids. The inch and a quarter main line reels up on the drums with a grind of gears, a behemothic sputtering of exhaust steam. Continuous vibrations disturb the air and communicate themselves to the earth over a wide radius. The cable runs away into the shadowy places of the forest. It recedes therein, chattering, whining; it comes forth dragging the huge sticks to the base of the sky-line pole; and the logs go thence, dangling, sliding, gouging holes in the hillside. It is all noise, effort, confusion, humming of lines, hiss of steam, bull-blocks screaming: a deafening uproar until a stop signal brings a hush that by contrast is solemn, as if that powerful machinery were a heart that had suddenly stopped beating.

Rod found his man at last and returned. They were living in the old Thorn house, taking their meals in a small room off the main mess-house, where the crew bolted its collective food in occupied silence, putting all its energy into the business of eating, and reserving a free and unrestrained mode of conversation for the ease of the bunkhouse. A steamer had touched and gone while he was absent, passing north through the rapids on the afternoon slack. He found Isabel Wall on the caulk-splintered steps, teaching young Roderick a whimsy she had picked up somewhere:

> Poor Robinson Crusoe!
> What made the poor man do so?
> He was a Robinson I know
> But that's no reason he should crow.
> I wonder why he Crusoe?

She was making the boy letter-perfect in this. Andy Hall sat on the step below her, smoking a cigarette in contemplative silence.

"They'll be through at Valdez tomorrow," he informed Rod.

"So soon? I thought they had a week to go."

"They made time," Andy commented tersely.

"Well, better load the working gear on floats and get it up here," Rod told him. "Have 'em begin on the cedar hollow."

"I put the fallers in there this afternoon."

Rod smiled. It was almost unnecessary to tell Andy Hall what should be done. Sometimes it seemed as if Andy had a mysterious prescience. Then Rod would recollect that they had discussed such a move long before. Or it was the logical move which Andy merely anticipated. In either case Andy always knew what he was doing, and why; nor did he ever hesitate to take the initiative.

Rod leaned back in a grass chair, clasped his hands behind his head, stared across the channel at the flash of the sun on the windows of Hawk's Nest. Behind him, in a west-facing room, he could hear the staccato of typewriter keys, tapping out the last chapter of Mary's second novel. He wondered, if things had been different, if he would have succeeded in that outlet. No, he decided. It would have been a splendid thing to try. He had been eager to embody and interpret the spirit of the pioneers. But he doubted now if he had the peculiar creative gift of making words transform his imaginings into a reality that would convey stark passion and stirring deeds. And Mary had that gift, beyond a doubt: not only the inborn faculty of perceiving, but the torturing necessity to transmit, to release through patient drudgery at her chosen medium, that sense of life as a vast conflict in which man struggles with his fellows, his gods, and his passions, sometimes to victory and often to defeat.

No, he had the vision, the perceptive faculty, but not that uncanny power to capture and pass it on. Such vision as he had must find its outlet in action less subtle, more practical. He would never write the stories he had dreamed; he knew that now. But Mary would; she had her wings. He was proud of her flight. Only, sometimes, when her work took her into a brooding remoteness, a spiritual detachment that thrust not only himself but every material consideration temporarily aside, he wondered if the artist could ever function except as the supreme egotist, if the true artist must not by some obscure compulsion subordinate everything to the imperative demands of his art. Even so, he knew that he would rather have only such portion of his wife as he could share than the most complete possession — body, soul and brain — of any other woman he knew. Mary would always understand. In any crisis she would always have courage and confidence. She was his windward anchor. He loved her not for what she did and said but for what she was — herself.

Young Roderick picked up a stick from one corner of the porch.

"Gotta go to work," he informed them gravely.

"What at?" Isabel inquired.

"Scalin' timber," he replied. He danced off down the path to the beach, chanting:

> Poor Robinson Crusoe.
> What made the poor man do so?

Already incorporating the reality of his environment into the child-world of make-believe. Rod smiled. He had done the same thing himself, alone, happily, through just such hot, smoky, August days long ago. The boy clambered over a heap of stovewood, measuring with his stick, making marks on a bit of notepaper just as the scaler did who walked the boom with pad and pencil and a six-foot scaling rule.

For a time the murmur of Isabel's and Andy's conversation accompanied Rod's thoughts. He continued to stare across at Hawk's Nest. A problem pressed him for solution, a question which involved closely that grey house with its glowing roof of red tiles, from behind which rose the conical top of the great cedar, in the shadow of which so many Norquays took their last rest.

He was approaching a critical stage in his affairs. He did not know how much longer he could carry on. Producing costs were overtaking market prices, and would soon pass them. Only by a foresighted contract with a Puget Sound pulp mill had he kept going so long. In a month that would expire. It could not be renewed on the same terms. The great pulp plant in Phillips Arm, which the Norquay Trust had financed and which had never ground a ton of pulp until Rod forced it into production, offered him prices he couldn't take on the wages paid and hours worked. He wouldn't know where to turn soon, unless he abandoned his present policy, cut wages to the bone, got into line with the other employers. That seemed to him like a breach of faith. He had made a fortune on the labour of his men already; that he was poorer in funds than at the beginning did not alter the case. The Norquay Trust had swallowed the profits. It would swallow a vast sum yet before its appetite was glutted. It hurt him to think of these men paying for Grove's mismanagement by lengthened hours and shortened pay. Nor did he wish to shut down and wait a turn in the market. A shutdown meant a cessation of revenue; that in turn might precipitate the disaster he had struggled so hard to avert. It was a very real difficulty.

He was stirred out of these reflections by a silence which had all the effect of a disturbing sound. He came back to the immediate present. Isabel still sat on the step, a dainty figure in a blue sweater and pleated tan skirt, staring after Andy's retreating figure.

"Your right bower," she said complainingly, turning to meet Rod's gaze, "is the stupidest man I know."

"You're a mile off the mark," Rod contradicted.

"He is," she repeated. "He's afraid of me."

"Andy Hall," Rod answered dryly, "is not afraid of anything or any one, least of all a harmless person like you."

"He's in love with me," Isabel said coolly. "And he's so afraid of me that he hasn't sense enough to see that all he has to do is to hold out his hands and I'll fall into 'em like a — a ripe plum. Can't you give him a hint, Rod?"

"Haven't you scalps enough at your belt without Andy's?"

"If I give him mine in exchange, that's fair enough," Isabel murmured.

"Do you really mean that?" Rod asked.

Isabel got out her cigarette case and deliberately blew smoke rings before she replied.

"I don't know for sure," she said at last. "Sometimes I think so, and again I'm not so sure. I could tell better if *he'd* ask me. It isn't that *I* wouldn't like to. It's simply that I have qualms of conscience sometimes about wishing myself on a man like that. I'm so damned useless, Rod."

"I don't think that men as a rule love women and marry them on the basis of their usefulness," he returned. "I'm certain Andy wouldn't. I must say it's rather odd to see you taking that slant at it."

"Oh, yes," she drawled petulantly. "I suppose you've got me labelled fragile, too. Just because a fellow's been brought up gilt-edged and has acted accordingly, is she to be credited with neither heart nor conscience, nor even common sense? I have come to the conclusion that I don't want to be a canary in anybody's cage, Rod. When I size up some of the horrible examples of how not to do it in my own crowd, I get afraid. I'm twenty-six years old, Roderick. Does it never strike you that a girl like me doesn't play a lone hand so long without good reasons?"

"What's that got to do with Andy?" Rod inquired.

"I'll tell you in words of one syllable and maybe you'll get it," she retorted. "Some years ago, if you recall the occasion, I was very much in love with your own distinguished self. I hope," she smile impishly, "it doesn't embarrass you to be reminded. It doesn't me, because I still think my judgment was good, even if I was out of luck. I've been in love probably half a dozen times since. And I always drew back at what the novelists call the psychological moment. Why? God knows. I don't. Something lacking, I suppose. Perhaps in spite of my giddiness I had a hunch that being in love with love isn't quite the same as being in love with a person. Then the war took all the likely ones away, and a good many of the best of them didn't come back. And something has happened to those who did come back. They're either so keen on the make they daren't take a girl seriously, or — or they've gone bad; the bloom's off 'em. Not one of them looks good to me. Nor the life they live. I hope I don't sound preachy. But some people who are rotten with money — especially those who've made it so fast they haven't had time to grow up to it — are rotten with other things, too. I may look like what Andy calls a charming, innocent parasite. I like to think of myself as charming. My instincts at any rate are innocent. But I do object to the role of parasite. I don't want to be one. I've never done anything useful, even for myself, but that isn't saying I don't want to — even if it's no more than to comfort and pet some man and hearten him for whatever sort of job he has in hand. I've never worked, but that's no sign I wouldn't if I knew where to start in. I'm not lazy, nor am I too fastidious for workaday life. That's what it's got to do with Andy Hall. I like him. I'd hate to tell you just how much; you'd blush. And he likes me. I know that, although he's the best little sentiment-represser I've come across. He's afraid of me, or he's afraid of what I am. I mean I think he doesn't see me just as a woman but as part of and more or less inseparable from a certain background — a background he doesn't like and doesn't trust.

"You see," she went on more hurriedly, her voice becoming a little uncertain, her, eyes turned steadfastly on the swirls and foaming overfalls the flood now made strongly in the rapids, "I get so infernally lonesome and discouraged sometimes. I'm tired of froth. I don't like the giddy pace most of 'em go. I don't want to be like Laska, soured on everything, so that she lives on cocktails and cigarettes and jazz. If she sits still long enough to think, she's apt to cry. If I don't find myself happy in the jazz age, Rod, at least I belong to it sufficiently not to be afraid or ashamed of my own thoughts and feelings and desires. I'm a normal female person. A woman can't escape the implication of a man, nor vice versa. Most of 'em go it blind. I'm not made that way. I don't know why, but it's a fact. Long ago I made up my mind that if I couldn't find the real thing in my own crowd, I'd go outside, just as you did."

"And then," she made a little gesture with her hands, "remember the day Andy showed Mrs. Hector Emmert his medals and made that passionate little speech that she said was sedition? Well, I warmed up to Andy Hall right then and there. Two years. I'm no nearer him now. He holds himself in. He won't let go. What can I do?

"I'll tell you," Rod said impulsively. "Andy doesn't know you. You don't let go yourself."

"Fiddlesticks," she retorted. "Two years. I think I'm shamelessly transparent."

"Two years? I've known you more than ten," Rod countered. "I've learned more about you in ten minutes than I did in all the time before. So imagine his handicap. You're a rich man's daughter. You've had every social advantage. You belong to a class that taken by and large Andy Hall not only dislikes but despises for its stupidity and arrogance insofar as it deals with working people."

"Oh, yes, the well-known capitalist class," Isabel said impatiently. "But you're one and he likes you."

"I come in a different category," Rod answered grimly. "I despise the tin-horn capitalist whose only god is capital more than Andy Hall does. It's part of a social theory with Andy. It's a personal feud with me. I'm suffering from the manipulations of that type of gold-digger. It has just about ruined me and has caused me to risk all that several generations of honest, generous-minded men built up, including a home many of us love — and a reputation for integrity besides. But Andy happens to know me as a man apart from my present dubious position as a capitalist. He doesn't really know you as a woman. He may be in love with you. Probably is, because you are an attractive little devil —"

"I thank you very much, kind sir," Isabel interrupted mockingly.

"But," Rod went on unheeding, "unless he were absolutely sure you would, as Christ told the man who wanted to be saved, 'Leave all that thou hast and follow Me,' a donkey engine couldn't pull a declaration of any sort out of him. Don't you see? Andy's full of sinful pride. He's class-conscious. He knows your kind of people better than you do, and he knows they regard him as belonging to an inferior order. He would chew his heart up and spit it out in little pieces before he'd let any flirtatious daughter of the idle rich have it for a curio in her collection. You've talked and laughed with him here in our house. You call him Andy and he calls you Isabel. But remember that he knows what manners are, and that being genial, even pleasantly intimate to the point of plaguing him the way you do, doesn't really mean anything. He's my trusted superintendent, and he draws a corking good salary which he faithfully earns, but he knows that wouldn't prevent a person like you from cutting him dead if he met you in, say the Vancouver Hotel Dubarry Room, hanging on the arm of, well, Sir Earnest Staples of Government House, Victoria."

"Never," Isabel protested. "I'm no snob."

"I didn't say you would. But it's been done. You've seen that sort of thing pulled," Rod continued. "Andy knows he doesn't belong in your crowd. What's more, he doesn't want to. He has seen quite clearly from the outside what you've seen from the inside, and come to the same conclusion. But he doesn't know you've arrived at such a conclusion. I didn't know it myself. You poke fun at them, of course. But you play the game with them right along, and you camouflage your real attitude toward life with Andy, with me, with us all. In fact, you'd have a hard time convincing any one, offhand, that you ever had a serious thought in your life. So how do you expect Andy to take you seriously?"

"But must one pull a long face and go about spreading the philosophy of disillusion and appealing for sympathy?" Isabel protested. "I can't help it if I'm mostly a cheerful idiot. How *am* I to make Andy understand that — that I — that —"

She choked up. And Rod felt intensely sorry for her at that moment. But he knew of no way to help.

"I said I'd tell you, and I'll try," he went on gently. "If you really do love Andy Hall and want him, you had better sometime just put your arms around his neck and tell him so."

Isabel looked away. A deep flush coloured her white neck and spread upward until it was lost in the roots of her yellow fluff of bobbed hair.

"Oh," she whispered, "I couldn't do that."

"That's the best way," he said kindly. "Andy has all the finer instincts. But he has a lot of inhibitions you don't know anything about. I don't think you really understand class feeling, Isabel. You seem to be free of it altogether. But it exists. Believe me, I speak both from experience and observation. It is next to impossible to build a bridge across a definite social gulf. You have to jump it — from one side or the other. People are apt to deny this in a supposedly democratic country. But it's truer than they think. You put Andy in dress clothes and turn him loose in your own crowd, and he'd get by with very little coaching. But he wouldn't stick. He'd say it was shoddy. Which you and I and Mary are agreed it is. But in contact with intellect, art, real achievement in the best sense, Andy not only asserts his equality, but would get a glow of enjoyment out of the association. Andy Hall's character is sterling, and that's above any class distinction. If Andy really cares for you, Isabel, I'd say you were justified in going to extremes to let him know where *you* stand."

"I can't go all the way myself," she whispered, and fell silent, staring moodily over the channel waters. Then she got up and went inside.

CHAPTER XXVIII

A DAY OR TWO later Rod came back to that conversation.

"I keep thinking of Laska," he said to Isabel. "Is she really so soured on things as you declared? Is she deliberately hitting the high spots just for the kick there's in it?"

"I'll tell the listening world she is," Isabel replied.

"I wonder why?" Rod mused. "She's free, young, and well-off. At least, she has all the advantages of wealth."

"Several whys," Isabel answered. "Her mind isn't healthy. It's twisted, or tainted or something. She started out several years ago with a lot of sentimental illusions. Matrimony, as she experienced it, was — well, unsatisfactory. Laska backed the wrong horse in the marriage race, and didn't discover it until too late. You don't mind my saying that Grove was a good deal of a mucker in his private life?"

Rod shook his head.

"I'm not particularly sensitive about what you say of him."

"Well, it's true. Did you know that Laska was really in love, very much so, with Phil?"

"I suspected it."

"She was always rather a queer fish," Isabel continued. "Good, generous impulses mixed up with very uncertain ones. She liked them both at first, about fifty-fifty, I think. She may have married Grove simply because he asked her first. He did have a way of making women like him — all kinds of women — for a while. Perhaps the fact that he was elected to be the biggest toad in the Norquay puddle influenced her. I don't know. I'm sure she thought it a fine thing to be mistress of Hawk's Nest and all it implied. Being chatelaine of a place with dignity, the permanence of age, all the indefinable things that Hawk's Nest makes you feel are part of it, must have appealed to her. But when she found what she was really up against as Grove's wife, how very different it turned out from the thing she dreamed it would be, well, it was the most natural thing in the world for her to look back longingly at Phil and to be intensely sorry for herself. Self-pity is a very demoralizing sort of thing. Phil looked like pure gold alongside what she'd chosen — no woman who lived with one man and knew the other could help seeing and feeling that. To know that she could have had Phil if she'd so chosen made it worse.

"Of course there was no turning back. It isn't done, you know — short of open scandal, or a perfectly insufferable outbreak of some sort. She had cooked her goose. In an extreme she might have divorced Grove. But she couldn't possibly marry his brother afterward. Nobody would have stood for that. So she just had to sweat. And that makes any woman sour, or hard, or reckless.

"You know how Grove performed," Isabel pointed out. "He was a very untidy person — morally."

Rod nodded assent.

"A man like that should never marry," Isabel continued sagely. "He was like a small, very headstrong boy with toys. Women were toys. When he got tired playing with one, he chucked her away and got another. He did that before he married Laska, I suppose. As soon as the novelty of her wore off he went right on — as usual. Everybody knew it. No one could do anything about it. He was fairly adept at keeping his affairs *de coeur* out of sight. There were a few explosions, to my personal knowledge. Then Laska finally settled back into a state of contemptuous resentful indifference, and let him go his own gait.

"But it made her suffer intensely, and it has given her a nasty taste in her mouth — and she has all the conventional reactions. If she had kids or work, anything real to take her mind off herself, she might come back to normal. As it is, I shouldn't be surprised at anything that sister of mine might do. She's all tension. She goes on hitting the high spots because she's got to do something. It's rotten, but so long as she can't get a kick out of anything else, why I expect she'll go on. I don't mean that she's dabbling in muck. Her instincts are fairly decent. But she's hovering on the ragged edge."

"Pity, isn't it?" Rod commented. "One can't take people by the scruff of the neck and set them right, even if one is sure of one's own standards and profound wisdom, which no one ever really is. When it comes to a showdown most of us have to dance according to our bent, and pay the piper when he presents his bill."

"That's the devil of it; that inconvenient bill," Isabel said lightly. "That's why I've got fussy about how and with whom I dance. There's not much fun dancing alone, but there's nothing but grief in dancing with a death's head wished on you for a permanent partner. That," she confessed naïvely, "is one of the reasons I like Andy Hall. You couldn't conceive of Andy being a bore, or a failure at whatever he undertook or cheating. I hate cheats. Even the unconscious ones. And there's a lot of 'em about."

Rod forgot this under pressure of other things. It was all true, even if unpleasant, and he had more pertinent affairs in hand, keener problems that involved himself, people who were still entangled in the Norquay Trust, the men in his employ who laboured faithfully because they had somehow acquired the assurance that he could keep the wheels turning when other camps shut down. They seemed to proceed on the assumption that being on the Norquay pay roll bestowed upon them immunity from the paralysis that crept over the body of industry.

To go on as he had begun was more than a material necessity. It had become a matter of pride as well as a necessity. He had fashioned a productive machine that worked now with automatic precision. But without continuous operation this machine would fall to pieces with his first task a little more than half-done, and his second task, which had been forming in his mind nebulously from the beginning — that of perpetuating this machine for the benefit of every unit therein, himself included — receded into nothingness. He had no philanthropic experiments in mind, but he did have an economic and industrial theory which he believed would work. Unless he could shake off the deadly weight of the Norquay Trust, it would crush him financially. To disband the organization now would destroy what he had been at great pains to create. His men wouldn't understand failure. They would classify him as another false alarm, another promiser who failed to perform unless it was to his own advantage. He knew that once he got the white elephant off his hands, all he needed was his men and machinery to go on indefinitely, to build up slowly on a solid basis. But the price of continued and unquestioned leadership was victory in this first battle. And the chance of continuous progress to victory began to seem more remote.

The bottom had fallen out of everything. The brief post-war orgy of production had run its artificial course. The industrial war babies had died of inanition. Exchange that fluttered like a wounded bird killed international trade. Europe was steeped in poverty. The waste of war could not be repaired until the wrangles of peace subsided. Instead of subsiding, the quarrels over peace became more acute. While the politicians thrust and parried, industry languished. In the domain of timber only first grades and pulp wood commanded a sale, and both on a falling market. The camps were shut down, the mills were silent. Neither camps nor mills would operate unless a profit seemed sure, a good safe margin. Few of them had the incentive to go on, such as drove Rod Norquay. He had to go on so long as he could clear a dollar, even fifty cents a thousand. He was butchering his holdings, but every dollar that went into the Norquay Trust brought him nearer a clean slate.

But even Rod's narrow margin was vanishing. Second-grade stuff accumulated on his hands. He could only renew his pulp contracts at a loss. And he was fighting to make good a loss. Unless he could hang on for the turn in the market tide that must come . . . His dilemma was very real.

He could do two things. He could shut down. Six months' non-production and he could say goodbye to every hope of a passable end to this adventure. Hawk's Nest and the ultimate sale of his standing timber might square the Norquay obligation. It would leave him picked to a skeleton. Or he could revise his established policy, cut wages to the bone, drive labour with a whip, fight them when they protested, go through the ugly stages of strikes, sabotage, hatreds, clashes, diminished output; in a word precipitate the industrial warfare which had made the coast a Bedlam for the single-track minds on both sides. And that also would ruin him.

September brought him to the stone wall. He came back from a business trip to town, depressed, uneasy. He knew that a good many people would consider his scruples unfounded. But he hated to cut wages. He had made such enormous profits on the labour of these men. He knew it. He knew that they knew it. It was not the way an employer should feel. It was not in line with the common conception of property rights. Nevertheless that was how he felt. However he came by it, his instinct was patriarchal. His men had become an aggregation of human beings for whose welfare he was to a certain degree responsible. He didn't know whether or not they shared such a feeling. He was too sensible to expect that sort of response. But certainly loyalty of a definite sort had manifested itself during an unsettled period in complete absence of friction. They had never made an unreasonable demand.

To keep going necessitated drastic reductions. Would they stand it? Rod had very few illusions about men of any sort. They might not be able to envisage what he did — a permanent benefit to be derived by all who stood by the ship if the ship weathered the storm. He could not mislead them by promises. He was fundamentally incapable of making promises he could not guarantee to keep.

He called Andy Hall into conference, explained in further detail just what conditions they were faced with. In the midst of this he saw Andy's attention waver, his eyes turn. Rod's gaze followed the direction.

Isabel Wall had been at the Euclataws two weeks. She was walking now slowly along the beach, bare-headed, her yellow hair glinting in the sun like spun gold, her skirt fluttering in the wind. A queer expression hovered on Andy's face.

Rod uttered another sentence softly; asked a question. Andy did not seem to hear.

"Damn it, never mind Isabel!" he broke out in exasperation. "Any time you want her you can have her, so for God's sake come out of that trance and listen to what I'm saying."

Andy glared at him, not so much in anger at the outburst as in sheer amazement, tinged with hopeful eagerness.

"What did you say?"

Rod began where he left off.

"I heard *that*," Andy told him bluntly. "I know it anyway without telling. I asked what you said about *her*."

"Oh, hell!" Rod threw up his hands. Then he got hold of himself. Something in Andy's eyes — a curious illuminating recollection of himself sitting in the stern of his canoe long ago, staring back through a moonlit night at Oliver Thorn's house with a strange fever in his blood, a dull ache in his heart.

"Lord, Andy," he said with rough kindness. "Does that knock you all in a heap? You're not generally so slow." He paused an instant, then repeated Isabel's own words. "If you weren't stupid you'd see that all you have to do is to open your hands and she'll fall into 'em like a ripe plum."

Andy matched glances with him for ten silent seconds. Rod smiled wearily. His impatience had burned out. Then a flush dyed Andy's fair, freckled skin.

"Shoot," he said presently. "I'm listening."

Rod continued.

"Simple. Leave it to the men," Andy counselled. "Don't make any arbitrary statements about either hours or wages. This bunch is wiser to conditions in general than you'd think. Show 'em your hand and give them the option of deciding what they want to do. Better let me handle them myself. Will you back up whatever I say or do?"

"Yes, your judgment is as good as mine where they're concerned."

Andy wrinkled his brows for a minute.

"I have a hunch they'll stand for pretty nearly anything you want to do, if they know your reasons," he said at last. "Be a pity to bust up a crack crew. I think they kinda feel that way themselves. It's a cut or a shutdown anyway."

Rod confirmed this.

"Well, we'll see tonight."

Hall went away. Rod watched him follow alongshore after Isabel. They disappeared together over a mossy point. His glance came back along the booming ground, followed the shore. Rod junior played on the gravel with the small son of a hook-tender and the equally small daughter of a high-rigger. A dozen houses where married men lived with their families faced that strip of shore. Clothes fluttered from taut lines. It neared five o'clock. Supper fires flung blue pennants from various chimneys. Over in the messhouse a flunky sang at his work and dishes clinked. From far up on the wooded slopes came shrill whistle blasts, the throb of machinery, all muffled in the deep cool forest over which was spreading a blight of raw stumps, broken branches, a litter of destruction.

He went into the house. Mary sat with a few letters in her lap, the gleanings of that steamer's mail. She looked up at him expectantly. He shook his head.

"Can't tell yet where we'll come out," he said.

"It's getting to be a sort of a nightmare with you, isn't it, Rod?" she said wistfully. "The whole thing."

"Oh, well," he replied absently, "another year, maybe sooner, it'll be finished — win, lose, or draw."

He lit a cigarette, drew a whiff or two, sat with it forgotten in his fingers till the stub burned him.

The long quitting blast went echoing up and down the channel. Men came pouring off the hill. The supper gong clanged, a prolonged and resonant metallic vibration, like an anvil under quick strokes of a hammer. Rod and his wife and boy walked to the small dining room set apart for their use. And still Andy and Isabel remained somewhere beyond that mossy point jutting like a green tongue into the sea.

Not until Rod and his wife were back on the porch and the last logger long since smoking in the bunk house amid a drone of talk did the twain appear. Andy walked straight on to the camp. Isabel perched herself on the top step. She regarded them with a heightened colour, an obvious repression, a look in her eyes as if she had beheld wonders.

Mary looked after Andy, back at Isabel.

"I'll go along to keep you company," she suggested. "I'm not the least bit hungry."

"Are you ill?" Mary inquired teasingly.

Isabel shook her head until the bobbed yellow hair stood out like an aureole.

"I never felt better in my life," she declared.

"I shouldn't be surprised," Rod ventured, "if you acted on the suggestion I made a few days ago."

Isabel looked blank for a second. Then she remembered.

"I didn't have to, Mr. Roderick," she said defiantly. "So there."

"Ah," Rod declared. "I perceive something has happened."

"Sagacious man," Isabel retorted. "Marvel of penetration, aren't you? What do you suppose happened, now?"

"Tell us," Mary suggested. "You're bursting with something."

Isabel arose, spread wide her short skirt, made an elaborate curtsey.

"Dear friends, I wish to announce my engagement to Mr. Andrew Hall," she said with adorable whimsicality. "Wedding gifts of articles useful in housekeeping on a small scale will be appreciated."

Then quite suddenly in the midst of her smiles a bright wetness welled up in her eyes. Her lips quivered. Mary put both arms around her.

"I'm gladder than any Pollyanna that ever blithered gladness," Isabel blubbered from this shelter. "And I don't care who knows it. Say, Mary, did it affect *you* this way?"

The two women disappeared within. Young Rod climbed on his father's knee and demanded to be told the story of Paul Bunyan and his famous camp in Michigan where the loggers were ninety feet high and twenty-four feet across the shoulders, and the cook coasted over the top of his kitchen range on roller skates of a morning to fry acres of hot cakes for the breakfast of these lusty men. Young Rod grew heavy-eyed listening to this gorgeous embroidery of fertile fancy on commonplace facts and presently went his way to bed.

Rod sat alone on the porch in a twilight that filled his eyes with a vista of pearl sky and purple hills, his ears with the song of the rapids that had crooned him to sleep when he was little like his son. There was a grateful hush, as if the mountains said their evening prayers, and the smell of the forest mingled with the dank kelp smell as the falling tide bared a weedy shore.

Andy's voice called to him in the dusk.

"Come on over to the office. There's a delegation to talk to you."

In the plain room where during working hours the bookkeeper cast up the camp accounts four men sat at a table. They greeted Rod pleasantly and came at once to the point.

"We've talked this over," one said. "Hall's told us how things stand. We don't want a shutdown. We want to keep workin'. For pretty near two years now we've set wages and hours. Whatever we asked we got without any argument. Now that times are bad again, we're willin' to leave it to you. We figure that eight hours is a long enough day. You set the pay."

"That's good enough," Rod answered. "But the cut may jar you. Things are at rock bottom. Nothing that we use, food, supplies, machinery parts, has come down a nickel. It seems a shame to cut wages, but unless timber prices go up, there's no choice."

"Uh-huh," one grunted. "How much of a cut do you figure will let you get by?"

"Twenty per cent," Rod told them bluntly.

"Well, that is pretty stiff," the chief spokesman commented. "Still — we won't go back on our word. Times are bad."

"I want to keep the outfit running," Rod said. "I can't do it on a losing scale. I'll post up a new wage schedule tomorrow. If a turn for the better comes, wages will go up again. I can't go any further than that."

"That's fair enough. Guess that's all. Good night." They nodded and filed out. Andy and Rod stood looking at each other.

"I figured that was about the line they'd take," Andy said. "I simply gave them the facts. Told them it was up to them whether the camp shut down tomorrow — the best camp in the country. And that if it did shut down for any length of time, it might never open again under the same management. Then they barred me out of the meeting, and chewed it over themselves. And there you are."

"Isabel came home manifesting unmistakable symptoms," Rod said slowly. "This seems to have been your big day all around, Andy."

They shook hands on that.

CHAPTER XXIX

THROUGH THAT DISASTROUS autumn of 1920 — when the logging camps of B.C. were given over to watchmen and the sawmills were silent storehouses of idle machinery, and the owners of both sat in clubs and homes, cursing labour, the government, that vague entity called the consumer who had mysteriously ceased to consume, raving about confiscatory taxation, bewildered and resentful in the face of a retrograde swing of the commercial pendulum — the Norquay machine functioned without a single creaking joint, on into the winter season through sodden weeks of mist and rain until a deep snow in January buried the gear and froze the water pipes that fed the donkey engines. Then even the hardiest logger was glad to stay indoors.

A certain percentage of the younger men, with good money burning their pockets, went to town, victims of the inevitable reaction from the grind of work. But most of the crew followed a wiser counsel and stayed in the camp, played poker in the bunk houses, read books and magazines, organized stag dances. Some of the married men built float houses on rafts which could be moved when the camp changed, and brought their families there to live away from rent and fuel costs in town. Their joint efforts persuaded the provincial government to establish a temporary school. So by degrees the camp began to take on the aspect of a community.

The shutdown was comparatively brief — five weeks. Then rains wiped out the drifts, banished the frost. In the dripping forest where fog wraiths hung like smoke among the tree tops, axes clacked, saws whined, cables hummed, and the logs came down to the sea.

Where the logging industry in great part had stopped dead before the barrier of unprofitable operation, Rod did not even slow down. It was not a question of a profit. It was simply a matter of turning trees into cash to replenish the plundered coffers of the Norquay Trust. Every boom that sold in the market lessened somewhat his obligations, once his men agreed cheerfully that a lowered wage was better than idleness. The reddest radical among them believed in him sufficiently to go ahead on the assurance that wages would automatically keep step with prices for the product of their labour.

In few other organizations that Rod knew did such a feeling prevail. Where it had play there was a minimum of dispute, a maximum of production. But it was rare. His affairs took him into Vancouver a great deal. He had kept up membership in a club to which his father and grandfather had belonged. And in the club quarters which served him as a hotel he came into casual contact with sundry pillars of British Columbia industry. The amount of invective poured on the head of things in general was a revelation.

These worthy gentlemen over their wine and cigars affected to believe the State, the home, the nation, reeled to ruin before union wage scales. The rancor in their voices when they spoke of working-class demands amazed Rod sometimes. But as he listened, he perceived that this rancor was impartially distributed over many things, upon the government, upon taxation, upon affairs in Europe upon the gaunt spectre of the Lenin-Trotsky regime; there seemed no end to their grievances. And he perceived further that this uneasy spirit lay in the fact that the sweeping tide of war prosperity had slacked suddenly where they had childishly believed it would surge on to greater heights — and that this slackening was unprofitable. If the stagnation kept up long enough, they must shrink to a lesser stature, some to ruin. They were uneasy. Some, committed to great undertakings, were palpably afraid.

If they could keep wages down and prices up! They did not say so openly. They did not correlate the two objectives. They merely brightened at any prospect of better selling prices for their various products, greater demand, and frowned in distress over labour costs. They said labour would have to come off its high horse, and they said it with a good deal of unnecessary vehemence. Quite unanimously, almost instinctively, they were bitter against any man who did not agree with them.

They said, "Men won't work." That was a lie. Rod Norquay had proved it. His men had worked; and he had in his crew a score of agitators blacklisted in other camps. No. Men who had seen wartime wages easily overlapped by wartime living costs would not work for a driving employer under conditions arbitrarily dictated; not unless the whip of necessity lashed them to the task. And when they had to, inevitably they laid down on the job. That was the root of the trouble.

"You could open your camps and start your mills tomorrow," Rod broke into a conversation at his elbow one day, "if you'd base your tactics on the fact that men are men and not beasts of burden. I'm doing it and making money. I've done it right along. There's no magic about it. I simply accept present-day conditions, instead of mourning for the good old days when a logger was something less than a dog in a kennel. The trouble with you people is that you're hogs by nature. You're not satisfied to have your snouts in the trough. You want both feet in."

He walked out on the street, leaving them insulted and indignant. But he did not care. He was in one of his moods, in one of those momentary surges of passion that overtake the hard-pressed man. He saw everything in such moments with a distorted clarity. The motives and aspirations of such men seemed mean beyond words. If it had been possible for him to stay long at such a pitch of emotion, he would have hated them as heartily as they hated him.

They did hate him. Chiefly because they distrusted him, because they couldn't understand his motives. For a long time they had believed that he was a fool about money, a sentimentalist who was sinking a great fortune into a bottomless pit. Then because they saw no sign of collapse, they credited him with ambitious schemes which aroused their cupidity, and finally their antagonism when he continued to play a lone hand and succeed where they, with their little combinations, either failed or were afraid to run a risk of failing. He would enter no arrangement designed to put labour in its place. He would have nothing to do with employers' associations. He stood out a lone figure, carrying on his shoulders the burden of the Norquay Trust and in his hands a producing organization whose efficiency they envied and could not duplicate by their methods.

All that winter Rod heard hints, snatches of conversation; he watched, listened, made mental notes. He heard the complaining of the pinched industrial barons. They blamed the war now. *C'est la guerre!*

But it was not the war. They were reaping, all civilization was reaping, only seed that had been sown long before the war. The worthy bourgeois learned nothing, but he did forget many things. Chiefly he forgot, or perhaps had never learned, that the war did not create greed, ineptitude, blundering, injustice; the war didn't endow man with a tendency to snatch at chestnuts in the fire and complain loudly when he burned his fingers. It seemed to Rod utterly childish to blame the war for individual or even national folly. The war had its own burden of iniquity to bear. The war created nothing and destroyed nothing that had its root in the human heart. At the worst it had only deflected certain things, released pent forces and passions.

He considered. Grove would have made as great a mess of his ambitious schemes if no cannon had waked echoes in Flanders. He had been a victim of his own weakness. A weak, vain man with great power in his hands, and a group of strong, predatory men filching it from him on the old principle that "he shall take who has the power and he shall keep who can."

This was the law that seemed to rule modern industrial society. Right has always rested on power; it cannot be otherwise. Very well then. Let them live by the law. Rod could not help a sneer when he saw these aspiring minor plutocrats wince as the shoe pinched them, the shoe which they would have fitted on other feet without a qualm, if they could.

Nevertheless the muttered growling of various influential persons echoed in his ears now and then. He heard it directly. He noted the effect of it in different aspects of his more or less complicated affairs. There were influential cliques in Vancouver who took it as a personal grievance that the Norquay estate — which was Rod himself — would neither heed their Jeremiads concerning labour nor deviate from a settled policy.

It takes so little to arouse the ugly devils that lurk in men. They tried to make a feud of what was only a feeling of irritation. They attacked him. When they went that length, Rod struck back with whatever weapon lay to hand, and he had not a few in his arsenal. They couldn't hurt him; they could at most annoy. And so presently, Rod, finding no cracks in his material armour through which a spear could be thrust, ceased to be troubled by their futile activities. He despised their stratagems, and mocked at them, and confounded them with a waspish sarcasm whenever he encountered them in person. Undoubtedly in that year he earned something close to hatred from a certain group of men who five years earlier would have been aghast at such a state of affairs.

About certain phases of this Isabel Wall kept him duly informed. But in the spring of that year she married Andy Hall — and was herself immediately cast out from among the chosen people. Which circumstance only moved Isabel to amused laughter. But it stirred Rod and Mary to admiration. In this final step Isabel seemed to have burned all her bridges with a high heart. They were quietly married and came to live with Rod and Mary for company's sake — since the two husbands were necessarily absent a great deal of the time.

Not long after that the last stick of the last Norquay timber on Valdez, that noble stretch of fir and cedar Oliver Thorn had husbanded so long, found its way to the boomsticks. When the first crew was ready to shift its donkey engines and coils of cable, Rod said to Andy Hall, "Have that outfit loaded on floats. Take it over to Mermaid Bay and make a high-lead setting a little back from shore to the right of the landing. Better start getting these camp buildings over there too."

Andy stared at him.

"You're not going to cut *that* timber?" He waved a hand across the channel, where the dusky forest massed behind the red roof of Hawk's Nest.

"Why not?" Rod asked. He wondered if Andy shared a feeling that stirred, he believed, in no breast save his own and Mary's.

"It's a damned shame," Andy muttered.

"No choice."

It was the simple truth. Rod looked across at Valdez often in the next few weeks — perhaps to turn his eyes from the desecration at hand. He did not expect any save himself to feel such a sentiment, to feel a physical shrinking every time a faller lifted his long-drawn cry of "Tim-*br-r-r-r*," and the sobbing swish of lofty boughs sweeping in a great arc and the crashing thud marked another tree prone. Valdez was a waste. Where living green had clothed the hills there lifted stumps, torn earth, bald rock ledges. Desolation. The Granite Pool lay in its cliffy hollow, bared to the hot eye of the sun. The deer and the birds had withdrawn to the farther woods. Animal life banished, vegetation destroyed. Barren. Bleak. Ugliness spread over square miles. Soon Dent Island would be like that. Hawk's Nest would stand bleak and bare on a stripped promontory. If man were immortal, surely the troubled spirits of his dead kinsmen must hover dumbly about the spot. But they were as powerless as he.

He had walked out to see the first tree thrown down, and he had overheard one faller say to his mate, looking up at the stone house and lifting his face to sniff the sweet smell of lilac blown to him across the lawns by a June breeze:

"By God, it's almost a crime to cut these trees."

But, as he had said to Andy Hall — no choice. Upon that twelve hundred acres the trees stood bough to bough — clean, straight, tall, enormous of girth, and sound to the core. From the level centre of the island an easy slope fell away to the water on every side. For a mile back from Hawk's Nest to walk abroad was like walking in the nave of a Gothic cathedral. Perhaps the Goths in their northern fastnesses first saw those pointed arches in the lofty symmetry of fir and pine. For a hundred years the Norquays had warred on the thickets and undergrowth. They had cleared away the dead trunks and the rotten windfalls. The floor of that forest was the floor of a park. Bough to bough the trees stood in endless ranks. Man was a pygmy among them. Dim aisles ran out into shadowy perspective. Only on the southern fringe bordering the house and lawn had the forest been thinned to let in sunshine and become clothed with grass. All the rest was carpeted with moss.

No logging crew on the Pacific Coast ever put their gear into such a logging chance. Twelve hundred acres of fir and cedar, few less than four foot thick at the base, thousands that three men touching fingertips could not span, clean straight trees that lifted a hundred feet without a knot or limb, and another hundred above that bared their heads to the sun. Their feet in perpetual shadow; their heads upholding the sky.

Except on two or three hundred acres of jungle at the northern end there was nothing in all that stretch to hamper a rigging-slinger with his snaky cables. The fallers could lay a tree where they wished. The high-lead gear could snatch the logs out at top speed. Rod could imagine old Jim Handy, the human logging machine, looking with glad eyes on such ground and such timber. Records would be made there. Big days that the loggers would talk about in years to come, days when more timber would go down to float within the boomsticks than ever was moved by a crew of men between sun and sun.

And that was why they were there now. He had hoped to save a part of this. But the pressure was too great. He had to have a given amount of revenue within a given time. Only by this means could it be secured. It was fortunate for him that he had this resource, doubly fortunate that it would go out on a rising market; for 1921 marked the turn of the tide.

All lost save honour! He smiled at the self-righteous expression. He could strike an attitude and utter that worn phrase. It was true. But was it valid — either the attitude or the phrase? Yes, for himself. He was throwing away every material advantage that men live, work, fight for, plan and scheme and struggle to attain. And he did not do it because it was a reasonable, logical course. He did it to gain peace with himself, to retain his own self-respect. He was so made that he could endure anything but the thought of meeting an enemy and skulking away in the face of danger, of treachery to a trust, of taking an unfair advantage. Yet there were times when he felt that it was too great a price to pay for another man's blunder. And then he would feel as if he had done something, or contemplated doing something, of which he was ashamed. He began to realize that the cheerful giver gives nothing of value compared to the glow he gets in giving; and that the man who can cheerfully sacrifice his dearest possessions has never yet been born.

They were living once more in the old house. For how long Rod did not know and he tried not to think. The outcome was still uncertain; and where uncertainty lingers so does hope. At least, it was very pleasant to be there.

Late one afternoon when the Dent Island operation had got well under way, a fog swept like a wet smoke through the Euclataw Passage. It lifted, broke, opened and closed as if it were of two minds whether to lay over the channel a veil of obscurity or disperse in torn fragments. While it hovered and shifted thus uncertain, and the tiderace in the rapids slacked, a white yacht nosed into Mermaid Bay and felt her way alongside the float.

It was the *Kowloon,* come back like a ghost of other days. From the porch Rod, Mary, and Isabel recognized her through the fog haze as Grove's old yacht, which Laska had come into as the major portion of her husband's estate, and sold to her father.

"I wonder if they've come to hold out the olive branch to an erring daughter?" Isabel said lightly. "Dad might — possibly. Still, I don't think he'd care to trespass on your bailiwick, Rod, even for that."

"What has very likely happened," Rod shrewdly surmised, "is that she's on her way somewhere north and has simply taken shelter on account of the fog. This passage is dangerous in thick weather."

He sauntered away to the workings after a little. The *Kowloon* was of no interest to him, save as a reminder of old days. At the inner end of the bay already a widening field of stumps lifted flat heads among a litter of discarded tops and broken boughs over many acres. With tools and machinery his loggers were eating into the heart of that ancient forest as a mouse gnaws into a slice of cheese.

The fog lifted and closed intermittently. Rod came back in the course of an hour to find a stout figure with a cigar jutting from its teeth standing in the edge of the logging watching the high-lead donkey spit smoke and steam and shudder under enormous strains.

John P. Wall greeted him impassively. His small grey eyes met Rod's for a second, wandered off among the stumps, the dimly seen men, the black iron monsters huffing and puffing, the reddish-brown logs floating by hundreds in the bay, swept over the unkept grounds rank with grass, the grey stone house casting a great shadow, and came back to Rod.

"Damn shame to do this," Wall flirted one hand toward the untidy logged-off ground.

Rod shrugged his shoulders.

"I'll give you two hundred thousand for Dent Island just as it stands," Wall offered abruptly. "Take your outfit and go log somewhere else. Two hundred thousand cash."

Rod looked at him. A hundred and fifty thousand would shift his last burden. That was the maximum he could realize from his timber, if he sheared Dent Island as a farmer shears his sheep's fleece in the spring. And with the forest stripped, Dent Island had no money value. It would consist only of an old stone house standing gaunt amid a few acres of grass, its background a stony stump-littered waste. Whatever associations Hawk's Nest had for him and his could be less than nothing to John P. Wall. What stirred the man? Had his iron bowels been moved to compassion? Was he obliquely trying to make amends? Or did he think that by purchase he could put on the intangible mantle the Norquays had woven about themselves in five generations?

Rod smiled wanly.

"Why should you wish to buy Hawk's Nest at more than its market value? Does your conscience hurt?"

"Conscience?" A flicker of expression crossed Wall's heavy face. "No. Don't use it in my business. Took a notion to the place. Always did like it. That's all. You're destroying it."

A glow of anger began to burn in Rod, and mixed with it a detached wonder at the type of man before him. He could imagine Wall viewing him with impersonal pity, and brushing him aside in pursuit of his own ends. There was a pachydermous quality in the man. He couldn't be hurt. He had no qualms. For him the world of humanity was not made up of men and women who had good impulses or bad ones, wisdom and folly, conditioned by many things. No, to him the world was made up of two kinds of people: those who could get what they wanted and those who couldn't. For Wall there were no fine distinctions, no ethical hazards in which a man might lose his soul. The firm grasp, the unrelenting hold, justified itself. Anything profitable was good business; anything unprofitable was bad business. Rod looked at him and wondered if Wall carried that remorseless philosophy into his social life, his family life; if he applied it to his pleasure, and in what degree. And if he did whether he found the balance in his life's ledger to lie on the credit or the debit side.

"You're reckoned wealthy, aren't you?" Rod said to him. "Three or four millions?"

"Something like that," Wall answered indifferently.

"I wonder if it has ever occurred to you that there are things money can't get you?" Rod said quietly. "This place happens to be one of those things."

Wall chewed his cigar, impassively reflecting. Rod turned away.

"Three hundred thousand," Wall said suddenly. Rod shook his head.

"No use. I wouldn't sell Hawk's Nest any more than you'd sell one of your ears. I was born here. My people have been born and lived and died and are buried here. Very old-fashioned notion, of course, but it happens to mean something to me. And please remember this, Wall. If it had to pass out of my hands, you would be the last man in the world I'd care to have hang up your hat here and call it home."

He left Wall to reflect on that.

A shrill blast from the high-lead donkey put an end to the day's work. Men came stringing out of the woods. In twenty minutes more the supper gong clanged.

As they sat at dinner Rod told Isabel of her father's offer. Isabel smiled cynically.

"Don't ever think the idea of any sort of restitution occurred to him,

Rod," she declared. "He wouldn't even understand the idea of such a thing. He has always admired this place, secretly longed to have something like it, and he has discrimination enough to know he couldn't create it in his lifetime. He'd buy Hawk's Nest like a shot. He has dreams of founding a Wall dynasty, I really believe. A place like this, made to order, with its history — why, he'd gloat over it. The parvenu idea of acquiring prestige by purchase — by proxy. I know I sound horrid, but it's true. He thinks the Norquays have gone to seed. And that the Walls only require a proper background to be somebody. It's amusing and sometimes almost tragic — this social pushing, this itch to be thought something you aren't, to make a big splash. Did he seem keen on it, Rod?"

"Rather."

"Mamma's been priming him," Isabel nodded. "I've heard her talk about the possibility — since you've been supposed to be in deep water. She thinks Bob's a perfect gentleman — even if his father isn't quite — when Robert's merely a good little spender. Poor old daddy. He's the best of the lot, because he just naturally can't help being a ruthless old pirate, and he never held a grudge in his life against anyone who beat him at his own game. He's a bear at making money and mom's a bear in society, and they've raised Bob and Laska and me to be bearcats of one sort and another too. Some combination."

Isabel applied herself to the salad for half a minute.

"Suppose you go aboard the yacht with me and I'll introduce you to Dad," she proposed mischievously to Andy.

"I have no objection," he returned calmly. "Neither have I the slightest desire to meet your male parent — whose only merit in my eyes is that he *is* your parent. I couldn't use him in my business, and it's a cinch he couldn't use me in his."

"He might," Isabel teased. "He has lots of irons in the fire and loads of money. You sure did marry money, Andy, old scout."

"Well, I have irons in the fire myself," Andy retorted imperturbably. "And without any hankering for loads of money I expect to get all I need."

The pair of them sauntered off after dinner, still facetiously debating what they called the possibilities of a Hall-Wall entente. Rod and Mary went out on the porch. The rapids murmured in a rising key. Young Rod, who had learned to read under his mother's tutelage, curled up in a chair with a book of fairy tales. The sun dipped below the jagged backbone of Vancouver Island and the afterglow lingered, a radiant tinge over the blurred slopes that lifted to high mountains on the mainland shore.

About the head of the bay were clustered compactly the numerous portable buildings of the camp — bunkhouses, messhouses, storeroom, isolated small dwellings. A short slope bright with low salal brush dipped to the water. On that gentle pitch numbers of the men often clustered in the evening, sitting on their haunches, lying stretched on their backs, spinning Rabelaisian yarns, Homeric tales out of their woods experience, talking about their work, the war, economics — all the infinite variety of futile gabble and profound wisdom that is embodied in a group of skilled men following a risky outdoor calling. The Pacific Coast logger is no mere beast of burden. He is master of an intricate technique as applied to the handling of enormous timbers by powerful and complicated machinery. The B.C. woods is no place for the sluggish of brain or hand.

Wall himself was heavily interested in timber and had been for years. There were probably fifty men in Rod's crew who had drawn Wall paycheques in their time. And there was not a man there but knew the Wall camps and knew little good of them. They had an evil reputation. Probably Wall himself had never seen the interior of a single one of his camps. He had no personal interest in such matters — only, in results. He got results through superintendents, who in turn passed the buck to logging bosses. And these again, because *their* jobs depended on high average production, drove without mercy so long as they could hold the job. There was a sardonic saying along the coast that every Wall camp always had three crews: one coming, one going, and one on the job.

The loggers frankly hated Wall and all his works. Whereas they liked Rod Norquay. Moreover, now in the third year of Rod's regime, very nearly every man there understood the situation. They were for him, to a man. Rod represented to them the very antithesis of everything

John P. Wall stood for. And no mean portion of Rod's crew were intellectually capable and emotionally impelled to make out a very black case against the John P. Walls of industry.

A little cluster gathered on this slope between camp and tidemark. The cluster grew till the limited area was black with men in caulked boots and Mackinaw clothing, men with unshaven stubble on their chins and strong calloused hands. They sat and stood there without the customary shouting and laughter. It seemed as if every man in the camp had been drawn to look silently down on the white yacht.

The *Kowloon* stretched her graceful length along the landing. Her paint was like virgin snow, and from stem to stern she glistened with brass and copper and varnished teak. On her forward deck two or three of her crew in spotless white ducks leaned on the rail, looking at the men ashore. Aft a gramophone exhaled the latest jazz. There were guests present, and now that the fog had gone with the sun, they were on deck, dipping and swaying and gyrating to the music.

Suddenly a man on the bank began to sing. A solitary voice, a rich baritone, it cut across the canned syncopation and lifted with the diapason of the rapids as a tonal background.

There was nothing strange in that. Men often sang there, soloists and impromptu quartets. They sang to amuse themselves, or because they were happy, for any or all the reasons that move men to song. It was not the fact of the man singing. It was his song.

> Ye sons of freedom awake to glory.
> Hark! Hark! What myriads bid you rise.

The third line came with a volume that burst the evening hush like the roll of drums. From a hundred-odd throats it poured in rhythmic unison, with a passionate earnestness, and something akin to a threat.

> Your children, wives, and grandsires hoary,
> Behold their tears and hear their cries.
> Shall hateful tyrants mischief breeding
> With hireling hosts a ruffian band
> Affright and desolate the land,
> While truth and liberty lie bleeding?

To arms, to arms! Ye brave.
The avenging sword unsheathe.
March on. March on. All hearts resolved
On liberty . . . or death!

The last word struck like the blow of a ponderous hammer falling on muffled iron. Then silence — as if it had been halted by some invisible conducting baton which had welded that impromptu chorus into a single harmonious whole to chant that old, old song of revolt against oppression.

Who that has ever heard a marching regiment sing the Marseillaise but knows the clang of its ending, like the snick of a breech-bolt or a great sword clashed home in its scabbard.

No one moved. No voices lifted in words or laughter. Rod, sitting with his chin in his palms, listened with a curious tension for a break in that sudden hush. The massed group on the bank remained immobile, very quiet, as if something profoundly sobering had come over them.

And in the midst of this strange quiescence a gong struck faintly, deep in the bowels of the *Kowloon,* and when the deckhands flicked off the mooring lines she backed slowly out into the channel, out into the gathering dusk, the jazz tunes stilled, her guests standing quietly in a group by the after rail.

CHAPTER XXX

AS THE REAPING MACHINES pass over a field of wheat at harvest time mowing swath after swath until there is nothing left but bristling stubble, so the men and machinery under Rod's direction mowed the forest, harvesting that great crop which the centuries had matured. Day by day the logs poured into the booming ground. Week by week tugs departed, towing enormous rafts. The mills chewed up these logs and spewed them forth as squared timbers, in wide boards and narrow, in beautifully finished materials out of which carpenters in far cities fashioned roofs over the heads of other men.

To Rod these trees had been living things, dumb giants brooding over the earth they shadowed. He had stood among them with a humbled spirit. As a child he had moved in that silence and shade with a strange awe, with a mysterious sense of possession and of being himself possessed. A childish fancy? Perhaps. But it lingered still, recurred often. He could imagine the spirit of the forest putting forth a voiceless protest at all this havoc. He could dismiss these fancies intellectually, but his mind was powerless to put aside emotion. His brain could support action with the stern logic of necessity; it could not always banish the pang from his heart.

If it were sentimentality to regret ravished beauty he pleaded guilty. He recalled the protest that burst from a million throats when the cathedral of Rheims crumbled under shell fire. Here was something as beautiful, as inspiring, as much a glorious monument of the centuries as anything of wood and stone wrought by the hands of man. Here was a majesty of form and a beauty of colour man might copy but could never surpass. It was being obliterated with considered purpose.

Mary encompassed it in a sentence, with a sigh.

"It is like seeing a painting you have treasured in your home for a lifetime ripped out of its frame, defaced, torn to bits by some vandal."

Summer merged into autumn. September rains rolled up a veil of smoke from scattered forest fires. The coastline emerged clear and sharp from the blur. The maples put on their russet gowns. Equinoctial gales harried the coast briefly and left still days shot through with a waning sun. And whether in sun or storm the wheels on Dent Island turned unremittingly. With sweaty bodies and untiring tools of steel the loggers plied their trade. The booms accumulated and went their way. Money poured in. From the material angle Dent Island was a gold mine. But like mines that have been, the vein was pinching out.

On a day in October Rod saw the last of the great booms draw clear in the wake of a steam tug. Before it was out of the Narrows he passed it on the *Haida*, southward bound. Very soon now he could write *finis* to another chapter in the sequence. Slowly, with a pent eagerness, he was placing his levers to right the inverted pyramid.

He knew that before he returned the last tree would fall, would be snatched seaward by the shuddering main line. His crew would gather all their gear on the beach, coil the cables, blow down the donkey boilers. But he would not be there for those obsequies. He had other ghosts to lay.

He stood on the deck looking back. The *Haida* had not yet cleared the inner harbour. East and west the waterfront spread away for miles in a darkness thickened by the city smoke, a black pall jewelled with deck lights, emerald specks, ruby gleams, dots and squares of yellow, brilliant lines of arc lights, scintillating, imprisoned lightning. Behind that line of dusky wharves, where vessels from far ports disgorged their freight with groaning cargo winches, rose the banked and terraced lights of the town. Great electric signs blazed on warehouse roofs, on every vantage point, proclaiming to all and sundry that "Smith's Coffee," "Brown's Tobacco," "The House of Jones," "Your Credit is Good," were epochal affairs, worthy to be written in letters of fire against the sky.

But from that flaming galaxy one — that, like the name of Abou ben Adhem, had been above all the rest — was missing now. It had greeted the incoming mariner and the tired commuter on the grunting ferries for twelve years. It would never glow again.

The Norquay Trust Company was no more. It was as dead as the man whose futile ambition had given it birth. Its great seal would never again be affixed to any document. With a deep personal satisfaction Rod had wiped out its corporate existence. Legally, honourably, painlessly, he had put it to death.

He stared over the rail. The hive! He seemed to hear the drone of countless creatures armed with invisible stings which they plied upon each other vindictively, unthinkingly, often without knowing what they did, as they buzzed about their sustenance-seeking, marching antlike in the streets, dumb swarms driven by instinct. Ants in the streets, factories, shops, flies clinging in clusters upon motive things of wood and iron called street cars. They came out of nothing; they were bound nowhere. They desired only to be fed, to sleep, to be amused; and their food, their slumber, their amusements were not means to an end; they were the end in themselves. Spiders in offices, banks, above the swarm, yet seeking only what the swarm sought: spinning their webs, enmeshing material things beyond their utmost need, themselves becoming enmeshed and destroyed — their souls if not their bodies — in their own web.

The hive! The futile swarms buzzing in the market place. In a moment of despondency he wished that he might never see it again.

He smiled in the dark, a grimace of utter weariness. Why couldn't he think of them except as agitated insects? A mood — a mood.

His job — that job — was done. Looking back at the lucent glow above the city, that lingered as an impalpable sheen in the sky after the *Haida* put the Brockton Point light abeam and the inner harbour was shut away, he felt a sudden relief. His life was his own once more, as much as any man's may ever be. He had shifted the weight off his shoulders. He was going home. After that —

Well, he wasn't certain. He had a plan, a program. It might come to something worthwhile. He hoped it would; he believed it would. If he had little faith in the value of much that men struggled for, he still believed in man. But whatever his future might be, it must be one of action. He could never be passive. To dream without doing? To contemplate, with contemplation as an end in itself? No. To be a passionately interested bystander, critical, puzzled, sympathetic, deprecating, uplifted or disgusted according to the momentary mood and impression, to the winnowing of events through the sieve of his intellect, but nevertheless a bystander aloof from the common, troubled stream of life — he could never be that again. He doubted now that he ever had been. He had only thought himself a watcher on the bank. He had been sweeping along in the current unaware. It couldn't be otherwise.

He was very tired. When the *Haida* cleared the outer harbour and met the full strength of a westerly swell in the Gulf he went below and turned in.

Daybreak in Ragged Island Pass! A wave of light and colour spanning the Gulf, lighting up the snowy peaks on Vancouver Island. A blend of misty shores, grey-green sea, hills that faded from olive to purple, from purple to delicate lilac and merged with the horizon as faint blue patches far off, on the edge of things. Then the sun stabbing in golden shafts through notches in the Coast Range, hunting black shadows out of every gorge, touching each wave crest with a sparkle. A morning breeze flicked the sea with touches of white, and set the *Haida* lurching, plunging, flinging fan-shaped bursts of foam off her bows, arching iridescent sheets of spray in which small, elusive rainbows gleamed.

At ten in the morning they ran the south narrows of the Euclataw with the ebb an hour gone, rolling, twisting, yawing widely as they sheered off wicked swirls and were shot at last on a straight current between the two Gillards and into the mouth of Mermaid Bay.

The house was silent, empty. It was silent and empty enough at best, its quiet corridors flanked by rooms that were never opened, in which ghostly shapes of furniture stood in dim light like swathed mummies. But the rooms they did occupy were empty. Rod went out quietly and sat down on the porch steps. Here presently came Stagg in overalls, his long dark face a healthy brown from self-appointed outdoor tasks.

"Mr. and Mrs. Hall and Mrs. Norquay went in the little launch on the morning slack to see the rapids run, sir," he informed Rod. "They weren't expecting you today."

Rod nodded. They had gone to watch the Devil's Dishpans spin, the great boils heave roaring up out of that cauldron, to listen to the loud song of pent waters released. He wondered idly if young Rod would some day run those rapids for sport with a girl in a canoe as a companion on the adventure, as he and Mary Thorn had done so long ago. It *was* long ago. He didn't trouble to cast up the years. He had a feeling of being separated from that time by something more profound, more significant, than calendar years.

He looked over at the camp. Figures of men moved about. Gangs were stowing gear on the beach. Cold donkey engines stood dead on their skids — round-bellied monsters with smokeless stacks pointing skyward. Miles of steel cable, main lines, haul-backs, high-lead gear, skyline rigging lay about. At least he had his tools! Tools and the men to use them. Men with the bark on: the shock troops of industry, a battalion under his hand, eager, skilful, disciplined, confident in him. What more did he want?

Then his eyes turned slowly northward, regretfully. *That* was the sum of his striving.

He had paid his debts. He faced the world with a great, empty stone house and twelve hundred acres of worthless land: worse than worthless, for its stony ribs, the melancholy stumps, the nakedness and the waste bred an ache in his heart. It had been so beautiful, and it was now so indescribably sad. Like a woman's lovely face ravaged by smallpox. It was hideous and must remain so until the kindly seasons clothed it anew with saplings which his grandchildren might see as another forest of lusty trees. But he would never look north toward the green palisades of the mainland without a touch of sadness, a pang of regret for that stately forest destroyed to preserve a tradition, to discharge an obligation, to live with honour in his own sight.

Tradition, obligation, honour! Royal words falling into disuse, uttered with an easy smile and facile lip service — sound without substance. But they had been more than words; they had been vital things to other Norquays as well as to himself. They remained so to Rod. He believed they held their old significance to many men, even in a world that worshipped Mammon above all other gods.

One pair of weak hands could destroy so much. Power in weak hands had torn down the work of four generations. But it could be rebuilt. Like the saplings, he and his could grow slowly to the old stature. Place and prestige could be grasped again, if he wanted them — if they seemed worth reaching for. He was not sure he wished to grasp either in the accepted sense.

He rose and walked out a little way, turned to look at the house. That was built to endure. A pardonable pride, the glow of a fierce possessive affection warmed him. Hawk's Nest would hatch an eagle yet. Norquay children would still romp in those wainscoted hallways. Some day it would come back to its old warmth and cheer, its comfort and security. Its blazing windows would be a mark for vessels running the rapids by night. The voices of friendly people would ring there, and laughter and music, so that sadness would keep aloof with its sombre garments.

Rod did not see in detail how he should accomplish this. But he had hope and courage. He knew what to avoid. He had been bitterly schooled in the way of a world which had abandoned the old faiths to pursue *things.* Nature had not fashioned him softly, even in bestowing upon him the rare gift of perception. The blood in his veins was the blood of men who did not suffer patiently at the hands of their enemies. He had no wish for a beak and claws to rend and tear. But he would sharpen his weapons and use them with a will on the Walls and Deanes and Richstons of the world if they got in his way. And he was confident that in such a battle he would never lack followers who knew the fight was fair.

He wanted no great thing of life save such reward of industry, initiative, ordered effort, as would turn this silent grey house into some measure of its old aspect and atmosphere; so that when his time came he could lie down content, knowing that for all that had been given him in the way of affection, trust, service, he had given some measure of return. His gods were not material gods. He did not wish his children to worship at a material shrine. Comfort they should have. Luxury they might desire and enjoy. But only if they gave something in return. If he had been minded to inscribe a motto for his house Rod would have written: "You cannot get something for nothing — soon or late there is a price to pay."

He would like to leave Roderick Thorn Norquay something to carry on. But what he most desired his son to carry on was chiefly such wealth as he could carry within himself: an ideal of uprightness, a sense of kinship with his native land, the perception that externals are only the husks of life, a soul that would not quail before disaster or swell too proudly if all the world lay at his feet.

Rod smiled over his musings. He was just turned thirty, and he stood there thinking of what he should like to leave as the spiritual heritage of his son. He had years and years and years ahead of him yet, and task upon task.

He swung on his heel. His eye touched lingeringly on the waste land, passed on to the men stowing the logging gear on the beach. Tools were there, and energy — in abundance. It was enough.

"Three generations from shirt sleeves to shirt sleeves," Rod said to himself whimsically. "We beat the average. It took us five."

And after a little reflective pause, he said aloud in a tone of conviction:

"There's one thing to be said for shirt sleeves. They give a man room to swing his arms."

THE END

ABOUT THE AUTHOR

Bertrand W. Sinclair (1881–1972) was born in Edinburgh, Scotland and immigrated to Canada with his mother in 1889. At age fifteen, he ran away from home to become a range rider in Montana for several seasons and then lived in California for a number of years. He returned to Canada in 1912, settling first in Vancouver, BC. He began his literary career by writing short stories and "novellettes" for such magazines of the day as *Popular Magazine* and *Adventure*, making his living as a freelancer. He soon became well known for his numerous novels in which he depicted the lives of ranchers, loggers and fishermen. With many of these, Sinclair was enormously successful; *North of Fifty-Three*, published in 1914, is said to have sold 340,000 copies. Both *Big Timber* and *North of '53* were made into silent movies. After 1922, he made his home in Pender Harbour on the Sunshine Coast and also worked as a commercial fisherman on his boat, the *Hoo-Hoo*, until the age of eighty-three. His VHF radio broadcasts to fishermen, known as "The Sinclair Hour," were widely listened to and respected. For further information, see Betty Keller's biography: *Pender Harbour Cowboy: The Many Lives of Bertrand Sinclair* (Victoria, BC: Touchwood, 2000).

Marquis imprimeur inc.

Québec, Canada
2011

Imprimé sur du papier Silva Enviro 100% postconsommation traité sans chlore, accrédité ÉcoLogo et fait à partir de biogaz.